T0329244

Amanda cracked open the bedroom door. It was Frank. . . .

"I shouldn't have blown up that way," he whispered through the opening. "As a diplomat, I'm supposed to be able to handle delicate situations."

She shook her head. "Don't."

"Tact is somehow more difficult when people you really care about are involved," he said, looking into her eyes.

Something caught in her throat. She swallowed. Swallowed again. It didn't go away.

In that moment an acknowledgment passed between them that Amanda welcomed joyfully—but also feared with all her heart. She felt excited in a way that she hadn't felt in years. Excited by the nearness of this very special man who was leaning into the narrow opening of her bedroom door as if by sheer will he could pass through it and into her life.

He belongs to someone else—to my best friend, a warning rang in her head. She let her eyes slip away from his, and pressed softly against the door. "Good night, Frank," she whispered. . . .

Books by Kathryn Jensen

Sing to Me, Saigon
Couples

Published by POCKET BOOKS

COUPLES

Kathryn Jensen

POCKET BOOKS

New York   London   Toronto   Sydney   Tokyo   Singapore

This book is a work of fiction. Names, characters, places and incidents are products of the author's imagination or are used fictitiously. Any resemblance to actual events or locales or persons, living or dead, is entirely coincidental.

An *Original* Publication of POCKET BOOKS

POCKET BOOKS, a division of Simon & Schuster Inc.
1230 Avenue of the Americas, New York, NY 10020

ISBN: 978-1-4767-2811-7

First Pocket Books printing January 1995

10 9 8 7 6 5 4 3 2 1

POCKET and colophon are registered trademarks of Simon & Schuster Inc.

Cover design by Carl Galian

Printed in the U.S.A.

To Bill—
A man who waltzes like a dream
and
Whose intelligence, wit, and
kindness have made my world
a happier place.

With love,
K.

Acknowledgments

My gratitude to John and Polly Clingerman for sharing their real adventures in the U.S. Foreign Service and helping me to breathe life into the characters of my imagination.

Sincerest thanks to John and Barbara Patillo of Towson Dance Studio, in Maryland, and Debby Green for sharing their love of and expertise in the beautiful world of ballroom dance.

And, finally, as always, I am indebted to Linda Hayes, my agent, and to Columbia Literary Associates, Inc. for giving me the chance to tell this story.

Say thou lov'st me while thou live,
I to thee my love will give,
Never dreaming to deceive . . .

—Anonymous

No married woman ever trusts her husband absolutely, nor does she act as if she did trust him. Her utmost confidence is as wary as an American pickpocket's confidence that the policeman on the beat will stay bought.

—H. L. Mencken

COUPLES

1

1965

Saturday dawned crisp and bright, a perfect Connecticut spring morning. A perfect morning for dancing.

Amanda Weitzer hefted her tote bag stuffed with the gear of her profession: soft pink leather ballet slippers; blocked satin toe shoes; black high-heeled, suede-soled ballroom pumps; two towels; a change of clothing; and a peanut butter sandwich and apple in a brown paper sack for lunch. A navy blue cardigan sweater was draped around her slim shoulders and framed small dancer's breasts. She wore a wraparound denim skirt to modestly cover her black leotard and pale pink tights.

As she pirouetted out the front door of the wood-frame duplex on Bank Street, she caressed the vellum envelope nestled in her skirt pocket and knew it was going to be a good day, a glorious day! Caroline was on her way home.

The moist breeze off the river tasted thickly of salt and fish, with a nip of fuel oil. She waltzed down the cracked cement steps, practiced a graceful heel turn with a handsome imaginary partner, and swirled along the narrow flagstone walk edged by Olga's fading tulips. All the way to the studio, where she taught six days a week, Amanda hummed, stopping only when she passed people on the sidewalk for fear they'd think her mad.

Throughout the morning's ballet, tap dancing, and jazz classes of her tiny students, Amanda wondered about Caroline's news, "news too delicious," teased her note, "to be shared on paper."

By the middle of the afternoon, Amanda found it impossible to keep her mind on teaching. She played 45 rpm records at 33, sent young dancers off wearing perplexed expressions to practice the wrong steps, totally forgot one class's routine, then was unable to find her notes. She ached for the day to end. But, perversely, by four o'clock when she was introducing her last adult ballroom class to proper waltz position, she prayed Caroline would be just a few minutes late. She desperately needed at least a few minutes to splash cold water on her face, apply a touch of makeup, and change into the flowered sundress rolled up in her bag, for Caroline was bound to be dressed to the teeth.

At the end of class, she hastily bid her students good-bye, seized her tote bag, swung around, and there was Caroline Ann Nesbit in a navy and white Chanel suit. She could have been on the cover of *Vogue.*

"Darling!" Caroline squealed, rushing at her with arms flung wide.

Amanda held back, feeling dried sweat pull against the skin between her shoulder blades, suspecting she probably didn't smell too great either.

"Oh, *come on!*" wailed Caroline. "You aren't going to ruin the stupid suit with one little hug!"

Laughing, they embraced like schoolgirls. Amanda spotted the diamond as they stepped apart.

"Jeez!" she cried. "You did it. You went off to college in search of a husband, and you found him!"

Caroline beamed at her. "It took almost three bloody years, my dear, but he's perfect . . . and well worth the effort. I had to come home to tell you all about him."

"I'm so glad you did," Amanda said, deeply pleased to see her friend so happy.

Caroline Nesbit was blatantly materialistic. However, her obsession with money, expensive clothing, frivolous toys, posh parties, and exclusive schools had never bothered Amanda. They were Caroline's birthright, for she was the daughter of very wealthy parents. Seeking wealth out in the men she dated had therefore seemed natural. It became a game they'd played while they were teenagers—one they both poked fun at and neither took seriously. The Caroline Amanda knew and loved had a brilliant mind and spirit; she was compassionate, fun-loving, and had shown Amanda horizons that the daughter of middle-class German immigrants would never believe existed. Caroline taught her to reach for her dreams.

Caroline's concern over money did have its serious side, however. Amanda knew, even if her friend never admitted it, that Caroline longed to pass along the family heirlooms to her own offspring, to teach her children the niceties of playing contract bridge, yachting on Long Island Sound, and serving spicy shrimp cocktails and chilled martinis on the lawn of a summer house. It was the life she'd grown up with and desired to continue, not simply because she was a snob, but because to accept less would reflect poorly on her distinguished family.

"Well, look who's here!"

Both young women turned. Sara Stevenson, a petite redhead who looked much younger than her thirty years was coowner of the Stevenson School of Dance along with her husband, Doug. She approached the two girls from the dim sawdust- and perspiration-perfumed corridor between practice rooms.

"Caroline's come home to flash her rock at us!" Amanda announced.

"A diamond? Only twenty-one, and you're engaged?" Sara reached out and seized Caroline's left hand to examine the enormous round stone. "It's lovely," Sara commented sincerely.

"Three full carats on the nose!" bragged Caroline with a satisfied nod at the dazzling blue-white stone set in platinum.

"You are incorrigible," Amanda scolded. But she had to touch the ring, too, feel the cool, sparkling gem with the pad of her index finger.

"So, what are you girls up to tonight?" Sara wanted to know.

Sara herself wore only a simple gold band. Doug had never been able to scrape enough cash together to purchase such a luxury as a diamond for the wife he so dearly cherished. They lived happily but on a perilously thin shoestring budget. Amanda studied Sara's face for any sign of envy or regret. She found only happiness twinkling in Sara's clear blue eyes as she looked up from Caroline's hand.

"I'm taking Amanda out for dinner. Would you and Doug like to join us? We'll go to the Lighthouse Inn."

"Another time," Sara said quickly, although she undoubtedly knew there would be no second offer. Caroline's social whirl rarely involved anyone so down-to-earth as a dance instructor or, in Doug's case, a department store clerk. Amanda had always been the sole, unexplainable exception. "You two need time to catch up," she added.

Caroline turned to Amanda. "Want to go home to change first?"

Amanda made a swift mental survey of her closet under the eaves of the old wooden house on Bank Street. She hadn't expected the Lighthouse Inn, which was quite refined compared to the local restaurants she frequented—Howard Johnson's and the Puritan Diner. It didn't take her long to conclude that nothing would quite live up to Caroline's Chanel suit.

"I brought a casual dress and jacket and a pair of flats, if that's good enough," she said.

"Perfect."

"Come upstairs to the apartment and use my shower if you like," Sara offered.

"Thanks. I'll be down in a minute," Amanda promised Caroline.

"No hurry."

But there was a hurry, at least in Amanda's mind. A sense of urgency to hear how Caroline's master plan had fallen into place, who her mysterious fiancé was, what he looked like, and all the intimate details of their courtship.

Being around her girlhood friend, she felt young again, although she could hardly be considered old at twenty-one.

Nevertheless, working long hours at the studio, spending austere nights with her parents, Olga and Bruno, who, now in their sixties, were making her begin to feel as if her parents' years were rubbing off on her, draining her energy and robbing her of years that should have been carefree.

Even the name they'd chosen for her made her feel aging and spinsterly. Amanda. To her, it exuded a whiff of stuffy attics, china dolls, and bits of Grandmother's yellowed lace. In first grade, she'd been the only child whose parents had gray hair.

When she turned twelve, she tried to forget her name and her parents' control over her by asking her classmates to call her Mandy. That was the year she'd met Caroline.

Caroline had wrinkled her nose in distaste at the nickname. "Mandy," she groaned. "That sounds positively gauche." Caroline used words like that. *Gauche. Avant garde. Lingerie.* Words that dripped with sophistication. "You should go by your proper Christian name," she advised. "It's much less common sounding."

Not wanting to appear common, Amanda had resumed using her full name, but she was never the same after meeting Caroline. This sophisticated young girl had touched her life, subtly yet irrevocably altering its course for the first of many times.

Amanda showered then dried off with one of Sara's worn terry cloth towels, not much thicker than a dish rag but bleached a pristine white. She slipped into clean underthings and the cotton dress, not too badly wrinkled from a day squashed at the bottom of her bag. A field of orange poppies over an off-white muslin background remained vivid after four years of wearings and washings. It might be a little early in the season to go sleeveless, but with its short, fitted white cotton jacket, this dress was the best she owned for evening wear. She had three glittering hand-sewn ballroom gowns, but they were inappropriate for anything but competition costumes.

The Capezios, supple red leather with little tassels at the toes, had been a graduation gift from Caroline. The two girls often stopped to admire them in the window of Bremmen's Shoes, two doors from the studio down State Street.

Amanda had loved the little thin-soled flats that resembled ballet slippers. To her mind, they were the epitome of casual glamour. She'd seen them advertised in the Sunday magazine supplement of the *Hartford Courant.* However, they'd cost an outrageous twenty dollars, a sum she had never paid for a pair of shoes and simply couldn't afford.

Caroline bought them for her on the spot, brushing aside Amanda's protests. "They're an early graduation present! Shut up and put them on."

Although the Capezios were nothing out of the ordinary to Caroline, to Amanda (then sixteen) they meant the world. They signified quality, something beautiful to cherish that would last for a very long time, unlike the cardboard department store shoes Olga bought her that held their shape for only a few months of hard use. Since that day, she'd felt she owed Caroline something precious and important. For the time being, she hoped that her friendship was enough, for it was all she had to give. Now, six years later, she'd graduated high school, worked fifty hours a week, and her financial status had changed very little, for most of what she earned she paid to her parents for room and board.

Finally dressed, her soft brown hair brushed out over her shoulders, Amanda at last bid Sara good night and ran downstairs. She found Caroline in the second-floor office, gazing out onto State Street through the wide picture window. The glass was hazy with tiny handprints and forehead smudges from students watching for their rides home.

"Here comes Doug," Caroline murmured.

Amanda went to stand beside her. A tall man with thinning hair walked slowly up the street. He was only forty-five, but his bent stance and the fatigue that showed in his face made him appear much older.

"Do you remember the summer we turned fourteen?" Amanda asked softly.

Caroline laughed. "We both had wild crushes on poor Doug!"

"Silly, weren't we? Such pests."

"I don't know how the poor man survived our rapturous stares. More than once I caught him blushing."

"Did he really?" Amanda asked, amazed.

"I swear. Red as a beet with a sunburn."

This evening, however, Doug Stevenson only faintly resembled the younger man who'd waltzed breathtakingly across ballroom floors with his lovely Sara in his arms to the applause of audiences in New York, London, and Paris. As Amanda watched, he climbed the gently sloping sidewalk as though it were a mountain. Step by step, placing his feet with consideration, he made his way up the drive. For the first time, it struck her that he might be ill.

"Let's go," Caroline said, suddenly impatient. She extracted her car keys from her purse on first try, a feat Amanda had never in her life accomplished. "We'll give Doug a wink for old times' sake on the way out."

Amanda shook off her momentary twinge of concern for Doug's health and laughed. "Oh, you're wicked." As exhausted as she was at the end of her own workday, she probably looked no better than he did. Poor man.

Despite her threat, Caroline behaved herself, merely showing Doug her ring. Amanda told him they were off to a celebration dinner.

"Congratulations," he said solemnly. "I hope you'll be very happy. Have a good time tonight, girls." He started past them along the sidewalk, but at the last minute turned to Amanda. "How was the day? Very busy?"

"No more than usual. Twelve classes plus the private lessons. Sara and I are both dog tired, but there were no crises. I think I have the easier schedule, teaching ballroom privates all afternoon."

"I know," he said thoughtfully, "I've tried to convince Sara to switch off with you, take fewer or smaller ballet classes. But she won't hear of it."

"She loves ballet . . . and the little ones."

"Yes, she does," he murmured. Turning, he opened the studio door and started up the long, dark flight of stairs.

"Still having money troubles, are they?" Caroline asked as he disappeared and they moved down the street.

"Always. I think Sara realizes they can't afford to limit class size or offer fewer sessions and still pay the mortgage. One day she told me that if she could attract enough new students, she'd insist that Doug quit working at Kresge's and go back to teaching again."

"Must be degrading, a grown man running a cash register and stocking shelves. What about the Saturday dances?"

For years, Doug and Sara had sponsored socials open to the public. They played an odd assortment of records from 1930s big band jazz to lilting old-fashioned waltzes and lively swing. Young men from the nearby Coast Guard Academy and the naval base were attracted by the chance to meet local girls. And those high school girls who were less popular with their own age came seeking "older men" for dates. For a time, Saturdays at the Stevenson School of Dance were quite popular, and at three dollars a head, the evenings brought in welcome extra income.

But the three-story red brick building had aged, becoming drearier each year. There was little money available for fresh paint and renovations, both sorely needed. Ballroom dancing fell out of fashion with the American public during the rock 'n' roll era of the sixties. Amanda and a few hundred others still clung to the elite world of professional dancers who competed all over the world. In countries as diverse as Japan, England, and Russia, partner dancing was considered an art and supported by the governments. In the United States it was a fading memory.

Amanda sighed. "Not many were coming to the dances, so Doug stopped having them. Most people who want a night out these days go to one of the bars down by the river—the Cave, Ship's Mate, the Last Bastion. They have light shows and live bands."

"Too bad," Caroline murmured, casting Amanda a wistful glance. "We shared some good times at those dances."

Amanda grinned, warming inside at the memories. "Yes, we did."

The white clapboard-sided restaurant in no way resembled a lighthouse, authentic or otherwise. The Lighthouse Inn was nevertheless lovely, with real candles burning in each of its tall windows, elegant maples forming a double row of leafy sentries along a semicircular drive of crushed limestone, and head-high mountain laurel in full, fragrant blossom cultivated across the front and along the sides of the building. A subtle old New England ambiance had been created inside with floors of oak boards and spacious rooms with high ceilings and plenty of walking room between linen-covered tables. The lighting was subdued, hiding the cracks that had spread across the paneled walls, but not so dark as to obscure a diner's view of the delectable food. The main dining room smelled of bayberries, cloves, and the inn's own fresh-baked rolls.

Since dinner was Caroline's treat, Amanda splurged and ordered her favorite: a half-dozen enormous broiled stuffed shrimp. The entrée was accompanied by a generous baked potato, a mountain of sour cream, and tiny green peas mixed with baby onions. Caroline selected a French veal dish with a light wine-and-lemon sauce. They decided on an imported Chablis to have with their meal.

"Tell me all about *him,*" Amanda demanded as soon as the waiter left with their order.

Caroline smiled, her eyes sparkling. "Frank Donnelly is ideal—everything I've ever wanted. He's brilliant, a talented diplomat fourteen years older than I, but then he'd have to be older to have an established career. His family is old, old banking money, residents of the Hamptons." Caroline rapidly nibbled a crusty roll.

Amanda was too excited to eat. Details first, food later. "What else?"

"Frank owns a house in D.C., Georgetown, actually," Caroline continued. "When he's in the country, he stays on Long Island with his family as much as possible." She lowered her voice, as if she were about to breach national security. "He's the only child, so the estate will be his one day, and, oh, it is exquisite! You've *got* to see it, Amanda."

"Does Frank spend a lot of time abroad?" she asked, knowing how Caroline adored traveling.

"He's been assigned as a political aid to Kissinger, negotiating with the North Vietnamese. If they can get the Communists to sit down and talk, he says we may avert a war or at least keep the United States out of a major conflict in Asia. Paris has been mentioned as a possible location for the discussions and you know how I love the city." Her eyes sparkling, Caroline polished off her roll and reached for another, tore it apart, and slathered the soft insides with butter. "After that, who knows? Frank's destined for great things, everyone says so. Ambassadorships all over the world. I'll be entertaining royalty!"

"Sounds ideal for you," Amanda agreed. Such a lifestyle was so foreign to her. She felt out of her comfortable, small-town element just talking about formal dinners and diplomatic receptions.

Their meals arrived, and for several minutes they ate in silence.

Finally Caroline spoke again. "When you meet him, you'll see, Amanda. He's everything I've ever wanted in a husband, but . . ." She hesitated. "The package—you know, how he looks and behaves sometimes—it's just not quite what I'd imagined."

Amanda recalled their teenage days. "You wanted Rock Hudson in a tux."

"Yes." Caroline cracked a smile. "But it's amazing how few really gorgeous guys there are in Washington. I think when God passed out the brains, he saved the hot stuff for the other poor schmucks."

Amanda laughed till her sides felt as if they'd burst. At last she caught her breath in shuddering gulps and looked soberly at her friend. "Is he good to you?"

"Spoils me rotten."

"Does he love you?"

Caroline took a quick sip of her wine. "Of course he does. How could he not?" She beamed confidently.

She's right, Amanda thought. Caroline was beautiful, well-bred, intelligent, and—looking through the eyes of any man with a normal libido—sexy as hell. She'd be the belle of the diplomatic ball no matter where she was in the world. A prize for the career-conscious foreign service officer.

For dessert they both had rich vanilla ice cream laced with crème de menthe followed by two cups of the most delicious coffee Amanda had ever tasted. Full and rather sleepy, she strolled alongside Caroline to her car, a shiny, new white Porsche 911s with glittering chrome spokes and tan leather interior. The night was still and warm. Above them a black, black sky glittered with thousands of silver stars. The air was scented mountain laurel, roses, and wild mint.

They sat in companionable silence in the car, gazing up at the heavens. Amanda wished on a star. She didn't envy Caroline her money or her future, but she wished she too were in love and that someone would love her . . . or just be right for her. A partner to go forward with through life, she thought, that would be wonderful.

After a while Caroline asked, "Am I greedy to want so much?"

"Yes," Amanda said but lovingly added, "I guess we all are selfish, though, each in our own way."

"Not you."

"Of course, me. My parents still badger me to go to college and become a teacher like Bruno. Academia is the only world they know. It's what they want for me, but I've been stalling them for years. I have no interest in that kind of life—treatises, lectures, long moldy discussions about why someone long dead used the word *placid* instead of *peaceful* in his translation of Goethe." She shrugged. "It leaves me cold."

"You want to dance," Caroline stated knowingly.

"Silly, isn't it?"

"Not at all."

"But impractical. I'm not interested in performing other than at ballroom competitions, which are the most exciting times I can imagine. And I just adore hanging out at a studio all day, all night. Sara and Doug's place is where I grew up. Music and dancing make me happy."

"So do it. Say, the hell with them!"

Amanda touched the velvety soft leather where her hip pressed into the seat. "Maybe I should. I think I could support myself teaching dancing if I built up a larger list of private ballroom students. But I also want a family. I want to have children while I'm still young, but kids cost money. Sara and Doug struggle to keep the studio going and feed just the two of them."

"Why do you think they never had children?"

"Doug in particular has strong feelings about providing children with the right kind of home. I think he feels he's somehow shortchanged Sara."

"That's stupid."

"But it's what he feels. That's what counts."

Caroline looked at her for a moment, her blue eyes sharp, discerning. Then she started up the car and began driving. "What about your love life?"

Amanda shrugged. "I'm very busy."

"That wasn't the question."

"I go out once in a while."

"How often is 'once in a while?'"

Amanda sidestepped the issue. "You know I've never dated around a lot."

"How about once in a leaping blue moon?"

"It doesn't usually work out," Amanda whispered, watching the dark shoreline through the passenger-side window. A few fishing inboards were moving upriver, their red and green running lights streaking the wavelets.

Caroline persisted. "You mean, like Mark or Tim?"

"More or less." Amanda shifted self-consciously in her seat.

Mark Mitchell, a dashing young Coast Guard cadet, had been her first love when she was still in high school. Tim Polchevski had been her dance partner for a year, an arrangement that had inevitably developed into a romance, only to be painfully broken off when he dropped her for another partner—more accomplished as a dancer and, she suspected, more experienced in other ways as well.

"I'm not ready for anything serious," she said quickly, hoping Caroline wouldn't pick up on the conflict between her family plans and reluctance to commit herself to a relationship. "Anyway, most of the men in this town are just passing through. Between the Coast Guard and the navy—"

The Coast Guard Academy was straight up the Thames River on the New London side where Amanda lived. A naval submarine base was almost directly across from the academy in Groton.

"I wouldn't be too quick to dismiss a navy man," Caroline pronounced in a firm tone. "They can make excellent husbands. Marriage is very important to their careers. The right wife can be a real asset."

Amanda squinted suspiciously. "Since when have you started viewing sailors as prime matrimonial material?"

Caroline waved off her criticism. "I'm not talking about *sailors,* I'm talking officers. Listen"—Caroline fixed her with a bright-eyed glare—"Frank and I will be throwing a little engagement bash at my parents' house in a couple weeks. A young navy officer will be attending—what a coincidence, but there you are!"

Amanda gave Caroline a drop-dead look. "I don't like being set up."

"It's not a setup, I swear. Brother, are you ever paranoid! Just be his dinner companion. You know, even up the boy–girl ratio." Laughing, Caroline pulled a slender cigarette from her purse, lit it, and puffed. "What harm can it do? Let him show you a good time. You'll enjoy the party more—and you *have to* come." She blinked at Amanda through the smoke. "You're my best friend. Be there for me."

Amanda smiled. "Of course I will."

Amanda shut the front door of her parents' house and dropped the nubbin of the rust-pitted brass chain into its slot. Barely two feet behind her were the stairs leading up to the bedrooms. Inches from her right shoulder stood a yellowing papered wall that separated the two sides of the duplex. There was hardly enough room to shrug out of her jacket and hang it on the tottering coat tree.

Coming home, she always felt as if the ugly little house had been hungrily waiting to swallow her up. The exhilaration of being with Caroline dissolved into the gloom. She hadn't drawn three breaths and already she felt as if she were suffocating.

This is my home! It should be a happy place.

On her right when she turned around was the parlor. Behind that, through a narrow doorway, was the dining room, which was never used for serving meals. The table, always prepared for the remote possibility of hosting a family feast, was covered with a tablecloth Olga had crocheted from fine strands of ecru cotton thread. However, not much of her creation was visible.

Bruno taught German language and history at the local community college. Books, legal-size note pads covered with his indistinct scrawls, and student theses and tests occupied every square inch of space. Stacks of term papers and weighty tomes mysteriously shifted from place to place on the table or were occasionally replaced by different stacks. But no spot, over the course of many years, was ever made available for plate or cup.

In the parlor where Amanda now stood, the light from the old Philco television illuminated every item in an eery vacuum-tube glow. Above her head and encircling the room on a shelf eighteen inches from the ceiling was Olga's bottle collection. Below one section was a maple china cabinet, its joints parting with age, weakened by the constant dampness of the river. One pane remained cracked where little Amanda had fallen against it while learning to walk. Inside, piles of china dessert plates, demitasse cups, wine glasses, and beer steins filled the shelves, so many and so crammed together that it was impossible to admire a single piece. Although none of the items were expensive or of especially high quality, the collection was Olga's pride.

A sonorous snore issued from somewhere close by. Amanda's glance swung around to a green horsehair armchair. Bruno snorted twice, stirred, coughed, then drifted deeper into sleep, his gray head resting on a tasseled antimacassar.

How very old he looks. Too old to be my father.

He and Olga had met late in life, both displaced persons following the Second World War, people of German ancestry who'd been living on a piece of Czech territory known as the Sudetenland. They were suddenly without a country, without a home. They'd come to America on the same ship, courting during the passage. He'd been forty-seven when Amanda was born, and Olga had been just six years younger.

The cigar Bruno had been smoking had died out in his hand, depositing a gray drift of ashes on the braided rug beneath his limp, ink-stained fingertips. His snores filled the little room with his presence in sleep, just as his cold austerity and gruffness did in waking moments. Amanda stood watching him, taking in the puckered face with its blue and red veins showing through thinning layers of skin, like the minuscule threads implanted by the mint in a new dollar bill.

She took the cigar from his wrinkled fingers and placed it on the glass rim of the wobbly smoking stand nearby. For a moment longer she gazed down at him as if in motherlike appreciation of the rare peacefulness surrounding her slumbering child.

At last she turned off the TV and, lifting the crocheted afghan from the back of the sofa, spread it over him, tucking it around his arms and chest, up under his chin.

"Sleep tight, you old goat," she murmured tenderly, knowing if he heard her, he'd be furious.

"Is dat you, Amanda?"

She jumped, then placed the voice on the second floor. "Yes," she answered in a hoarse whisper up the stairwell. "I'll be right there."

Before going to her mother's room, she detoured through the kitchen. The refrigerator was full of Olga's specialties, a mixture of German and Czech dishes. Tonight: white sausages, Kartoffel salad, and Mohn strudel. Amanda cut herself a portion of the poppyseed pastry.

Eating in bed was a terrible vice. However, she was helpless to break the habit that had become an enjoyable part of her nightly routine.

She climbed the stairs; placed her snack on her bedside table, a cardboard pedestal disguised as a table by a piece of sheeting; pulled down the thin plastic roller shades; clicked on the ceiling light, which was the only illumination in the room; and, finally, continued on to Olga's room. Beneath the door shone a yellow strip of light. Olga was an insomniac and often read through the night.

Amanda tapped lightly. "Papa's asleep," she said, walking in at a signal grunt.

"I know."

"Can't we help him up to bed?"

"Try if you vant," Olga replied dispassionately, still concentrating on her German-language newspaper.

She was thin as a wheat stalk, pale and wrinkled, and worked herself to a frazzle cleaning a house that didn't need to be cleaned. As a girl she'd been taught to be a good German wife, and she was incapable of breaking the habits of a lifetime. However, she drew the line at providing other services for her husband. They'd had separate bedrooms for as long as Amanda could remember. She couldn't recall them ever touching one another.

"I won't break my back dragging him up dose stairs," Olga replied when Amanda continued to look at her hopefully. "He'll just cuss you out for thanks."

Amanda winced. "Maybe you're right." Bruno was not a gracious waker.

"You were teaching very late tonight?" Olga said, a distinct question in her voice.

"Caroline's home. We went out for dinner after my last class."

"Oh. And how is your *hochnasige Freundin?*" Olga's voice was predictably frosty. She had never approved of Caroline. "Your high-nosed friend" was a relatively kind epithet for the wealthy young woman from the other side of the river, whom Olga had always considered snooty.

Amanda refused to be baited. "Caroline is getting married."

"Married? Ach, so young?"

"Not everyone waits as—" Amanda realized almost too late that she'd been about to say something cruel. "A lot of people marry in their early twenties. I think she told me her fiancé is in his early thirties."

Olga shrugged, thrusting her nose back into her newspaper. "Who knows," she muttered in German. "Maybe it will work."

2

Caroline lay in bed smiling at the ceiling for no reason other than the fact she was delighted with the way her life was coming together. She'd worked hard to prepare for marriage —the right education at the right schools, proper contacts carefully nurtured with the appropriate sorts of people, practice in every social grace and point of etiquette. All toward one end: to become the perfect wife. The amazing thing was, she didn't object to the label, for Frank Donnelly was the ideal husband.

Well, *almost* ideal. In bed he was a gentle lover and careful to satisfy. He was—frowning, Caroline shook her head—*uninspired* was the word that came to mind. However, she refused to listen to her fretting subconscious. To be uninspired would mean Frank was, perhaps unknowingly, less than captivated by all she had to offer him, or he wasn't truly in love with her. And she would accept neither possibility.

Well, love isn't everything, and the same goes double for sex, she consoled herself, rolling over between the silky sheets on her Queen Anne bed. She'd had lovers who could perform for hours, leaving her panting, drenched with sweat, and dizzy with spent passion. But they hadn't possessed Frank's potential for giving her everything she ever dreamed of: a family that would form the roots of a prestigious Nesbit–Donnelly dynasty, houses around the world from which she could play hostess to the world's heads of state. Power and distinction were, to her, the ultimate turn-ons. Better than sex, which was saying a helluva lot.

Too excited to sleep, she tossed back the sheet and went to the dresser to brush her hair for the third time. The silver-plated boudoir brush had been her high school graduation gift from Amanda, one she suspected had been saved for from pocket change over a period of many months, which made it far more precious to her than the solid silver antique set that had belonged to Grandmother Nesbit.

What would she have done without Amanda, her down-to-earth, ever-loyal friend? Amanda who had supported her through every crisis, never criticizing, never asking more of her in return than companionship.

Feeling warm memories wash over her as she rhythmically brushed her chin-length honey gold hair, Caroline closed her eyes, recalling summer nights from their girlhood with a vividness she could almost touch.

She and Amanda had occasionally been allowed to spend a night at the studio. After Sara and Doug retreated to their apartment on the third floor, the two girls sat on the old stage that had hosted dance bands in the '30s and '40s. They played records on the turntable used during lessons, experimenting with new steps, talking about everything: the paralyzing fear of someday needing to wear braces on their teeth, the boys they were dating or hoping someday to date, their dreams for the future.

"Do you want Elvis, the Platters, or Pat Boone?" Caroline asked, dealing out Sara's collection of glossy black 45s like a deck of cards on the dusty wooden floor around her.

"Some of each," Amanda proclaimed eagerly. It was 1960, they were sixteen years old, and their music of choice was a mixture of pop and blues-rock: Elvis—"Don't Be Cruel," the Platters—"My Prayer," Bill Haley and His Comets—"Rock Around the Clock," Chuck Berry—"Maybelline," Pat Boone—"I Almost Lost My Mind,"

Frankie Lymon and the Teenagers—"Why Do Fools Fall in Love?"

These songs were a far cry from the Tchaikovsky, Chopin, and Strauss to which she and Amanda danced during their ballet and waltz lessons. But together they drank in every primordial drum beat and thrilling violin crescendo of rock tune or classic alike. Amanda, especially, seemed nourished by any kind of music, and Caroline suspected that dancing was more than just her hobby. It was her freedom from a stifling existence, living day in and day out with two old people who merely tolerated each other; spoke in the obscure, chilly language of scholars; and had never understood a young girl's talent or dreams.

The two girls talked most often about boys, a topic that never wore thin on Caroline, possibly because she was deprived of male contact. She attended Griswold Private School for Young Ladies in New London. Longing to meet boys was the main reason Caroline had come to the studio and started taking lessons, although her mother considered learning to dance part of "rounding out" her daughter's social education. Caroline had discovered that all Stevenson students were invited to Saturday night dance parties, which were eagerly attended by young men, to her way of thinking much more sophisticated young men who'd already graduated high school—sailors and Coasties.

But on these special sleepover nights, it was just the two girls alone. And when they became too exhausted to dance to their records in the empty ballroom or even to sit up any longer, they pulled cushions off the couch in the waiting room; lugged them up onto the roof where the flat, tarred surface held the day's heat; and stretched out under a thin blanket to ward off the river's snappy breeze. The air smelled of the nearby sea, baked tar, the spicy red geraniums Sara grew in immense wooden tubs on the rooftop, and of the French fries, codfish cakes, and baked beans swimming in thick molasses sauce that the Puritan Diner, next door to the studio, served up until ten each night.

From the roof they could see the Thames, named for the more famous river in the original London. They watched the lights of a ferry heading for Block Island and listened to a submarine chug upriver toward the naval base, its engines throbbing in the darkness like the heartbeat of some enormous beast. Eventually, amid a dozen whispered good nights and lying within arm's reach of one another, they drifted off to sleep. And when dawn arrived, the slow purple glow made the world visible again. Like magic.

Caroline gently set down the silver brush and sighed. She still considered those nights the very happiest of her life, which was perplexing to say the least, for they had nothing to do with either men or money, her chief interests in life.

The house on Eastern Point possessed only two floors but appeared larger, for it stretched out as long as any three of the neighboring homes. Its weathered gray shingles, the color of sun-dried driftwood, were framed with white trim and washed-blue shutters. Its name, Gray Cliffs, suited it although the brief rocky bluff at the far end of the manicured lawn was hardly high enough to be called a cliff. Still, the structure itself had the right appearance in color and design. The attached garages resembled scrubbed-out caves, spacious enough for six automobiles. Eight massive stone chimneys, leading up from grand fireplaces within, topped a slate roof. It was an estate worthy of Vincent Nesbit, president of Universal Shipping, the largest government contracting firm on the East Coast.

Wearing a cream-colored cocktail dress edged with delicate gold braid, Caroline stepped through French doors, which were blown about by white gauze curtains. The veranda overlooking the ocean had been opened up for the engagement party, window panes exchanged for screens. Tables were set up inside and spilled out onto the velvet-soft lawn, each covered with a pink damask cloth that was weighed down against the brisk ocean breeze with Paul Revere silver, Waterford crystal, and translucent English bone china.

Caroline spotted her parents in the middle of a cluster of guests—the Emersons, who'd driven up from New York, and Dr. and Mrs. Paul Zintner—and walked over to play the proper hostess. While she chatted lightly, she anxiously scanned the crowd, aware of her own elevated pulse singing in her ears. Frank hadn't shown up yet, although he'd called to say he was running late, and neither had Amanda. She wanted them at her side. She wanted the reassurance of their presence to make this day real and to reassure her that she was, in fact as well as in theory, doing the right thing. She nodded at Walter Emerson's comment on the race riots raging in Watts. Twenty thousand national guardsmen had been called out to quell the violence in the L.A. ghetto. She elegantly lifted a glass of white wine to her lips and complimented Maxine Zintner on her new social column in the *New York Times*. But all the while she was thinking, *Where are you, Amanda? Frank, please . . . please get here soon!*

At last she caught a glimpse of Amanda's slim figure weaving among the guests, and she felt instantly calmer.

Amanda's arms and shoulders were lightly tanned from taking her lunches up on the roof of the studio. The sun had also brought out her freckles, which weren't the kind that appeared as distinct dots but rather formed a dusky Milky Way across the bridge of her nose, spreading over her cheekbones and making her look tanner than she really was. She never wore makeup during the summer, except a touch of mascara and lip gloss.

Caroline raised a hand and waved. Hastily excusing herself, she met Amanda halfway across the lawn.

"I thought you'd never get here!" she hissed in her ear. "Frank's late, too. I'm going to kill him!"

"No, you won't," Amanda assured her. "He undoubtedly has a good reason."

"Like saving the free world from the Communist menace?" she said.

"That's a fine excuse." Amanda grinned, and Caroline could feel her sizzling nerve ends begin to cool down as the wine took the edge off her tension and her friend's teasing soothed her.

She looked at Amanda, only then realizing how ill at ease her friend appeared. "Relax. They're just people," she whispered.

Amanda winced. "Rich people aren't just people. I feel so unstylish." She had worn the same orange-flowered dress she'd chosen for their dinner weeks earlier, but this time spruced it up with white pumps; a choker of white plastic beads, the kind that popped apart so that you could adjust their length; and matching button earrings.

Amanda, thought Caroline, had a knack for making herself look pretty with dimestore accessories. "Don't worry about the dress." Caroline squeezed her hand reassuringly. "You look fantastic."

"Good afternoon, ladies."

Both women swung around to face a tall man with trim blond hair. His aqua-blue eyes peered straight into Caroline's, delivering a sensual jolt to her system, and she thought, *How lucky you are, Amanda. He's just my type: bronzed, muscled, and full of fun. But I'm giving him to you, my dear.*

"Amanda, I'd like you to meet Lieutenant Robert Allen. Robert, my best and oldest friend, Amanda Weitzer. Oh, there's Frank!"

Amanda barely got out her hello to Robert before Caroline dashed off between tables toward a distinguished-looking man wearing steel-rimmed glasses and a dark suit.

"So that's the lucky fella," Robert commented lightly.

"Must be," Amanda murmured as Caroline lifted her cheek for a welcome kiss from her intended.

She remembered the vague reservations Caroline had expressed the night of their dinner at the Lighthouse Inn— something about Frank Donnelly's appearance or manner. At the time, Amanda had assumed he must be somewhat homely, at least ordinary looking or perhaps bore some serious physical defect. Studying him from a distance, she had to admit that he possessed rather sharp features and he wasn't very tall, standing only a couple inches above Caroline in her heels. But he radiated an aura of authority and intelligence that gave him a smoother and more impressive presence.

Looking even more nervous than before Frank had arrived, Caroline pulled him toward them and made introductions all around.

"I'm glad to meet you, Frank," Amanda said, laying her

"Only in ballroom competitions. Waltz, tango, rumba . . . that sort of thing. It's quite different from doing a Las Vegas-style stage show or dancing with a corps de ballet or some other kind of touring company," she explained. "Most of the audience and all of the judges are made up of other dancers."

"I see." His eyes dropped to the glass of warm champagne she'd been nursing for the past hour. "Let me get you a refill before the bar closes."

He caught up with the bartender who was packing away bottles, slipped him a bill, and came away with a fresh magnum of Dom Perignon. Popping the cork with expert ease, he dumped the dregs from her glass on the grass, then refilled it and his own crystal flute with the luscious bubbly stuff.

"I don't suppose you have a competition coming up that I could observe," he asked.

"Not for a couple months, I'm afraid."

"Pity. By then I'll probably be out at sea again." Her heart thrilled at the look he gave her—lingering, flirting just a little beneath pale masculine lashes.

She cleared her throat, hoping her voice wouldn't crack when she spoke. "I'll let you know when one comes up," she promised. "If you're really interested."

"I'd like that."

Men in overalls scuttled around them, folding tables and chairs, tossing napkins and tablecloths into huge-wheeled hampers. After a few minutes, Caroline and Frank rejoined Amanda and Robert.

"We have plenty of time before dark," Caroline chirped. "Let's play badminton or go for a swim or . . . no, maybe croquet, oh I love croquet, although we'd have to set up wickets—"

"She's higher than a kite," Frank informed them, chuckling at his bride-to-be. "Calm down, darling, we have the rest of our lives to tackle every sport known to mankind."

"I know. I just want to—"

"Excuse me, miss." A maid stood in front of the French doors. "Mr. Donnelly has a telephone call. The gentleman says it's urgent."

Frank gave Caroline a look of apology. "Sorry, I'll be right back."

Leaning against the trunk of an old maple tree, Caroline watched Frank disappear through the door.

"Well," she asked slowly, "what do you think? I know you're both dying to talk about him."

Caught by surprise, Amanda didn't know how to reply.

"Come on!" Caroline wailed, "Tell me!"

"Well, he's a very unusual man . . ."

"Unusual." Caroline savored the word.

Robert smirked. "She means *boring*, my dear. He's dry as old shoe leather."

Amanda scowled at him. "I didn't mean boring at all. He's just . . . I don't know . . . It's as if his mind's in a dozen other places even while he's carrying on a charming conversation. If you really want to know what I think about him—compared to most of your men, Caroline—he's incredibly cerebral, but, I suspect, *never* boring."

"Most of your men?" Robert raised a taunting eyebrow. "Is the list terribly long? Maybe Frank should be apprised of those who've gone before him."

It was the first time Amanda had ever seen Caroline blush.

"Whether there's a list or not is none of your damn business," Caroline snapped. "Besides, my past doesn't matter to Frank." She looked pointedly at Robert. Amanda spotted Frank crossing the yard toward them. As he neared, Caroline said, "He loves me . . . and I love him."

"I'm glad to hear that," Frank said dropping a kiss on the nape of her long neck, which was still pink with annoyance.

Caroline affectionately glanced over her shoulder, but when her eyes met Frank's, she gave an involuntary shudder, and her lips instantly straightened. "Something's wrong," she guessed. "What?"

"I'm sorry, darling. I have to return to Washington."

"Now?" she cried. "But you were planning to stay the"— she broke off—"to stay until tomorrow."

Amanda knew Caroline too well to miss her cause for disappointment. She'd been looking forward to sleeping with Frank at Gray Cliffs, since they'd have the house to themselves for the night. Amanda pretended to be busy observing a bubble as it slowly rose through her champagne.

Frank wrapped his arms around Caroline, reassuring her with a hug. "It seems Mr. Kissinger is meeting with President Johnson first thing tomorrow morning. I'm expected to be there."

"Oh, damn." Caroline pouted. "Well, I'll drive you to the airport."

"Don't bother. I've already called a cab. It's on the way."

"You're sure?"

"Absolutely." He gave her an encouraging smile then turned to Robert. "Good to meet you, Lieutenant. I hope we run into each other again."

"Likewise," Robert murmured, holding out a hand to shake.

"And Amanda . . ." Frank took her hand with cool aplomb and lifted her fingers to his lips for the briefest of kisses in the Continental manner. He fixed her with a steady, sincere gaze. "Caroline has so often and warmly spoken of you. I'm glad we've finally met and only wish it had been under more relaxed circumstances."

Amanda nodded. "I hope both of you will come back often to Connecticut, so we can keep in touch."

"I'm sure we will. And maybe someday you'll be free for lunch." He winked over her shoulder at Caroline then leaned forward to whisper in Amanda's ear loud enough for everyone to hear. "You can fill me in on my lovely new wife's vices."

Amanda nearly choked on a laugh. *So, the diplomat has a sense of humor!* she thought delightedly.

Caroline let out a comical yip of dismay. "If you think I'd leave you two alone together for more than five minutes, forget it!"

A horn honked from the front of the house. Looking forlorn, Caroline took Frank's arm to walk him to his cab.

Amanda sat down with a sigh on a wooden chaise lounge and closed her eyes against the orange glare of the afternoon sun, absorbing the sudden stillness that always followed Caroline's departure.

"Frank has quite a handful there, don't you think?" Robert's voice sounded amused.

She opened her eyes to find him seated on the foot of her chair, watching her intently, and decided she didn't want to analyze Caroline behind her back as they'd done with Frank. "You don't seem like anyone I've ever known in the navy," she commented.

Robert chuckled. "A diplomatic change of topics if ever I've heard one." His eyes were a mesmerizing color, made bluer by the reflections off the water. A crisp dimple was centered precisely in the middle of his chin, and his cheekbones were unusually pronounced for man—all of which produced a very dashing package against his dress uniform. "Loyalty to an old friend is an admirable trait. But I still think he's in for trouble. Caroline's quite a woman."

"Maybe he's quite a man," she countered.

"Touché." He hesitated for a moment, looking as if he were about to say something more, but at last decided against it. "As to the navy, I suppose I am somewhat different from most commissioned officers. I take the whole military thing a little less to heart. I don't intend to make a lifelong career of the service. In fact, I've been thinking of opening my own business at the end of my commitment."

"What kind of business?" she asked, interested.

"One possibility is a sporting goods store. After living in this area for several years, I've noticed that there's a lack of good ones close by. I'd carry the usual equipment for kids' team sports, then add on for adults. With the baby boomers due to start coming of age, I figure on a strong recreation market for adults."

Amanda nodded. "I'm impressed." She found his plans quite fascinating.

"Well, it's just a pipe dream for now," he admitted with a boyish shrug. "Pulling it off will take a lot of hard work."

They talked for a while longer, sitting on the same chair beneath an arbor covered with wisteria that filled the air with its heady scent, rivaling the pungent snap of salt from the nearby sea. A thick carpet of grass sloped down toward the horizon, diagonal stripes of light and dark green shifting in the warm breeze.

Feeling incredibly mellow, Amanda let her head drop back against the sun-warmed wooden slats. "How did you come to command a ship at such a young age?" she asked.

"I'm twenty-eight, and I received the necessary education and experience from attending the Naval Academy. Besides, the navy isn't exactly overflowing with prime officer material these days. The situation in Vietnam makes for scanty recruitment. Guys are nervous, not knowing what they might be getting into."

"From the little bit Frank mentioned today," she observed, "I'd say things don't look as if they'll improve very soon."

"So he says . . ." Robert muttered, bending down to pluck a strand of grass. He raised it to his lips and chewed on it while watching her face. "What about you? Any long-range plans?"

"The only thing I truly enjoy is dancing. It makes me feel alive and apart from all the nightmares in the world— earthquakes, wars, disease, things we can't really do anything about. I mean, I'd be thrilled if I were terribly clever at medical research and could devote myself to finding cures for illnesses. But I've never been especially good in school, just an average student." *Much to Bruno and Olga's disappointment,* she thought ruefully.

They talked a little while longer, and at last, Caroline rejoined them. She looked like a totally different person. Her pretty eyes were dull, her walk stiff. She kicked off her shoes and sprawled disconsolately on a white wrought iron chair.

"I don't see why Frank has to do this," she grumbled. "He's spoiled the whole weekend."

"Frank's job sounds pretty important," Amanda pointed out.

"I suppose." Caroline groaned, shoving her toes through the grass, her gold ankle bracelet glinting in the sunlight. Slowly, her eyes flickered up at Robert. "I really did want the four of us to have the rest of the day together."

"I'm not disappointed." He leered at her playfully. "I now have *two* beautiful ladies all to myself. Just think of the tempting possibilities!"

29

Caroline shot him a cold glare. "I'm not going to be very good company," she announced, standing abruptly. "Why don't the two of you go for a swim or something." She marched off toward the house.

Amanda started to go after her, but Robert grasped her arm. "Leave her alone. She's just upset that she doesn't come first—before Kissinger and America."

Amanda frowned at his open disapproval. "That's a rather callous thing to say."

He shrugged. "How long have you known Caroline?"

"Years. Since we were kids."

"Then you should have learned by now that her foremost concern is always for Caroline Ann Nesbit."

Irritated, Amanda nevertheless sat down again on the chaise. There was a good deal of truth in what he said, and she sensed that he wasn't trying to be cruel, just matter-of-fact in summing up the situation.

She squinted up at him. "What makes you think you know her so well?"

"While I was at the academy in Annapolis, Maryland, I often squired dear Caroline around to various Washington functions. And since then, a few other times." There was a tinge of bitterness in his voice, and Amanda wondered if they'd been more than casual friends before Frank came along. "Caroline is a glorious girl," he continued, "but she's self-centered."

"She is, but she's generous, too. And such fun to be around that it more than makes up for her shortcomings." Amanda chewed her lip thoughtfully. She wanted to stay around long enough for Caroline to cool down, and Robert had surprised her by being wonderful company, even if he was somewhat critical. "How about going for a swim before it gets dark?" she asked.

"I haven't brought any trunks."

"The Nesbits keep a selection of bathing gear in the bathhouse." She pointed toward the private beach. A striped cabana had been erected above the high tide line for the season.

"A swim would be perfect," he agreed.

They took turns changing. Amanda went first, choosing one of Caroline's discards: a white maillot with a halter neckline that reminded her of something Marilyn Monroe might have worn. She felt primitively sexy in it, and Robert gratified her by emitting a low wolf whistle as she stepped out of the tent into the sunshine.

He donned a conservative blue-and-white pair of trunks. His arms and shoulders were a golden tan, his chest and back ridged with muscle. *He's gorgeous!* she thought, and she couldn't completely ignore the sensual tug deep within her as she watched him fold his clothing and place it beside hers on a flat rock.

They swam the length of the beach, racing from a stone breakwater to the end of the dock where the Nesbits' boat, *Precious Cargo,* was moored. The ocean was chilly, as New England waters are even during the height of summer, but Amanda welcomed the invigorating tingle it lavished on her skin. She needed this physical outlet to squelch her sudden attack of lust.

However, Robert did nothing to help her calm down, for he flirted with her shamelessly, diving between her bare legs, popping up in the white-nipped surf, his hair slicked back with sparkling droplets, his lashes long and darkened by the water.

Eventually, the salty water and exercise sapped her energy and helped cool her sensuous thoughts about Robert's body. She was breathless and shivering by the time Caroline hailed them from the pebbled beach.

"Hey, you're both going to shrivel up and disappear if you don't come out!" She was wearing a silky peach caftan that billowed about her like a pastel cloud. She looked radiant.

"How long have we been swimming?" Amanda asked.

"Over an hour." Caroline tossed Amanda a towel as she stepped out of the water. "I took a nap. Everything looks brighter now."

One thing about Caroline, she never stayed angry or in a testy mood for long. Amanda put an arm around her, and the two women climbed the wooden stairs built into the rocky ledge with Robert trailing behind.

"He'll be back soon," Amanda murmured.

Caroline sighed. "You know how I am. I make plans, and they damn well better work out."

"Some things in life you can't plan."

"Not many, if I have any say in the matter!" Caroline ground out, but Amanda could tell that, in her own way, Caroline was poking fun at herself.

They spent the last few hours of daylight sipping gin and tonics fashioned by Robert, snacking on leftovers from the party, and playing a cutthroat game of croquet during which Robert knocked both ladies' balls over the side of the cliff. When it finally grew dark, Amanda announced that she'd be leaving since she had to teach an early class the next morning. Robert and Caroline escorted her to her car, a second-hand Rambler with more rust than chrome.

"I'll be going now too," Robert said. "I have to get back to the base." He touched Amanda on the arm. "I'd like to call you, if that's all right. Maybe we could go see a movie or something."

"I'd like that," Amanda replied softly, her heart doing little leapfrogs in her chest.

Caroline was a mite tipsy. "See?" she slurred ecstatically. "I told you, one look at Amanda and you'd forget all about—"

"She *is* lovely," Robert cut in, opening the car door for Amanda. He leaned in through the window after she was settled inside and, looking somewhat frustrated, whispered, "I'd kiss you if we didn't have an audience."

Before Amanda could react, he'd stepped back, and she wasn't sure she'd heard him right. She turned the key in the ignition and drove down the long drive of crushed oyster shells. Halfway across the Gold Star Memorial Bridge, she decided she had indeed heard him correctly. She turned the radio up loud and sang all the way home.

3

Lieutenant Robert Allen whistled a jaunty tune as he strolled into the lounge of the Bachelor Officers' Quarters at the U.S. Navy Submarine Base in Groton, Connecticut. It was a little after eleven P.M., and the Bachelor Officers' Quarters was deserted.

Someone had left the TV on. CBS News was showing a clip of Johnson's address before Congress. Robert paused to listen, lighting a Camel cigarette, then hung around as a file tape of a B-52 bomber replaced the president's jowly visage. More air strikes had been called.

Man, he thought, *am I ever glad I'm not a pilot or some poor foot soldier.* Fortunately, a lighter story followed. A young designer named Bill Blass was predicting that the miniskirt was on its way out.

Damn shame, he mused. *What's a leg man to do?*

Robert grinned, tossing his head back and savoring the image that had just slipped into his mind. Amanda Weitzer had great legs. Must be her dancing, he guessed, shutting off the black-and-white set and continuing through the lounge to his room.

He lit another cigarette from its predecessor and made

himself a Beefeater martini. Brit gin was expensive, but what the hell. The military gave its folk great discounts on booze, so a guy could afford to drink like Rockefeller. Besides, they owed him at least a few simple comforts while he was in port. Three long months jammed inside the steel hull of a sub got pretty damn boring.

But now he wasn't bored. He was fidgety, keyed up. He thought about Caroline, whom he'd just left at Gray Cliffs. She was a great gal, but he'd never deceived himself by thinking she wanted him for anything more than an occasional escort to a party or a casual roll in the hay.

She'd probably introduced him to her dancer friend as a consolation prize, hoping he wouldn't make a scene after breaking the news to him that she was getting married. She really needn't have worried.

Robert swallowed a third of his drink, following it with a long pull off the Camel. No matter. He was glad he'd met Amanda. She was pretty and interesting and possessed a wholesomeness, which hinted that she probably could cook up a storm as well as keep a tidy house, unlike dear Caroline who was hopeless without a maid and cook.

It occurred to him, not for the first time, that he was tired of living in one-room, mint-green-walled barracks. He considered what a pleasant change it might be to come home to a little wife in a comfy Cape Cod cottage with white eyelet curtains in the windows, rose bushes out front, and maybe even a couple of kids. Why not go for the whole shebang?

He prepared a second martini, drank it slowly, feeling himself gear down enough to slip off his shoes and stretch out on the bed. Before he had the chance to dwell any further on his future, he was fast asleep.

The next morning Robert telephoned Amanda at the first of the two numbers Caroline had given him. An old woman answered.

"This is Commander Robert Allen. I'm trying to reach Amanda Weitzer," he explained politely.

"She isn't here," the woman replied in a guttural accent.

"Oh. Do you suppose she might be at the dance studio?"

"Das Kind! She is there all the time, only comes home to sleep." The woman hung up on him.

He stared at the receiver as the dial tone blared at him. "Super home life," he muttered, trying the second number.

This was considerably better. A younger woman's voice answered. When he asked for Amanda, she told him in a pleasant voice that Miss Weitzer was with a class and would return his call at her next break.

Feeling frustrated, he paced the lounge, fending off would-be telephone users for half an hour before the phone jingled.

"Robert! It's good to hear from you." Her voice floated through the receiver to him like a whisper of fresh air, a little out of breath with anticipation, or possibly it was just the aftereffects of exertion. Whatever the cause, she seemed happy to hear from him, and her excitement made him feel a little light-headed himself.

He envisioned Amanda swimming with him at Caroline's beach, her dainty, erect nipples showing through the white nylon of her swimsuit, her face aglow with salt spray and sunshine.

Robert asked her out to a movie and late supper that night, and when she accepted, he felt unaccountably as if he'd run a race and won a gold medal.

They ate at a place called Abbott's in Noank, which was a quaint seafaring town dating back to the seventeenth century. The houses of whaling captains could still be seen along the shore, white and square and sturdy with their widow's walks perched atop them like frilly hats.

All of the seating at Abbott's was outside—picnic tables with brightly colored canvas umbrellas stuck through a hole in their middles to provide shade during the heat of the day. Now the umbrellas were folded, revealing a sky studded with brilliant white stars. The tables stretched out over an acre along the banks of the Noank River.

Robert ordered a pair of boiled lobsters, coleslaw, fresh-cut fried potatoes, and, as an appetizer while they waited for their dinner, a basket of steamed mussels and clams accompanied by plastic cups of drawn butter. Amanda and Robert broke open the hot shellfish and ate the sweet insides, licking melted butter from their fingertips while watching sailboats drift upriver from a day out on the sound. Inboard motors on fishing trawlers chugged in the dusk. Running lights struck long ruby flashes across the ripples produced by passing boats. Soft, rhythmic ripples of the water lapped against the pier where the catch of the day was wheeled on dollies straight into the kitchen of the restaurant. The night cries of the gulls settling down as darkness thickened mingled with the smell of concentrated salt and gasoline from the motorboats, hot shellfish, and the fruity white wine Robert had brought to accompany their meal.

It had been a long time since Amanda had enjoyed herself so much. Robert was entertaining, delightfully glib, and attentive, all the more so after several glasses of the wine. Amanda felt light-headed, lighthearted, and when he moved around the table to sit beside her instead of across from her, she felt . . . ready.

Ready. That was the only way she could explain her feelings. She wondered how he planned to approach her. Would he take her hand softly in his? Would he slip his strong arms around her and draw her close, disregarding their fellow diners? Would he wait until they were alone again in the car, then turn onto a quiet dirt lane and ask if he might kiss her? And she? What should she do? Play coy and initially rebuff him? Or melt into his embrace and allow nature to take its course.

She found it impossible to keep her mind on their conversation. There was absolutely no doubt in her mind that the young navy commander would be a skillful lover. But perhaps her mood was coloring her view of him. She hadn't been intimate with a man since the breakup with her old dance partner, and that had been over a year ago.

Somehow, the meal was finished. Mounds of shiny red lobster, black mussels, and pearly clam shells were piled on plastic plates and discarded in a trash barrel. They climbed into Robert's Corvette and drove. He continued to be as casually talkative as before, and Amanda's heart thudded in her chest so hard that she was sure her ribs would crack at any moment.

The night had turned cool and densely black with vivid stars above. Before Amanda knew it, they'd arrived in front of the duplex on Bank Street and were walking up the front steps. Robert shook her hand and bid her a polite goodnight. She closed the door behind her and stood in the parlor, wondering why she was there and not parked in some lovers' lane in Robert's arms.

She was in shock. What had gone wrong?

"Damn," she muttered, leaning against the front door.

She glanced down at the tote bag still looped over her arm, stuffed with sweaty leotards and tights. She felt destitute, unloved, deserted. There was nothing to do but drag herself upstairs to her room, wondering how she could have misinterpreted his interest in her.

Robert asked Amanda out every evening the following week. When he went to pick her up on Friday, she was teaching a private lesson in the large ballroom instead of using one of the smaller practice rooms, so he lingered in the doorway unobtrusively watching. The man she was talking to looked like a truck driver—burly, roughly shaven, with enormous forearms. *What a joke!* he thought, looking forward to seeing how Amanda would handle the oaf on the dance floor. Robert was shocked when the guy seized Amanda in his arms and whisked her gracefully across the floor in a sensuous tango to "Hernando's Hideaway."

A little flame of jealousy licked his heart. Whereas Amanda had been merely pretty a moment ago, she now seemed irresistibly seductive, a beautiful, daring temptress as she danced the intimate adagio, so much so that he had to remind himself that this was the same sweet girl who'd sedately dined across the table from him all week. If she had interested him before in other ways, now he *wanted* her. And the urge was all the more intense since he hadn't had sex in nearly two weeks. Unusual for him when he was on shore duty.

When the music stopped, he stepped out of the shadows, feeling pricklingly possessive.

Amanda looked over and beckoned to him with a warm smile. "Come here, Rob. I want you to meet Nick Plucinski, my dance partner."

"Partner?" he asked warily. Perhaps he had a rival?

"We dance together at professional competitions," she explained. "Nick teaches at a studio in Hartford. We take turns commuting to practice."

"Glad to meet you." Nick held out a thick hand.

Robert shook with him. "You dance very well," he said as the other man flung a towel around his sweaty neck and sat down on a folding chair to change into street shoes.

"Thanks. I've been at it a few years, but Amanda here makes me look good."

"Yes," Robert agreed wholeheartedly. It occurred to him that, dancing with Amanda, any man would look damn good. He pictured himself spinning her across the floor at the Officers' Club Christmas Ball.

"Same time next week at my place?" Nick asked.

Amanda nodded. "I'll be in the city early to do some shopping, so we'll have a good long time to work."

Robert watched him leave, then turned back to Amanda, wanting to ask her to clarify her relationship with Nick but knowing he didn't have the right—just yet.

"I'll wash up and be right down," she said, straightening from unbuckling black high heels, giving him a soft smile. He impulsively grabbed for her and, pulling her against his chest, kissed her hard on the mouth.

She leaned away, gasping, a little flustered, but with a promising look of curiosity in her doe-soft eyes. "What was that for?"

He realized belatedly that they hadn't kissed before and some smoothing over might be necessary. "You were . . . fantastic!" he pronounced, grinning.

"Ah, so you like the tango!" She laughed at him.

"I like the lady dancing the tango."

"You must have Latin blood in your veins," she teased. "Give me a couple minutes to change, okay?"

While he waited for her, Robert walked around the ballroom floor. Any wall not concealed with mirrors was covered with photographs that had apparently been shot at competitions. In many pictures, there was an elegant young couple perhaps ten years ago and still strikingly handsome in more recent pictures. There were also many photos of Amanda posing with various partners. Sometimes she appeared shockingly daring in abbreviated sequin-studded Latin costumes that featured nude-colored fabric inserts. In other views she was demurely angelic in a fluffy white waltz gown. Either way, she looked delicious.

Eventually he strolled out into the office where the Stevensons greeted him. This couple, whom he recognized from the photos on the wall, seemed to take a proprietary interest in Amanda, and so he treated them to the same gentleman-officer routine he always dished out when confronted by the parents of a girl he was dating. Just like his old midshipman days at the academy. He'd learned then that you could get away with just about anything if you polished up your manners. He asked the Stevensons if he might use their telephone and made a call. At some point while he'd been watching Amanda and Nick, his plans for the evening had changed.

Amanda joined them. She looked like the girl next door again in a cotton skirt and peasant blouse, her hair pulled up from her nape with a bright ribbon, little tendrils slipping out to brush her shoulders. They said their good-nights to Sara and Doug and went on their way.

A few minutes later, Robert took Amanda's hand as they strolled up State Street. "I changed my mind about the movie tonight," he told her. "I don't feel much like James Bond."

"I thought you loved Sean Connery. You're not ill, are you?" she asked, looking concerned.

"No. I just want to take you someplace special. I made reservations at a restaurant I think you'll like."

They passed the Garde Theater and rounded the corner to a little restaurant called the Tide's Edge. It held only a dozen tables, and the menu was limited, but the food was consistently top-notch—a mixture of Continental and American cuisine. Every time he'd brought a woman here she'd melted in the intimate atmosphere. Of course, he blew forty bucks on the meal, but it always paid off in bed.

"This is absolutely delectable," Amanda pronounced through a mouthful of veal. "I should have dressed up for a night like this."

He reached across the table and took the fingertips of her

left hand in his. "You look gorgeous just as you are." She blushed, actually blushed! Gratified, he carefully continued. "I like you an awful lot, Amanda. I suppose you've guessed as much, since I've asked to see you just about every night since we met."

She didn't say a thing, just watched him with a soft upward turn to her lips that wasn't quite a smile, as if she didn't dare show him how pleased she was.

Robert refilled their glasses with wine and continued. "I think we're getting to know each other pretty well. I was hoping you'd agree that we're . . . well, ready for the next step in our relationship."

"Next step?"

"Yes." He looked down at her fingers, lightly clasped on the tablecloth. Was she nervous? Would she be offended, fly into a rage, turn him down cold? Why was this so much more difficult than the other times? "Listen," he pushed the words out, "I've heard of this really nice spot up near Rockport. I've always wanted to take a long weekend and drive up to Maine, but it seemed a silly thing to do on my own." Actually, Caroline had taken him there, and he'd longed to go back ever since. But why quibble over details when weaving a good story? The hotel had been classy, made him feel like a goddamn admiral, but now Caroline was out of the picture. "I wanted to share it with the right person," he finished, raising his eyes to meet Amanda's at last.

She seemed to be deep in thought.

He cleared his throat when she still said nothing. "Would you go away with me for a weekend? If you like, we can reserve two rooms. The important thing is we'll be off on our own, have plenty of time to talk and . . ."

Amanda observed Robert, her heart tripping over itself. His bright white teeth, his ingenuous blue eyes sparkling with humor; everything about him was vivid and alive, like the new color TVs in the display window at Moier's Electronics.

Suddenly she wanted to be with him, to be entertained by him, and to be hugged and share his happiness and be touched and—oh, hell—to be made love to. She needed someone, and for a long time just anyone wouldn't do. But Robert wasn't just anyone. He was intelligent and funny, and he had a good career (albeit one she'd never considered for a potential partner). Above all, he was the most attractive man she'd ever known.

Amanda smiled at him. "I'd love to go . . . and one room will be just fine."

Robert grinned, relieved. He hadn't been looking forward to spending an entire weekend with a woman who wasn't game for a good time, but he'd felt compelled to take the chance. If Amanda was wife material, he had to be sure they were compatible in every way before he tied the knot. Sex was too important to leave to chance.

4

For the first time in his life, Frank Donnelly was doing something that pleased his old man: He was marrying Caroline Nesbit. Maybe, at thirty-five, he'd grown tired of resisting his family's expectations. Or maybe it all came down to having Donnelly blood running in his veins. Whatever the reason, knuckling under this time actually seemed the smart thing to do.

There had been a succession of intelligent, well-bred young women in his life. Many had been quite beautiful, and he'd even considered marriage on one or two occasions but never with much enthusiasm. Something had always been lacking in the privacy of his heart if not in the public forum of a drawing room. After a while, he became convinced that he was searching for someone who didn't exist.

Then along came Caroline. She was passionate, bright, and attractive—a dazzling flash of a woman who offered an effective counterpoint to his naturally reserved nature.

She'd been floating through elite Washington social circles while still in college and was a sought-after date for the whirl of embassy and congressional receptions and balls. His eye had first been drawn to her at a charity affair sponsored by the Greek ambassador, then a number of times afterward.

Even before he asked her out, somehow he knew she was going to play an important role in his life. She had a certain knack for making a man see that what she wanted was best for him as well. And he hadn't even tried to elude her charms, for being with Caroline was a truly stimulating experience—in many senses.

His parents adored her; his colleagues thought she was perfect. He himself found her as adept in bed as she was in a receiving line. He asked Caroline Ann Nesbit to marry him three months after their first date.

Frank looked up from his desk and out the window of his office. From here he could see the Capitol. The sun caught it just right, reminding him of golden-domed temples of the Orient. Inevitably, his mind followed his heart back to the first time he'd seen that part of the world. An argument with his father had indirectly sent him there.

He'd been eighteen years old. It was New Year's Eve 1949. His father, a prominent senior financial officer at Chase Manhattan, had insisted that he major in finance at Yale. Frank didn't want to be a banker. He wasn't quite sure what he did want, but it would have nothing to do with banking, that much he was certain.

After a particularly nasty shouting match with his father, he'd stormed out of the house, and, in a fit of adolescent fury and pride, he'd enlisted in the Marines. Nine months later, he was boarding a ship in Kobe, Japan, bound for South Korea. His life had changed forever.

Frank was more than excited. He felt virile, pumped up, ravenous for battle. For weeks he'd intently listened to Walter Cronkite's reports on the six o'clock news: Communist insurgents from North Korea had invaded the south; the United Nations was meeting in an emergency session to decide upon a response. He overheard barracks rumors: Truman was prepared to send U.S. Marines to aid the Allied forces, but he still had to deal with Congress. No one seemed capable of making a quick decision. All the while, Frank, like so many young men before him, ached for a chance to prove his manhood on the field of combat.

On June 25, 1950, all speculation ended. North Korea

launched a massive attack on Seoul, and three days later, Communist troops overran the capital of South Korea. Throughout the summer he and his comrades-in-arms, boys he'd grown closer to in spirit than he'd ever been to his own family, drilled in hand-to-hand combat at Parris Island. They were shipped from South Carolina to Kobe and waited some more, drilled some more. Finally, the moment they'd been preparing for arrived.

The First Division made a perfect textbook amphibious landing at Inchon, South Korea, on September 15. They then marched east toward Seoul, encountering only token resistance, and by September 28 the combined UN forces had recaptured the capital allowing Syngman Rhee's government to return.

They didn't stop there, though. General MacArthur ordered the First Division Marines to push north across the 38th parallel into North Korea.

On October 15, Truman and MacArthur arranged to meet on Wake Island while all the world watched breathlessly. The general ordered his plane to circle the island until Truman had landed, wanting to make the president wait for him as a measure of his own power. He then pressed for permission to use nuclear weapons on Mongolia, because the Chinese were supplying both men and arms to their Communist allies. Without the delivery of a decisive and crushing blow, he argued, they would continue their aggression until the entire world fell under the evil shadow of socialism. Not wanting to risk a third world war, Truman refused.

Two willful men had played out a power game to a standoff, an unsatisfactory conclusion for both.

It was sometime shortly after Wake, as the icy winds swept down from the Changpai Mountains, that Private Donnelly realized something was terribly wrong. A division of Marines could march sixty miles in twenty-four hours. But the First Division was inching north at barely ten miles per day, even though MacArthur had ordered them to chase the Communists straight across the Yalu River into Mongolia. Why were they moving so slowly?

One particularly bleak afternoon, Frank was delivering a message to the operations officer. As he approached Lieutenant General Bowser's tent, he overheard him complaining to one of his staff.

"We can't drag our feet any longer. Command is on to us. The order is move, and move fast. Straight north."

"What about the recon flights?" demanded the other officer, sounding angry.

Frank stood shivering in the frigid blasts of arctic air, yet he was unwilling to step into the tent and end the conversation. He walked past the sentry and glimpsed Bowser through the flap opening, shaking his head worriedly.

"Our pilots report massive Chicom troop concentrations just the other side of the Yalu."

"They might join in the fight. Shit, General! We might be walking into an ambush!"

"Or it might just be a show of force," Bowser said thoughtfully.

Frank felt a lump swell in his throat, nearly closing off the air to his lungs. For the first time, a terrible thought occurred to him: *We could all die here tomorrow!* He never said a word to anyone. There was nothing a nineteen-year-old grunt could do.

Thanksgiving Day was miserable. The Chosin Reservoir plateau, where the First Division had camped to celebrate the holiday, was four thousand feet above sea level and assaulted by the coldest winds yet. The good news was, for the first time in months the Marines were served something hot and tastier than the usual flavorless C rations. But the luscious slices of turkey dripping with steamy gravy froze solid before they could cut them. The best anyone could do was suck on chunks of meat like a Popsicle.

Unbelievably, the temperature plummeted still further below zero during the course of the day. Then the first wave of Communist Chinese soldiers struck. MacArthur's high command denied their existence—despite overwhelming intelligence to the contrary—right up to the moment of the ambush. By intentionally placing his own men in jeopardy and daring the enemy to make a move, MacArthur hoped to

45

force Truman to give him the bomb and his very own war. Instead, Truman fired him. But that didn't help the men trapped at Chosin.

Frank fought for his life and those of the boys around him. Admirably disciplined, the twelve thousand-man combat division held together despite overwhelming odds, battling bravely in frozen ditches and across ice-encrusted fields. Constantly under attack, they retreated in proud, orderly fashion for thirty-five bloody miles on foot, carrying their wounded and dead while defiantly singing an obscene ditty.

As Frank tearfully shouldered the body of a boy who'd beat him at cards the night before, he cursed glory-hungry generals and nearsighted politicians. He vowed on the day they met up with the relief column in Chin-hung-hi that he'd somehow find a way to make peace work. No more war games. No more MacArthurs. No more Frozen Chosins.

Sara was delighted to hear about Amanda's travel plans. "Don't worry about a thing. I'll try out some of our older students as assistants to cover our beginner classes. That's how you got started, remember? It's good experience for them. You can reschedule your adult classes. Go! Have a wonderful time."

Dealing with Olga and Bruno was a little more difficult.

"You are going off with a strange man to Maine? Dat must be at least three hundred miles!" Olga gasped. "Do you hear this, Bruno?"

"Bitte?" her father grumbled from the midst of his papers in the dining room. He was teaching two summer semesters. Because each was only four weeks long, a mountain of student papers had to be read and corrected all within a very short time. The courses were different from his usual ones, so he had to also prepare lectures. He seemed to never close his beloved volumes of Goethe and Nietzsche.

"Your daughter is driving in an automobile with a strange man to Maine," Olga informed him in German. "They will stay in some filthy motel, no doubt."

Amanda rubbed the bridge of her nose and squeezed her eyes shut, guessing what was coming.

Bruno appeared in the kitchen doorway. "Tell him you cannot go."

"Why?" Amanda asked.

"Your father says so," he intoned, thick brows bristling over black, black eyes. "Tell him your father forbids it."

"I'm twenty-one. I can make my own decisions." She would have understood if she thought they were truly worried about her. But Amanda knew from previous experience that their only concern was that she might embarrass them or disturb their routine.

Bruno looked over his glasses at her, the eyebrows that had always frightened her as a child lowering ominously.

"Tramps sleep with men dey aren't married to! You are sleeping with dis man while living under my roof?" he bellowed.

"No. I'm not sleeping with him, Papa," she said, trying out a gentler tone. "But I'm not a virgin either, and I haven't been for years."

As soon as she'd spoken, she knew she'd made a dreadful mistake. There was dead silence, then Olga let out a shuddering breath.

Bruno looked at Olga. "Dis," he stated, pointing a thick finger at his wife, "ist your fault, *frau*. You say, 'Dancing lessons vill help her come out of her shyness, help her make friends.' Vell, dis is the friends she makes. Letches! She might as vell live in a combine with hippies!" he finished in a roar with a flourish of waving hands as if he were a crazed orchestra conductor.

"That's a commune," Amanda corrected, "and I'm not—"

"Shut your mouth!" he ordered, stepping forward, his face dark red, temples pulsating. "My father would have thrown such a daughter into the street!" He stepped forward, drawing back his hand, and for a moment she was certain he was going to strike her.

Amanda curled her fists at her sides in defiance, as she'd done when he'd berated her for average grades although she'd tried her very best to succeed in elementary school, as she'd done when they'd argued about her working Saturdays during her high school years at the studio, as she'd done when she refused to attend college and sit in a classroom even one more day after she'd graduated from high school. And he had struck her those times, a fierce, shaming slap across the cheekbone that she added to all of her other reasons for defying him and clinging to her dreams.

She didn't flinch. Slowly, Bruno's hand dropped in a dismissing wave. He turned away from her, crossed the room, and returned to his papers at the dining room table.

Amanda shook her head. It seemed to her that she'd never been able to please them. Even if she agreed to turn down Robert's invitation, they would remember only that she'd considered going, which was as bad as the actual act.

"You'll go," Olga muttered bitterly. "You are a stubborn girl. But it's wrong."

"I never said I intended to *sleep* with Robert," Amanda protested. But of course that was exactly what she hoped for.

Olga refused to look at her, one woman sensing another woman's desire and perhaps despising her because she no longer was capable of feeling such passion herself.

There followed a full week of tension in the Weitzer household, all three residents avoiding one another whenever possible, being stiffly polite whenever contact was unavoidable, like at the dinner table. "Pass der salt, please. Tenk you, very much."

But Amanda was determined not to disappoint Robert or herself.

Saturday arrived clean and bright after a July shower. The grass in front of the little house was damp and the kind of vivid green one only sees after a thorough rain. When Robert pulled up in front of the house in his Corvette, Amanda carried her suitcase down the steps into the foyer, aware that her parents were ignoring her departure by busying themselves like a pair of moles somewhere in the recesses of the duplex. *How much of life they miss,* she thought. She called out a cheery good-bye for effect but got no answer, and so she let herself out the front door, troubled by their coldness but nevertheless determined to enjoy her illicite weekend.

Robert grinned at her, his eyes twinkling. He took her suitcase, popped it into the little trunk, then held the passenger door for her while she climbed in.

Her heart was all ajangle with excitement as they drove, chatting about the weather (how beautiful it was), discussing the history of Rockport (Amanda had looked up the town at the library in a tour book), and talking about the navy.

Robert thought that he might be given command of another boat. There was a chance of his sailing for Asia, which brought up Vietnam. Amanda was able to comment in fair detail about the political situation there, for she'd started reading the newspaper every day—a new habit she'd developed since Caroline's engagement. If her best friend was marrying a career diplomat, she, Amanda, would have to keep up on world events so as not to appear totally ignorant. She was finding the Paris Peace Talks surprisingly interesting. Several evenings while devouring a description of each side's demands, she wished she knew Frank well enough to call him and ask questions. To witness, to be part of such momentous events firsthand fascinated her, which in turn amazed her for she'd always detested history in school.

After driving for almost an hour, they'd reached northern Rhode Island. Robert pulled off the road into a public rest stop surrounded by a thin grove of maple and evergreen trees.

He rubbed his eyes and stretched his long body in the driver's seat. "I didn't get nearly enough sleep last night. Guess it's caught up with me."

"Would you like me to drive?" Amanda offered. "You can nap."

"No. I just need a little break. Come on, I've brought snacks for the road."

He reached over the back of the seat and retrieved a wicker hamper.

Delighted with his plan, Amanda climbed out. "We're in luck: picnic tables." She pointed at the little cluster in a clearing close by. A family of five with a dog occupied one and were gaily munching away on sandwiches.

Robert pursed his lips. "Kids and a pooch. They'll start

squabbling as soon as they're full, and the dog will be all over us, begging for scraps. Let's find someplace a little more private."

"All right," she agreed.

They located a footpath through the trees. Robert hiked onward, dissatisfied with the first stretch of grass they found, which was littered with other people's trash.

"It's disgusting how people dirty up pretty places like this," Amanda commented, marching along happily at his side. Sunlight filtered down through the leaves overhead, and she felt relaxed and happy.

Robert switched the basket to his other hand, took her hand in his, and began humming. When they finally stopped, he glanced around approvingly. "This is more like it," he exclaimed, setting the basket down in the grass. They'd come nearly a quarter mile from the parking area, and from where they stood, Amanda could see a farmer's field edged in barbed wire. The air smelled of hay growing in warm sunshine, of tree bark and sweet wild flowers. Speckles of sunlight filtered through the generous tree limbs above. It was ideal, romantic, and utterly theirs.

Robert was all business now. He unlatched the hamper and pulled out a checkered cloth for sitting on. Next he extracted cheese, bread, a plastic sack of fruit, and a bottle of wine.

"You could feed an army with this," she teased as she curled her legs beneath her to sit.

He sat beside her. "A navy, madam," he corrected her.

They laughed, and their eyes met over the picnic basket, sharing the humor. Then Robert's glance darkened, and for a moment she thought the sun must have slipped behind a cloud, taking the blue out of his eyes. Then she recognized his desire, and all she could think was *Thank God he wants me as much as I want him!*

There were no tender caresses, only long, deep kisses as Robert pushed her back onto the checkered tablecloth, food and wine forgotten. His muscular body moved on top of her, pressing her into the soft woodsy loam and releasing the scent of pine needles. Then his hand was under her skirt, and his mouth covered hers. Distant sounds of traffic from the highway faded into a warm buzz in her ears. His hands trailed tantalizingly over her skin, while his mouth urgently slid over her lips, her throat, nipping at her nipples, moving downward. Amanda arched against the warm earth.

A sliver of consciousness intruded on her passion. She released her right hand from Robert's hip and reached toward her purse.

"It's all right," he whispered hoarsely, "I'll take care of it."

She relaxed again, letting Robert pull her panties down and off over her knees. He raised her skirt while unzipping and pulling down his pants.

"Oh, Amanda," he groaned, "you can't know how much I've wanted you!"

"I want you, too, Robert," she murmured, her eyes dropping to take in the stripped lower half of his body— lean, hard, and eager for her.

He entered her quickly without a condom. Puzzled, she looked questioningly up into his eyes.

"It's all right," he whispered. "Don't worry."

With long, full thrusts, he brought her to orgasm. She bit her lip to keep herself from screaming with delight. Almost immediately, he withdrew, clasped her fingers around him and came on her stomach. She watched him, mesmerized by the overt sensuality of his ejaculation. It had all happened so fast, yet she couldn't stop trembling for the longest time.

Amanda lay exhausted but satisfied, breathing raggedly, happily dizzy, and throbbing warmly inside. She wanted more than anything to curl up in the sun-dappled shade and nap in Robert's arms.

He laid a hand on her arm. "Hey," he chuckled, "get dressed. Someone could come along. We're lucky we weren't interrupted a few minutes ago."

"Mmmmm," she mumbled but didn't move.

Robert grasped her hand and pulled her into a sitting position. "Let's go, pretty lady."

Opening her eyes, she scowled at him with mild irritation. She felt like basking in their carnal afterglow. He, on the other hand, looked ready to scale Mount Everest. Nevertheless, she realized the truth in what he was saying.

They dressed and ate, then started out again, taking Route 1 around Boston before hitting the New Hampshire border. "We'll stop for gas soon," he told her.

They were talking less, but the silences were companionable. She snuggled down, curling around the awkward stick shift between the seats, and laying her head in his lap to take a nap. It was going to be a wonderful weekend, she decided contentedly. They were so very good together. No man before had made love to her as Robert had. He seemed to know precisely how to touch her, just what to murmur in her ear at the ideal moment to arouse her to her fullest. She was so grateful for his attention she could have cried. It had been a very long time.

Amanda awoke and sat up when she felt the car slowing down. They were pulling into a gas station. Robert filled the tank while she dashed for the ladies' room, used the toilet, washed her face and hands, brushed her hair, and put on a little lipstick.

When Amanda returned to the pumps, however, the Corvette was no longer there. Confused, she stood in the middle of the pavement, looking around at the beehive activity of refueling automobiles and scurrying travelers, and finally spotted the little sports car behind a few gnarled elm trees in back of the garage. It was almost completely screened from other vehicles. Robert, she reasoned, must have moved it out of traffic while he used the men's room.

Amanda walked across to it and found he'd left the car unlocked for her. A moment later, she spotted him jogging toward the car. Grinning impishly at her, his blue eyes alight, he leaned in through the open window and nuzzled her neck.

"I can't get enough of you," he growled in her ear, then nibbled its tender rim.

Amanda feigned shock. She was immensely pleased and flattered by his playfulness. "We'll be at the hotel in a little over an hour," she teased, ruffling his thick dark hair.

"I can't wait an hour for you." He tickled her in the ribs until she crumpled to one side in her seat, helpless with laughter.

Robert ran around the car and slid into the driver's seat,

at the same time adjusting it all the way back. He pulled her over to sit on his lap. Before she'd fully recovered from her giggles, he started unbuttoning her blouse.

"Robert!" she gasped.

But his hands worked magic on her and she had no real desire to stop him. She reassured herself that they couldn't be seen from the parking area or highway. Even then, the possibility that they might be discovered only added an element of danger to their play. In seconds she was as wildly involved with his body as he was with hers.

And his was an incredibly beautiful body—what she could glimpse through the openings of his clothing. He was deliciously tanned, with only a small white rectangle of skin across his hips. He had smooth, wide shoulders, naturally toned muscles, a washboard stomach, and a sexy line of soft fur running from his throat to the thicker matting of his crotch.

Still half dressed, they somehow made love in the front seat of his Corvette. And they had sex for a third time as soon as the bellboy left them alone in the spacious room that overlooked the rocky Maine coastline, a fourth time directly after dinner, and—she wasn't sure if it was a dream or not—she thought he woke her during the night at least once.

By the end of the weekend, the two days were a steamy blur in her memory. It seemed that whenever one of them looked at the other, they threw themselves into one another's arms dissolving in kisses and touches that peaked in the ultimate passion. They took time out only to eat, hit a tennis ball around on a clay court for a half hour, and stroll twice on the hotel beach.

Monday morning Amanda woke in her own bed, pleasantly sore in unusual places, dreamy, still feeling the pressure of Robert's hands on her and in her. There was a ghost of concern in her mind, not that she might have become pregnant, for he seemed to have an endless variety of methods for avoiding that problem, either by withdrawing at the last moment or by showing her ways to stimulate him without resorting to actual intercourse. And he never failed to please her.

No, her concern pertained to deeper aspects of their

developing relationship. For although they had discovered everything there was to know about each other's bodies, neither had learned anything more about the other as a person. She made up her mind that the next time they were together they would have a long talk about everything that was important to each of them. They would have to get to know each other. Sex was fine, was great! But more was involved in a relationship if it was to have a chance of lasting.

Amanda saw Robert nearly every night for the next three weeks. Unfortunately, talking was one thing they didn't do much of. He took her to dinner. He drank a couple martinis before dinner and wine with the meal, and she kept him company by having more than she had intended. Then he'd drive to a secluded area off the shore road, they'd park and make love, then he'd take her home.

She wanted to ask him a hundred questions, but she hesitated to interrupt the heady flight of their romance. Why mess with such a good thing? she rationalized. She was enjoying herself thoroughly. And Robert was madly in love with her, he said so frequently. She craved the intensity of their lovemaking. Asking what flavor ice cream he liked best or his political opinion on Vietnam or the upcoming presidential election seemed trivial beside the immensity of their love. The outside world could wait.

The outside world didn't wait for long. Before Amanda knew it, Caroline's wedding was only weeks away, and she had asked Amanda to be her maid of honor. There were fittings for the gowns, and Caroline insisted upon her being present not only for the maid's dress, but for three of her own fittings, which took place at a New York City dressmaker's. There were two rehearsal dinners and four showers (all of which Amanda was expected to attend). Caroline repeatedly called her for major and minor emergencies—only lavender, no pink, orchids available for the church!—or just to oooh, ahhh, and ogle an especially extravagant gift (or singularly stupid one) that had arrived that day.

"Just think!" Caroline cried, aglow with excitement as

they sat together in her parlor and she unwrapped a third Waterford crystal vase. "Someday this may be you!"

"I seriously doubt it," Amanda replied. "My parents don't have the Nesbit connections. If I marry, Olga and Bruno will invite a dozen stodgy professors and hold the reception in the dining room." She wondered if their only daughter's marriage would be cause enough to break out the "good" china. She suspected it wouldn't.

"How grim," Caroline groaned.

"I don't mind. I can accept them being the way they are as long as they don't interfere with who I want to be." Amanda set the three vases on a table that now displayed thousands of dollars worth of silver, crystal, and Irish linen.

"Well, cheer up," Caroline said. "I think Robert really likes you! Maybe he'll ask you to marry him."

The idea had occurred to Amanda. She'd been seeing him for several months now, and he'd proposed a second trip to Maine. But until Caroline's wedding was over, she couldn't concentrate on anything else. She was, in fact, more nervous than the bride, keyed up to the point of mild nausea many days. Between teaching a full schedule, dashing off to rehearsals, and shopping with Caroline for her trousseau, she was in a constant state of exhaustion.

At last she took a day off and told everyone—Caroline, Robert, and Sara included—that she needed time to recoup. She slept until ten o'clock in the morning. She made herself a breakfast of French toast, bacon, and butter sautéed cinnamon apple slices with fresh brewed coffee. Bruno was teaching, and Olga was meeting with her literary critique group at the library, so Amanda, blissfully, had the house to herself. She brought her calendar down to the kitchen and opened it beside her plate. While she ate, she tried to create some order in the next few weeks.

As she searched out chores she might have overlooked and needed to reschedule, flipping the pages backward over the past month then the one before that, she became aware of one date that should have been foremost in her mind.

Her last menstrual period had been two weeks before her trip to Maine. Since then she'd missed one period, and now was several days overdue for her second. Her body was normally as dependable as the sunrise.

Feeling suddenly short of breath, she again flipped through the month of May in the wild hope that she'd written her usual *P* very small on one page and overlooked it, or she'd recall a couple days of cramps that she'd forgotten to mark down.

But it was no use. The fact that Robert had withdrawn from her before each of his orgasms had lulled her into a false sense of security. She'd assumed impregnation was impossible. Something must have gone wrong! Robert must have miscalculated . . . oh, God!

Suddenly her queasy stomach, fatigue, and, now that she thought of it, the acute sensitivity of her breasts, made a different sort of sense.

Amanda made an appointment with her gynecologist for the next morning. By the end of the week, test results combined with her examination left no doubt. She was pregnant.

Amanda had put off seeing Rob until the test results were in, wanting to be absolutely sure before she turned his world upside down. Now that there was no question, she called him and suggested they go out for a quiet dinner that night. He was enthusiastic and promised to pick her up at the studio.

All day long, Amanda kept her secret. To tell Sara or Caroline before she'd broken the news to Robert didn't seem right. Strangely, she wasn't afraid of his reaction or of her own situation. She was happy to know that she would have this baby. To start a family in her early twenties was exactly what she'd hoped for. The only wrinkle was that she happened not to be married at the time.

However, as thrilled as she was, she couldn't very well let on that she was pleased until she saw Robert's reaction. If he didn't want the baby, that would end their relationship. She would refuse to have an abortion, and she wouldn't be able to bear seeing him, the father of her child, if he had rejected their baby.

By the time eight o'clock, the end of her teaching day,

rolled around, she was in a cold sweat. As Robert walked her to the Corvette, she felt as if her knees would buckle beneath her she was so nervous. She stopped abruptly beside the car door, resting her fingertips on the curved glass pane, and studied her reflection—slim and young. How would she look eight months' pregnant? *Funny, but nice,* she thought, smiling.

"Don't you want to get in?" Robert asked.

She shook her head. "Let's walk for a while."

"Reservations are for eight-thirty."

"I know, but I have something to tell you," she said softly. "I don't want to talk in the car."

He looked at her solemnly. "You were too busy to see me for the last few days. If this is going to be a good-bye speech, you can tell me right now. I don't need the kid glove treatment."

Oh, Robert, how wrong can you be? She smiled softly at him. "You know how I feel about you. It's not that, but it is . . ." She was at a loss for words.

"Serious?" he asked.

"Yes."

He nodded and offered her his arm. They walked down the length of State Street, past Moier's Electronics, the shoe store, Kresge's, Rexall Drug, the News Center with its hundreds of magazines and newspapers, and, at last, the bars that nestled next to the railroad station and docks. They walked out onto the long wharf cars drove across to board the Orient Point ferry four times a day during the summer months, once daily during the winter. Amanda stopped walking and turned to face Robert, a lump in her throat, the muscles across her shoulders taut with worry despite her own joy. She realized in that moment that it wasn't just the thought of losing him, but the fear of hurting him that tormented her.

"I've been trying all day to think of an easy way to say this," she whispered. "I can't."

"It *is* that you don't want to see me anymore," he stated, sure of himself and looking bleak.

"Oh, no!" She smiled, tears filling her eyes, and reached

up to gently touch his cheek. "It's not that at all. I like being with you. I want things to stay just as they are, but I'm . . ." *Say it. Just come straight out and say it!* "Rob, I'm pregnant."

He blinked, looking almost comically dazed. "You're kidding, right?"

Despite her desire to reassure him, she was a little miffed. "Of course I'm not kidding. I wouldn't joke about a thing like that!"

"I see." Releasing her, he squatted and picked up a pebble lying on the wharf. He looked away from her and across the river at the ships in dry dock at Universal Shipping, then threw the rock as far as he could.

Amanda's heart sank as surely as the pebble he tossed into the wavelets. "I have no intention of forcing you to marry me," she choked out the words quickly. "I don't want that. I just have to know how you feel about being a father, because I'm going to have this baby. I won't get rid of it . . . but I'll need to find another place to live, because my parents will be impossible about this. If necessary, I'll raise the child by myself—"

He stood up in front of her and put his palm over her lips, silencing them. "Don't be so defensive. It was my fault. I said I'd take care of things. I didn't, unless . . ." He looked at her with obvious meaning.

"No!" she protested. "Of course, I haven't been with anyone else!"

"Sorry, I had to ask." He looked thoughtful for a minute. "Well, I have to tell you, I've been considering marriage anyway. Being with you makes me think it might be a pretty good deal. I guess this just moves things along a little faster." He grinned at her. "Marry me, Amanda?"

Her breath felt as if it had been sucked out of her lungs. All indecision vanished, and her joy instantly tripled. Suddenly, everything seemed so much simpler. Rob wanted their baby! He loved her, although he hadn't said as much in his proposal. But he'd said so enough times when they'd made love, and she felt that he must care deeply for her to commit himself in this way.

Amanda threw her arms around his neck and squealed,

"Yes! Yes, of course, I will marry you, Commander Robert Allen!"

Caroline's wedding was set for the third Saturday in August. During the week before, Amanda and Robert took their blood tests and applied for a marriage license. They intended to leave directly from Caroline's wedding reception and drive to a little church in Hampstead, Connecticut.

It was Amanda's wish that they be married without her parents present. She could too vividly imagine their reactions. For once in her life, she refused to allow her joy to be soured by their complaints and dire predictions of disaster. Robert would have preferred to simply be married by a justice of the peace in New London, but Amanda wanted the church, even if there would be no guests to speak of.

Sara and Doug accompanied them to serve as witnesses. They used Amanda's old but reliable clunker since the Corvette wouldn't accommodate four. The little wedding party tooled gaily through the summer countryside to the tiny stone church. After the short ceremony at which Robert placed a slim gold band on Amanda's finger, they piled back into the car and drove south to Essex and the Griswold Inn, where they ate their second bridal dinner of the day.

Amanda's only regret was that Caroline could not be at her wedding as she had been at hers. However, Amanda felt she had to be practical. Before long Robert would leave for sea duty. Besides, she admitted to herself, she would feel better having a ring on her finger before her middle started to swell noticeably.

Her own wedding was far simpler than Caroline's, but Amanda didn't care. All that mattered was that she and Rob were happy. Together, they'd look forward to their baby's arrival. Although finding the man of her dreams hadn't come about quite as she'd expected, she was content.

5

Amanda couldn't believe she'd gone so long without having this baby. At two full weeks beyond her due date, she felt like an overfilled water balloon, and she couldn't remember the last time she'd found her toes without help to put on ballet slippers.

Sara commandeered advanced students to work as demonstrators for Amanda's classes, but Amanda insisted upon personally supervising until she delivered. She propped herself up beside the record player and directed a nine o'clock ballet class as usual this Saturday.

"*Pique . . . pique* turn again . . . and glissade ensemble," she chanted to the beat of the music. "Lovely, Janet. That's right, Patty, use your arms but soften the elbows. Like this."

"Les Sylphides" played in the background, weaving a dreamy melody to capture the children's feet. There was even a boy in the class, which was unusual for a small-town studio. He was tall for his age, agile, and, at ten years old, had developed a promising masculine grace.

"Very nice, Alex. Put some real power into this leap. Height. More height!" she encouraged.

By continuing to teach, she kept herself from going crazy. She and Rob had moved into a dingy efficiency apartment near the naval base until an apartment became available at the beginning of their second month as a married couple. The single room was clean but the furniture was worn by decades of temporary occupants. It did not feel like a home. At last they had been able to move into one of the modest apartments provided for officers and enlisted men with families, and that seemed better. Rob left for sea duty on the *Neptune,* the submarine under his command, with a crew of one hundred sixty. And Amanda waited alone for her baby.

Robert was somewhere in the middle of the Atlantic Ocean—exactly where, Amanda had no clue. Routes patrolled by nuclear submarines were kept secret, because they carried nuclear warheads and were intended to provide a first line of defense against an aggressor. As her due date approached, arrived, and passed, Amanda needed as much emotional bolstering as possible.

Her parents didn't make this last stage of her pregnancy any easier on her.

"There must be something wrong," Olga fretted. "No woman in my family ever carried a child so long. Are you sure that the doctor knows what he's doing?"

No, Amanda wasn't sure. But she certainly couldn't afford to lose confidence in the professional who was supposed to deliver this baby any day now.

"Maybe I calculated my conception date wrong," she said and hoped Olga would let it drop.

When she didn't, Bruno was the one who unexpectedly silenced her. "Leave her alone, Olga," he said gruffly. "It'll come when it's ready." Amanda could have kissed him, but he spoiled whatever shred of kindness he'd been able to dredge up from his thin spirit by adding with a woeful glare over the rims of his spectacles, "She'll have more than she can handle then, let me tell you. Twenty years of raising a child, only to discover it will do what it wants and ignore everything she teaches it."

Sara was her savior. She proved eternally calm and sensed that a level-headed, unemotional approach to mother nature's delay was best. Although she'd never had a baby of her own, she intuitively sensed Amanda's needs.

She kept Amanda busy but also forced her to take

ten-minute breaks between classes to put up her feet, and she often stole moments from her own classes to rub Amanda's back or run into the ballroom to give her a quick reassuring hug.

"I'm as thrilled with this baby as if it were my own," she confessed to Amanda in the midst of one hectic Saturday. "You are like a little sister to me, which makes me an unofficial aunt, and that pleases me more than I can say."

Normally Amanda taught ballroom in the afternoons and evenings. But since she'd grown too awkward and big to efficiently partner anyone, she traded classes with Sara. Saturday at three o'clock, she took on an adult beginner ballet class. Most of the women took the lessons for exercise or to fulfill girlhood fantasies of becoming ballerinas.

"Rond de jamb and *rond de jamb* and—that's right, ladies—gently lift the leg, placing the ankle on the barre, and—*oh!"*

All eight women froze in bizarre positions and stared at their exceedingly pregnant instructor with concern.

"Was that a contraction?" the closest one asked timidly.

"I—I don't know. I've had little contractions for months. This seemed different. Maybe it was just a hard kick." She tried to relax. The muscles in her abdomen rolled, knotted, and gripped tight as a clenched fist. "Oh . . . no!" she gasped. "It wasn't . . . a kick."

Amanda fell to her knees, breathless, her limbs incapable of supporting her under the sudden downward pressure.

In the next moment, she was surrounded by her class, ready to assist with advice or more if called upon. Six were veterans of childbirth with families of their own.

"I'll get Sara," someone called out, running toward the front practice rooms.

"Breathe slowly. Relax."

"If you feel like lying down, go ahead."

"Here's my sweater, dear. Use it as a pillow."

They all offered well-intended advise, but what Amanda really wanted was Rob, which made no sense at all because he would have been less help than the least experienced of them. Still, she yearned for her handsome husband to bend over her, to whisper encouragement, to tell her she was beautiful in her whalelike awkwardness and pain, to tell her he cherished the gift she was about to give him.

However, he was thousands of miles out at sea, unreachable except for the Familygram that would be sent after the baby was born. She admitted to herself that even if he had been here, she wasn't sure that she could really count on his enthusiasm, for when he'd left a month ago, he still hadn't fully adjusted to the idea of fatherhood.

Sara arrived in the ballroom and clasped Amanda's sweaty fingertips between her two cool palms. "I've called the hospital," she murmured. "Your doctor will meet us there."

A pain shot through Amanda's lower back and rounded her belly in a wave. For a moment, Sara's sweet face blurred. "I—I don't know if I can even stand," Amanda said, feeling foolish, helpless, and frightened all at the same time.

Another contraction.

She gasped. She didn't know a hell of a lot about the birth process, there simply had been no time to attend classes. But these damn contractions seemed awfully close together.

Another!

"Ah!" she shrieked, stuffing a fist over her mouth to stifle her scream. She was embarrassed that she was unable to calmly endure the pain in front of the other women.

Then everything began happening so fast she was only vaguely aware of each step. Her water broke, and she instinctively brought her knees up, bracing the soles of her shoes on the splintery wood floor. Two contractions overlapping one another. Unbearable pressure. Another contraction! She panted to try to catch her breath.

Sara took charge. "Maryann, here's the doctor's answering service. Call it. Give them this address and tell them he *must* come here. Amanda can't possibly make it to the hospital. The ambulance service number is taped to the phone. Call it. Maybe they can get a medic here faster than the doctor. *Now, everyone out!*"

"Sara," an older woman's voice interrupted. "I've had five of my own."

Sara reached up and dragged Linda Garfield down to the floor beside her. "Okay," she said. "Linda, you're our expert

63

until the pros arrive. *Now—everyone else out, and I mean it!"*

Linda was a large-boned, gravel-voiced woman in her forties who didn't have a clue how to dress to diminish her size. She wore a gaily flowered leotard with coordinating purple tights. Regardless of her gaudy outfit, she was the comfort and experience that Amanda and Sara both needed.

Linda told Amanda what to expect and to not push just yet. She sent Sara off for a cool, damp cloth and wiped Amanda's temple while whispering soothing words. Then she ordered Sara off to fetch a clean cotton blanket to spread beneath Amanda. Without her, Sara knew she would have fallen to pieces inside, although for Amanda's sake she would have continued to pretend confidence.

There, on the worn wooden dance floor of the Stevenson School of Dance, over layers of rosin and wax chips and the dust of a thousand dancers' slippers, little John was born. The ambulance arrived ten minutes after the work was done.

Sara visited Amanda and her baby son every day at the Lawrence Memorial Hospital, which was just five miles from the studio and four from her parents' home. Olga and Bruno came only once, bringing a jade plant in a ceramic pot. Olga detested flowers. Both she and Bruno were allergic to various pollens. The plant, Amanda supposed, was to be brought home to their house along with the baby.

"You can't go back to that apartment alone and care for a newborn," her mother fussed. "And you certainly can't afford a nurse on a navy man's pay."

"Do you want me to come home, Daddy?" Amanda asked.

Bruno lifted one shoulder and looked away. "I have a lot of work to do. It won't help my concentration, having a squalling infant in the house." He received a jab in the ribs from his wife's pointy elbow. "But we'll make do, I guess," he added quickly.

Even Olga must have thought that he sounded cold. "The baby will stay upstairs," she told him. "It will sleep most of the time anyway."

Amanda winced at the thought of her child, stored away unlovingly in an out-of-the-way room. "Why don't you come to my place and stay with me for a week or two?" Amanda asked her mother. She had no real desire to share her private domain with a sour Olga. But she felt incredibly weak. What if Olga was right? What if she couldn't adequately care for little John on her own?

"Come to that drafty little apartment?" Olga huffed as if her own home were a palace. "There's hardly room for you and the baby. When is that husband of yours due home?"

"Three weeks," Amanda replied wistfully. At least she had the satisfaction of having called Olga's bluff. It was clear her mother had no interest in leaving the duplex and her husband's dour company to warm up to her grandson.

Amanda summoned up a weak smile. "The baby and I will be fine on our own."

For the next twenty days, Amanda slept when she could, which wasn't much at all. She nursed and bathed John and changed his diapers what seemed a hundred times each day. She laundered by hand his tiny buntings, undershirts, and socks as well as the cloth diapers. The newer disposable diapers were too expensive, and she couldn't afford a diaper service. She had no washer or dryer, and venturing off to the base laundromat seemed too exhausting an expedition with her newborn son.

She rocked John to sleep, worrying about his snorty little breaths and panicking whenever she couldn't hear him breathing in the night from the dresser drawer where he slept beside her bed. She was tempted to ask for help from her neighbors, all navy wives. The little bit of contact she'd had with other women in base housing before John's birth had been pleasant enough. But having been rejected by her own relations somehow made her want to tough out these first difficult weeks on her own. Perhaps this was a symptom of the stubbornness Bruno had always accused her of, or maybe it was just something she had to do to prove she was truly independent.

John cried when he was hungry, but he also cried after nursing and fussed himself into shallow sleeps from which he soon awoke screaming again. When she took him to the doctor, he became concerned that John had lost rather than gained weight. He told her that her breasts were producing insufficient milk and advised her to switch to formula. She spent hours sterilizing bottles and mixing formula but was gratified when the baby finally accepted the substitute milk and began sleeping with satisfied little snores after gorging himself. The added benefit was that she finally caught up on her own sleep.

Amanda's breasts ached as the milk dried up. She packed ice bags on them and took showers throughout the day to soothe them and ease her frayed nerves. She desperately wished she could be in the studio with Sara. She missed Sara's companionship, the students, the music, and the exhilaration of dancing.

Amanda spent her evenings alone with John, rocking him while watching old musicals on TV that she'd loved as a child. Gene Kelly in *An American in Paris* and *Singing in the Rain*. Fred Astaire and Ginger Rogers in *Top Hat, Flying Down to Rio,* and *The Gay Divorcé*. The music was impossible to sit through. She sang "Puttin' on the Ritz" and whirled across the cramped living room with little John cradled in her arms.

"Your first dance lesson," she cooed at him, nuzzling his button nose with her own.

On the twentieth day, she found she was able to move around the apartment at close to her normal pace. She discarded the horrid donut pillow she'd sat on to cushion her poor stitched-up bottom and tossed worn maternity smocks and elastic-bellied slacks into a sack for the navy wives' clothing drive. She planned to have more babies but intended to save up for nicer clothing by then.

She could foresee Robert's pay increasing over the years, according to the standard military pay scale, and when she returned to teaching, she'd be able to provide a comfortable second income. She envisioned a new order developing in her life. There was so much to look forward to, and she felt so fortunate to have found Robert, who was making her dreams of a family a reality.

* * *

Amanda spent all of the Thursday prior to her husband's return in joyful preparation. She pulled down, washed, and rehung the curtains in all four rooms. She vacuumed, then scrubbed the kitchen floor to remove dribbles of sticky formula.

After lunch, a package arrived from Caroline. Inside was a pretty lavender night dress and a Congrats! card. A brief note had been penned across the back in her friend's elegant script: "For the new mommy—can't believe you did it in under an hour! That must be a world's record! I'm next—due in January."

Amanda called Caroline later that day, although she couldn't easily afford the long-distance charge to Europe. Frank was posted in Italy as a political officer at the U.S. consulate in Naples. The two women gaily swapped news and gossip for a half hour. Amanda decided she'd have to somehow cut back on groceries to pay the bill when it came. But she'd have happily eaten peanut butter sandwiches for a week to chat with Caroline this way, as if they were two schoolgirls again, living in neighboring towns.

"I'm a nervous wreck," Caroline moaned across the line. "Either I go home to have this kid, or they fly me to the American hospital at Weisbaden a month before my due date. I'll be damned if I'll spend Christmas in a military hospital!"

"So, you'll come home?" Amanda gasped with delight.

"Absolutely. Actually, once Mother found out the alternative, she insisted. Even before I got pregnant, she'd been nervous about the student riots in Europe. The Red Brigade and all. You must have heard about Aldo Moro, the president. They kidnapped and killed him—ruthless punks! Frank and I came across a Communist Party demonstration the other day when we were walking after dinner, and we had to turn back. It's all very bothersome."

"And Frank? How is he? Will he be able to come home with you?" Amanda asked. John was napping on her tummy, his little mouth sucking pleasurably on his tiny fist.

"Frank's fine. We think he'll be able to use his vacation leave to stay with me until after the baby's born."

"That's nice," Amanda murmured, then fell silent. Was she just a little jealous? she wondered. Yes, she had to admit that having Rob around then would have been nice, but he'd be home before long, then they'd be a real family.

On the morning of the *Neptune*'s return to port, Amanda arrived at the dock along with a couple hundred other wives, mothers, girlfriends, and offspring. She cuddled John in her arms, shielding him from the sharp February wind that whipped off of the Thames River. She'd dressed him in a fuzzy blue bunting that had a drawstring closure at the foot end and a cozy hood to protect his little head from the bitter cold.

The conning tower of the *Neptune* glided into sight downriver at precisely ten-thirty, right on schedule, which led Amanda to believe that the ship had been lingering in Long Island Sound in order to arrive right on the dot of eleven.

The sun made a valiant attempt to warm the crowd. The moist river air smelled of salt, the old wood of the pier, and butter and hot corn kernels. An enterprising vendor had set up a makeshift booth and was selling small paper sacks of popcorn to restless youngsters. Flags waved in little hands, smiles broadened, and cheers filled the wintry air as the great gray-hulled ship drew near, guided by a chugging tugboat. Many of the crew stood in dress uniform on the sub's deck.

A lump formed in Amanda's throat when she thought she spotted Rob. *Three months,* she thought, tears stinging her eyes, *it feels more like three years.* So total was his isolation during a mission that he hadn't been able to write to her or she to him. They'd parted with promises to look forward to the good times they'd share when he returned.

Now, she hoped she wouldn't disappoint him, for her figure was still far from its svelte prebaby form. Her stomach felt flaccid, like an empty potato sack, even though she'd performed her sit-ups faithfully, morning and night.

Amanda became aware of John squirming in her arms. She glanced at her watch—almost his lunchtime. This child never stopped eating! Without taking her eyes from the docking vessel, she snatched a bottle from the open diaper bag slung over her shoulder and wedged the plastic container under her chin, leaving one hand free to wave.

As the ship swung closer, she could at last make out her handsome husband standing beside an open hatch. He spotted her and, in a very uncommanderlike move, leaped high into the air, returning her wave with both arms flailing. Tears of happiness trickled down her cheeks.

Why does it take so long to park one damn boat? she fretted. Her heart pounded and her ears rang with the shouts of other women and their children as they also spotted the special men in their lives.

At last the ship was secured, gangways lowered, and men began streaming off, seabags slung over their shoulders. Robert was one of the last off, saluting a fellow officer who stood at attention on the dock. Amanda waited patiently in a sea of hugging families. Finally, Robert was there, too, holding her close to his starched white uniform, kissing her deeply until she had to push away to catch her breath and protect John from being crushed.

"Your son!" She laughed, holding the baby out for him to take.

He hesitated, looking endearingly bewildered.

"You hadn't forgotten, had you?" she teased. "We're a family of three now."

"No. No, of course not. I just didn't think you'd bring it with you, you know, the crowd and cold weather and all. I—"

"You what?" she asked, still amused by his confusion.

"I thought you and I . . . we'd be alone first. Celebrate a little." His hands cupped her hips and pulled them toward him suggestively. "Then I'd meet the little cuss."

She gave her young husband a steady look. "I'm afraid you're about to suffer a rude awakening, Commander. A baby is a twenty-four-hour-a-day job."

Robert's face fell.

"Don't worry," she promised cheerfully, "I've lined up a baby-sitter for Saturday night. We'll be able to spend some time alone together then. But isn't it wonderful? We're a family! I love having you home and having John here with us. The three of us," she murmured, content in Robert's arms, with John in hers.

Robert looked down at the tiny creature snuggling at his wife's breast. His wife! How had he come to have a wife and a child? Well, of course, he knew *how* if one was speaking simply of the order of events in his life. It was just that it happened so fast! There he'd been, shacking up with a cute dancer one weekend, and the next thing he knew he was stepping off his ship into a family man's life! Responsibility weighed on him like a lead anchor.

He knew guys—men under his own command—who looked forward to this moment of reunion with their loved ones. Before today the only welcome homes he'd received were from one or another of his girlfriends. Usually not the same one two tours in a row, which was fine by him. No ties, no trouble. His girls were just as enthusiastic as any of the wives here and a whole lot less demanding. If any of them got too serious, he cut the anchor line and drifted free.

Still, Amanda was a good-looking woman; he could have done worse knocking up some navy groupie. As she hugged him, he felt her warm breasts crushing against his abdomen. They were larger than he remembered. He relished the idea of fondling them—the sooner the better.

"The kid looks tired," he observed, catching the baby in the middle of a yawn. "Is it time for his nap?" he asked hopefully.

Amanda smiled at him. "John never sleeps for long during the day. A half hour or so at a time."

"That'll do fine for starters." He winked at her wickedly.

Back at the apartment, Amanda settled a dozing John in his crib. Then she and Robert strolled arm in arm into the bedroom. He caressed her through the apricot silk blouse she was wearing, asked if it was really "all right," and told her to tell him if he hurt her.

Although it was somewhat premature for her to have intercourse, she didn't object. She was as thrilled to be with Rob as he appeared to be with her. Genuinely touched by his concern, Amanda promised she would let him know if she was uncomfortable.

Robert made efficient love to her, his orgasm arriving

70

after only five minutes. She didn't protest to ending their lovemaking so soon after they'd begun. Her flesh felt tight and unpliant, still sensitive. She found it impossible to relax and enjoy the experience. It did hurt, but not so much that she felt the need to ask Rob to stop. After all, she'd planned her husband's homecoming to be very special, warmly romantic, and perfect in every way. Nothing short of unbearable agony would have caused her to refuse him.

"I'll put the steaks on," she said, sliding out of his arms and off the bed.

He smiled lazily at her as she pulled on a pink chenille robe. "Steak?" He grinned. "A dinner fit for the returning warrior."

"Exactly. Steak, lyonnaise potatoes, homemade popovers, and fresh asparagus tips, with a spinach and mushroom salad for first course."

"Heaven . . ." he murmured, stretching his naked body across the rumpled sheets.

Her eyes drifted over him hungrily. Oh, how she wished she could roll with him in wild passion, be rough and brazen, and demand that he satisfy her. She wanted to be made love to fiercely, to feel him fill her instead of wincing at her stretching stitches.

No matter, she told herself as she walked into the bathroom, John would wake up any minute, wanting to be fed again. Besides, she had other treats lined up for Rob this evening.

"I'll mix us a couple of drinks," Robert called through the closed door.

"Fine," she answered.

When she joined him in the living room, he handed her a glass of crystal-clear white wine. He held a martini in his right hand, sipping thirstily.

"Don't fill up on drinks," she cautioned. "I have a lion-sized dinner for you."

He toasted her. "Whatever the cook says."

By the time the steak emerged from beneath the broiler, though, Robert was on his third martini, and she knew she'd be wise to quickly sit him down to some solid food if she expected a sober companion for the rest of the evening.

"We can eat now," she called out, placing a platter of sizzling meat surrounded by crisp-topped potatoes on the table.

Robert grinned at her, easing an arm around her waist. He crunched her between his pelvis and the kitchen counter, kissing her on the mouth with rising passion. A piercing wail filled the apartment, and he jumped away from her.

"The baby," she said, drying her hands on a kitchen towel. She slipped away from him, flung open the refrigerator door, pulled out a bottle of formula, then deftly thrust it into a pot of warm water before dashing from the room.

With consternation Robert watched her pink chenille rump disappear around the corner. He waited for her return, listening to her cooing and gurgling at the child in the other room. He felt annoyed but, after a minute's thought, decided there was, after all, no rush. He fixed himself another martini, took it into the living room, and stretched out in the Naugahyde recliner. A few minutes later, Amanda breezed through the room with a crying baby in her arms. She hushed him lightly, as if she didn't really mean it, and passed Robert a smile en route to the kitchen.

A minute later Amanda returned with a bottle stuck in the kid's face. Robert observed them for a while, feeling hungry himself in spite of the numbing alcohol, wishing some of her attention could be coaxed his way.

"Would you like to feed him?" she asked, beaming at Robert as if she were offering him a second portion of filet mignon.

"Huh?"

"Your son, would you like to hold him while I finish putting dinner on the table?"

He blinked at her, for the first time realizing what she had in mind. She expected him to take over some of her chores, to do domestic stuff! *Him*—commander of a nuclear sub! But the drinks numbed his anger, quelling any desire to set her straight, at least for the time being.

"Sure," he said magnanimously, swallowing down the remaining few ounces of his drink. "Give the little sailor here."

She settled the baby in his arms, showing him how to hold

the bottle, and reminded him to stop every now and then to burp the child. She draped a clean cloth diaper over his left shoulder for this purpose.

Robert looked down at his son. *I ought to feel something,* he thought blandly. *I ought to sense he's mine and feel protective and proud and . . . Dammit,* he thought, *I don't think I can do this.* He felt caged, forced, unnatural. It had always been him, him alone. He hadn't wanted to change his whole goddamn life when Amanda came along. It had just happened. And now everything seemed beyond his control.

He stared with disgust at the sucking lips surrounding the rubber nipple and his son's scrunched-up pink face and felt miserable. Hell, the kid didn't even look like him.

"Is dinner ready?" he called out, anxious to have an excuse to put the little baggage down.

"Almost," Amanda called from the kitchen.

"But *you* eat on demand," he muttered at the baby.

Feeling sorry for himself, he stood up, walked over to the couch, and laid John on a cushion, propping the bottle in his mouth with an embroidered pillow.

"There," he stated, "good as ever." He opened another bottle of wine, poured a glass, took a long, satisfying taste, then refilled his glass and a second for Amanda.

She'll just have to learn how to take practical shortcuts like this, he mused. *Then she'll have more time for us.* It would be just like it was before.

Amanda immediately sensed Robert's dissatisfaction with his new family, but she chose not to remark on it. They ate dinner. Her husband described how well the cruise had gone and confessed sweetly how much he'd missed her, especially at night. Three months was a long time.

"I'm glad you have at least three months in port before your next sea duty," she said, chewing a bite of juicy steak. "Where did you take the *Neptune* this time?"

"Sorry, babe," he said, gesturing at her with his fork, "classified."

"Oh. Of course."

This trip really hadn't been all that secret. Nevertheless, it was easier not to tell her about their stopover in Newport News, Virginia, where minor repairs on two missile tube hatches had turned into eight weeks in dry dock. As it turned out, he could have been home for his son's birth, but he'd had no desire to hang around Amanda during those last weeks of her pregnancy. She was already as big as a barn when he left, and the doctor had told her she shouldn't have sex toward the end anyway. Better to stay away, take care of his recreation elsewhere, then return a father after the fact. He was sure he'd have been no help to her anyway.

Amanda ate slowly, absorbed in Robert's stories of the sea. He told her sad, charming, funny, outrageous incidents featuring his crew on board the *Neptune* as they patrolled the Atlantic. She'd go crazy shut up inside a submerged steel trap beneath tons of water. She felt guilty for cursing his absence while she was in labor and during the long nights of soothing a colicky infant. Her husband was, after all, only doing his job and supporting his family.

He poured her more wine at the end of the meal. Mellow as a summer peach, she reached across the table, and they held hands.

She felt utterly complete as a woman. Her child slept on the nearby couch, where she'd bolstered him around with soft cushions to keep him from rolling. Her husband sat across the table from her. She lived in a simple but safe home away from her disapproving parents. Life was perfect. Almost.

She did miss the studio. Missed Sara and Doug even more, because since the baby had come, she hadn't driven across the river to New London. Now that she was feeling stronger and adapting to the baby's schedule—and he to hers—she was beginning to fit a few little luxuries back into her life, like a hot bath while John napped or a few minutes spent in the base library, selecting a good novel before she had to escape to the car with the fussy little man. Soon she hoped to return to teaching. Then life would be ideal.

Robert's first week at home was one of readjustment for all. Amanda realized that one reason she had been looking forward to her husband's return was not only his companionship, but the relief of sharing some of the tasks of parenthood. Robert, however, did not seem inclined to help out. He hated changing diapers and always found ways of avoiding that task. If pressed, he would occasionally feed John or hold him while Amanda prepared his bottle or cleaned. But he immediately put the baby into the crib as soon as he began to cry. He never washed out bottles, did laundry, or performed any chore remotely domestic. Amanda wondered how he had ever survived before they'd married and she had taken over all of the housekeeping duties.

After a week of running herself ragged while Rob lounged around, expecting to be waited on, Amanda grew impatient. She understood that he had to learn how to be a father. After all, she'd had several weeks' head start getting a grasp on motherhood. But she had envisioned a different kind of relationship for them as husband and wife, more like the one that had blossomed so beautifully between Sara and Doug. A partnership of loving equals.

Amanda recalled one Friday night that would linger in her memory forever. She'd taught toddler ballet in the afternoon, then taken her own ballet lesson with Sara, and finished the day with a private ballroom lesson with Doug—this time, the flowing international foxtrot that would later become her strongest competitive dance.

After changing into street clothes, she'd followed the music back into the ballroom to say good night to Sara and Doug before starting her walk home.

The lights had been dimmed to a soft yellow glow in the huge, high-ceilinged ballroom. A Paganini violin concerto played on the phonograph. Doug held Sara in his arms, waltzing across the broad expanse of floor—she in her working leotard with a flowered scarf tied like a sarong around her slender hips, her butter-yellow hair loose around her long throat, he in his department store slacks and short-sleeved sport shirt. They might have been Prince Charming and Cinderella in disguise, so beautifully did they move through the intricate natural turns, double reverses, chassés and whisks, and liquid hesitations of the classic waltz.

Sara's eyes sparkled adoringly up at her husband with a light they'd never lost after all these years. Amanda wanted *that*. That breathtaking joy of being swept into her man's arms and carried through life on a cloud fashioned by Paganini, Strauss, or even Glen Miller.

Perhaps that was why her first lovers had been dancers. It was only later that she found that simply being able to glide around a floor to music wasn't enough.

One morning over breakfast, Amanda brought up the subject she'd dwelled on for three days. "Rob, are you planning anything for today?" she asked.

"No. Not a thing," he answered, looking interested. "Thought I'd just unwind a bit this morning. Head on over to the gym to work out later in the afternoon, then go on to the club—unless you have something better to offer."

The Officers' Club had become an almost nightly stop for him. Sometimes she resented the fact that he needed the camaraderie of other men more than he wanted to be with her. Other times, she was so exhausted at the end of a long day it was a relief to get him out from under foot and have the little apartment to herself.

"I was thinking," she began hesitantly, "I'd like to go to the studio today . . ."

He sipped his coffee and looked puzzled, as if thinking, *What does this have to do with me?* "Fine with me, sweetheart," he answered finally.

"If I leave around ten o'clock and get back by two, do you think you could handle John?" she asked, kicking herself for sounding as if she were begging. After all, Robert was the child's father, and she deserved a break now and then.

Robert put his cup and newspaper down. "You want *me* to take the baby for *four hours?*"

She took a deep breath. "Yes."

Robert shook his head, his lips lifting in a half smile.

"What does that smirk on your face mean?" she demanded, angry all of a sudden. "You don't think you should have a hand in raising your son?"

"Of course, I do," he bit off. "But you picked a hell of a time to spring this on me."

"Spring it on you! You've had over nine months to get used to the idea of fatherhood."

"I don't mean *that!* I'm not stupid." He glared at her.

"I've just spent three months crammed inside an iron sardine can with eighty men. I come home needing a rest, wanting to make love to my beautiful wife, and have a little fun. I find some broad who's obsessed with motherhood and can't find the time to be with her husband . . . and, on top of that, she intends to dump her kid on me and take off for half a day."

"Obsessed?" she choked out. "Do you expect an infant to fend for himself?"

"Look, I don't mean to upset you," he pronounced in a coolly controlled tone that sent her blood pressure skyrocketing. "I just think you could arrange your schedule a little more efficiently to include my needs." She didn't announce what immediately came to her mind: that Commander Robert Allen might physically be a grown man, but he was talking like a selfish child. "We can afford to put the baby in the nursery for four or five hours a day," he added reasonably.

"The base nursery!" she gasped. "Do you have any idea what that place is like? I checked it out before John was born. They're understaffed and overbooked. Children under two years of age are put in a crib for their entire stay, no matter how long. That's no way to treat a child—like a caged animal."

"A baby-sitter then. Call some teenager to come to the house on a day like this when we have separate plans. After all, we need our freedom."

Amanda's heart fell. It wasn't supposed to be like this. A marriage should be sharing, helping each other to grow and reach each of the partners' fullest potential. "I thought you said you had nothing special planned," she pointed out weakly.

Robert shoved himself up out of his chair. "Geez, babe, what's happened to you? Before I left for sea duty, you were a fun kid. Now you have a baby, and you're constantly nagging me! I work hard, round the clock for months. I come home to demands!"

"You came home to a woman who loves you and your baby son," she corrected him in a strained voice. "Some men would be proud."

"I am proud!" he protested. *"Of course I'm proud!* Don't accuse me of not being a good husband and father." He shook a finger in her face. She had to resist the impulse to knock it away. "I put this roof over your head, didn't I? You have your baby and everything you need for him. Isn't that what you wanted?"

Amanda nodded, feeling numb.

Robert let out a long-held breath, his eyes still dark and snapping with anger. "I really thought that having a kid would settle you down to a normal life," he said, sounding exasperated.

"Normal?" She stared at him, hopelessly lost.

"Yeah, normal. I mean, what adult woman runs around the country dancing for a living—other than a stripper."

Amanda's mouth hung open. "Robert, let me remind you that my dancing was once very appealing to you."

"It was," he admitted. "But a man expects his wife to behave appropriately."

"Appropriately?" A sinking feeling seized her stomach. Her fingers knit over her still-soft belly, by habit resting on the shelf that was no longer there. From the nursery John gave a soft waking warble. Reflexively she glanced toward the room, then turned back to her husband. "What have I done that's inappropriate in your eyes?" she asked tightly.

"It's not just me," he said defensively. "Some of the other guys, well, it's no secret that their wives think you're a snob. You don't join their clubs, take part in the family support activities on base."

"I don't enjoy making ceramic kittens, knitting sweaters, or planning teas. I'm just not very good at any of those things," she admitted. "But I love to dance."

"Right," he said darkly. "I know the truth about why that is, and so do you." Again, with the pointing finger.

"The truth?"

"Be honest, babe. You like the attention . . . displaying yourself . . . letting strange men hold you. It's disgusting, a perversion, a—"

"That's enough!" she choked out, suddenly aware that she couldn't reason with him. He was so insecure in their relationship that he was unable to trust her. She made a hasty decision. "I'm going to visit Sara for a few hours today. I haven't seen her in weeks. I'll take the baby with me."

Immediately Robert was all sweetness. He came over to her and put his arms around her. "I don't want to end your friendship with Sara. I know how much you like her. I'm not being unreasonable. I just don't feel confident taking care of the baby alone," he admitted sheepishly. "I might do something wrong . . . hurt him."

Amanda's heart went out to Rob. So that was what had been bothering him. He'd used every male ploy except coming out and admitting the truth. He was just plain scared.

Well, parenthood was scary for her, too. She couldn't forget the terrible things he'd accused her of, but she could forgive him. She took two steps forward and lapped her arms around his neck. As if on cue, John began squalling in earnest from the other room.

"Don't worry," she whispered, kissing Rob on the cheek, "you'll do just fine." She would let some time pass before trying again to involve Rob in his son's care. Perhaps she'd rushed him into a challenge he wasn't yet ready to handle.

6

1968

The villa overlooked the sparkling blue Bay of Naples and, in the distance, the low silhouettes of the islands of Ischia and Capri. It's red-tiled roof and cool stucco walls basked in the noonday summer sun—a dust particle of calm and beauty in a universe of turmoil. Vietnam had by now become a full-fledged military conflict involving thousands of American soldiers and tearing the United States apart emotionally as well as politically. College campuses erupted in protest against the Asian war and racial discrimination at home. Europe, too, suffered its share of political violence and economic unrest.

Naples, however, remained a lady, providing visitors and natives alike with a surfeit of sunshine, quaint shops, and delightfully rich food. In Caroline Nesbit Donnelly's case, the city also served as a convenient home base for frequent shopping and sight-seeing sorties across the Continent.

She and Frank had resided in Italy for over eighteen months. Frank's post as political officer at the U.S. Consulate General was supposed to extend for another six months, with the possibility of a second tour, which was marvelous as far as Caroline was concerned because life couldn't have

80

been better. She had three servants—a housekeeper, a cook, and a governess to care for Jennifer, their daughter.

Her own duties, as wife of a professional diplomat, were numerous and challenging: entertaining visiting government dignitaries and their wives, accompanying her husband to public events, hostessing parties for four or four hundred guests. But she still had plenty of time to read, visit her hairdresser—a darling named Adolpho—drive up the coast to Rome for long, leisurely shopping sprees, or lunch right here in town at Sabatini's with other American and foreign diplomats' wives.

The villa was regally situated atop a lush hill not far from the ominous slopes of Vesuvius. Almond blossoms framed a picturesque view of lean white ocean liners, tiny bright-sailed skiffs, and tourist-packed ferries in the turquoise harbor. The Donnellys' home was a far grander residence than was had by most of the consulate staff. Other political or economic officers at Frank's level kept modern, tastefully furnished apartments in the business district, but Caroline had insisted that some of her own money be used to lease the villa she'd fallen in love with the first day they'd arrived in Naples. Except for the three months she'd returned to the States to give birth and recover from the birth to her daughter, she'd stayed the whole time in Naples, not caring to go home for holidays.

Jennifer Ann had been born just over a year ago at George Washington University Medical Center in D.C. In Caroline's view, having a baby was a disgusting experience. After nearly ten hours of excruciating pain, insensitive doctors, and pain-in-the-ass nurses, one tiny, ugly baby had finally popped out of her ravaged body. She'd immediately informed Frank that he could forget about trying for a son; she was absolutely not going through *that* again! If Frank was disappointed, he didn't show it, for he was thoroughly enchanted with his tiny daughter.

Italy was an easy place to raise a child. Experienced governesses came cheap, not that Caroline and Frank found it necessary to count pennies. Her quarterly stock dividends from the portfolio her father had given her as a wedding present paid for the house and live-in domestic help. Frank's salary from the U.S. State Department took care of their clothing, food, and as much travel as they liked. They lived not lavishly, but well. She couldn't complain.

Caroline languorously stretched her svelte body on the cushioned chaise and rolled over onto her back. She wore the bottom only of her bikini, which in itself was a concession to Frank. He was a bit uncomfortable with her sunbathing totally nude since the patio was only semiscreened by a line of graceful linden trees from the neighboring villas and the streets on the hill below. But everyone here went topless on the beaches. So, she thought, what the hell.

Caroline felt free and easy, deliciously uninhibited and sexy as the strong Mediterranean sun toasted her body. She wished Frank were here to take the pleasant edge off her hunger.

She spent another hour in the sun, then plunged into the pool to cool down and, wrapping herself in a thirsty velour bath sheet, went inside to check on Jennifer.

"El dormira, Signora," Margarita whispered when she cracked the door open.

Caroline nodded and tiptoed in to look at the soft blond head resting in the crib. She touched a curl, moving it off the child's lightly perspiring forehead. This was when she enjoyed having a baby. Sometimes she held the little girl to her breast as she slept, just to feel her breathe, to remind herself that they were of the same life, the same blood.

Unfortunately, once Jennifer woke up, Caroline could stand to be around her for less than an hour before she lost patience with the child and sent her away with Margarita. Children were so illogical, so loud and obscene. Having been raised by a nanny, she herself had only a tenuous mother–daughter relationship to model this new one after. Caroline and Madeline Nesbit had spent little time together until Caroline reached her teen years, when she suddenly took on the social role of an adult. Since then, they'd become almost close.

Raising a child, Caroline believed, was best left to a professional.

"Will you dress Jennifer for the party at three, Margarita?" she asked.

"Si, Signora."

"And be sure to feed her before you bring her downstairs. I want our guests to see her at her best. She gets restless and whiny on an empty stomach."

"We will stay only *picollo minuti,"* Margarita promised.

Satisfied that one detail had been resolved, Caroline retreated to her own room. She bathed in tepid water laced with Chanel No. 5 and shaved her long legs and her underarms. She took her time drying off. It was the warm, slow time of the day when a hot Italian sun slanted through the metal shades. Most of Italy still followed the centuries-old custom of a daily siesta between noon and three o'clock, a gloriously civilized practice. Caroline napped for an hour then rose and arranged her hair in a sophisticated twist, baring her long, silky nape.

As she was adjusting the last hairpin, a car pulled into the courtyard. She peeked out a narrow slit in the shade, looking down at the top of Frank's head as he climbed out of the gray BMW.

She loved him with surprising fervor. But she took care not to demonstrate her affection too obviously, for she sensed the danger of losing her own identity in the strength of Frank's. Emotion was a luxury she couldn't afford. Nothing was more important than keeping a firm command on the course of her life. To do that she must also control other people.

Marriages, she firmly believed, were destroyed by two diseases. Familiarity and boredom. She'd witnessed her friends' flaming love affairs cool after six months, slip into a lukewarm matrimonial state, then, after a couple years, disintegrate into bitter ashes of alienation and indifference as both parties searched elsewhere for stimulation.

That wasn't going to happen to her and Frank. By remaining somewhat illusive to him, by sheltering parts of her life and her heart from him, she would *make* this marriage survive. They'd been married almost three years now. So far so good.

83

As Frank's trim, conservatively suited shoulders disappeared beneath the stucco archway over the front door, she breathed in the flower-scented air and tried to think only pleasant thoughts.

Caroline felt a curl of desire in her stomach. They'd made love two nights ago, and after a lazy morning of sun and swimming, she was ready for him again. But she'd learned the pattern of Frank's sexual appetite. Twice a week seemed the optimum for him. He liked to build a hunger and then spend a couple of hours in bed, satiating himself with her.

Their lovemaking was good for her, too, but she'd had to learn to pace herself. She'd always treated sex rather like an afterdinner mint. It was an added sweet to top off a pleasant evening if her date appealed to her. And, generally, she didn't date men who would repulse her if she ended up in bed with them.

Because her relationships had lasted no more than a few months each, she'd never experienced the deeper stages that followed unleashed passion. To be perfectly candid, she missed that shot of pure adrenalin and scintillating wildness of a new and untested lover.

Many times since their marriage, she'd been tempted to return to familiar habits. Old lovers wanted to remain "friends." Interesting strangers lured her with provocative glances and veiled propositions. She got prickly all over on hearing a polished British accent, watching an Austrian skier's physical prowess on the slopes at Innsbruck, studying an Italian gentleman's tight bottom in a scanty bikini that revealed everything. But she had Frank, and she'd been faithful to him because she had too much to lose by fooling around.

She drew in a deep breath, let it out in a long, cleansing whoosh, releasing a dozen scintillating fantasies and directed her mind toward the evening ahead. She dressed in a sophisticated but deceptively casual white gauze dress she'd bought in Rome. The fabric contrasted dramatically with her tan shoulders. Strappy, heeled sandals and a splash of colorful wooden beads at her throat and wrists completed the casual outfit.

At last there were footsteps outside her door. "Is that you, darling?" she called out. Glancing in the mirror, she checked her reflection one last time.

Frank stepped into the room and eyed her appreciatively. "You're all ready."

"And *you* are running late," she chided mildly. It was, after all, her job to keep him on schedule.

He glanced at his watch. "So I am. Pity." He gave her a roguish glance to let her know he was interested, then took her in his arms.

"Now, we don't want to shock the guests," she teased, running two slender fingers up his beard-stubbled cheek. He must not have shaven that morning. She added seven extra minutes to his preparation time. "Who's coming besides Professore Montcare and his wife? When you called, you said to expect six for dinner."

"Congressman Mark Holliman and his wife, Virginia. They're on vacation and stopped by the consulate this morning. You don't mind an impromptu luncheon like this, do you? I know it was short notice." He released her and slipped off his jacket, tossing it on the bed.

"Don't worry. Everything's been taken care of. Cook got started right away, with only a little grumbling. And Francesca had to be hurried through her dusting in order to have time to polish the silver. Other than that, no emergencies!" She was good at managing people and was proud of her ability. "The Hollimans are Washington movers, so I hear," she commented, slanting him a speculative glance. "His friendship could be very important to your career."

"We aren't really friends, more like acquaintances in related lines of work."

"Still," she persisted, "a contact is a contact. It's rumored he'll run for the Senate next term. After that, who knows?" She flexed her manicured fingers. Power had always been a guaranteed turn-on for her. "Who else should I expect?"

"Rami and Yvetta Grazi."

Caroline's smile faltered. "Do you think that wise?"

Frank loosened his tie as he walked toward the armoire that served as a closet. "Rami is a brilliant Romanian artist."

"And a dangerous dissident."

"Dissidents aren't all necessarily dangerous," he corrected her gently. "They disagree with their government's current policy. If the current government was a democracy instead of a socialist regime, who knows what dignified post he might hold."

"Then why is he running away?" she asked.

"He's not running. He lives in exile while he tries to raise funds to support an alternative government for his country—"

"A revolution—" she huffed in distaste.

"Hopefully not. Romania has been Communist for some time now. Rami believes that orderly change is possible if the ruling class loosens its control over the populace."

"So you are helping by giving him legitimacy, by granting him the United States government's blessing."

"Not officially."

Her mouth went dry. Could Frank be acting outside of department policy? "Be careful, darling," she cautioned. "Don't take chances, your career is too important to risk for some gypsy gunrunner."

Her comment reminded him of her upper-class bias, and Frank grimaced at her choice of words. "I will be careful. All I'm doing is helping Rami to meet a few people in power in non-Communist countries. Men and women who might be able to advise him. A little money wouldn't hurt his cause either."

Caroline pressed her palm over her stomach. She wondered if she was developing an ulcer. Frank's tendency to flirt with the underdogs of the world had put his career at risk before. She could foresee trouble.

Considering her options, Caroline watched Frank undress. He wasn't an especially tall or large-boned man, but he ran three miles every day and did isometrics to keep fit. His body was sleek, devoid of any fat.

Naked, hard as an athlete, he loped for the shower, calling over his shoulder, "Pick out something comfortable for me, okay?"

She had severe second thoughts about a quick tumble on the bed. But time was really too short.

With a sigh, she opened the double doors of the armoire

and, without conscious effort, decided on white linen slacks and a pale blue shirt that wouldn't clash with her dress. Frank had wonderful taste in clothing but rarely bothered to put much thought into assembling an outfit. How other people saw him didn't seem to matter to Frank. He was too busy dealing with the politics of nations, too involved in other people's lives, to focus on anything so inconsequential as his wardrobe. That's why he needed her—the perfect foreign service wife.

She chose fabrics for his suits; made appointments for fittings with the tailor favored by the foreign service officers —Gino, on Via Vendetto—ordered shirts to match the finished garments; selected ties, socks, and shoes. But her expertise was not limited to the clothing closet. She drew up menus for receptions her husband would host, instructed her cook and the assistants he would hire for a special occasion, ordered and supervised the placement of floral arrangements, coordinated the decor of their houses. This one and their permanent home outside of Washington, D.C., in plush Potomac, Maryland. Balancing all elements of a diplomatic life was hard work and required more imagination and ingenuity than most people imagined, but Caroline was good at it, and Frank appreciated her hard work, always congratulating her for a job well done.

She was no fool. She kept an eye out for telltale signs of marital discontent and restlessness. She knew that before they'd met, he'd never lacked willing hostesses, and she suspected that many of these lovely young women had doubled as mistresses. More than one tale of a broken heart had reached her from veteran foreign service wives, and she herself had intercepted many a wistful gaze directed at her husband during department functions.

Frank stepped out of the bathroom, still toweling off from his shower. Caroline sat on the edge of their bed and unabashedly admired him, allowing herself to look forward to the next time he'd make love to her. She felt satisfied that her life was in order.

Congressman Mark Holliman was rail thin and considerably over six feet tall. His wife, Virginia, was a petite woman. They looked like a ladder and a step stool when they stood side by side. He was politically ambitious but had proven willing to listen to experts and await a propitious time for his ascent to power. Frank thought Holliman's civil rights voting record and programs to help the poor were laudable. The congressman had a reputation for fairness. To date, however, he had had very little exposure to international relations. Frank had decided to remedy that situation.

Rami Grazi was the grandson of a former premier of Romania. He and his wife were both small, dark, and quiet. Like little mice, they hovered around one another, as if unsure of their surroundings, and were exquisitely careful of everything they touched. Frank knew they made Caroline nervous, but he believed it was important that these two men should meet, and so he'd arranged the informal supper. It worked out better than he'd expected. The professor and his wife telephoned their regrets at the last moment, due to a family emergency, which left a more intimate group.

The six adults visited on the patio beside the sparkling pool. When Jennifer appeared in her governess's arms, she instantly became the center of attention. However, as soon as Cook arrived with the first course, Margarita returned for the child as she'd been instructed.

Frank shooed the woman away and sat his little daughter on his lap, where she perched contentedly, sucking on bits of bread that he fed her as Cook served the meal.

Caroline slanted him a vexed look. "You'll spoil her, darling. Being around strangers for long overexcites her." She couldn't fathom why he fussed over the child so. Even Jennifer's occasional tantrums didn't seem to faze him. He simply hauled the child onto his shoulders and, singing loudly, produced fully as much noise as she did. She eventually stopped crying out of curiosity to see what her father was doing.

The congressman's wife leaned forward and tickled Jennifer beneath the chin. "What a delightful child," she purred. "So well behaved."

Jennifer drooled bread mush down her chin, the front of her dress, and onto the knee of her father's five-hundred-dollar white linen pants. He casually mopped up the dribble with his napkin while continuing to chat with the congressman.

Caroline rolled her eyes at the sky and gave up.

The Donnellys' cook was Sardinian and when given full rein was capable of producing a sumptuous feast in the tradition of his native island. This evening he had prepared *culingiones,* a ravioli stuffed with spinach and cheese; a delightful salad of marinated fresh tomatoes, artichokes, and ripe olives; *porceddu,* which was savory roast pig; and *carasau,* or "sheet music," a paper-thin bread the shepherds took with them when they left their homes in the mountains to follow their sheep.

As they ate, Frank and the congressman discussed the race riots that had newly broken out in major American cities over the past summer.

"We're doing our best to make changes that should have been made decades ago," Holliman stated. "But any change takes time, and people are naturally impatient." He looked at Rami, his expression watchful, intent. "Your own countrymen are learning the same lesson, are they not?"

"Yes," Rami replied, his dark eyes shining. He had a rough beard but no moustache. A sinuous scar traced the right edge of his jaw. The off-center bump on his nose looked as if it were a souvenir of an unset break.

Caroline shuddered. Such a brooding, unpredictable man. She didn't like having him in her house, her garden, or anywhere near her family. Next time Frank suggested inviting the man to dinner, she'd definitely put her foot down.

"Yes, we are impatient," Rami repeated in heavily accented English. "We have been impatient to see change for many years. And now it will be worse since Nicolae Ceauşescu became president of the State Council last year. People are afraid to challenge him."

"I thought Communism was the preferred form of government in Eastern Europe," the congressman's wife remarked. "It seems to have such a strong backing."

Rami leaned forward in his chair. "Some people believe Ceauşescu will deliver us to prosperity. I do not think so. He uses Communism the way a king uses a monarchy to gain wealth for himself and his family. He lies to us, his own people. He bleeds us of all hope. You will see what he does to Romania. In time, only the wealthy elite of his supporters will survive. We will be his slaves!" He slapped his damask napkin fiercely against the tabletop.

The napkin cracked like a gunshot. Caroline jumped and aimed a glare of distaste and urgency at Frank that said, *Do something!*

But before Frank had time to consider acting, Yvetta's hand settled on her husband's arm like a little bird, fluttering to light on a branch in a storm. He looked at her, his expression softening as a message of strength passed between them.

Rami released a loud breath. "I'm sorry. You are right, Congressman. Of course change does take time. But when there is no meat, no fresh vegetables or fruits to be bought anywhere, when everyone is an employee of the government, but there is not enough work to keep everyone busy for more than a few hours a day, and what little is done is done shabbily, for lack of pride, when a man curses the government for his family's destitution and he disappears from his home in the night, never to be heard of again, then, my dear sir, it is very difficult to wait."

The American politician looked steadily at the other man. "That is a reasonable assumption."

Frank intentionally remained silent throughout the interchange between the two men. To even the most observant student of human nature, he seemed totally absorbed, playing with his little daughter on his knee. Meanwhile, a special bonding had taken place, one that might last a lifetime. It was a bonding he'd deliberately nurtured. Holliman was destined to rise in the United States government—how high no one could predict. But if Frank pegged him right, he'd someday chair the Foreign Relations Committee. He might very well prove a powerful ally for anticommunist factions in Eastern Europe.

Since his experience in Korea, Frank had mellowed some in his opinion of politicians. Not much. Just enough to allow himself to see ways to use them to make things happen. He'd also met some very good men who cared as much as he did about people and the quality of their lives. He'd bet his inheritance that Holliman was one of these men—tough, brilliant, compassionate, and stubborn. A mixture of pluses and minuses that, for once, weighed out on the positive side of the scale.

Margarita returned again for Jennifer. This time Frank kissed his little daughter on top of her curls and allowed the woman to take her away. He had work to do.

The men sat, smoking pungent Virginia hand-rolled cigars and drinking Yugoslav wine while learning more about one another's countries. Rami and his wife had friends in Yugoslavia, and their fund-raising journey had taken them there before they'd traveled on to Italy.

The ladies excused themselves and moved inside, out of the Mediterranean breeze. They freshened up, then adjourned to the sitting room. Virginia Holliman asked the names of Caroline's favorite shops in Rome, London, and Paris—all cities she'd hit while on their European junket.

"And you, Yvetta, don't you just adore Rome!" the politician's wife asked, trying to include the other woman in the conversation.

Yvetta smiled patiently. "Rome is a very exciting city. But it is hard to see so much wealth when our people have so little," she answered in a quiet voice.

Caroline suspected the little gold digger was laying ground to beg for a handout. She had no intention of lending the use of her home to a pair of money-grubbing peasants. Besides, what if Frank picked the losing side? Then where would his career be? She quickly changed the topic of conversation.

7

Amanda tried to love her life as a naval officer's wife. She attended auxiliary meetings, learned to play a passable, if not brilliant game of bridge, took up ceramics long enough to make Robert a chess set and her mother a vase, which Olga immediately nested in her glass china cabinet among other treasures that would never be used. She contributed to bake sales, helped out at the co-op nursery school off-base, where many of the officers' wives took their toddlers to play with children their own age. She served as a welcome lady on the submarine base hospitality committee.

The women she met were generally pleasant to be around, sometimes intelligent, occasionally truly talented, but she missed the activity of the studio, the excitement of preparing her ballroom students for the pro-am competitions in which they danced with her. She also longed to return to the professional comps she had danced in ever since her eighteenth birthday.

Her partner, Nick, had been disappointed when, four months before John's birth, Amanda informed him that she'd be dropping out of competition.

"Where will I find anyone as good as you?" he moaned.

"Flatterer," she accused good-naturedly. "It won't do any

good, Nick. I want to stay at home with the baby. No long-term sitters the first couple of years. But I'll be back," she promised him.

"Call me when you're ready," he told her, wrapping her in a bearish hug meant to last the duration.

Now, three years after John's birth, she sometimes drove to New London to spend an afternoon with Sara, visiting with her between classes. They both watched with delight as John bounced on his chubby baby legs in perfect rhythm to whatever music was playing.

Sara always told her how much she missed her, which broke Amanda's heart. "Come back," Sara urged. "You don't need to pay a sitter, bring John with you!"

But Amanda knew her return to teaching would be sure to provoke another scene with Robert.

Her husband went out on other cruises. Each time, Amanda was achingly lonely while he was away and agonizingly tempted to take Sara up on her offer.

"Just a couple classes a week," Sara pleaded. "God knows I could use the help, and you could use the exercise. You're turning into walking flab."

"I am not!" Amanda objected, highly offended. Her waist had pinched down to a modest twenty-five inches. Of course, it used to be twenty-three inches, but she doubted she'd ever return to her prebaby shape. "I can't come back, not now."

"When?"

"After . . . after . . . I don't know. It's so difficult to work around Robert's schedule when he's at home."

"So just teach when he's gone."

"Once I come back, you know I won't want to stop."

"So, why stop?" Sara studied her expression. "It's that husband of yours, isn't it? He doesn't want you to be here."

"He wants me with him. That's natural," Amanda defended Rob. "I'm sure Doug wouldn't like you skipping out of town every night and all Saturday."

"But Robert is out in the middle of an ocean for three months at a time! Why sit at home?"

Amanda considered her point, which had a lot of merit. "Maybe you're right. I could teach just while he's gone." She knew he'd be furious even then, but there was no reason why he had to know what she was doing every moment of her life when he wasn't around.

She brought John with her to the studio in February as soon as the *Neptune* put out to sea. At first she took over only a few classes. Sara set up a playpen in the corner of the ballroom nearest the record player. John was so enthralled with the students that he stood with his little chin hooked over the top edge, gazing with fascination at them for hours on end.

Sometimes Amanda let him join a class. He'd mimic the older children, making them laugh. They adopted him as their mascot and lead him around by the hand. During her private ballroom classes later in the day, Sara took John upstairs with her, fed him dinner, and laid him down on her own bed, where she read to him and cuddled him to sleep.

"I've never seen Sara happier," Doug told Amanda after several weeks. "The time taken out of classes to rest and play with John brings a bloom to her cheeks. Have you noticed?" Yes, she had. Sara did look sublimely relaxed and in marvelous spirits. "I wish, in some ways, that we'd had a child," Doug admitted.

"She's a natural mother." Amanda worked up the courage to ask the question she'd pondered for as long as she could remember. "Why don't you now? Why not have a baby? You're both still young."

Doug looked thoughtful. "Long ago we made the decision not to have kids. I don't really regret it. I hope Sara doesn't." His gaze shifted away from Amanda, toward the photos lining the office wall.

Amanda didn't press him for an explanation. Doug and Sara were devoted to one another, that was all that really mattered. As Caroline had said, their not having children probably had to do with money. Besides, sharing John on an almost daily basis seemed to fill that void in their lives. Amanda felt warmed by the joy her little son brought to these two special people.

After reacclimating herself to working, Amanda began telephoning some of her private ballroom students who'd dropped out when she stopped teaching. They were delighted to hear she was back. Three signed up for lessons with her immediately.

She called Nick, who told her that he'd been competing with a young woman from New York City. They'd danced well at several national competitions but had failed to make the final cuts and, therefore, took no awards.

"If it had been you and me, Amanda, we'd have had a shot at placing in the finals."

"Maybe, Nick," she said, laughing. It was exciting to dream about again wearing a glittering gown with feather boa hem and shear sleeves studded with dainty hand-sewn seed pearls, to envision herself twirling around a chandelier-lit ballroom in the arms of a gentleman in black tails and white tie. So romantic, this extension of her girlhood fantasies, Saturday afternoons daydreaming through yet another 1930s musical as Fred and Ginger flickered across the screen of the Philco in her parents' dim parlor.

Returning to dancing was all the more appealing since there had been precious little romance in her life of late. Robert loved "dances" at the Officers' Club, but they were of the drape and shuffle variety performed to popular slow music or the disconnected gyrations of rock and roll. And there was always considerably more booze flowing than graceful gowns.

Other young officers flirted with Amanda, sometimes innocently, other times in more purposeful ways that let her know they'd be available when Robert was next out at sea. It was the navy's version of wife swapping. Flagrant affairs and divorce were frowned upon among commissioned ranks; a stable family life was considered necessary to an officer's career. Nevertheless, the attitude remained that boys will be boys, and so a little fooling around on the side, if done prudently, was looked upon as not unhealthy.

On bad days, Amanda felt somewhat used. She was providing a service to Robert and receiving scanty benefits. But she told herself that she loved him and he must love her, for he always came home to her and their sex life continued to be satisfying. What he was giving her was a whole lot more than Bruno had ever given Olga. Within her realm of experience, their marriage was working.

With increasing anticipation, Amanda looked forward to the day when Rob's commission would expire, just three years away. Then they'd open his sporting goods store. Once he'd become involved in a venture he loved, she had no doubt that she'd be able to teach him to understand her own passion for dance.

With twenty days remaining until Robert's return, Amanda and Nick stepped up their practices to three times each week in preparation for the Atlanta Open International Competition, which would take place later that spring. Because she had to truck John around with her and the drive to Hartford took three hours round trip, Nick offered to do all the commuting. His wife, he said, didn't mind as long as Amanda was his partner. The two women had met numerous times and struck up a comfortable friendship.

Before John's birth, Amanda and Nick had won several local modern and Latin competitions. Modern dances consisted of the waltz, quick step, foxtrot, tango, and Viennese waltz. Latin dances on the official syllabus were the rumba, cha-cha, jive (a fast version of swing), samba, and *paso doble,* which was a dramatic dance mimicking a Spanish toreador leading the lady through graceful moves as if she were his cape. Amanda and Nick always entered as a ten-dance couple, a strenuous ordeal often drawn out over two days. Amanda felt most adept at the modern dances, whereas Nick adored and excelled in Latin routines. Together they were developing into a strong team.

The year before Amanda had married Rob, she and Nick had scraped together enough money for plane fare to California and placed in the finals of the West Coast International Championship. However, they were beaten out of fourth place by a talented Canadian couple. Now, years later, when Jacques and Françoise De Lorme toured U.S. studios, performing and instructing, she and Nick booked a series of lessons with them. Even after splitting the hundred-dollar-an-hour fee, Amanda was strapped for cash for months. But the result was even more promising teamwork for her and Nick.

Never had they won a top-four slot outside of Connecticut, but now Amanda felt sure they had a chance of placing first or second, if not at Atlanta, then very soon. As for Robert, even if she had been able to contact him on the submarine and tell him that she intended to resume competing, she'd have waited so that she could talk to him in person.

On the day of the *Neptune*'s homecoming, Amanda cleaned the apartment from top to bottom, baked a deep-dish apple pie and a ham, made candied sweet potatoes—one of Robert's favorites—then spent a long, luxurious hour soaking in a tub of bubbles, applying perfume and makeup, doing her hair, and dressing for her husband's return.

She kept John up all day, skipping his customary after-lunch nap on the theory that he'd be ready for bed early. She set the table with fresh flowers, candles, and the only crystal she owned; chilled a magnum of imported champagne; and placed another set of candles on the dresser in their bedroom, all to create the perfect atmosphere for an intimate evening. She wanted to please Rob, not because she needed his approval, but because he was her husband, the father of her son, and she loved him. She wanted the two of them to be happy. The rest, she was convinced, would follow.

The *Neptune* put into port at three P.M. on that April afternoon. The ecstatic greetings of families and friends had become a familiar but no less moving routine for Amanda. Women around the world welcomed their men home in this universal fashion: with tears, shrieks of joy, kisses, and long embraces. It was a ritual of life to be savored, cherished, and kept in the heart forever. As her arms came around Robert's shoulders in his navy whites, the fingertips of her left hand smoothed the fine short hairs below the rim of his cap, and he smiled down at her. Their lips touched, a surge of warmth and desire swelling within her breast, and tears tumbled from beneath her lashes. Everything beyond the next few hours that she'd spend with her man suddenly seemed unimportant.

"Was it a good mission?" she asked as they walked holding hands toward the car. Robert was carrying John who waved a shiny red, white, and blue pinwheel on a stick that Amanda had bought him at the Rexall down the street from the studio. The little boy's cheeks were pink, his hair a rumpled dark nest of curls, cookie crumbs stuck between his chubby fingers. He looked absolutely beautiful in his navy blue corduroy playsuit, and Amanda was filled with a blissful sense of fulfillment. *My family! How could I ever want for more?*

And yet she did, God help her, she did. She wanted to reclaim the part of her life that had made her the person she was. She slanted Rob a hopeful look as he answered her question.

"Good cruise? Yeah, good as they get I suppose. Damn long though." He turned to her. "Oh, babe, it felt so long without you."

She smiled, excited too. "Guess we'll just have to make up for lost time," she said coyly.

"You bet!" He grinned. His blue eyes met hers, pulling her in, promising her fun and satisfaction, and she decided to wait until tomorrow to discuss Atlanta.

At home she put the ham in the oven. She'd already studded the firm pink flesh with cloves, smothered it in a brown sugar and mustard glaze, and precooked it. She turned the gas burners on low beneath a pan of sweet potatoes and turned the champagne in the ice bucket while Robert changed clothes. He came out of the bedroom with John by the hand, walked over to the bar, and mixed himself a drink, then invited John to add the olive and stir it for him.

Amanda eyed the generous-size glass with concern. Each time Robert came home, he seemed to drink more than when he'd left. She didn't like the pattern she was witnessing, but so many other wives treated their husbands' heavy drinking as a male prerogative.

Amanda herself rarely consumed more than one glass of wine during an evening. She wasn't fond of the loss of balance and disorientation that accompanied drinking alcohol. A dancer spent her life in pursuit of balance and precision of movement. To do anything to the body that destroyed this vital poise seemed unthinkable to her.

"I'll have dinner ready in a minute," she called out, speeding around the kitchen.

Robert sat John on the couch and turned on the TV, finding a channel showing cartoons. Having occupied the little boy, he strolled toward the kitchen and intercepted Amanda between the sink and stove, curling an arm around her waist.

"Don't be in such a hurry," he coaxed. "Come sit down a while."

"Aren't you hungry?" she asked, mentally counting off the minutes before the food would be overcooked.

"Hungry for you."

She smiled and touched his cheek. "John is—"

"Busy playing," he finished for her in a throaty whisper. "Come on, what will you have? Wine? A gin and tonic?"

It would seem rude not to have anything with him. "Champagne," she said with a sigh.

"Champagne it is." He retrieved the bottle, popped the cork with a flourish, and poured her a glass. Gulping down his own drink, he served champagne to himself as well.

"To us," he said, raising his glass.

"To us." She tasted the pale bubbles and let him draw her into his arms, kissing her lips, her throat. His teeth nibbled at her nipple through the fabric of her dress.

A rush of heat shot through her breasts as he began caressing her and unbuttoning her blouse. Amanda caught her breath, and the real world spun back into focus.

"Rob!" she gasped, sliding a look at three-year-old John. He must have sensed something interesting was in the works and was observing his parents with cool childlike wonder. "The baby—we can't . . . you know . . ."

Robert shook his head at her, still smiling rakishly, and kissed her on the lips hard. "Can't you stop being a mother for ten minutes?" he asked as he pulled away.

"No . . . yes! That's not a fair question," she objected. Her own desires were no less urgent than his. She'd gone without sex for three months, too. She'd missed the electric thrill of a man's hands on her body, missed having a man's warm, protective body beside her in bed. Still, that didn't justify their behaving like animals in front of their child. "In an hour I can put John to bed," she promised. "Then we'll have the rest of the night to ourselves. I've made you a lovely dinner."

Robert stepped back, casting her a petulant look. "Put him to bed now, why don't you?"

"I can't just dump the child in his bed. He has to have supper and a story and—"

"Oh, for godsakes, Amanda. Are we back to this again?" He picked up his glass from the table where he'd left it before embracing her and walked away in search of a refill.

Frustration boiled up inside her. "Do you think I don't want to go to bed with you? Do you think I'm not just as eager as you?" she demanded.

"Babe, I don't know what to think. It seems to me that you should be ready to please your husband about now. You've had a couple of years of playing mommy," he pointed his glass at her, nearly slopping its contents over the edge. "Remember what being a lover is like?"

Amanda felt as if she'd been slapped in the face. "Of course I remember!" she snapped. "I want that, too. But if we can just wait a few—"

"Christ!" he exploded, dashing the glass on the floor where it exploded into a hundred pieces. "Wait! Be patient! How about a little spontaneity around here? Are we going to fuck on a timetable the rest of our lives?"

"Robert!" she warned between gritted teeth. It had just occurred to her that the shattered crystal stem had been one of the set Caroline had presented to them after their wedding. Her heart crumbled even as her own anger mounted. "Robert," she repeated, forcing a calm tone. "I love you, and I want to make love to you worse than you know. But I'd just planned on everything being perfect tonight."

Robert rolled his eyes toward the ceiling, a gesture he never used unless he was borderline drunk. It irritated her no end that he was not only ruining his own homecoming, but tomorrow morning would blame her for his disappointment. She'd done everything she could to make this a special night. Now she was afraid the damage was already beyond repair. She looked at him, at a loss for words to express her misery.

"All right. You win." He held up both hands in a sign of defeat. "We'll eat. Then we'll put baby to bed, and we'll go into the damn bedroom and make respectable love like respectable adults." He glanced down at the shattered crystal on the tile floor with detachment, as if it were part of the furnishings and had no connection with him. Stepping over it, he picked up her glass and filled it to the brim with champagne.

"Let me know when dinner's on the table." He took a swallow. "I'll be watching the news. Cronkite and Vietnam are at least mildly entertaining."

Amanda counted to ten. She counted to ten again, breathed deeply, and, after a few minutes, felt her pulse lower.

It wasn't hard to understand why Rob was acting this way. As had happened before, he was feeling slighted, as if he had to compete with John for her attention, and the alcohol was distorting his judgment. If he'd been sober, he'd never have considered making love to her in front of their son. But the little boy in Rob was sensitive to all rivals—even a child. And, like a child himself, he wanted what he wanted right now! There was no reasoning with him.

Amanda stared at the glass shards near her feet. *I'm not going to clean that up,* she thought stubbornly. *He did that, not me. He can clean it up!*

She finished setting the table, served the food, and called Rob and John to the table. John sat in his high chair on her left. Robert sat across from her. While she fed John from her own plate and nibbled at dinner, Robert ate two servings of everything, accompanied by a rosé wine he selected from the teakwood wine rack he'd bought in Spain. She sipped at a half glass, whereas he drank as heartily as he ate.

At the end of the meal, Rob mutely picked up his glass and the bottle with its remaining contents and retreated to the living room. She could hear the TV program switch from *Gunsmoke* to *Peyton Place* while she changed John into pajamas for bed. The little boy was mellow and warm in his pj's and snuggled up beside her on his bed for a story, dozing off before the end. He whimpered in token protest when she gently shifted him beneath the covers, but he didn't open his eyes.

With a deep sense of relief, Amanda softly shut his door and walked the few feet down the hall to her own bedroom. Most of the tension had evaporated from the little apartment. She quickly slipped off her clothing and slid into a cool mint green peignoir with lace inserts over her breasts and delicate rosebud trim at the neckline. The nightgown wasn't expensive, but it was feminine and softly seductive.

She spritzed scent at her throat, in the narrow valley between her breasts, and under the nylon hem in the general direction of her crotch. She fluffed her hair, checked her subtle makeup, and, at last, strolled into the living room with the hope firmly implanted in her mind that she had saved the evening through her patience. She would make up every lost moment of waiting to her husband. She intended to make love to him in the ways she'd learned most pleased him, and she felt her own anticipation swell in response to her imagination.

Amanda paused at the living room doorway to observe the sleek back of his head. Rob's feet were propped on a hassock, the champagne glass perched, empty, on the padded sofa arm.

"Robert," she whispered, posing in the doorway. "Darling," she repeated when he didn't move.

After a moment longer, she frowned, and a chilly feeling crept up her limbs toward her stomach. She slowly walked across the room and rounded the end of the sofa.

Rob was sound asleep.

Amanda smothered an almost overwhelming urge to scream, weep, or throw something in frustration. She stood numbly for several long minutes, then picked up his glass and the empty bottle wedged beneath his hip and took both back to the kitchen. Without thinking about what she was doing, she pulled out the dustpan and whisk broom from the pantry and swept up the shining slivers of glass on her floor. She clicked the dead bolt on the front door, turned out the lights, and crawled into bed—alone.

The next morning Amanda was up early with John. They went through their usual routine of dressing and breakfast. She took him outside, and they walked down to the playground where he could work off some of his early morning energy. By the time they returned to the apartment, it was ten o'clock and she could hear water running in the shower. She belted John into his high chair and gave him slices of fresh apple and a handful of raisins to snack on, then knocked on the bathroom door.

"Coffee?"

"Great!" Robert called out.

A few minutes later he appeared in his robe, his hair still damp. He kissed her on the cheek, accepted the mug of coffee she offered, and took a seat at the kitchen table.

Amanda looked at him sideways, gauging his mood. Sunny but unstable, she decided as he popped two aspirin in his mouth and washed them down with coffee.

"Do you want breakfast?" she asked.

"What do you have?"

"Eggs, cereal and fruit, or pancakes if you like. They won't take long."

"I'll just have toast. My stomach's a bit queasy this morning."

"No wonder . . . all that booze," she stated matter-of-factly.

He studied her over the rim of his mug as he raised then slowly lowered it. "You're not going to start that again, are you?"

"No," she said. "I guess not." But she was going to start something else. She'd have to put aside her aversion to his drinking for the time being, because those discussions always came to a dead end. But another part of her life wouldn't wait. "Rob," she began, "I'm going back to teaching at the studio. Actually, I already have . . . on a part-time basis."

He silently sipped his coffee, concentrating on a chip in the porcelain.

"Robert, do you hear me?"

He let out an impatient sigh. "I thought we'd settled this."

"*You* assumed we'd settled it. I postponed returning to my profession until John was older. Listen," she continued urgently, "we can use the money from my teaching. Every time I dance in a pro-am competition, my student partner pays me twenty-five dollars per dance. That's darn good money—three or four hundred dollars for a day's work!"

"We'll get along fine without it," he said blandly. "It's petty cash, not an income."

"Competitions combined with a regular teaching schedule could provide a modest second income," she persisted.

Robert's face pinked with anger. "Jeez! What's with you? Other navy wives don't work. Not *officers'* wives anyway."

Amanda swallowed, trying to control her desire to reach out and strangle him on the spot. "Rob, please be reasonable. Dancing was my life before I met you. I don't want to lose it."

"You're a mother now. You should have outgrown this . . . this fantasy."

"Your career is important to you," she pointed out. "Mine is important to me."

Glaring at her furiously, he shoved his mug away. "Career! You call squirming in some guy's sweaty grip a career? I call it indecent!"

They were back to that again. What had been intriguing, perhaps even a turn-on for him before marriage, was now lewd. His possessiveness colored her love of dance in tawdry hues. He was blind to the grace, creativity, and innocent fun in what she longed to do. She might as well have sold herself on a street corner.

Sadly, she realized that not only was dancing a crucial part of her character, it was one she wanted to share with her child. John should learn that life wasn't just Mommy cooking and cleaning and Daddy drinking and playing softball with the guys.

"Be reasonable," she pleaded. "You're away for months at a time. I need more of a life than this apartment and John. I didn't think I would, but I do. I tried, really tried to fit in with the other wives. It didn't work."

Rob glared at her. "It didn't work because you didn't make an honest effort. This is incredibly selfish of you, Amanda. You disappoint me. Now that you have a husband and a son, you can't play around with life like when you were a kid. You're being irresponsible, selfish . . . *damn selfish!*" he repeated for emphasis.

Tears welled up in her eyes, and she clutched the back of a kitchen chair, her knuckles turning bone white. "I am not" was all she could choke out. For several seconds her mind refused to produce anything beyond blank denial. Then she began to speak again with deliberate forcefulness. "I won't neglect either of you if I dance. I can take John with me. He loves going to the studio, and I'll be home for supper most evenings, which is the only time you're around anyway."

He shook a finger at her. "Don't try to shift the blame. It won't work, babe."

"Who's talking about blame? I just want you to be fair about our marriage."

He let out a weary groan. "All right. Go back to teaching, but no more competitions."

She stared at him, dumbfounded. "You're dictating to me? You're commanding me not to compete?" she demanded through gritted teeth.

He must have realized the level of her rising anger. Walking over to her, he put his arms around her waist and drew her close. "I'm asking, okay?" he said, suddenly sweet. "I'm asking you not to compete. Sure I want you to be happy, but there has to be some, well, some common ground to our relationship. Besides," he hesitated, turning her chin up with one finger to gaze into her tear-filled eyes, "do you have any idea how it makes me feel to see you in another man's arms, wearing one of those . . . those skimpy costumes?"

Something inside of her softened. "Oh, Rob." His jealousy wasn't logical. She'd been totally faithful to him and intended to remain so. "I didn't mean to hurt you," she murmured. "Please don't worry about me and other men. I'm perfectly satisfied with you. Besides, dancing with a man is not the same as having an affair with him."

"I've seen how they look at you," he persisted.

"It doesn't matter," she soothed.

"So you're still going to do it?" he asked softly.

She swallowed. "Yes. I have to—for me. But I promise that working at the studio or performing in comps won't interfere with our family life. I'll always have time for you, darling."

He grimaced. "Sure, squeeze me onto your dance card."

He was bitter now, but she'd prove to him that she was right.

"I'm not baby-sitting for you," he stated abruptly. "And I'm not footing your travel or costume bills or any of that crap."

"The dancing will pay for itself," she assured him.

"Well, I suppose you'll do what you want . . ." he grumbled, sounding remarkably, frighteningly, like Bruno. He stalked out of the room.

The following months were strained. Amanda tried to accommodate her teaching routine to her husband's work schedule, but his days while in port were unpredictable, split between administrative paperwork, teaching younger enlisted men, and leave time. He worked rotating shifts—days, swings, mids—and often went out drinking with his buddies when he was off-duty. He'd show no interest in spending time with her for four or five days, then, without notice, announce that they'd be going out that night. More than once she had to call Sara and cancel a class at the last minute.

Amanda's rehearsals with Nick suffered because she found she was unable to throw herself heart and soul into their routines with Rob's accusations ringing in her ears. She began questioning her own motives for her attraction to dance. Could Rob possibly be right? Was her fascination a form of perversion, a means of cloaking sexual experimentation? Did she experience an illicit thrill from the closeness of a man's body?

Nick was patient with her but noticed the difference.

"You're not concentrating," he complained. "And you're stiff as a board!"

They had been working on a tango routine that involved intricate partnering and dramatic coordination of movements. Their hips must be tightly positioned facing one another. She must lean back into the crook of his right arm at an angle that pressed her right breast against his chest. She'd never been particularly aware of this contact or the brushing of their thighs or Nick's palm low on her back. All that had simply been part of the performance. Now she felt oversensitized.

"We're out of synch from start to finish," he pointed out in exasperation after a grueling three-hour practice session. He looked her steadily in the eye. "What's wrong, Amanda?"

"I'm sorry, Nick."

"Is it me?"

"No. Your lead is perfect. I can tell you've been working very hard on the routine. It's fantastic."

"Is little John all right? Not sick or anything?" The mischievous little boy could be a distraction. Sara kept him upstairs in the apartment while Amanda and Nick worked.

"No, he's fine," Amanda said.

"Husband trouble then?" he guessed. "I was afraid of this. I've lost more partners to jealous husbands."

Nick's wife, Susan, was an administrative assistant for an insurance company executive in Hartford. Although she was a nondancer, she never missed a competition. Susan cheered Nick on with enthusiasm, jumping up from her table in the audience to clap and shout out his number. And she always warmly congratulated Amanda when they did well as a team. Why couldn't Rob be like that?

"He'll come around," Amanda stated with more confidence than she felt. "Come on, let's try the routine again. We only have two weeks before Atlanta."

As the days passed, Amanda grew increasingly nervous, knowing she still was unable to give their routines her all. She wrote to Caroline, feeling the need to dump her emotions on an impartial party. Rather than write back, Caroline telephoned.

"You're crazy, you know that?" Caroline demanded. "Why do you let that jerk dictate what you can and can't do?"

"Rob's not a jerk. He's my husband, and he loves me."

"Then he should want you to be happy. Dancing makes you happy! What's the big deal?"

Amanda just shook her head, unable to offer a reasonable explanation for Robert's personality.

"Do you have a girl to take care of John?"

"No."

"You mean, not full-time . . ."

"I mean *never*. I assume by 'a girl' you mean a nanny or someone like that. I'm not in your financial situation, dear," Amanda pointed out wryly. "Once in a while, I hire a teenager to stay with John while Rob and I spend a couple of hours at the Officers' Club. But that's a luxury."

The line was silent.

"Caroline, you still there?"

"I'm here." She rumbled the words down low in her throat, the way she'd done when they were girls and she was annoyed. "I just can't believe you've turned into this—this . . . domestic slave, carting a kid around everywhere, no time for yourself."

"I wanted a family. I expected to take care of my children. John is an easy child—so beautiful, cheery, and full of fun. He's exhausting sometimes, but I wouldn't trade him for anything in the world."

Caroline sat on the other end, listening to her friend. She herself had never felt the intense tug of emotion Amanda spoke of. In many ways that made it difficult for her to sympathize with her. On the other hand, she thought it might be nice to feel so overpoweringly connected to another human being . . . her child, her husband. Full of love, no reservations, no misgivings.

She suffered frequent anxiety attacks about her coolness toward Jennifer. Caroline suspected she might be one of those women who should never have had a child; she just didn't know what to do with the kid! Maybe she'd feel differently about a boy, but she'd never know, because she wouldn't be having any more.

Caroline forced her thoughts back to the matter at hand: Amanda's problems. "What you need is a vacation," she decided. "Come visit me. Come stay in Naples with us. It's glorious here!"

Amanda choked. "Naples! I'm scrimping to afford gas money to the comp in Atlanta next week."

"I'll pay your airfare."

"The baby, Rob . . ."

"All of you can come. I'll pay for the whole goddamn family. Okay?" She was exasperated with Amanda's lack of adventure. Or was she really so poor she couldn't afford to hop on a jet now and then to pop in on friends? What an incredibly drab existence! "Come," she pleaded. "Come, come, come!"

"I have students booked for classes through the summer, then a very important comp to prepare for in Montreal in October."

Caroline groaned. "Geez, I miss you. And we're leaving Italy in November."

"You are?"

"Yes. It looks as if Frank will either be stationed in the Belgian Congo or Vienna."

"Quite a contrast."

"Needless to say, I'm pulling for Vienna with both hands and feet," Caroline commented dryly. "Africa would be a nightmare."

"Well, I'll pull for Vienna, too," Amanda promised.

"I have an idea! What about Christmas? If we're in Vienna, you could visit us there! Oh, that would be wonderful—the holidays in Vienna, so refined. And Jennifer's governess will take care of John, too. You won't have to lift a finger while you're here."

"And if you're in Africa?"

"Don't even think it," Caroline warned. "Deal? Vienna at Christmas?"

"I wouldn't feel right asking you to pay for us. We can save up . . . maybe. I'll ask Robert."

"Don't ask. Tell. And if there is any question of money, please call me. I'll send tickets."

"All right," Amanda said softly, gratefully. "I'll call you in a week or so and let you know how he takes it."

To Amanda's surprise, Robert accepted Caroline's invitation with unbridled enthusiasm. "Vienna!" he cried. "I've never been there before."

Amanda tenderly stroked the stubble of his beard. "It will be a chance for us to be together, away from our jobs, in a new setting."

He gave her a flirtatious wink and poked two fingers between the buttons of her blouse. "I can think of all sorts of interesting possibilities."

Amanda smiled. Somehow she'd find a way to make their marriage work.

8

By the day before the Atlanta competition, Amanda knew she and Nick could have used another month of practice. However, they had no choice but to go with what they'd learned and hope for the best. All of Amanda's amateur partners had decided the trip to Georgia was too far to travel for a quick performance on the dance floor. Although the extra money would have helped with expenses, at least Amanda wouldn't be distracted by having to perform in the pro-am events. Unfortunately, that also meant she wouldn't make any money unless she and Nick placed in the finals.

Nick and Susan took turns driving the '59 Ford station wagon, while Amanda entertained John in the backseat. When John napped, they talked through each of the ten routines. Susan was a valuable critic. Having watched their final rehearsals, she was able to offer a number of suggestions for improvement.

The drive seemed endless but John was surprisingly good, having only a few cranky sessions. Amanda tried to get some rest while he slept, but she ended up with a lot of time to think. Too much time. She dwelt uneasily on her marriage . . . her family . . . her future.

She had never intended John to be an only child. When

she was young, she had longed for a brother or sister, envying kids from large, boisterous families.

Although Robert was finally adjusting to John's existence, he still didn't do much in the way of helping with unpleasant household chores—wiping up the little boy's gooey fingerprints and spills, doing a load of laundry, or even washing his own dirty dishes after eating a sandwich in front of the TV. But he cheerfully took his little son for walks and had taught John how to put together a wooden jigsaw puzzle and showed him how to clap his small hands together to trap a rubber ball in the air. Those precious times, when Amanda unobtrusively watched them together, were her happiest. She and Rob continued to make love when their work schedules cooperated. If Rob seemed not as passionate as he'd been early on in their courtship, that seemed natural and didn't concern her. She tried not to think too often about whether or not he had been faithful to her. A sixth sense warned her that this many hours spent with "the guys" might not be so innocently spent.

As Amanda, Nick, and Susan drove south on I-95 through South Carolina, Amanda forced her doubts out of mind and concentrated on happier things. Having John with her at the studio had worked out far better than she ever could have predicted. In another year or two he'd be able to wander between classrooms and take part in some of the classes. It was a wonderful atmosphere in which to raise a child, with so many other children to socialize with and so much to do.

Her mind skipped ahead. If she and Rob were going to have a second child, it should be soon for practical purposes. As long as Robert was in the navy, her prenatal visits and hospitalization would be paid for by the government. Afterward, while Rob was starting his business, money would undoubtedly be tight. It would not be a wise time to extend their family. But if they did have a second baby, Amanda was confident that she'd be able to continue teaching, and the new little one would be welcomed by Sara and Doug, who had all but adopted John. Amanda felt infinitely fortunate to have them. She couldn't imagine working a "normal" job—nine to five every day of the week, sitting at a desk, and leaving her children with strangers.

And then there was Caroline, she thought with a smile, another of life's happy surprises. She thought about her friend's invitation and looked forward to flying to Europe— her first vacation of any kind since the impromptu honeymoon she and Robert had taken to western Connecticut. Her life seemed to be settling into some sort of order, albeit with some resistance from Rob. He continued to drink too much, was away from the house more than she liked, and each ninety-day sea tour seemed to drive a new wedge in their marriage. She hated his being away, but even worse was the readjustment period when he returned. However, most importantly, they were working on their marriage.

Yes, she thought as Nick took the exit off the interstate into Atlanta, having another child soon might well fit into the scheme of things.

Atlanta sizzled in June. The lovely old southern city shimmered in a shockingly bright sun. Cramped and exhausted from the long drive, they passed up the opportunity to drive around in search of elegant columned plantation mansions and went straight to the hotel.

The Regency was already teeming with competitors. Bellboys careened through the lobby, pushing luggage carts loaded with gowns, tuxedos, and sequined costumes too fragile and splendid to crush into suitcases.

Most of the costumes had been individually fashioned by designers in England or New York, who specialized in ballroom attire. Ron Gunn, a London tailor, was making a name for himself by constructing special tuxedos with lapels that remained unrumpled and shoulders that lay flat despite their occupants' raised arms during a performance. Seamstresses specialized in designing off the shoulder gowns of flowing layers of chiffon and tulle trimmed with delicate feather boas, iridescent bugle beads, hand-sewn sequins, and aurora rhinestones. The dresses flatteringly slenderized and emphasized a dancer's every graceful move. Each unique gown cost thousands of dollars.

Amanda had spent years experimenting with fabrics and patterns, learning to sew her own gowns because she knew she'd never be able to afford custom-made costumes. By ordering special materials and trims directly from a New

York City distributor, she found she could create a gown for a few hundred dollars—money hard come by from her teaching and performing fees. However, the right costumes were a necessary investment in her career.

Nick, Susan, and Amanda checked in at the front desk. They followed a bellboy to their rooms, unpacked, went downstairs to the café for a quick lunch, then rode the elevator back up to change for their first round of dances. Susan sat John on her lap at a table near the edge of the dance floor so he could watch his mother. They clapped and shouted Amanda and Nick's number—28—hoping to direct the judges' attention to their favorite couple. After all five international modern dances were over, six couples of the thirty-eight entries were announced as finalists. Amanda and Nick were among them.

Although they were jubilant, within an hour they would have to repeat their routines, dancing against some of the best professional dancers in the country—the waltz, quickstep, foxtrot, tango, and Viennese waltz. At the end of the long day, Amanda and Nick had placed third and, although Amanda was somewhat disappointed and thought they could have done better, Nick was ecstatic.

On the second day, the Latin dances were scheduled, and Amanda was a nervous wreck. The category included rumba, cha-cha, jive, samba, and *paso doble.* Rob's jealous outbursts were largely aimed at these routines, which were choreographed to show off the female dancer's figure and showcase her sensual grace. If performed correctly, all the dances were beautiful, exciting, and exotic. But because Amanda felt her husband's disapproval, even at this distance of nearly a thousand miles, she moved stiffly and made mistakes, which prompted errors from Nick. They failed to make the cut.

Nick was understanding but noticeably disappointed. During the long drive north through Georgia, South Carolina, and North Carolina, he talked about what he should have done differently when all the time Amanda knew (as she suspected Nick knew) that their discouraging finish was completely her fault.

When they hit the Virginia border, she came right out and

told him so. "For the Montreal comp, we'll do better," she promised him. "I can't let worrying about Rob's opinion of my career mess with my mind this way."

For the next few months Amanda worked on involving her husband in her dancing. She repeatedly asked him to come and watch her practice or to take lessons with her so that they could dance together on social occasions. She hoped that by learning a little about the art form that she so loved, he would in turn learn to appreciate it.

"I dance just fine," he told her gruffly. "No one does that stuff you do at the Officers' Club." He gave her a shrewd look. "They're all fags, you know—those guys who like that ballroom stuff."

She couldn't resist. "I thought you were concerned about my having an affair with one of *those guys.*"

"Hey," he retorted, "maybe some are AC/DC."

"Oh, good grief!" She gave up after that.

Having tried her best, Amanda in good conscience now turned her mind totally to rehearsals for the next comp.

By October, in Montreal, she was relaxed and resolved to place in the finals in both categories. She and Nick took a second in modern and a third in Latin. Given the tough level of competition, they were thrilled. They immediately began making plans for next year's comps. And, on the reputation they were gaining in the New England area following their wins, both she and Nick signed up several new students apiece.

"Competing is really starting to pay off," Amanda told Rob excitedly. "More students means a higher, more reliable income."

"Look," he said smugly, "you don't have to try to justify yourself to me. Be honest, babe. You want to prance around in pretty dresses. Let it go at that, huh?"

A terrible fight ensued.

From that moment, Amanda vowed never to discuss her dancing with Rob again. It was her private world. If he didn't appreciate it, the hell with him. Not the most mature reaction to criticism, she admitted, but the only one that was genuine. At least they wouldn't have flaming arguments every other week.

Thanksgiving was close at hand. The navy assigned Rob to temporary duty in Annapolis, Maryland, at the Naval Academy. He called three days before the holiday, saying he was sorry to disappoint her but he couldn't make it home as he'd hoped. Amanda tried to take the news in stride but spent a miserable Thanksgiving Day at her parents' house.

To cheer herself up that night after she'd put John to bed, she made herself a cup of orange-spiced tea and started making plans for Vienna. Her mood instantly improved.

They would leave for Europe on the fifteenth of December and return on the second of January. She made a list of clothing to pack—her own and John's—and another of presents she would either buy or make for Caroline, Frank, and Jennifer. By one o'clock, she was so excited she couldn't sleep. Just the thought of seeing Caroline again made her feel light-hearted. She wanted to get to know Frank better, and it would also be her first chance to meet their daughter. Christmas in Vienna promised to be a dream come true. When she finally drifted off to sleep, it was to the strains of a waltz by Strauss.

Commander Robert Allen had rented a sleek new Buick as soon as he got off the plane at Baltimore–Washington International Airport. His temporary teaching assignment at the academy involved only light duties; he'd have plenty of time to kill.

He knew his way around the quaint seafaring town that had survived as the capital of a modern state. The academy was composed of immaculate, squat brick buildings surrounded by a series of iron-rail and brick walls with intermittent guardhouses. The rooming house he'd booked into was a graceful white Colonial listed on the Historical Register. He had to park three blocks away because cars were restricted from the section of town where the old cobbled streets endured.

As soon as he hung his uniforms in the closet and tossed the rest of his clothing into a dresser drawer, he called Ted Streeter. They'd hung out together during their academy days and graduated in the same class. They met at their old hangout, a bar on High Street.

116

"How long you in for, sailor?" Ted roared, slapping him on the back.

"Four weeks. Admiral Max asked if I'd like to be a guest speaker for a couple of his classes."

"The wife and kid along?"

"Naw. The little woman's obsessed with playing mother and doing her own thing. You know, the independent type. Trying to prove something."

Ted shook his head. "You're lucky. Laurie tails me like a foxhound. Wish she had a hobby or something."

Robert chugged his beer. "Women. Can't live with 'em. Can't live without 'em." He looked slantwise at Ted. "You up for a night on the town?"

"When was I not, my good man?" Ted grinned. "You still got numbers? Laurie trashed my little black book. Course a few special ones are branded in the old brain." He tapped his skull.

Robert pulled a worn leather address book from his pocket. Big red *X*'s slashed through all of his old girlfriends' names but failed to obliterate the entries. One night before his wedding, he'd sat down with Amanda and made a ritual of the crossing out process, letting her watch him draw each bright X while he explained that he had no use for other women now that he'd found her. The funny thing was, at the time he had meant it.

For the first six months of his marriage, Robert had been absolutely faithful to his wife. He'd surprised himself by discovering that he'd grown loyal to her in some strange way he couldn't quite fathom. She was sweet, graceful, and perpetually cheerful—a unique woman in his experience. But sometime during her pregnancy, he'd grown restless and the need to break loose had seized him, tearing him out of the easy pattern of their domestic life. He took advantage of his trips away from home, searching out a nice-looking, similarly restless lady for a night on the town.

Rob sometimes wondered if he were addicted to sex— he'd read about cases like that—but if he were, it didn't bother him because *sexual addict* was just a label some tight-ass psychiatrist (probably a woman) had slapped on some lucky group of guys who'd succeeded in beating the curve by getting laid five times as often as the rest of the male population, which made him feel pretty special.

Everyone knew it was a man's prerogative to bed different partners during his lifetime. His old man had been quite adept at fulfilling his destiny. He slept around and didn't care who knew it. Eventually his wife, Robert's mother, left them both. Robert wouldn't have chosen to go with her anyway. He worshipped his father, a navy noncomm. Just the same, her disappearance from his life hurt.

I'll never be the one left behind again, he thought. That was why he was so careful about Amanda. No girls on the side in town. He'd be considerate and separate his women by plenty of miles. This arrangement complicated life, but he figured he owed his wife a certain amount of discretion, more than his old man had given his mother. He'd do what he had to, to keep Amanda happy. But he wasn't going to let her turn him into a wimp, into some henpecked hubby.

Rob and Ted met the girls for dinner at the Dusty Rose. Sherry was a young LPN at Anne Arundel County Hospital. Diana was a veterinarian's assistant.

"Sure, we like to party," they said, giggling. They shared an apartment nearby, where they all would retreat afterward, a mite tipsy from the night's revelry. It was Robert's idea of the perfect evening.

Vienna in December was stunning. The Ringstrasse, which encircled most of the inner city with its tidy individual channels for pedestrians, automobiles, horse-drawn *fiakers,* trees, and park benches, sparkled with new snow. Amanda took one look around and loved what she saw: a sophisticated, glossy city kept spotlessly clean and brimming with history. On their way in the taxi to Caroline's flat in the 19th District, the driver took the long way around to point out the exquisite Opera House, gracefully spired St. Stephen's Cathedral, the grand Hofburg Palace, and the two singularly most famous pastry shops (in all of Europe, he claimed) Gerstner's and Demel's—the last, home of the famous Sachertorte, a rich chocolate cake layered with jam.

Frank was at the embassy when they arrived, but Caroline rushed out to the curb to greet them with squeals of delight.

"Amanda, look at you—so gorgeously slim and healthy looking! And this must be John! Oh, what a little gentleman you are! Jennifer will just eat you up. Robert, how are you?" She raised her cheek demurely for a hello kiss. "And how was the flight? You took Pan Am?"

"Yes. Eleven hours, but we're here." He looked around, blowing his frosty breath into the sharp air, looking up and down the street of dignified baroque Austrian houses. "Nice section of town."

"Most of the international community resides in Grinzing. Make the driver help you with the bags. Amanda, John, come inside out of this cold."

Amanda followed Caroline inside, leaving the luggage to two able-bodied men. Robert had been in an excellent mood during the flight. For the first time in years they'd actually had long discussions about news, Hollywood gossip, food, sports, and plain old nonsense, anything that came to mind. Of course, she'd steered clear of the danger topic—her dancing. But, all in all, it had been a delightful way to get reacquainted.

Caroline divested Amanda and John of their coats, introduced Jennifer, with whom Amanda fell instantly in love and had to pick up and cuddle despite the little girl's protests. Then they all went on a tour of the house.

"The good news is Austrian flats have soaring ceilings, hardwood floors, are never more than five stories up, and—at least those leased by the diplomatic corps—come with tasteful furnishings so you don't have to truck your own stuff all over creation."

They walked into a spacious parlor decorated in cream, mauve, and gold. Amanda drew a long, slow breath, taking it all in: antique sofa, dark wood tables, lustrous porcelain figurines. Caroline's touch was definitely here, although the furniture might have been chosen by someone else.

"It's lovely, Caroline."

"I didn't get to the bad news yet." She gestured with one hand, and they traveled down a short hall. "There are no closets, in the bedrooms or anywhere else, so you cram all your hangable clothing into garderobes. We have a W.C.— water closet, toilet and sink only—and a bathroom with a tub, sink, and bidet. These two doors here." She led on to a bedroom—hers and Frank's, Amanda guessed from the lavish decoration. "Beds are wood with wire frames to support two little mattresses to make up one double. It's so silly. These people are the ultimate sophisticates, yet can't begin to figure out how to make a comfortable bed!" She shook her head, laughing.

"But you like it here," Amanda pointed out.

"I adore it. I'd stay here forever. Unfortunately, the department doesn't like to keep its people in any one spot too long." She shrugged. "Who knows, maybe we'll get London, Paris, or Madrid next!" She glanced at Amanda's thoughtful expression. "I'm sorry, I do get into myself, don't I?"

Amanda smiled. "You always did, but I don't mind. I like to see you this happy. And I'm just thrilled to be here." They hugged, and it felt like old times, as if they'd put something back together the way it should be.

It was going to be an even better holiday than Amanda had envisioned.

Caroline watched Frank play with John and Jennifer, tickling them mercilessly until, squealing and gasping for breath, they ran to hide behind the sofa. Moments later they were back for more of the same inane torture. It seemed to her a stupid game—noisy, nerve-wracking, with no point at all and never any winner. Her gaze traveled to see if Amanda's reaction mirrored her own, but her friend sat comfortably on the floor near Frank's knee, contentedly sipping a cup of tea, smiling at the children's antics.

Every now and then Amanda murmured a cautionary, "Maybe you'd better calm down, John . . . Look out for the pretty vase on that table. . . . Oh, Frank, he's going to wet his pants he's laughing so hard." But she was laughing, too, and clearly had no intention of putting a stop to their madness.

Caroline knew Amanda, and she was sure that her happiness at this particular moment wasn't an everyday occurrence. After being with Amanda for a week, Caroline was all the more convinced that her friend and Robert were terribly mismatched as a couple. Amanda was a hard worker, dedicated to her dancing and determined to make her marriage work. Robert was an overgrown, if adorable, child who had no idea what he wanted out of life. Amanda was fighting an uphill battle with him for a husband and paltry military pay to live on. In one of her letters, she mentioned that she'd turned down an offer to teach at another studio in Hartford, a much larger city where she might expect to find more and higher-paying students. That was probably a decision based upon her absolute fidelity to Sara and Doug, but it might also have been another point of contention between herself and Robert.

Caroline shook her head, regretting that she'd ever introduced Amanda to Rob. If she'd known the girl was so ripe to marry, she'd at least have picked a guy with oodles of money. But she knew Amanda. Stubborn as Amanda was, she never gave up. What Amanda couldn't change, she'd overlook or work around. No matter how bad things got, she would never throw Rob out. Her loyalty to those she loved was boundless. How many times as girls had she, Caroline, hurt Amanda's feelings, only to be welcomed back as a cherished friend?

Caroline turned back to watch her husband and best friend playing with the children. Still no point to the silly game, still squeals, lunges, giggles, hiding. She couldn't make herself join in, in fact, had never been able to tolerate the way Frank lost himself in play with Jennifer. It was as if the two of them were broadcasting on a secret wavelength, and she was incapable of picking up the frequency. She felt left out at those times, just as she did now.

Needing to pull some attention away from the children, she asked casually, "Where's Rob?"

Amanda deflected a wandering leg as John tumbled across the carpet and into her lap. "I think he said he was taking a walk."

If Caroline knew him at all, his outing would include a stroll down one of the narrow alleys off the Karntnerstrasse, which was lined with intimate bars. He'd sit at a tiny table for a while, munching hot almonds, listening to the piano player, and drinking a white wine, perhaps Durnsteiner, then try to pick up one of the girls of the demimonde who were unlike hookers of any other city in that they accepted as clients only those gentlemen whose looks they liked. Robert would have no trouble picking one up.

"It's awfully cold out for a walk," Caroline remarked dryly. Wasn't Amanda at all suspicious? *Come on, girl, demand that the son of a bitch shape up or clear out!*

"He doesn't mind the cold," Amanda said with a dim smile. "He needs some time away from the kids, you know how it is."

"I know." But the governess had spirited the little monsters away for most of the week, so Rob couldn't be all that stir-crazy. "I'm getting some coffee. Anyone want any?" Caroline asked halfheartedly, backing out the doorway.

"None for me," Amanda answered, nodding toward her half-full teacup.

Frank didn't respond. John had gleefully sneaked up on him from behind. Now his short arms were locked around the diplomat's neck. Jennifer shrieked with delight and joined in the attack, attempting to pin her father to the floor.

Caroline pressed four fingers of one hand to her temple and, lowering her head, walked away. Her ears were ringing. She didn't know how much more of this she could take. One kid was bad enough, two was a zoo. That reminded her of another problem. Frank wanted another baby. She couldn't bear the thought of a second child cluttering their life even further.

Caroline passed through the swinging door into the tiny kitchen. Austrian kitchens were typically so small you could barely turn around in them. She liked Italian kitchens better. Whole families could live in them and did if they were of the lower class. Farmers brought their mules and goats inside to keep them from being stolen during the night.

Hot coffee sat in the Braun brewer where the cook had left it before departing for the night. Caroline took a white china cup from the cupboard, dropped two saccharin tablets into it, and added a spritz of milk from the pitcher in the little European-size refrigerator, then the steaming coffee.

Trying to clear her mind, she buried her nose in the fragrant steam and inhaled.

"Something wrong?"

She looked around to find Robert in his heavy coat, cheeks pink from the cold. He took off his gloves and smacked them together to knock off the snow before stuffing them into his pocket.

Caroline produced a plastic smile. "No. Of course nothing's wrong."

"Good. Got some of that for me? Smells great!"

"Help yourself," she offered none too graciously. She wasn't about to wait on him the way his wife undoubtedly did.

He hunted through cupboards for a coffee cup. She didn't help by pointing out which one they were in. Finally, he found the right door, selected a generous mug, and poured himself coffee. He unzipped his coat and leaned back on his elbows against the countertop to observe her sitting at the table.

"We were good together, Carrie."

"Don't call me that!" she snapped, shooting a worried glance toward the kitchen door.

She refused to look at him. A minute passed . . . another. Then she heard his shoes pad damply across the tile and stop behind her chair. One hand came down to close warmly around the curve of her nape, massaging softly.

"Brings back memories, doesn't it?" he whispered.

She shivered. In the three years since she'd been married, she'd let no man other than her husband touch her. Sometimes she felt proud of her accomplishment. Other times she just felt bored with the sameness—the same lover in the same bed, looking up at the same ceiling. Frank was a considerate partner, no doubt about that. He'd learned her preferences, her little perversions, and how to use both to please her. But nothing quite compared to the sheer animal jolt of being undressed, caressed, and entered by a new man. She missed the danger and adventure. And yet, Caroline reasoned, giving in to that hunger could cost her dearly.

Robert's fingertips veed together and traced a path down the back of her neck to the collar of her dress. "Memories are strange things, Carrie. We never lose them. Even when we want to throw them away, they come bouncing back." He paused and, in the pocket of his silence, she could hear her heart thudding in her chest. "All those parties in D.C. and Annapolis, then the long, steamy nights afterward. Morning came, we hadn't slept. Remember?"

She let her head drop back as he massaged her shoulders. How could she forget? Robert was sexy and fun, the perfect escort to receptions or bedrooms. But he hadn't been born to the right family, and his earning potential was severely limited. The best he'd ever be was commander in the navy. She understood herself well enough to know that wasn't for her.

"The night of your engagement party . . ." he whispered in her ear. "Your parents' house . . ."

She felt liquid. "You met Amanda there."

"Yes," he breathed, letting the image of the day linger in her mind. Pale pink tablecloths, glittering crystal, a champagne toast, congratulations, wealthy and powerful guests, and Amanda's wide brown eyes staring with fascination at Robert Allen.

But she'd only intended for her friend to have a fling! Just get laid a couple times, have a few laughs. In return for the favor, Amanda would be weaning Robert off of his affair with Caroline. She certainly didn't want any scenes between an ex-boyfriend and her fiancé.

Who gave a damn if her methods were a little underhanded. Amanda would have a good time, and Robert would etch a new notch in his already well-notched belt. Everyone benefited.

Then another image flashed across Caroline's mind: Amanda in her car, Robert flirting with her through the window as Caroline stood behind him, pretending not to notice. A fickle breeze swept off the sound, and Caroline caught the scent of dried salt mixed with musk from the short blond bristles at the back of Robert's neck. Amanda pulled away. She and Robert had waved and walked back together into an empty house.

"Oh, God . . ." she moaned, setting down her cup with a clink.

He put her thoughts into words. "We slept together that night."

"For the *last* time," she said firmly. "It didn't seem wrong to say good-bye."

"You weren't married then. It was okay."

"My best friend was falling in love with you."

"Hey, no one knew how it would turn out. Don't start feeling guilty about something that happened almost four years ago." He pulled a chair alongside hers, sat down, and swiveled her around to face him. Holding her stone-cold hands in his, he looked in her eyes and said, "We were great together. We could be again."

She yanked free of him. "You're crazy," she hissed. "We're both happily married."

"Happily?" he asked quirking a brow. "Does Frank give you everything you need? *Everything?*"

Rocketing out of her seat, Caroline slapped him across the jaw and dashed out of the kitchen and down the hall. She locked herself in the W.C. Her mind was racing, but not as fast as her heart. Had Frank or Amanda heard them? No, Robert's and her voices would surely have been masked by the play screams of the kids. Even the slap, which had landed with considerably less impact than she'd intended, must not have been heard, or there would have been a reaction by now.

Caroline splashed cold water on her face to cool the burning skin, a second too late realizing that she'd destroyed her makeup. Staring with dismay into the mirror, she watched her mascara and eyeshadow run into a ghoulish gray mess beneath her lashes.

What should she do about Robert? Tell Frank . . . after all these years? Confide in Amanda that her husband had been and still was a flagrant womanizer without a moral bone in his body?

Frank's reaction was unpredictable. He might blame her for Robert's proposition, thinking she'd encouraged him, or hold their previous affair against her, even though it had ended—albeit with a fiery bang. On the other hand, if she said nothing to Frank, Robert certainly wouldn't either. He wasn't the petty or vindictive type to confess past sins to Frank in order to embarrass her. More likely, he'd let her rejection slide, continue to put on a proper front, and wait in the wings until she came to him. Which, of course, she would never do.

Caroline pressed her hand over the burning spot in her stomach; took three deep, calming breaths; and willed her pulse to slow down. Damn him for pulling something like this! Never would she risk the life she'd dreamed of and worked for and loved! She was a diplomat's wife, and by God, she could be diplomatic about this whole mess.

And what about Amanda? That was easy. Learning of Robert's past association with her best friend was one thing, but telling her he was probably fucking every skirt in sight *today* would destroy her. And she'd never let Amanda down. Never in a zillion years.

So, the answer was no in both cases. She would tell neither her husband nor her friend.

Peeking out of the W.C., Caroline ascertained that the hallway was clear. She could hear Robert's deep voice, laughing with revolting facility from the parlor, probably over something silly the children had done.

She ran down the hallway to her bedroom, shut and locked the door behind her, threw open the window, and breathed in the crisp Austrian air spritzed with tiny flakes of snow. She had to get a hold of herself, patch up her makeup, and return to the living room completely unruffled.

"I shouldn't be this rattled," she told herself. "Men make passes at me all the time. Robert's no different from any other male."

She firmly took Kleenex in hand and began wiping off smeared makeup.

The following week was one of the most difficult for Caroline in her adult life. She did everything she could to keep busy and avoid Robert. She thought of him constantly.

No matter where she was in the flat or what she was doing, alone or with Amanda and the children, Robert would appear. The warm gazes he gave her made it clear he knew that she was thinking of him. They also conveyed that he was still open to renewing their affair.

The mere sight of Amanda made Caroline feel dismally

guilty. She went out of her way to entertain her friend lavishly—taking her shopping, buying her expensive gifts after lying about the prices, arranging teas for her to meet other wives in the international community, treating her to pastries at Gerstner's. She even broke one of her most strictly enforced rules and allowed the children to eat their meals with the adults and stay up late into the evening playing games in the parlor. She felt protected from Robert's veiled seductive glances by their presence. She was terrified of what might happen if she were caught alone with him again.

On New Year's Eve the two couples attended the traditional ball at the Hapsburg emperors' Summer Palace. Having been forewarned to pack for formal occasions, Amanda had brought a luscious peach-colored ball gown adorned with a creamy lace collar that fit snugly around her slim throat with matching lace trim at the cuffs and hem— one of her homemade creations. The dress, although designed for competitive wear, easily blended with the Viennese gowns. Robert wore his dress white uniform, Frank, tails and white tie. Caroline chose a wine red velvet gown with cap sleeves and crystal droplets sewn in a delicate web over the bodice. She wore long white gloves, wine satin pumps, and, for jewelry, a diamond choker, bracelet, and earrings Frank had bought her for their second anniversary.

The orchestra played danceable renditions of popular music—the Beatles' "Day Tripper," The Mamas and the Papa's "Dedicated to the One I Love," Aaron Neville's "Tell It Like It Is," tunes by the Turtles, Left Bank, the Seekers, the Casinos—interspersed with traditional waltzes, courtesy of Strauss—"Tales from The Vienna Woods," "An Artist's Life," and "The Blue Danube."

Robert liked the rock and modern ballads and danced aggressively, asking each of the ladies in turn at their table to be his partner. And they all accepted because, as the wife of Ambassador Bruckner put it, "He's such a likeable chap and so irresistibly handsome as well."

He only waltzed with Amanda once, under duress from Caroline in the form of a vicious kick beneath the table. His movements were stilted and forced. Nevertheless, he was in a party mood—slick, confident of his physical prowess, definitely in his element, and attracting more than his share of wistful glances from women at other tables as he and his wife moved across the polished wood floor.

Since balls were de rigeur in Vienna, Caroline and Frank had had plenty of practice. One had no choice but to learn to waltz. And Caroline was fortunate, because she'd taken lessons as a teenager.

Caroline glanced across the table at her friend, knowing how frustrated she must be without a partner capable of leading the beautiful dance properly. She'd seen Amanda perform the Viennese at an exhibition, and it had been an awesome experience. The young woman simply floated, her heeled slippers skimming the floor as a serene smile lifted the corners of her lips. No effort seemed to be involved. Yet even experienced amateurs tonight left the floor panting from the exertion of keeping up with the swift tempo and swirling steps.

Caroline observed Amanda as yet another waltz swept couples from their seats and into one another's arms. Her friend eyed the revolving figures with obvious longing while Robert chatted up the ambassador's pretty young sister.

Why does she let him get away with that? If he were mine, I'd rattle his damn teeth for ignoring me!

Caroline jabbed Frank in the ribs. "Ask her to dance," she hissed.

Frank looked doubtful. "Do you think Amanda wants to? She and Robert have only danced a couple of times."

"Do ducks swim?" she demanded. "This is a woman who'd rather stop breathing than sit still when music plays."

Frank obligingly stood and walked around behind Amanda's chair. "Would you care to waltz, m'lady?" he asked.

She looked around and up at him, suddenly aglow, and Caroline knew she had done at least one good deed for her friend. Frank opened his arms to Amanda. She stepped naturally into them, taking her position in the curve on his right arm, resting her right hand in his raised left. Caroline settled back into her seat to enjoy watching them twirl across the room, disappearing amidst a rainbow of organdy, velvet, chiffon, and jewels.

Frank looked down self-consciously at his feet as they rounded the first corner of the grand ballroom of the Summer Palace.

"Don't do that, Mr. Counsel," Amanda murmured beneath the flowing tide of music.

He laughed and straightened abruptly. "The cardinal sin of dance, huh? I don't usually peek, but I felt a little out of position for some reason."

She gave him a patient smile. "This is where I should be, way over on your right side. You're accustomed to holding the lady in front of you, but believe me it's easier to dance this way—less tripping over your partner's feet and it looks much nicer. I hope you don't mind my offering a little creative criticism. I'm afraid it's the teacher in me coming out."

"Not at all. I appreciate any pointers you're willing to give." He brought them to a jerking halt, then laughed as another couple nearly crashed into them. "Whoops, close call. I have to admit, though, it is a little stressful to be dancing with a professional."

"Relax," she advised, "you're doing great."

Her posture, as they'd begun to dance, was at once assertive and responsive, allowing Frank to lead but stepping swiftly and decisively between his feet to spin them around nearly a hundred eighty degrees with each three-count.

They were soon whizzing past other couples as he led Amanda in the classic one–two–three rhythm, revolving rapidly to the right, then reversing direction so as not to render them hopelessly dizzy.

"Relax still more," she whispered in his ear.

He loosened his hold. "You do this without any effort at all," he commented, slightly out of breath already, although he was in excellent physical condition. "Everyone else huffs and puffs, while you glide across the floor like an angel on ice skates."

She laughed, gazing up into his eyes, and he wished he could tell what she was thinking. Suddenly, she said,

"Caroline is a very lucky woman. I'm so glad she's happy. Thank you."

"Thank you? I love my wife. I shouldn't have to be thanked for being decent to her."

"I know . . . you don't . . ." She looked flustered as she spun around the room in his arms. "I just wanted to let you know what a relief it is to see her content."

He caught the shadow that crossed her expressive brown eyes. "And are you as happy with your life? With your marriage?" As soon as he'd spoken, he thought, *What a stupid, insensitive thing to ask.* The question was far too personal. He hardly knew her. Or was that really true?

Reading her letters had been unconscionable. Her confidences were intended for her girlfriend, not for him. But ever since the day they'd met at the engagement party, he'd been eaten up with curiosity about Amanda. She'd been fresh, natural, athletic, and feminine in a delightfully old-fashioned way, so unlike the T-shirted, protesting young women who marched across American campuses, so unlike her refined, pampered, fashionably stunning best friend who was the perfect mate for him. Or so he'd thought at one time.

Funny, he mused, how you can figure all the angles, know in your gut what's right for you, and go after it, only to find that something elemental is missing. Something you'll never be able to put your finger on no matter how hard you try. And, sadly, something definitely was missing from his marriage.

Some days he felt as if he had half a family, as if Caroline wasn't even part of his and his daughter's life. She seemed to detach herself emotionally from them. Other times Frank decided he had the best of all possible marriages to enhance his career—a charming, attractive, and highly efficient hostess, in-laws with wide political and financial alliances, a beautiful child to love and be loved by, and an experienced, willing lover—whom he happened to have married. Yet he would have settled for a woman more in tune with his temperament, a nurturing partner who loved people as he did. For he'd come to realize that all of Caroline's talents were skills she had learned, but to love thoroughly, selflessly,

130

was a gift that comes from the soul. Caroline, he feared, was incapable of true love.

As he'd read Amanda's letters and, later, watched her play with Jennifer and John and laugh at his silly jokes, he'd realized the simple joy of being around a woman who saw fun and happy possibilities in everything around her.

The waltz rose to a heady crescendo of violins, then was suddenly over. He released Amanda and offered her his arm. They'd ended up on the far side of the crowded ballroom, facing a long hike back to the table.

Amanda hadn't answered his question.

"Listen, forget what I said back there . . . about your marriage. It's none of my damn business."

"You're right," she said mildly, "it isn't. Besides, who wants to talk about anything so . . . so ordinary on a night like this. Oh, this place is thrilling! I never thought I'd waltz in a real palace!"

"I wish I could have done you justice," he said, glad that she hadn't been offended and had easily moved on to another topic. "My dancing leaves much to be desired."

"Anytime you want a lesson," she replied pleasantly, "it's on the house."

"Hey, I'd like that. Think you could teach me something dramatic, perhaps a tango to shock the folks back in D.C.?"

"You cut quite an elegant figure already," she remarked, smiling at him. "But I suppose I could give you a pointer or two."

The expansive floor was clearing, but slowly. He guided her between chatting couples.

"When is your next competition?" he asked.

"October, in Boston. What a wonderful time to travel north—the leaves will be turning beautiful colors . . ."

His face lit up as if she'd painted a most appealing picture. "When in October?"

"The fifteenth and sixteenth. Why?"

"I'll be in the States for three weeks out of that month— two of them in D.C., then home to visit my folks on Long Island. Boston is just a short hop north from Long Island. Are spectators allowed at these competitions of yours?"

"Of course," she assured him, looking pleased. "If you

and Caroline can come for only one day, though, make it the fifteenth. That's when we dance in the modern category. You'll see some gorgeous waltzes."

"Caroline will be staying in Vienna. She isn't crazy about zipping back and forth across the Atlantic for rushed visits. But I'd enjoy seeing you dance." He hesitated. "Will Robert be there?" He'd distinctly disliked the man after meeting him at the Cliffs, and his opinion of him hadn't improved after reading Amanda's letters.

"No," she replied without offering any explanation. "He doesn't attend comps."

"Well," Frank said, "I'm not going to miss out."

It was January 1, 1969, the day before her guests were due to depart for the States, and Caroline was a bundle of nerves. She dashed around the flat picking up things, putting them down before she had a chance to use them, then forgetting where she'd laid them. She was frantic that the dinner—her last with Amanda for God knew how long—be perfect. She made certain to never let herself be caught alone in any room in the house except for her own bedroom, and then she locked the door. She didn't trust Robert to honor her wish to be left out of his romantic games. She wanted him *gone!* Out of her house, out of her life! He was right in one way. Her marriage had never totally satisfied her, but she was convinced that her relationship with Frank was close enough to perfect. When so many pieces of the puzzle fit, why fret over one or two missing ones?

They all ate dinner—delectable roast goose with all the trimmings—then Amanda read stories to the children in front of the fireplace until they nodded off and were carried to bed. The adults played canasta. At the end of the fourth hand, Amanda smothered a huge yawn.

"I'm sorry," she apologized. "I know it's only ten o'clock, but I'm exhausted. I guess it's the thought of the long plane trip tomorrow. Are you ready for bed, sweetheart?" she asked Robert.

Caroline flinched. How obscene, wasting endearments on

that manipulative bastard. For the hundredth time, she seriously considered taking Amanda aside before they left and confessing everything to her. The truth might shatter whatever shred of happiness her friend held on to, but wouldn't she be better off knowing in the long run? *As soon as I can get her alone,* she thought, *I have to tell her everything no matter how much it hurts her.*

Caroline stood up, avoiding Amanda's eyes. "I'm tired, too."

Frank looked at his watch. "Just as well that we break up the card game. I have to prepare a briefing for tomorrow."

"What a shame," Amanda said. "We shouldn't have kept you at a silly card game when you had work to do."

He waved off her concern. "No problem. I'll see you all in the morning before you leave." He walked out of the room and down the hall in the direction of his study.

Robert turned to Amanda, a glass of brandy swirling in his right hand. "I'm going to take a short stroll down to the plaza. The cold will help clear my head before going to sleep."

"Your head would clear a damn sight faster if you drank less," Caroline pointed out testily.

"No doubt," he said, mock toasting her before setting down his empty glass and leaving the two women alone in the parlor.

Amanda sat very still. Caroline reached down to put an arm around her. "You all right?"

Amanda smiled weakly. "Sure. I guess my mind's already halfway across the Atlantic. I'm anxious to get back into the routine at home."

"Sure you are. Get away from nasty old Vienna with all its parties, free baby-sitting, and nothing to do but sit around, eat pastries, and talk."

Amanda laughed. As always Caroline saw right through her. "It has been two wonderful weeks. I didn't realize how badly I needed this trip."

"We both needed it. Seeing you always makes me feel so good," Caroline assured her. "Come on. I have to talk to you about something."

They walked arm in arm down the hall, Caroline searching for the right words with every step. Abruptly, Amanda stopped and turned to face her. "Before you say anything, I have to tell you this. Staying here with you, Frank, and Jennifer has meant a lot to me. I can't recall being this happy in a long time."

"I know, honey. I know," Caroline soothed, patting her on the shoulder while searching for the right words to tell her about Rob.

"I mean it," Amanda murmured. "I think coming to Vienna has given me strength I've needed to stick to my goals and work out my marriage." Amanda hugged her hard. "Thanks."

A few minutes later when Caroline stared at her reflection in the bathroom mirror, she kicked herself for chickening out, for telling Amanda nothing. And yet she had a sense, as one woman often does about another, that Amanda already knew most of the truth about her man. Amanda knew she'd married a dud. She knew he played around but, for reasons of her own, chose to ignore his infidelities.

Caroline smoothed cream over her face, thoroughly cleansing the fine skin, then finishing with a light night lotion.

There was a muffled knock on the bathroom door. She turned on the water in the sink, letting whoever was there know that the room was occupied. The knock sounded again.

"Shit!" she muttered under her breath. Then louder, "I'll be right out!"

Sometimes European flats—even luxurious ones—left a lot to be desired. Screw the bidet, which she'd never learned to use anyway. What she wouldn't give for a spacious modern American bathroom with a sunken bathtub, a hot tub, and sauna.

The knob turned, and Caroline belatedly realized she hadn't bothered to lock the door.

Robert let himself in, shutting the door behind him as he smiled at her cheerfully. "Hello, Caroline, my dear."

"What the hell are you doing?" she choked out.

"I decided this was the only room in the house where you

and I might talk in private." He shook a finger at her. "You've been avoiding me."

"With damn good reason—" She reached around him for the doorknob.

He blocked her with his body.

Caroline glared at him, furious with his games, but not so blinded with anger that she couldn't take in details. He was wearing charcoal gray slacks and a crisp white dress shirt with the collar unbuttoned to reveal a few strategically positioned chest hairs. She felt unaccountably claustrophobic and shaken.

"Let me out," she ordered in a low voice.

Robert's smile didn't falter. "Not until you tell me that you don't want me, that you'll never want me again."

"N-never," she sputtered, unable to get the words out fast enough. "In fact, never would be too soon!"

"Your eyes tell me different," he teased, brushing a platinum wave off of her brow. His hands seemed to drop away, but a second later she became aware of their warm pressure on her shoulders, then smoothing her upper arms. His thumbs traced mirror paths, whisper soft, along the sides of her breasts. Caroline's heart shot into her throat as a familiar heat spread from the inner most recesses of her torso and out through her limbs. *No*, she told herself, *I understand what he's doing. But there's no such thing as seduction. Short of rape, Robert Allen can't make me react to him . . . unless I want to react.*

She shut her eyes, blocking him out. But that was worse, for her sense of touch became acute and his hands suddenly felt as if they were searing the tender flesh. Gradually, his thumbs centered over her nipples, gently teasing them to firm peaks.

She swallowed a scream.

"What's wrong, Carrie? Why aren't you stopping me? Why aren't you calling out to your husband, Mr. Hotshot Diplomat?"

Oh, God, he had always had wicked thumbs. Wicked, wicked . . . wonderful thumbs. She recalled how he'd sometimes tantalize her, letting her see his erection, encouraging her to touch him, but refraining from entering her. He'd caress her deeply with his fingers, probing, titillating a bit more, finding that moist, most sensitive fraction of an inch of her anatomy until he'd driven her wild.

The memory burned within her. She let out a soft whimper of protest, but no cry for assistance, no scream of outrage, for then he'd stop teasing her, stop touching her like this, and losing the delicious rise of her arousal at this moment seemed a fate worse than death.

Caroline tried to think of Frank. But their lovemaking had long ago become too comfortable to produce the eroticism she craved.

"Why not call for help?" Robert repeated, moving so close she could feel the heat of his body through their clothing.

"Be-because I refuse to make a scene," she gasped. "Robert, stop that . . . please, oh, please . . ."

He shook his head slowly, side to side, his blue eyes riveted to hers, his thumbs sketching circles around her nipples. "Tell me you'll never want me again. Tell me and mean it. I'll go away forever."

She wasn't above lying, but what was the point? The man wasn't blind. She pulled herself together long enough to respond with a semblance of logic. "If we had an affair, Frank and Amanda would be hurt terribly. I couldn't do that to either of them."

"They would never know."

"They'd find out."

"Who'd tell them? Certainly not me. I'm the epitome of discretion, you know that from past experience. And *you* certainly aren't going to confess anything in a rush of guilt. Carrie, I know you too well." His hands were traveling again, this time downward. "You are far too practical and single-minded a woman. You go after what you want and don't let up until you've gotten it. And you recognize your needs. You need a man now. Don't you?"

His voice was mesmerizing. Yet she felt oddly clear-headed. *Yes, I do need a man, you bastard. Why do you have to be so damn good at this?*

His hands slid down her ribs, pressed in at her waist, and

molded her hips. As feverishly hot as she was, she shivered at his touch.

Dammit, he was right. He was the perfect lover. And despite the fact that there existed a difference of several million dollars of personal worth between them, they were two of a kind. If she were to ever take a lover, Robert would be the one. Not that she was going to take a lover, but if she did, if she decided that the time was right, she needn't fear disclosure or blackmail from Robert. He was simply too unimaginative. Robert was safe. He wouldn't bother bragging to his buddies about his millionaire mistress, because they already figured he'd slept with every woman on the planet. And she needn't fear his becoming possessive and demanding that she leave her husband for him because all he wanted from her was sex. He was, if she were considering a lover, ideal . . . which she wasn't . . . of course . . . considering a lover . . .

With a jolt of surprise Caroline realized that his right hand had shifted off of her hip and moved beneath her skirt hem. She sucked in her breath, biting down on her lower lip as his palm inched smoothly up her silken thigh, rounding its inner surface, his fingers stopping just short of her panties. Then she could feel his short nails brushing tantalizingly against the softly curled hair ends through the silk fabric.

Caroline squeezed her eyes shut, savoring the flash of intense heat, aching for him to touch her harder, to drive her to madness, to satisfy her . . .

"Robert, yes . . . please, yes," she moaned.

She wasn't aware that she'd actually spoke the words until his answer whispered in her ear, "Anything you want, Carrie."

He circumnavigated the crotch of her panties and sunk two wide fingers into her, as she arched against the wall for support. Her nails bit into the muscles of his shoulders beneath his crisp shirt.

"We were always good at reading each other," he whispered hoarsely in her ear, while moving within her, eliciting wave upon wave of unbearable pleasure.

She clamped her teeth tighter over her lip to stop herself from crying out in ecstacy.

"Remember how I taught you to do this for yourself? I'll bet when Frank's traveling on some high-priority diplomatic mission or when he's just too tired to love you, you do this to yourself . . . do what a man should do for you . . . what *I* can do for you."

She dropped her head forward, then picked it up with effort but was incapable of answering. How often had she wished for the carefree days when a one-nighter automatically followed dinner and an evening at a Washington function. Each new man—even if he weren't an especially adept lover—turned her on just because he was new. Robert, however, had the skill to outlast repeat performances.

His fingers pulsed within her. She grasped the back of his neck, pressed his head forward, and kissed him deeply, relishing the salty taste of his mouth, inhaling his fragrance, feeling as if she could devour him with her body. In a surge of sensation, her orgasms overlapped, climaxing in a single consuming rush of agonizing delight. Her body went rigid for an instant, then she slumped against him, struggling to breathe, trembling as if from the aftershocks of an earthquake.

"Oh, God, what have we done?" Caroline groaned softly.

She was still fully dressed, and he had never removed or readjusted one article of his own clothing. She hadn't even taken him in her hand, and that, she thought, was the cleverest part of his plan. For now she hungered to touch him.

Her hand moved as if of its own accord to press over his zipper. Beneath the metal grooves, she could feel his rigid shape.

"Not now," he whispered. "We must be careful."

"Yes." She swallowed. Her mouth felt horridly dry. "Careful," she repeated.

"Tomorrow morning," he said. "Before we leave for the airport, Amanda wants to take the children for a walk to get John settled down for the plane ride. I'll suggest she take Frank along while I finish packing."

"Yes." Everything was yes now. Could only be yes, as if she was capable of pronouncing no other word.

"While they're out, you and I will talk about how we can get together every now and then . . . to renew our old friendship. Then I'll fuck you so good it'll last until the next time we meet."

Caroline thought, *This is destiny. This was bound to happen no matter how I tried to prevent it. Let it be, girl. Enjoy him.*

9

As much as Amanda had loved being in Vienna with Caroline and Frank, she was eager to return home and throw herself into her busy schedule of caring for John, teaching, practicing twice a week with Nick, and keeping up with household chores—the daily routine that made her feel in control of her life and brought a reasonable amount of satisfaction. She was, she found, happiest when she was busy. Lazing around with Caroline had been delightful, but the lack of pressing tasks left her with too much time to think.

While in Vienna, whenever John and Jennifer were awake, Frank and Amanda had been the ones to entertain them. Robert completely divorced himself from their games as if they were beneath him. And, sadly, Caroline appeared to feel awkward around her own daughter, unsure of how to enjoy her. Amanda felt sorry for her and had tried every way she knew to help her loosen up but had failed.

Other troubling thoughts crossed her mind. It hadn't been lost on her that Robert found Caroline attractive. He didn't exactly leer at her, but Amanda remembered intercepting a prowling gleam in his eye more than once. At one time—

why did it seem so long ago?—those looks had been directed at *her*. She expected a marriage, even a sound one, to mellow, the passion to cool. But she'd hoped for a gratifying flare-up every now and then.

After they'd returned home and she had time to put her concerns in some sort of rational order, she decided that Rob's roaming eye might, at least in part, be her fault. She vowed to put more effort into her appearance when she was at home. She bought a sexy new negligee, put on a touch of makeup after cleansing her face each morning before starting breakfast, began wearing cologne again.

They had sex once a week on Saturday nights after Rob returned from the Officers' Club. It was fun, and Amanda looked forward to it unless Rob had drunk too much—then he fell asleep before much happened.

Sometimes on a weekday morning, though, when neither of them had to rush off to work early and John slept a bit later than usual, Amanda awoke, aroused by the warmth of a man in her bed. She slipped off her nightgown and luxuriated beneath the sheets, wishing that Robert would roll over, smooth his hands around her bottom, pull her to him, and make long, lazy love to her while the dewy morning air and soft sunlight spilled over the window sill.

To feel loved, totally loved, not simply possessed as if she were a chair or a job—that would be truly wonderful. Unfortunately, Robert seemed not to notice her efforts to lure him into a more romantic state.

On the positive side, however, he did put up less resistance to her spending time at the studio. From the lack of dirty dishes and glasses waiting for her on the kitchen counter, she assumed that he wasn't at home much of the time. She felt bad that they saw so little of one another, but perhaps they were better off that way. Other couples she knew of eventually got on each other's nerves and had terrible fights. At least they weren't fighting.

In February the navy sent Rob to supervise the fitting of a new ship in Scotland. He was there for a month, but his sea tours had accustomed Amanda to being alone. She and Nick took advantage of the extra time and doubled up on their practices. They decided if they did well in the Boston comp, next year they might take the plunge and enter the international championship in Blackpool, England—considered by many the Olympics of ballroom dancing.

Amanda continued to write to Caroline every month and received brief but always cheerful replies. However, while Robert was away (and Amanda most needed to hear from her), she received nothing from Caroline. In March, her letters started up again, full of political gossip and name-dropping, and were even longer than before. Amanda reciprocated with news of John—he was learning his alphabet and numbers—and of her new students, and of a dress she was sewing for her modern numbers, a fluffy, white creation as delicate as spun sugar. The months rolled on. If money was sometimes short, she made do . . . and as long as she was dancing she was never bored.

It was a sunny Tuesday in June when she picked up her mail at the base post office box and extracted a thick, cream-colored parchment envelope with a familiar embossed return address in Vienna. To her suprise, her own address had been drawn in smooth, precise, black letters in a hand that was not Caroline's.

Turning the envelope over curiously, Amanda walked down the sidewalk toward the apartment with John straggling along behind her, kicking pebbles and gaily singing, "Up, up, and away . . . boooootiful balloon!" as she read the letter inside.

Dear Amanda,

Although October is still some ways off, I thought it best to confirm our arrangements to meet at your competition in Boston. I plan to arrive in the city on the 15th as you suggested. I'll be staying at the Ritz-Carlton at Arlington and Newbury Streets. If you and your partner would like to stop over for breakfast before or dinner following your performance, I'd be delighted to play host.

Both Caroline and Jennifer are well. Jennifer asks for you often and misses our wild wrestling matches with John. We should try to get the two children together once in a while. John seems to have a reassuring influence on Jen, and she thrived on entertaining him.

For my part, I enjoyed finally meeting you under less formal circumstances than an engagement party or wedding reception. Your stay with us was immeasurably relaxing—a breath of fresh air. So many of our acquaintances in the service are obsessed with petty jealousies and maneuvering for next rung up on the career ladder. Socializing has become very tiresome, and it really shouldn't be.

Caroline has suggested that we make our family visits a Christmas tradition, and I couldn't agree with her more. Please consider the idea and let us know how the three of you feel about it.

> Cordially,
> Frank

Amanda folded the single sheet of parchment. *What a nice man,* she thought.

While John napped before they left for the studio, she brewed herself a cup of mint tea and sipped it while answering Frank's letter.

Dear Frank,

I'm sure that Christmassing annually with the Donnellys will be met with enthusiasm by Robert. He's spoken of our visit often since we returned home and more than once has expressed an interest in going back to Vienna to see more of the city. For myself, I can think of no happier way to spend the holidays.

Now, about Boston. Nick and I will have rooms at the Lenox. Not as posh as your hotel, but it happens to be the comp site, so by staying there, we'll get discounted rates and avoid driving back and forth across the city loaded down with costumes and makeup cases. I'll leave a message and a ticket for admission at your hotel. Breakfast, I'm afraid, will be impossible.

The morning of a comp I'm so nervous I can barely choke down a slice of dry toast. But with any luck, maybe we can all have a victory dinner.

Best to your lovely ladies!

Amanda

October

Frank found his ticket, along with a program, at the front desk of the Ritz-Carlton, just as Amanda had promised. Her hotel room number was penciled on the front of the program. Tucking both items into the front pocket of his carry-on bag, he headed for the elevator.

Just before leaving Vienna, he'd tried once again to convince Caroline to come with him. But she'd recently hostessed two dinner parties for him—very tricky affairs involving carefully designed seating arrangements to keep two rival politicians out of shouting range.

"I need some time by myself," she'd explained. "I'm simply wiped out, darling." And he didn't doubt it. There was a spa she favored at Lusat in the south of France. He suggested she treat herself to a week or two there, and she'd agreed that might be just what she needed.

Frank tipped the porter, closed the door, and immediately crossed the suite to the bedroom where he pried off his shoes and stretched out on the bed to study the competition schedule. The events appeared to have begun at ten A.M., with amateurs and pro-am teams competing first. For a moment, a pang of disappointment gripped him. What if he'd missed her performance?

His eyes drifted down the page. Amanda and Nick weren't scheduled to compete until six P.M. that night.

Smiling with relief, Frank lifted the receiver of the telephone beside his bed and dialed the Lenox, then asked the operator to ring Amanda's room. No answer. He left a message with the operator, letting Amanda know that he'd arrived and would see her later.

144

After a quick shower, he changed into casual slacks and a sport shirt, having determined he'd kill a few hours by revisiting some of his favorite places in Boston. Frank walked along the stately tree-lined streets of Beacon Hill, past the elegant brick townhouses of the city's nineteenth-century wealthy. He turned into the Public Gardens, pausing for a while to watch the famous swan boats glide serenely past with late-season tourists as passengers. Before many days, the venerable wooden paddle boats would be hauled out of the water for the winter. But today the weather was mild and perfect for a leisurely glide across the pond. He passed up a ride but purchased a tiny blown glass swan as a souvenir for Jennifer.

Because he rarely visited a city without spending an hour or more in its library, he crossed Copley Square and climbed the steps to the Boston Public Library. He was surprised to discover a remarkably fine collection of artwork that he'd missed on previous trips—some Daniel Chester French, an oil by John Singer Sargent, a rare Puvis de Chavannes. He only glanced at his watch when it was announced that the library would soon be closing.

Outside on the sidewalk, Frank got his bearings and determined that he'd have time to walk to the Lenox. On the way he passed a flower cart, the vendor closing up shop for the day as the air grew chill and dusk drew closer. On an impulse, he retraced his steps.

"How much for that bouquet of cut posies," he asked.

"Five dollars, sir," the blowzy old woman replied.

"I'll take them." He peeled off a bill and tucked the tissue-wrapped bouquet under his arm, striding down the darkening streets overshadowed by the Prudential building along Copley Place and finally to Boyleston Street.

It had occurred to him only on seeing the flowers that ballroom dancers, like ballerinas, might be given a bouquet, rose, or some small token at the end of a performance. For some reason, he suddenly felt it important to have something in hand to present to Amanda when she finished dancing tonight.

He timed his arrival at the Lenox for five o'clock, with the hope of getting a good seat. The moment that he entered the ballroom, it became clear that he'd misjudged the popularity of the event, for the room was packed. Few vacant seats were visible at any of the tables surrounding the spacious dance floor.

Hoping to spot Amanda, Frank scanned the crowd but could find her nowhere. Recorded orchestra music swelled from immense speakers placed at opposite ends of the ballroom. He tried to find an out-of-the-way corner in which to stand and watch the dancers warm up: men in tuxedos guiding ladies in ethereal gowns around the room in one vast counterclockwise circle.

At last he spotted a brunette whose bared, delicate shoulders and softly curved arms reminded him of a familiar picture: Amanda in her New Year's Eve gown, reaching out to pick up his little daughter and give her a good-night kiss. When the young woman turned sideways, he could see that it was indeed her, and she was lovely, although in a way he'd never seen her before.

Amanda's hair was arranged on top of her head in a sophisticated twist very unlike her everyday style that fell in loose natural waves around her pert oval face. She wore dramatic theatrical makeup that emphasized her eyes and lips. She looked deeply tanned, as did all of the dancers, male and female, and he suspected this must have been achieved through the use of body makeup, for he doubted that Amanda could have retained her natural summer tan this late in the year. She looked like a sophisticated fashion model but floated like an angel in her feathery snow-white gown.

The music stopped. Amanda and her partner lowered their arms and stepped apart. Then, looking apprehensive, she glanced around the room.

Frank raised an arm above his head. Amanda saw him. Grinning, she waved him over to a round table occupied by a half-dozen dancers in costume and their guests.

"Oh, Frank, I'm so glad you made it in time!" She gave him a welcome hug. "Flowers?" she asked.

He placed them in her hands. "I thought . . . you know, after the show . . . They're a little difficult to hide."

Amanda sniffed them happily. "I'd rather have them now. I may be so furious after we dance that I wouldn't appreciate them." She plucked a tiny sprig of baby's breath from the fragrant cluster and tucked it into the ruffle at her bodice. "For good luck," she murmured. "Here, let me introduce you to everyone. My partner, Nick . . . This is Frank Donnelly, Caroline's husband."

"Glad to meet you," Nick said jovially, holding out a big paw.

Nick wasn't at all what Frank had envisioned. He looked like a construction worker poured into exquisitely tailored formal wear. And yet he'd seen the man dance a few minutes ago, and there hadn't been a hint of bullishness about him.

"Frank! Frank!" John called, emerging from beneath the table where he'd evidently been listening in.

"Way to go, old man!" Frank scooped him up into the air, gave him a pretend toss toward the ceiling, then set him down. "How's it going?"

John hung from the crook of Frank's elbow, dangling his feet off of the floor. "Just great. Can I have more popcorn, Mom?"

"Sure. Just try not to spill."

He seized the bag from the tabletop and retreated under the table.

"He'll come out to watch us dance, but he really prefers his private hideout in a crowd like this," Amanda explained. Next, she introduced Nick's wife, Susan; another couple who were competing; and Nick's parents, who had flown in from New Jersey to cheer on their son.

"Are your folks coming, too?" Frank asked Amanda.

She shook her head. "They find little value in the dance world," she murmured. "Ooooh, Nick, look at Gary and Marilyn Saxon! Don't they look stunning tonight?"

Frank watched Amanda, recalling some of her letters to Caroline. She'd only infrequently mentioned her parents, and then with a sense of wistfulness. Although he couldn't imagine a couple not being proud of a daughter like Amanda, he assumed they were disappointed in her vocation. This made absolutely no sense to him. She worked hard, was beautiful, intelligent, genuinely caring, and successful at what she did. It amazed him that she always seemed so full of joy despite having an imbecile for a husband and insensitive parents. Looking at her tonight, it was difficult to imagine that she faced any adversity.

Perhaps that's why she dances, he thought, *to leave the pain behind.*

She cast him a final grateful look as she laid the bouquet gently on the table. "Sit right here, Frank. Nick and I have one more practice dance. Susan will fill you in on what's going on."

After watching for a minute, he leaned over and shouted over the music into Susan's ear. "They're remarkable! What dance are they doing now?"

"The quickstep," she told him. "It's rather old-fashioned. You don't see it much anymore except in exhibition. But it's one of my favorites—so energetic and bouncy. Just lovely when done right."

The steps were sometimes sweeping, sometimes skipping in coordinated mayhem. Amanda leaned to her left, gazing with a practiced rapturous expression over Nick's right shoulder. Her left hand rested lightly on his upper arm, the pinky daintily curled. Her right hand clasped her partner's left, which was raised in the line of dance as if pointing their way. Amanda's skirt billowed around her ankles like a marshmallow cloud, the tiny satin toes of her pumps peeping out as she tripped expertly through the rapid steps.

"Do you and Nick dance together often?" Frank asked.

Susan's green eyes sparkled, observing her husband with undisguised pride. "We dance socially. I've never been good enough to perform at a professional level," she admitted. "Ballroom competition is fierce. I'm too laid back by nature to enjoy it. But Amanda's amazing. Look at her! She seems like such a little powder puff of a woman, but she's tough as nails—a real athlete and aggressive as hell on the dance floor."

Frank watched Nick and Amanda weave effortlessly among other competitors on the floor. *She truly is remarkable . . . in many ways.*

Susan kept talking. "Nick jogs and works out with weights every day to keep in shape for this. It's grueling, like training for an Olympic event. They'll dance five modern routines today, five Latin tomorrow. If they make the semifinals and finals, they'll have danced for two to three hours each day with very little break."

"I can't imagine," Frank murmured. When time allowed, he played tennis. A couple of hours on the court just about knocked him out. This looked every bit as strenuous and demanding.

The evening was exciting and tense, and it flashed by all too quickly for Frank. By ten o'clock, Nick and Amanda had captured a first place in the professional modern division. The table erupted in jubilation. Nick hugged Amanda, then his wife, then his mother, then Amanda again. He was like a little kid who'd won a soap box derby.

Frank couldn't remember the last time he himself had felt this good. He was hoarse from cheering his favorite couple on, ecstatic at seeing Amanda so happy. He wished with all his heart that Caroline had been here to witness her friend's triumph.

"You did it! You did it!" he cried, clasping her to his chest when Nick finally released her.

"On to Blackpool!" Nick shouted, then turned to Frank. "Let's celebrate. Know any good restaurants in this town?"

Frank consulted his watch. Boston rolled up its sidewalks early.

"Everyone come to my suite," he invited. "We'll throw a private party."

"Really?" Amanda asked, beaming.

"Sure. That's why suites and room service were invented. Meet me at the Ritz, suite 710, after you've gathered up your gear."

He telephoned room service from the lobby of the Lenox. He felt as thrilled as a kid planning a friend's birthday party. *What to order? What to order?*

"I'd like a late dinner for eight," he began, thinking as he spoke. He was famished, and a juicy steak would hit the spot, but he had noticed how carefully Amanda ate while in

Vienna and wanted to offer her something that she could enjoy without guilt. "Let's start with a selection of your pâtés with thin slices of pumpernickel and wheat breads . . . light dips and assorted fresh raw vegetables . . . a chicken salad . . . a chilled fruit compote . . . and champagne."

"Will that be all, sir?"

Then again, she had adored Viennese pastries . . .

He ordered a chocolate Bavarian torte and two carafes of coffee.

He didn't question how or why he'd become so wrapped up in Amanda's victory. Maybe his reaction was similar to the vicarious thrill one experienced when watching a sporting event. The contagious excitement of competition, cheers from the crowd, and the sheer physical beauty of men and women dancing in one another's arms had left him breathless.

He took a cab back to the hotel, washed up quickly, shaved the second time that day, splashed his favorite aftershave on, and ran a comb through his hair. He didn't question why he was going to so much trouble. He wondered if Amanda would still be in her exotic costume when she arrived.

Nick and his wife showed up just as a waiter was rolling a cart loaded with food into the room. Frank tipped the waiter, and Susan took charge of setting the elaborate trays on a low table in front of a Queen Anne settee. Nick's parents showed up ten minutes later, bringing news that the other couple from their table, although they'd been invited, wouldn't be joining them after all.

A few minutes later, a soft knock sounded at the door, and Frank opened it to find Amanda and John standing outside, looking freshly scrubbed of theatrical makeup in her case and stale popcorn and cookie crumbs in his.

"Welcome!" he said, grinning and stepping aside to let them in. "The party is now complete! Let's eat, I'm starving."

"Me, too!" John crowed.

"I can't believe he's still hungry," Susan said, shaking her head. "All he did the whole day was eat!"

"The bottomless pit," Amanda commented, tousling his hair and watching him heap fruit on a plate.

"He looks tired," Frank commented softly in her ear.

"He is. It's been an exhausting day. Give him ten minutes on that sofa, and he'll be out cold." She smiled softly at the little boy.

Frank observed her expression, so full of love for her son. He marveled at the gentleness of womanhood mirrored in Amanda's sweet smile and felt warmed by it although it wasn't meant for him.

She'd changed into a silky cream jumpsuit, gold earrings in the shape of tiny knots, and a thin gold-chain bracelet. They looked like the real thing. However, Frank guessed the jewelry was tastefully chosen costume stuff, worth no more than the glittering faux diamond choker she'd worn during the competition. She didn't have much money of her own—he'd gathered that much while she was in Vienna—and her husband didn't seem the type to buy her anything of real quality. On her ring finger there wasn't even the smallest chip of a diamond—only the thin gold band. Frank had been surprised when Robert had willingly paid his family's airfare to Europe after Caroline had offered to send tickets. Perhaps that was where his male pride drew the line.

"How do you feel about your triumph, now that you've had time to calm down?" Frank asked.

"I'm still shaking," Amanda admitted. "It's wonderful . . . and so is *this!*" She began helping herself to a huge plateful of food.

Frank stood back and watched her while Nick talked at him about the comp. He nodded every couple seconds but stopped listening almost immediately. Amanda was stunning, her cheeks aglow, her eyes afire with remembered glory. As happy as she'd seemed in Vienna, not for one moment had she looked this alive. No, there was one exception . . . the New Year's Eve ball at the Summer Palace. When he'd waltzed with her, he'd glimpsed this rare and dazzling Amanda.

"So, tell me about tomorrow," he asked her when Nick moved away to take his turn at the serving table.

"The Latin." Amanda shook her head as she munched on a piece of fresh melon. "Here, have a bite. . . . This is scrumptious. . . . You said you were starving!"

He plucked a couple chunks of cantaloupe and one of pineapple from her plate and listened intently.

"The level of competition will be tough," Amanda continued. "The U.S. Latin champs are here, and all of the other couples are excellent dancers and determined to place well."

Susan was sitting on the sofa, eating. John had stretched out beside her but now scooted closer to rest his head in her lap. Nick's parents took their plates to nearby armchairs and listened in with interest as she explained the fierce competition they'd face the next day.

Nick came over to stand beside Amanda. "But we've been working on our routines. We have a good chance," he stated.

"Yes," she agreed, smiling at him. "We have."

"I wish I could stay through tomorrow," Frank said, smiling. "But my flight for D.C. leaves at noon. I still have several days' worth of work to finish before returning to Vienna."

Amanda felt an uncontrollable need to sit down. It had been a wonderful but long and strenuous day. Her legs ached, and her feet burned. Frank must have seen her looking around for a spot on which to collapse and hauled a chair from the dining table over to where she stood.

"Thanks," she murmured gratefully. "I'd love for you to be here, Frank. Maybe you'd bring us good luck for a second day. But I know you must be terribly busy. I promise to call and let you know how we did."

"I'd like that," he said.

She leaned into the tapestried cushion of the chair and propped her feet on the edge of the couch, for the first time taking in the room—a luxurious room by the standards of any hotel she'd ever been in. With food in her stomach, her throbbing feet off the floor, and Nick telling everyone stories of all the near trips and collisions averted that day and comparing the talents of the various couples they'd face tomorrow, she could feel herself relaxing.

Having Frank in the audience had been a delightful ego builder. The few times Robert had seen her dance, he'd always spoiled the experience with a snide comment about the minuscule sums of money she made for all her effort or a cutting remark about how immature she was to get caught up in this silly world. He often repeated his theory that Nick must be a fag.

But Frank had just sat back, absorbing the music and sights, and seemed to truly appreciate the hard work that went into the dancing. He made her feel worthy. He made her feel good all over. And, an hour later, when she lifted a sleeping John in her arms to haul him back to the Lenox, she thanked Frank once again for the party. As Nick drove through the dark streets of Boston, she thought, *What a lucky, lucky woman you are, Caroline. I hope to God you appreciate this man.*

10

As always following a comp, Robert took some time accepting Amanda back into his good graces. He made no secret that he resented her taking off across the country to pursue what he viewed as folly. For days he was moody and taciturn, moping around the house or disappearing without explanation. He'd walk over to the Officers' Club and drink with his buddies for hours or simply drive off in the 'Vette and not return until after midnight.

Eventually, the unspoken tension between them drained off, like rainwater after a spring storm, and a kind of practical accord settled over the apartment. Amanda could again ask her husband what he'd like for dinner without being snapped at. And he was moderately agreeable, even taking John off her hands for an hour while she prepared a meal or did laundry.

During these periods of truce, she thought a lot about their future as a family. She adored little John, but he was no longer a baby. She found herself observing pregnant women's bellies with envy and smiling at infants in the grocery store. Another little one, she thought, would provide John with a sibling and complete her family. After a second Christmas in Vienna with Frank and Caroline, she

154

was determined to discuss her plan with Robert, but he was preparing for another TDY, so she waited until he returned home late in March.

"I think we should have a brother or sister for John before too long," she suggested over breakfast one morning as a gray rain fell outside the window. She had thought of a hundred ways to bring up the subject more subtly, but experience had taught her that the direct approach was best with Rob. If she failed to come to the point immediately, he somehow took charge of a conversation and derailed it.

He bit into a slice of toast and turned back a page of the *New London Day*. "You want another one?" he asked.

"Yes, you know I do. We've talked about this before. I don't want John to be an only child, like I was."

"I guess it's okay."

It irritated her that he showed no real emotion on the subject of their family one way or another. He lifted his coffee cup to his lips, read his newspaper.

"Do *you* want another child?" she asked. "I mean, if you feel strongly about not having a second child, we shouldn't. But if we are going to add to our family, we should have the baby before you leave the navy at the end of next year."

"Makes sense . . ." he mumbled.

"Robert, are you listening to me?"

He lowered the paper. "Of course I'm listening," he answered dryly. "You want another kid. Fine. Two can't be much more trouble than one."

Although it hurt to hear him talk about their children this way, he was so much more responsive to John than her own father had ever been to her. Only recently had she realized that a man could be warmer or more loving than Robert.

Spending two Christmases in the Donnelly household had been an enlightening experience, as well as a little troubling. For Frank's pure joy in observing and interacting with the children made her start thinking. Could it be that there were other men like Frank and Doug? Men who could be masculine yet tender, who loved and enjoyed their wives and children openly without feeling threatened?

That possibility set her wondering in an even more disturbing direction. Was it possible she might have married

Robert for the wrong reasons: She was in a rush to have a family of her own and he just happened to be available? Or had she mistaken lust for love?

Well, the decision had been made, and she must shoulder the responsibility. Robert was a good provider, he was saving for their future, and he'd never do anything to knowingly hurt their child or her. These were his strong points, and she believed that she should concentrate on them and not be so hard on him. After all, she had her faults, too.

Meanwhile, since Robert had no objections to adding another child to their family, Amanda stopped taking the Pill and set her sights on completing their family. She also took the next step toward securing their financial future.

Since Robert's release from the navy was less than two years away, Amanda began scouting out likely locations for a sporting goods store. Whenever she found one that looked promising, she left a note or clipping from the real estate section of the local newspaper on the refrigerator. Robert pocketed the pieces of paper, thanked her, and said he didn't have time to check into them right away. He'd get to it.

"Don't you think you should start contacting a few banks to feel them out about the financing?" she suggested.

"I've got a lot on my mind right now," he replied. He'd taken over a couple training classes at the base, which included instructing young seamen in escape tactics from a submerged ship and survival at sea. She imagined the classes were rather stressful, because he came home looking exhausted. "There's just no time left for this now. It will have to wait. Besides, the savings account will more than cover a down payment."

Connecticut Bank and Trust statements arrived periodically, but they were always addressed to Robert. As a couple, they'd always paid one another the courtesy of not opening the other's mail.

The months passed. Robert prepared for another sea tour on the *Neptune.* She left a couple more interesting advertisements for him, knowing that once he left, another three months of location hunting would be lost.

"Get off my back!" he snapped. "It's my business, I'll take care of it when the time's right!" But his voice softened when he caught her crushed expression. "Hey, you have enough on you already. Let me take care of the money, okay? Oh, by the way, the paychecks are going to be direct deposited from now on into our savings. I'll make sure you get cash for household money, though."

She frowned. "I don't think I even have the CBT account number."

"Don't worry about it. The bank will issue you a draft while I'm away. It will arrive the usual time."

"But in case of an emergency while you're out at sea," she protested, "I should have access to that account."

He shook his head, sure of his male wisdom. "Not a good idea. We need to stay on budget. It would be just too tempting for you while I'm away to withdraw money for some little thing. Let's handle it this way since I have it all set up. Okay?"

She sighed, uncomfortable with losing control of their finances, but didn't want to fight over anything so trivial. "All right," she agreed.

It was September 1970 and John was almost four years old when Amanda found out that she was pregnant again. Rob had been on sea tour for over a month and had two more months to go. Since the *Neptune*'s mission was classified and contact with naval operations was limited to a periodic signal sent by the ship to a military receiving station, she had no way to contact him. However, she'd have chosen to give him the news in person anyway.

Amanda was terribly excited. *This baby,* she thought joyfully, *will be different. Rob is more mature and has been a father for four years.*

John had a birthday. She took the little boy to Friendly's for hamburgers and a candlelit cupcake.

She told Sara that she was expecting another child and received a warm hug and misty smile. "I hope it's what you want," she said softly.

"It is," Amanda assured her. "I really want another baby, and the timing is perfect."

She visited her parents and announced the news.

Bruno barely looked up from his texts.

Olga remarked, "Just what you need, another mouth to feed. Have you thought any more about going on to college?"

No, she hadn't. Her mood dampened, she needed a quick and powerful antidote for her parents' emotional poison. She called Caroline in Vienna.

The phone took a while to connect through a series of international operators. Then she heard the line click open.

"Bitte?" It was Frank's voice.

"Oh, I expected Caroline or your maid to pick up—" she laughed nervously. "Hi, this is Amanda!"

"Amanda? Is anything wrong?" Frank asked, his voice taut.

"No. Just the opposite really. I'm expecting our second child."

"You're pregnant?"

"Yes!" She laughed, happy again, knowing she'd have Frank's support.

"Why, that's wonderful news!" He hesitated. "How does Robert feel about it?"

"I'll be able to answer that question a little better in forty-five days. He's out at sea."

"Oh, I'd forgotten, you did mention his tour in your last letter. Does he want another child?" Before she could reply, he rushed on. "I'm sorry, that's rather personal. You don't have to answer."

She hadn't even considered not answering. It was incredibly easy to talk to Frank, as relaxing, although in a different way, as it had always been to talk with Caroline. She snuggled down into the worn arm chair in her living room with the telephone receiver cradled between her shoulder and ear.

"No, it's all right. Robert and I often discussed having a second child. He agreed that if we had another, we should have it before he gets out of the navy. That will be six months after this baby's born."

"Sounds as if you've planned well," he commented.

"What does Robert want to do after he's been decommissioned?"

"Go into business for himself. Remember how geared up he was about getting into sporting goods when we visited that first December?"

"That's just about all he talked about," Frank admitted dryly.

"Well, we have a savings account that he's been feeding since before we married. That and a modest loan will get us started."

At his end of the line, Frank grimaced. *Balls, bats, rackets, playtime gear of every sort—the ideal occupation for an overgrown child. Robert will buy his toy store and submerge himself in running it so that he can continue ignoring his wife and child . . . children.*

But he couldn't discuss his true feelings with Amanda. Although he felt intensely involved in her happiness and welfare, much as he would have if she'd been a younger sister or sister-in-law, the whole situation was different. In the case of family, he could *do* something to help out. He'd insist she spend more time visiting with him and Caroline to take a break from the jerk she'd married. Once in a while, like on her birthday or at Christmas, he might buy her something nice, something he picked out himself to let her know that he cared. Or he might consider establishing a small trust fund in her and her children's names, so that she'd have a small income independent of her husband. Being an only child, he'd never had anyone to be a big brother to. Looking out for her like that would have been nice.

But she wasn't family and his concern might be misunderstood, causing her more difficulty at home than she already had.

The line crackled, and he unconsciously gripped the receiver, afraid of losing the connection.

"Listen," he said quickly, "Caroline is in Paris visiting a girlfriend. Would you like the number there so that you two can have a chat?"

Amanda considered her phone bill, which would already

be high with one overseas call. "No. Just tell her the news when you talk to her next."

"I will," he promised. But the tinge of disappointment he'd heard in her voice kept him on the line. "You really are all right, Amanda?"

"Sure. It's just a little annoying, not being able to contact Robert at times like this. It's hard to be patient."

"Hang in there," he encouraged, trying to sound chipper.

"Talking to you has helped a lot," she admitted in a whisper, her lips brushing the tiny punch holes in the plastic instrument.

"Good-bye," he said.

"Good—" the phone clicked dead—"bye, Frank."

Slowly, Amanda hung up. She sat gazing at the phone for a long while, musing over their conversation, her eyes misting over. *It's hormones,* she excused herself. *Damn hormones.*

Frank stared at the telephone on his desk. He ran a wide finger around the dial three times. It took him several minutes' worth of dial tracing to start functioning again. He didn't want to call Caroline again. He was pretty sure of what would happen if he did.

But news of Amanda's pregnancy was important enough not to be put off for ten days until his wife returned home. The two women were extremely close, and Caroline's voice might be just the lift Amanda needed. He dialed the Paris number Caroline had left for him.

Frank listened to the distant buzzing. Once, twice, three times the signal rang through, his nerves prickling. Someone picked up.

"Allo?"

"Charmaine? This is Frank." His throat thickened. He cleared it with effort. "May I speak with my wife?"

"Oh, tch, tch, tch—too bad, Frank." The French woman sounded as if she were singing every word in a twittering soprano. "You just missed her."

"Where is she now, Charmaine? It's too early for the salons to open."

"Ah, Frank, *vous êtes très amusant!* Caroline walked down to the bakery for bread . . . *pour petite déjeuner.*"

"Walked? For pastries?" he repeated dully.

"Oui. She'll be right back. I will have her call you as soon as she returns."

"Merci."

Frank pressed the connect button down and sat, waiting, the receiver still in his hand. He was not a suspicious man. But it did seem an odd coincidence that never once during the past year when Caroline had taken off to visit one or another of her girlfriends or spas was he ever able to contact her directly on the first try. Always messages had to be taken. And *walk?* Caroline never walked anywhere in her life! She'd have ordered a delivery, sent a maid on the errand, or coaxed Charmaine into going in her stead.

The phone jangled. He removed his finger from the button.

"Hello, darling!" Caroline's voice was breathless. "I just got back in. These croissants won't do my figure any good, but they're scrumptious and so wickedly addictive."

"I'm sure they are," he replied dryly.

There was a speculative pause from her end. "Darling, is anything wrong?"

"No. Amanda called. I wanted to pass along her news. She's expecting another baby in April."

"She is! God, the poor thing! I'll call her."

At the chalet in the foothills of the Alps, Caroline slanted a look across the room at Robert. He was napping, nude, stretched out in a sunny patch on the thick, creamy Flocatti carpet where they'd made love. She'd leased the house for two weeks while his ship was in dry dock in North Carolina.

Caroline immediately decided she wouldn't be the one to tell Robert the news of his impending new fatherhood. He was a lousy actor and, most likely, would let on to Amanda that he knew, especially if he was displeased with her for getting knocked up. She'd call Amanda to offer her congrats some time when he was in a deeper sleep or in the shower.

"She wants the baby," Frank replied woodenly.

Robert stirred and stretched on the rug.

"Well, that's all that matters then, isn't it?" she stated quickly. "Listen, I've got to say good-bye so I can call her."

161

Frank's heart felt as if it were splitting in two. There was little doubt in his mind: His wife was having an affair. He loved her, had loved her from the moment he'd set his eyes on her . . . or thought he had. Did it really matter?

"Jennifer misses you," he murmured over the dull ache at the back of his throat.

"Oh, and—and I miss her too, of course . . . and you, darling," Caroline bubbled from her end. "Be back before you know it! I'll bring you both lovely presents."

"Fine." He couldn't make himself add "Enjoy yourself." He hung up, resting his hand on the phone, eventually letting it slip limply off.

Frank toyed with the perverted notion of ringing Charmaine's number again. If it was busy, he might comfort himself with the hope his wife had been telling the truth: She was actually in Paris where she'd said she would be and was calling Amanda to congratulate her. But if Charmaine answered the phone and failed to produce Caroline without some foolish excuse and several minutes' delay to track her down at some other location, well, he couldn't stand the finality of that evidence. To guess was one thing, to catch his wife in the act was—

"Aw, hell," he muttered, raking his fingers through his hair.

He wished he had someone to talk to, to confide in, but he'd never been a man for making close friendships. Inchon had cured him of that. One minute, you were swapping dirty jokes and slapping some fellow on the back. The next, he was inert matter lying on the frozen mud.

Frank decided he would do nothing for several reasons. Caroline was still the perfect hostess—the best sort of mate for a diplomat. More importantly, their daughter idolized her even though her mother spent little time with her. If it came to a divorce, Caroline would refuse, strictly out of spite, to let him have Jen. He knew her too well to think otherwise, and he couldn't bear the thought of being separated from Jennifer forever.

Frank felt sick, helpless, and furious. Whatever had possessed Caroline to take a lover? He prayed the affair would burn itself out soon. Then, if he could find the strength, he'd take her back without ever mentioning this day.

Two days before the Neptune's expected arrival in port, Amanda received a wire from Robert, informing her that he'd be flying up from Washington, D.C. His flight wasn't yet confirmed. He'd call from the airport for a ride.

Over the years, Amanda had lost touch with the navy community. She spent little time at the apartment on the base, John didn't attend nursery school there, she rarely bothered reading the submarine base newsletter, and her lack of participation in neighborhood activities and clubs had, in general, alienated her from the other wives. She lived in a different world, one she much preferred, and it wasn't unusual for a ship to put into an alternate port if maintenance became necessary, so she didn't bother to ask anyone what had happened to change the sub's itinerary.

After five years of marriage to Robert, she'd learned not to set her expectations too high. She didn't buy champagne or a special wine, hoping to discourage his overly robust drinking. She planned a simple meal of a tossed green salad, broiled cod fillets with lemon butter, and steamed fresh broccoli. She waited for Rob's call.

Contrary to his message, he arrived in a cab. He hugged John, then his wife. When he pulled back from Amanda, he poked her belly, which was just beginning to show.

"Put on a few pounds while I was away?" he teased. "We'll fix that with some exercise." He winked saucily at her.

"Exercise won't help." She saw a chance to make a game of her happy news.

"The kind I have in mind cures all ills, babe." Then his glance fixed on hers, and he knew. A look of incredulity crossed his blue eyes. "You're *not!*"

"I am," she said proudly.

But the smile she'd imagined blooming on his lips never materialized. Instead, he glowered at her. "Dammit, Amanda! How could you let this happen?"

"Let it happen?" she repeated numbly. "I stopped taking the Pill four months before you left."

"Shit!"

"Why are you so upset? We talked about this."

"We talked about having another kid . . . someday. *Someday* doesn't mean the first fuckin' chance you get!"

"Rob!" She collapsed on the sofa, tears streaming down her cheeks. Why did they never seem to be on the same wavelength anymore?

"We have plenty of time," he said, sitting down beside her. His voice was quieter, reasonable now that she appeared shattered. He put an arm around her. "I just don't think I'm ready for the added responsibility of another kid."

Her mouth fell open. She gasped. *"You . . . responsible?"* The two concepts didn't fit together.

"How far along are you? You could, you know . . . postpone it."

"An abortion? I'd never do that. This is our child we're talking about!"

"Oh," he said.

Be reasonable, she told herself. *Calm down. Think.* She breathed deeply for a good ten seconds to flush out the hysteria building inside of her and swiped at her wet eyes. "Robert, you agreed that we should have the child before you left the navy."

"So?"

"This baby will be born just six months before your commission expires. What could be better?"

He shifted on the sofa. "I've been thinking a lot . . . while I was out at sea . . . about—" He avoided her eyes. "About extending my commission."

"What?" She shot to her feet.

"Well, I have. We have a comfortable life. Why jeopardize it by gambling on some business scheme? Our medical bills are paid, we have inexpensive housing and access to subsidized clothing and household goods from the base exchange. I like my job, and I have plenty of free time to do the things I enjoy."

"Like drink?" she asked bitterly.

He pointed at her accusingly. "Now don't start that. I have to maintain certain social obligations. I have to take up the slack for my wife, who decided long ago she was too good to mix with navy people."

"That's not true!" she cried. He'd never understand. She didn't object to the people. It was the lifestyle to which she'd never been able to adapt.

She sobbed into her hands as John ran over and clung to her knees, scolding her, "Stop it. Stop it, Mommy!"

"Oh, go ahead and have your kid—your two kids. You always wanted them more than me anyway." Robert stood up abruptly. "But don't expect me to change my career for you. I don't ask you to stop dancing, do I? Do I?" he shouted, conveniently forgetting the grief he'd given her for years.

She was too tired, too emotionally drained, to respond to his petulant, childish questions.

"Well, I don't," he continued when she didn't answer. "So quit making demands on me. Stop trying to change me!"

She knew then that she had stopped loving Robert, possibly had never really loved him.

He walked out of the apartment, and a moment later she heard his car roar to life. She took John by the hand.

"Let's go read a story together," she invited him, walking toward her bedroom.

"Can I read this time?" he begged.

She smiled weakly. John had memorized *Green Eggs and Ham* and could glibly recite most of it by heart, which he called reading. Amanda cuddled her son on the double bed while he "read" in his high-pitched voice. And she let her thoughts drift, her pulse slowly returning to normal as her priorities regained their proper order in her mind.

She would have this baby on her own, care for it without a husband's help, and live out many more lonely nights. This was her reality. She figured the trade-off actually wasn't all that bad. By this time next year, she'd have completed her family. She'd still, God willing, have her dear friends: Sara, Doug, Caroline, and Frank. And she'd have her dancing. If she possessed all of these things, her life was indeed rich. Who needed a fairy-tale romance to be fulfilled?

11

Amanda faced each new day, resolved to keep her family together and to make the best of all that was good in her life. Her apartment was small but comfortable. She brightened it with lacy window shades to let in the clear Connecticut sunshine and bought fresh-cut flowers for her table whenever she could afford them. If the furniture was cheap (featherlight veneers with plastic topcoats purchased from a local discounter), she perked it up by sewing brightly patterned scarves and matching slipcovers. By cruising thrift shops, she was able to pick up a car seat, an almost antique high chair, a scratched end table, and a lamp that didn't work. She refinished the table and rewired the lamp by deciphering the instructions of a kit that were allegedly written in English by a Japanese factory worker. And she grew fat awaiting her baby's arrival with the belief that things could only get better.

Christy Ann Allen was born on April 17 at five in the morning, after her mother had been in labor for ten hours. Again, Robert was not present; the *Neptune* was at sea. But this time Amanda accepted her husband's absence with a fierce sense of pride. This was *her* baby. Robert hadn't wanted the child, had been consistent in showing no real interest in its progress during her pregnancy, and therefore she felt justified in keeping Christy to herself. And, as if someone in authority had been listening to her thoughts during the pain-filled hours in the delivery room, Christy was born with Amanda's lustrous dark hair and eyes, her mother's nose and mouth, and, perhaps, a hint of Bruno's brooding intelligence, but not one feature in the pinched little face reminded her of Robert.

If Amanda sometimes longed for an adult companion with whom to share the adventures and chores of each new day, she reminded herself that Rob was evidently doing the best he could simply by supporting his family. And, yes, he was more affable than Bruno had ever been. Although she never had much money left over after the bills were paid on the first of the month, she had to admit that she and the children didn't lack any real necessity. There was always a way to make do. She bought shopping bags full of fabric on sale at fifty cents a yard and sewed his-and-her rompers for the spring, little shorts and tops for summer wear, and pants with coordinated jackets for winter. She learned how to stretch a household allowance that seemed it could stretch no further.

There were only two extravagances in her life: her dancing and Christmases with the Donnellys. She used her teaching fees to cover travel expenses to comps and for shoes and costume materials. And she scrimped all year to put aside enough for their holiday airfare.

They spent a fourth Christmas with Caroline and Frank in Vienna, a city Amanda had come to love. She waltzed with the newly appointed ambassador, with Frank's junior colleagues, and with Frank himself.

By the next Christmas, however, Frank and Caroline had relocated in London. Amanda, Robert, and their two little ones spent a glorious week there. It was difficult to travel with little Christy, but Amanda wouldn't have passed up their holiday reunion for anything.

She was grateful that Robert was agreeable to these annual trips, for he always found excuses from doing anything else with her that included the family, whether it was a summer picnic at Eastern Point Beach or a night out at the drive-in movies with the youngsters bundled in their pajamas and armed with pillows and blankets for the backseat. No time seemed a good time for Rob. He was too busy with his duties or had already promised to play on the base softball team or must meet with his buddies at the club to celebrate someone's promotion, impending marriage, or birth of a child. And then there were the times when he was simply gone, without explanation, a prerogative he defended as an inalienable male right.

Amanda picnicked and movied alone with John and Christy, refusing to become a hermit because her husband wasn't interested in doing the same things she wanted to do. And she never lost hope that the future would bring exciting developments.

"I'm going to keep on saving," Rob told her when she asked if he'd ruled out the possibility of leaving the navy. "Even if the sporting goods business doesn't work out, we'll have something put aside for the future." He was up front about the money that he continued to hold out of his paychecks for their savings account: three hundred each month. It seemed an enormous chunk of their income and made budgeting a challenge, but Amanda knew that tightening their belts now was worthwhile if it provided them with a nest egg.

She concentrated on enjoying her children as they grew, and they grew so fast! Amanda took them to visit her parents at least once each week, usually on Sundays when Rob left for the afternoon to watch pro sports on TV at the club. Olga and Bruno seemed as much at a loss playing the role of grandparents as they had been in the role of parents. They were both in their seventies now, and Bruno had developed arthritis in his hands so that holding a pen was painful and marking his papers had become a grueling task. Olga seemed in good health but was as insanely protective as ever of her treasures.

"Now don't get too near that cabinet," she'd warn John in her thick accent. "Everything in there is very valuable."

He'd look at her with wide eyes, then gaze into the glass case at the stacks of dishes and glassware.

"Why don't we eat on those?" he asked, pointing to rose-bordered china plates.

"They are much too good for everyday use," she told him curtly. "Besides, I wouldn't dream of taking them out while you children are in the house. You are wild and destructive."

She was wrong. John was infinitely cautious while in Olga's house. He never broke a thing. Christy, however, was her grandmother's worst nightmare. She seemed bent upon fulfilling Olga's prophesies, for the little girl's coordination was unreliable, and she stumbled and dropped things constantly. She was probably no clumsier than most children at her age, but Olga viewed every spilled glass of milk, every trip over the curling carpet as a major disaster, and days spent at Grandma's became an ordeal for everyone. Amanda cut back their visits to twice a month, and neither Olga nor Bruno objected.

Bringing John and Christy with her to the studio was very different. There, Amanda could let them roam with the other children. Sara was easygoing, permissive, and cheerful about their expected childhood mishaps. The Stevenson School of Dance became for John and Christy as much their home as the apartment on the sub base, as much a delightful retreat as it had been for Amanda.

Another year passed. John turned seven and Christy, two. Christmas 1973 was in London, as Frank and Caroline had been fortunate enough to land a second tour in England. Fortunate in some ways but not in others—earlier that year the Irish Republican Army set off two bombs near Trafalgar Square, injuring two hundred thirty-four people. And around the world, things seemed no calmer. The Watergate inquiries continued to rock Washington, D.C. The war in Vietnam was winding to a dismal close.

Amanda continued to exchange letters with Frank, who wrote more frequently than Caroline and became more reliable in keeping Amanda up to date on family news. Amanda responded to his letters separately from her correspondence with Caroline, writing to his office address since that was the one he always used as his return address on his letters to her. She found his thoughts fascinating and continued reading the *New York Times* to increase her knowledge of world events. When she found a political situation puzzling, she wrote down her questions to include in her next letter to Frank, and he explained what he could. For someone who'd never earned above a C in her history and social studies classes in school, Amanda felt increasingly confident of her knowledge, which gave her a great deal of satisfaction. A most amazing by-product of her correspondence with Frank was that she actually enjoyed accumulating names, places, and dates that she'd considered a bore in school. They became real to her.

Because she wanted to share her new interest with Robert, she left the first few letters from Frank on the coffee table for him to read. This was a mistake.

"Why is he writing to you?" he demanded.

"The letters are for the whole family," she explained. "Listen to this: 'Caroline and I are planning a trip to Lucerne in the spring and possibly another to the French Riviera during the summer.'"

"Sure, he's bragging again about their money," he scoffed darkly.

"He's just relating family news," she objected.

"Let me see that!" He snatched the letter out of her hand. "What does this mean? This drivel about him being asked by the White House to address some delegation of African tribal chiefs and political types."

"I suppose the State Department feels he'll be valuable in helping them sort out their problems."

Frank had written about some of the terrible infighting between tribes and factions in the newly independent African nations. Atrocities—torture and cannibalism of their own people as well as foreigners—had been reported, and one of the department's goals was to try to stop these more or less isolated incidents from turning into another bloody civil war like the one in the Congo ten years earlier.

"Diplomacy is his job," she continued. "He's a wise man and talented negotiator. Those people are lucky to have him."

"Oh, like you'd know about something like that. Since

when is international relations one of your areas of expertise?" he demanded. "Boy, has he got you snowed under!"

Amanda could only shake her head. Why Robert should feel so threatened by Frank, she had no idea. Perhaps he envied Frank his money, his prestige, or his family name. But if he coveted anything any other man possessed, he never took steps to try to improve his own situation. He seemed perfectly content to allow his life to drift along on the course he'd set when he left the academy. The navy was comfortable for him.

In order to avoid further conflict, Amanda began reading Frank's letters the day they arrived then threw them into the trash along with the flyaways from magazines.

Sometime during the spring of 1974, a subtle change seemed to occur in Caroline and Frank's marriage. Although Caroline had always signed only her own name to her notes—a carryover from their correspondence as schoolgirls—Frank generally closed his letters with best wishes from both himself and his wife. Beginning that March, he signed only his name, although he continued to write of their joint activities and travels as he had before.

Throughout the summer, Frank's letters included some news about Caroline but more of his own personal reflections on his work and his daughter. He seemed deeply concerned about Caroline's callousness toward Jennifer and several times mentioned Caroline's solo trips to friends' homes and resorts, leaving the little girl in the hands of the household staff.

Amanda recognized that by writing to her, he was using her as his emotional sounding board. After some thought, she decided that this was entirely logical. She was, after all, his wife's closest friend. She would know Caroline best and might be able to give him some clue to her behavior. But Amanda also realized that she must offer her opinions and advice cautiously or risk hurting Caroline.

Two weeks before Thanksgiving on a bitter cold morning, Amanda walked with John and Christy, bundled in warm jackets and gloves, to pick up the mail at the base post office.

Among the usual bills and advertisements was an envelope from London with Frank's distinctive, bold handwriting on the front.

"We'll stop by the playground on our way home," she told John and Christy.

Amanda sat on a bench, while her two scrambled up the ladder to the slide. She smiled in anticipation of losing herself in Frank's words for a few precious minutes, pulled off her gloves, and sliced open the envelope flap with her thumbnail. Flecks of snow spit out of the clouds, dusting the paper in her hands. As her eyes swept across Frank's words, her smile stiffened, then fell away. It was the letter she'd hoped would never come.

Dear Amanda,

I must confide in somebody but have no one capable of understanding my pain, except you, my dear pen pal. You must by now know that I write with the heaviest of hearts.

My wife, you see, is having an affair or perhaps has taken a string of lovers. I can't be sure which. Damn it, I don't see why it matters—one is as bad as the other as far as I'm concerned. Everything she says and does these days points to some type of romantic liaison. Her periodic absences, during which she's difficult to reach, her coolness toward me and apathy toward our private life.

I hope the knowledge this letter brings won't harm your friendship with Caroline. You know her faults better than anyone, so you are probably not at all shocked. Perhaps you already know about this—she's written to you of another man in her life. I had believed she was happy with me and had changed her ways once we married. She seemed content enough in Naples and, for a time, in Vienna. But I'm convinced now that she doesn't love me.

On the other hand, she remains the finest diplomatic hostess on the Continent. Her smile sparkles, her wardrobe is impeccable, she charms rogues, dictators, and politicians alike. She's witty, a talented planner and delegator of tasks, and, God help me, I don't know if I could do without her.

This preoccupation of hers with other men has been going on for years now—possibly five, maybe even six, I can't say for certain. In the beginning, I was sure that after a few months whoever she was seeing would lose his fascination with her, or she would grow tired of him. Apparently not. I predicted that one year would bring her back to me, but no. Then I began to suspect that more than one man was involved, which is the likelier situation, considering how quickly she becomes bored with anything.

I have no interest in divorcing Caroline, so there is no point in hiring a seedy detective to gather evidence of her infidelity. Jennifer seems increasingly attached to her the older she grows, which is to be expected— Caroline is her mother. But the woman shows only superficial interest in her child. It breaks my heart.

I apologize for dumping all of this on you. It isn't fair, but I feel compelled. Forgive me—

Frank

P.S. Please do not discuss this with Caroline. My intent is not to point an accusing finger or use you to mediate my marriage. I just needed someone to listen, and you are there.

Amanda rested the letter in her lap, her hands trembling, but not from the cold. "Damn you, Caroline. The man loves you. Why are you playing games with his heart?"

Feeling numb and on the verge of tears, she stared sadly at the spiky male scrawls across the thick vellum. Frank must have been at his wit's end to bare his soul like this to her, to anyone. Of course he must have chosen her partly because of the geographical distance between them. There was little she could do to intervene with an ocean between them. Besides, he clearly trusted her to honor his request to not mention his letter to Caroline. That was the hardest part for her, to be placed between two people she loved. How could she choose? How take sides?

Feeling emotionally shredded, she watched her son and daughter play on the swings. John was eight years old now and loved to read. At the studio, he often spent hours on end with a stack of books he'd checked out of the library. One week he was into dinosaurs, another it was racing cars. He crammed his little mind with one topic, then started in on something new. He was doing very well in school, too. She was so proud of him. Christy was three and idolized her big brother. Amanda suspected that would wear off as soon as she got a taste of independence when she entered school. But for the time being they got along marvelously, and she was grateful for the companionship they provided for one another.

She looked up at the gray New England sky, so thick with clouds she couldn't make out where one ended and the next began, and she thought about Frank, about Caroline, about little Jennifer, who was so hungry for love from her beautiful mother. Was there some tactful way she could help any one of them without betraying another?

Perhaps when Jennifer was just a little older, Amanda thought, she might invite her to come and stay with her for a few weeks at a time, offer her lessons, or give her a part-time summer job to help build her self-confidence. Every Christmas Amanda was amazed at how increasingly bashful and nervous the little girl was becoming, which seemed strange for the offspring of a woman like Caroline.

As for Caroline herself, well, Frank had sworn Amanda to silence, so she couldn't confront her friend. But maybe there was some subtle way of warning Caroline that she was jeopardizing her marriage by neglecting her husband. She'd have to think about how to do that.

And Frank? He needed a friend, someone who could be close by for him, someone more than just a distant ear. Another man would probably be best. But she was neither a man nor was she nearby, so there was little she could do to help him except to keep on writing and let him know that she cared.

With a sigh, she heaved herself up off the cold wooden bench and took the children home. She made tuna-fish sandwiches for them. They sat at the kitchen table and ate

174

them with pickles and potato chips. Then she put Christy down for her nap and left a contented John to rest on his bed with a pile of books. An hour was their limit, but it would be enough time for her to answer Frank's letter.

Amanda curled up in a corner of the sofa with a pillow over her knees and a magazine balanced on top of it to serve as a desk. She gnawed the cap of her ballpoint pen, letting Frank's words of distress seep into the quiet of the little apartment . . . and she died inside for him. She knew why Caroline's infidelity affected her so deeply and Frank's pain touched her to the point of tears: because Frank's letter had forced her to look at her own marriage more critically. And her heart at last told her that Robert had never kept his marriage vows. Somehow, she knew this as surely as she knew that she loved her children. She'd held on to her sanity only by shoving that awful truth to the back of her mind.

She put her pen to paper and wrote.

Dear Frank,

I just finished reading your letter and have put John and Christy down for a rest. You're right—I'm not shocked. Caroline can be selfish and foolish, but she's always been fair with me. I had hoped she would be fair with her husband or at least faithful.

I can't offer you any advice—I'm so sorry. I know Caroline well enough to suspect that she will deny there are other men in her life and she will offer unarguable excuses for her behavior, then, almost certainly, continue doing whatever she damn well pleases.

However, I can, finally, be as honest about my own marriage as you have been about yours. It will be a relief to have someone to confide in. Perhaps it will give you some comfort to know that you are not alone.

I believe that Robert probably has had a number of affairs during our marriage, but at least he's kept them to himself. With all of his drinking, you'd think he might have let a name slip once in a while, but there hasn't been one. I knew when I married him that he was a ladies' man. I'd hoped, as every woman foolishly does, that the man she finds irresistibly sexy will cease being a magnet to other women. It's a game we all play . . . and lose.

But what hurts more than the suspicion of his infidelity is the day-to-day neglect of living with a man who really doesn't give a damn about what I do with my life as long as his house, children, and meals are in order.

When we met, we seemed to have so much in common. There were lovely qualities that we admired in one another and plans for an exciting future together. I'm afraid that all we really had was a simple case of lust. The possibility sends chills down my spine. I hate feeling this way! So cold, so at a loss. What do you do when you suddenly learn who the person you married really is—and that person disgusts you?

This sounds like such ridiculous melodrama on paper, doesn't it? But it's real life, it's true. Seeing it isn't all that difficult. The hard part is deciding what to do about the truth.

Divorce would destroy Rob's career. It would also mean that I'd need to take a full-time job, probably day work, in order to support myself and the children. However, I don't want to put John and Christy into day care. Keeping them with me while they're still young is important to me and, I think, to them, too.

So often these days, I sit here and say to myself, there are worse things in the world than a loveless marriage. I've learned to depend upon others for adult companionship—Sara and Doug, you and Caroline, Nick and Susan—and I do without the intimacy and caring of a strong marriage. I'm truly not unhappy, Frank. I have so much to be thankful for. The children learn something new every day; through them I always have a fresh outlook on life. And I have my dancing—always my dancing, thank God! Nick and I consistently place in the top three spots at most every comp.

Competing takes an incredible amount of work and isn't cheap, but I'll *never* give it up.

And, I remind myself, as you should, things do change with time. Someday Caroline will come to her senses. Someday Robert will grow up, realize that his children have become real people without him, and maybe he'll even appreciate the woman he lives with.

I look forward to seeing you all in Groton for the holidays. Caroline wrote that you would be at Gray Cliffs for a real American Christmas. In the meantime, take care of yourself, Frank.

Fondly,
Amanda

Amanda would always remember the month of May 1975. Years later, she recalled each of the *New London Day*'s headlines in tall black block letters, because they were fixed in her mind by the events to come.

U.S. MARINES RESCUE THE MAYAGUEZ FROM CAMBODIANS

BOSTON ORDERED TO BUS 21,000 CHILDREN

FORD ASKS CONGRESS FOR $507 MIL FOR VIETNAM REFUGEES

EPA ANNOUNCES DRINKING WATER IN 79 CITIES POLLUTED

The big movie at the Garde Theater was *Jaws;* Amanda's favorite song on the radio was a Neil Sedaka tune, "Laughter in the Rain"; and Sara started complaining of aching in her limbs.

"I guess I'm getting old." She laughed at herself. "I feel so tired all of the time, and my poor legs hurt like crazy."

"You're working too hard," Doug scolded gently. "Consolidate a few classes. Give yourself more time to rest in between."

"He's right," Amanda said. She'd noticed in the past year how sallow Sara's complexion had become. She was losing weight, too.

Amanda helped her reorganize their classes, grouping

more of the intermediate students together, doubling up on the beginner classes of four- and five-year-olds. The new sections were larger than either of them liked to teach, but the change created a few blessed holes in the schedule during which Sara could withdraw upstairs for a quick break.

Throughout the summer, though, she continued to look drained and, in time, was barely able to drag herself through the day. She took two aspirins every four hours for muscle cramps, but Amanda could tell that the mild medicine didn't help much.

There was a strange summer virus going around. The symptoms were aching in the joints, nausea, and fever.

"You should see a doctor," Amanda told her. "A virus could develop into something more serious."

Sara brushed aside her concerns. "I'm just a little run down. I'll try taking vitamins."

She took vitamins, got more rest, and the virus, if that was what it had been, seemed to clear up.

One humid August afternoon, Sara was teaching a class of advanced ballet students in the ballroom when Amanda returned from a front room to exchange her pile of practice records. Amanda sorted through albums while Sara fussed with the record player. Sara's hands shook as she lifted the needle onto a record. She grimaced, and beads of sweat broke out on her forehead. She dropped the stereo arm and the needle screeched across the black plastic.

"What's wrong?" Amanda demanded.

"I'm okay. I just have to finish this lesson, then I'll . . . I'll . . ." Sara's knees buckled without warning, and she would have fallen to the floor if Amanda hadn't caught her.

"Julie, Maryanne! Take over the class, please! You know what comes next. Barre work, then floor exercises . . ."

She helped Sara hobble out of the ballroom and up the stairs toward the apartment.

"Please, don't do this," Sara whimpered. "Please . . . I'll be fine. Doug will be so upset. I don't want him to worry."

"I'm calling him at the store," Amanda said. She herself

was sick with worry and wasn't going to let Sara talk her way out of being seen by a physician this time. "As soon as he gets home, we're taking you to the emergency room. Let *them* decide if you need a doctor."

Amanda paced the waiting area of the Lawrence Memorial Hospital Emergency Room. She'd left John and Christy with the high school girls who worked as teaching assistants at the studio. Sara was being examined in one of the trauma rooms with Doug at her side.

Amanda looked at her watch: two-thirty. They'd been in there for over an hour, and she hadn't heard a word from Doug or a doctor. She turned around, marched over to the nurse's desk for the third time, and asked, "Is Mrs. Stevenson still in the examination room?"

"Yes."

"May I see her?"

"You'll have to wait. The doctor's with her."

"Is she—Is there any information yet about—"

"You'll have to talk to Mrs. Stevenson about that."

"When?"

"When the doctor finishes with her."

She felt as if she could happily murder the woman if only she weren't so preoccupied with Sara's condition. Sara. Sweet Sara. What could possibly be wrong? She was only forty years old! Surely it couldn't be anything serious.

A hand rested on her shoulder, and she spun around, her heart in her throat. Doug stood in front of her.

"Is she all right?" Amanda demanded, her voice cracking. "Is she—"

His face was as white as the chalk she'd rubbed on the tips of her toe slippers when she was thirteen years old. Sara had painstakingly fitted her for that first pair. She swallowed, struggling to speak.

"Doug?"

"They're . . . ummm, keeping her to do a few tests," he managed at last.

"What kind of tests?"

"I don't know," he said with a vague gesture of his hand.

"I'm not sure I took in everything the doctor was saying. She has that virus again, but they think she may have had a mild heart attack, too."

"Heart attack?" Amanda gasped.

He nodded. She's always had a murmur. Some doctors said it was nothing to be concerned about. Others advised her to take life slowly, avoid any activity that might strain her heart."

"I wasn't aware of that," Amanda murmured.

"She never spoke of it to anyone except me. I tried to keep an eye on her. When she got tired, I made her take it easy for a while. She never listened, said exercise was good for everybody."

"Oh, Lord," Amanda moaned, hot tears swelling in her eyes.

Doug put his arms around her, and they comforted one another. His shoulder smelled of new shoe leather from the back room at Kresge's and of cigarette smoke and hospital disinfectant.

"Can I see her?" she asked at last.

"Tomorrow. An orderly and nurse are taking her up to a room now." He snuffled softly, and she didn't embarrass him by looking to see if he was crying. "She'll be okay," he murmured.

Amanda nodded. "Maybe she just needs some kind of medicine. I can take a couple more of her classes, and we could hire one or two of our teaching assistants to handle the beginner classes."

They were walking together toward the exit. Doug's long body slowly stretched upward out of its slump; he seemed somewhat cheered by her suggestions.

"A few years ago when she had a bad spell, I suggested we sell the studio. She never would agree to doing that."

Amanda knew how Sara felt, for she felt the same way. The studio was home. It had been home when she'd lived in the Bank Street duplex with Olga and Bruno. It was as much home to her now as her apartment on the base. More so.

She returned to the studio with Doug, retrieved her children, thanked the girls for watching them, assured worried students who hadn't already left that Sara would be fine, and climbed into her car. She was scared, sick at heart, and confused.

John and Christy rode quietly in the backseat, sensing something out of the ordinary in the air.

After ten minutes, John asked, "Will Sara be okay?"

"I don't know," Amanda answered honestly. "I hope so, darling." She tuned the radio to WSUB. Neil Sedaka was singing, making his comeback to pop music. She cried silently, dabbing tears from beneath her lashes with the back of one hand before the children could see them.

It was all she could do to feed John and Christy, see to their baths, and put them to bed. Once they were settled down for the night, there was not an ounce of strength left in her body. She collapsed on the sofa in the dark and sat there, hugging a throw pillow.

Sometime after ten o'clock, Rob walked in, humming. Amanda looked up from the sofa. He didn't see her at first, continued into the kitchen, and made himself a drink before returning to the living room, flicking on a light, and picking up the TV listings from the coffee table.

She laid aside the pillow, startling him.

"Geez! You scared the crap out of me! What are you doing here?"

The lump in her throat felt sharp and enormous. She couldn't speak. Tears spilled from her eyes.

"Oh, Rob, I'm so scared—"

He rushed to her, setting his glass down as he moved. His hands closing around hers as he sat down and looked up into her glistening eyes. "Is something wrong with one of the kids?" he whispered, glancing toward the bedrooms.

"N-no," she gulped. "Sara."

"What happened?"

"She's sick . . . in the h-hospital." She swallowed, forcing out the words in gulps. "They think . . . maybe she had a heart attack. Oh, Rob, it was terrible. I've never been so terrified in my life." She broke into sobs and he put his arms around her. It was the only time she could remember him showing any sensitivity to her at a time of stress. But at least he'd saved his best bedside manner for a true crisis.

"Calm down . . . calm down," he murmured into her

hair, rubbing her back in slow soothing circles. "She's in the hospital now. It's the best place for her; the doctors will watch her. Are they doing any tests?"

"T-tomorrow." Now she was hiccupping as well as crying but less hysterically.

"Good. This sort of thing happens. At least they caught it in time. Her doctor will put her on some kind of pills and make her slow down. I'll bet the woman hasn't taken a vacation in years."

Amanda pulled back to look up in wonder at Rob's face. How could she have missed this side of him? Perhaps this compassion was a quality she'd been blind to. Maybe there were other facets of his personality she'd failed to recognize and appreciate.

"You're right," she said. "Sara never stops."

"There." He drew his thumbs under her long lower lashes, wiping away moisture. "Told you so. Now, I suppose you'll have a busy day tomorrow, taking some of her classes, canceling others. Long lists of little brats to call and disappoint. Right?"

"Yeah." She gave him a small smile.

"So you'd better get some sleep." He stood and pulled her to her feet.

"Oh, Rob, thank you!" she cried, throwing her arms around his neck and holding him close.

"Thank you? What do you think I am, an unfeeling slob?"

She shook her head. There was hope for them after all. As long as he was capable of healing her pain, there was hope.

Amanda woke out of a deep sleep and sat bolt upright in bed, her heart hammering in her chest. Someone had picked up a ringing telephone, and the silence that followed had awakened her. She pulled on her robe and padded barefoot down the hallway.

John and Christy sat in the middle of the living room floor in front of the TV, still in their pj's with bowls of dry cereal in their laps. Rob was talking on the phone in a low voice. Her pulse slowed down, but she still felt shaken.

Amanda poured herself a cup of coffee while she listened in on her husband's end of the conversation.

"Of course. No . . . I understand. Hey, don't worry about it." His back was turned to her so that she couldn't see his expression, but his tone was taut. His left hand clamped the receiver tightly to his ear to enable him to hear over the TV. His right arm was raised, fingers laced through his hair and poised in concentration.

"Rob?" Amanda asked softly.

He turned, and the distress in his eyes told her everything. Amanda's stomach instantly catapulted to her heels. She thrust a fist against her mouth to stifle a sob.

"Yes," he said quietly into the phone, "I'll tell her. Look after yourself, Doug. Call if you need anything." He hung up and stared at the floor as if unwilling to meet her questioning gaze.

"Sara had another heart attack . . . last night after you and Doug left the hospital."

The room began to spin. Amanda stretched a hand out, grasped the back of a kitchen chair, and clung to it.

Rob continued in a tight monotone. "Apparently the virus that had been bothering her for a long time turned to pneumonia in a matter of hours. Sara went into shock, then her heart . . ." He lifted both hands, then let them fall to his sides. "Doug rushed back to the hospital as soon as they called him, but she was . . . she didn't make it, babe. Sorry."

The universe crashed down around Amanda. She tottered forward and sat down, oblivious to anyone or anything in the room.

Rob knelt beside her. "It's okay. Cry all you want."

"Is Doug . . . How did he sound?"

"Like he didn't know what hit him. I don't think he understands she's gone yet."

She nodded woodenly. Yes, that would be like Doug. Sara was the single most powerful force in his life. Her presence would linger for a very long time.

"Doug's closing the studio for a couple weeks until he decides what to do. He's planning on cremating her, having a service on Wednesday at the Congregational Church."

Amanda knew that the Stevensons weren't religious, but the old stone church at the top of State Street was the closest to the studio and its pastor's daughter had taken ballet lessons with Sara.

John came over, took her hand, and observed her with mature concern. "You okay, Mom?"

Not to be outdone, Christy leaped up, scattering Cheerios everywhere. "You okay? Everything okay?" she parroted in her four-year-old motherly voice.

"I'm all right." Amanda sniffled, tears clogging her throat. She hugged them both, silently thanking whatever power might exist for them. And for Rob. Today, she was even grateful for him.

Amanda called London that afternoon. It was the earliest she could make herself pick up the phone and speak without bursting into tears. In some ways she hoped that Frank would answer. After all of their shared confidences, she wanted to tell Frank how comforting Rob had been during these shattering hours. She knew he would be happy for her. But she also wanted to ask him about Caroline. Since some good news had unexpectedly come from her own marriage, the same might be true of his.

Caroline picked up. "Amanda!" she cried as soon as she heard her voice. "What a glorious surprise! I was just thinking about you, must have telepathy or something."

"Caroline—" she choked out "I'm afraid I have bad—"

"Oh, God! What's happened? You okay? The kids?" Her voice cracked. "Robert. Did something happen to Robert?"

"We're all well. It's Sara. She had a heart attack, then pneumonia set in overnight . . . so sudden. No one could do a thing . . ."

Caroline's voice was a mere whisper across the line. "Are you saying she died?"

As firmly as she'd prepared herself for the task, Amanda was incapable of answering.

"But she was so healthy and—and *young!*"

"Yes."

Dead air hissed between them, across the Atlantic. It seemed forever before either woman found the next word, then they began speaking in the code of two people already close who become still closer, nearly of a single mind at a time of tragedy.

"Doug?"

"He's holding up."

"Funeral?"

"Cremation. Small memorial service Wednesday."

"I'll be there."

"Plane tickets?"

"I'll get them somehow."

There seemed nothing more to say.

Although it was the end of August, the morning of Sara Stevenson's memorial service was cold, rainy, and miserable, which seemed totally appropriate. Amanda had asked Robert to accompany her to the funeral but later changed her mind.

"I have no one else to watch John and Christy. My parents say they are busy on Wednesday, and I can't very well take the children with me—they're just too young. Will you stay with them?" she asked.

"Of course." He thought for a moment. "Are Caroline's parents picking her up at the airport?"

"No. I called the house. The maid told me that the Nesbits are traveling somewhere in South America, and the chauffeur is on vacation. I suppose Caroline will catch a cab."

"I'll pick her up and bring her here so that the two of you can drive to New London together."

"You'd do that?"

He smiled and shrugged, looking pleased with himself.

Caroline's plane was due to land at ten-fifteen on the morning of the memorial. Since the service was scheduled for one o'clock, there would be plenty of time to visit and have lunch before they left for New London.

That morning Amanda moved around the apartment like a sleepwalker, making the beds, then carrying a load of clothes to the laundromat and back, forcing herself to eat a bowl of warm oatmeal without milk—the only substance her sensitive stomach had been able to digest for three days. She watched the clock, anxious for Caroline's presence and strength.

The rain stopped at nine-thirty, and Rob left for the airport soon after. Amanda changed into a simple black skirt and white blouse. She chose not to wear jewelry or scent. The world seemed colorless without Sara.

With nearly an hour to kill before Caroline arrived, Amanda flicked the TV between game shows and sitcom reruns while listening with one ear for John and Christy as they played outside with their friends. The hands on the clock passed ten-thirty, then eleven. A hazy sun emerged from behind black clouds. Worried that Caroline's flight might have been delayed, Amanda turned off the TV and stared out the window, as if her watchfulness would speed Caroline's journey. At eleven-thirty she dialed the airport, convinced that something was terribly wrong. On the second ring, tires ground to a halt on the asphalt outside.

Amanda lifted the white eyelet kitchen curtains to see Caroline in stylish mourning garb: a black sheath, a black poplin raincoat with silver buttons flung over her shoulders, shiny patent leather shoes on her feet, and matching clutch bag clamped under one elbow. Her cheeks were flushed when she burst through the kitchen door and into Amanda's arms. They wept, arms around one another. A part of their lives and all of their youth had gone with Sara. She had been teacher, idol, mother, friend, big sister, and coach to them, and she was gone, leaving behind two grown women who would never again look at a dancer without comparing her to Sara Stevenson.

Sara would never hold her arm so stiffly. Sara always completed her *tour jete* with an insouciant lift of her chin. No one waltzed as effortlessly as Sara. But Sara was gone.

Rob stood in the doorway, shifting from foot to foot, looking abysmally uncomfortable. "You two had better go along or you won't make it in time for the service," he said gruffly.

Amanda released Caroline and reached for her husband's hand. "We'll go now, darling." She turned back a second time before going out the door. "Thank you for watching the kids . . . and everything."

"No problem." He lifted a hand in parting.

* * *

Caroline sat stiffly on the torn vinyl upholstery of Amanda's station wagon. It had already been one hell of a day before the little prop jet had landed at Groton Municipal Airport—two days, to be more exact, for she'd begun her long flight home from London last evening.

Frank had wanted to come. *Thank God I talked him out of it,* Caroline thought grimly. Traveling with him had become impossible. When they were together, the tension between them was like a knife twisting in her gut. She suspected that somehow, somewhere along the way, he'd guessed that there was another man in her life. However, she was sure Frank had no idea that Robert was her lover—she'd been too careful.

These days, she and Frank existed in the same world, day after day, each performing his or her job with professional dedication. In public, they remained a celebrated couple and were invited to more foreign service functions and private parties than they could practically attend. But whatever warmth and trust had started to bloom during the earliest stages of their marriage had withered and died after a couple of years together.

She loved her job, being a foreign service wife, and intended to keep that position regardless of the cost. But she found it impossible to resist the exhilaration of an occasional liaison with Robert. Sometimes she and Rob couldn't meet for two or even three months, sometimes longer. Then she'd arrange a spa visit for herself and he'd take leave, telling Amanda he'd be on Tour of Duty or that his cruise had been extended. They'd spend an erotic week on the Italian Riviera or on an isolated island resort. They mated like animals, wildly, roughly, with sensual gratification their only aim. She was sure that she didn't love Robert any more than he loved her. But she craved him, lived for him, would have suffocated in a murky sea of boredom without the promise of his hands working their magic on her body again and again and again.

Now, however, as she rode in Amanda's rattletrap of a car, Caroline couldn't look at her friend.

I'm sleeping with your husband. I've let him fuck me for six—Jesus, is it six—years? I will continue sleeping with him because I like it. I may be reprehensible, but at least I'm sane. Besides, my dear friend, what you don't know can't hurt you, and if he weren't screwing me, he'd be on top of some cheap bimbo.

Caroline suddenly needed to talk to stop herself from thinking about how rotten she felt. "How's Doug?" she asked.

"Not good, I'm afraid." Amanda replied, steering onto the access ramp to I-95 that would cross the bridge over the Thames River.

"How will he handle the studio on his own?"

"I don't know. I don't think he's worked things out that far ahead yet."

Caroline's brain insisted upon bouncing between disturbing images. Robert . . . the station wagon . . . the interior of Robert's car a few minutes earlier . . . Frank . . . poor, dear, ignorant Amanda. If she and Amanda hadn't been best friends, she wouldn't feel so rotten. Caroline could almost blame *her* for the whole mess.

Then she thought of something that made her feel better. Today, as Robert had driven to the submarine base, she'd actually said no to him.

They had been pulling out of the airport parking lot right on schedule when Robert slid his right hand up her thigh.

"Not this trip," she stated firmly.

"Why not?" His guileless blue eyes turned on her in disbelief.

"I don't know, out of respect for Sara . . . for my and Amanda's friendship with her."

"Christ, you sure picked a fine time to develop principles."

She slapped his face.

"Geez, babe!" He nursed the side of his face with one hand.

She was indignant. "If I didn't have principles, I'd be bed hopping with half the diplomatic service."

"All right, all right!" He pulled onto the gravel shoulder of the two-lane road. "Shit, that hurts!"

They argued for almost an hour. He pleaded, threatened, cajoled, and in a last ditch effort attempted to charm her into a roadside quickie, but Caroline stuck to her guns. One had to draw the line somewhere. No fooling around this trip.

Now Amanda drove across the Gold Star Memorial Bridge, and Caroline clutched the door handle and desperately chattered on about anything that flitted through her mind to chase away thoughts that were too confusing to dwell on any longer.

Finally, they parked across the street from the church. "Will there be a reception for the family or anything back at the studio?" Caroline asked.

Amanda shook her head. "I'm sure Doug wouldn't be able to handle anything like that. Besides, the two of them were pretty much alone. Sara's parents died years ago. She told me once that she had a brother, but she'd lost touch with him. I think she said he was a forest ranger in Oregon or Montana. Doug has a sister in the Midwest somewhere."

"Maybe we could offer to take him someplace for a drink or a late lunch afterward," Caroline suggested.

Amanda looked doubtful. "Let's see how this goes first."

It was a beautiful service. The organist chose Stravinsky's "The Fairy's Kiss," a moving ballet based on Hans Christian Anderson's *The Ice Princess*. As the music filled the church, Amanda gazed at the mother-of-pearl urn on the alter and envisioned Sara—a princess in repose, her pale hair arranged around her gentle face, a smile sweetening her lips. But the vision brought no consolation for her loss.

Many of Sara's students and their parents came, bearing flowers they laid around the urn. The younger girls were in tears. Even their older sisters, who had often been Sara's and Amanda's assistants, sobbed soundlessly. To cover their puffy eyes, they wore dark glasses, evidently the only ones they had—modish beachwear with outlandish neon frames that were out of place in the dim chapel.

Amanda and Caroline held hands throughout the service, squeezing softly for strength when the minister spoke of Sara's goodness, her generosity, her beloved husband and adoring students.

Amanda couldn't bear to look at Doug, who spent the entire service bent forward in the front pew, his face pressed against his forearms.

189

She wondered fleetingly if Rob could ever be as shattered by her death and knew instinctively that he would not. Rob would miss her only in the most practical of ways. How would he take care of the children? How would he prepare meals, keep a house clean, launder the clothes now that he'd gotten out of the habit of doing such things for himself? Her insides ached with sudden realization. *As kind as he's been these past days, my husband doesn't love me.*

It was this thought as much as the emotional strain of Sara's funeral that made her decision easier. "I can't go anywhere to eat," she whispered to Caroline as they filed out of the church behind Doug.

"Are you sure? We could talk about the old days, the good times. That's what you do after a funeral. You heal each other," Caroline said softly.

Amanda smiled gratefully at her. "When did you become so wise?"

Caroline jerked her head around, her eyes flashing with incongruous anger. "I'm not very wise at all. It's just better to talk sometimes . . . better to talk than think too much."

"I know." Amanda draped an arm over Caroline's shoulders. "But let's talk back at the apartment."

"No! Not *there.*"

"Why not?"

"Robert—" Caroline blurted out, "and the children. We'd disturb them. I just want the two of us to be alone. Let's drive over to Gray Cliffs and hang out in my bedroom, like the old days . . . no kids, no husbands, just us."

"I'll call Robert," Amanda said.

They spent the rest of the afternoon with their shoes off, sprawled on Caroline's canopy bed, sipping white wine. They told stories about the studio, dances, boyfriends, and, most of all, Sara. Stories they both knew by heart because they'd shared the experiences. They laughed a lot and cried often. Eventually Amanda's appetite returned with a vengeance.

The cook wasn't working while the Nesbits were away. But Caroline found a generous hunk of Gruyer cheese in the refrigerator and eggs and a loaf of bread in the freezer.

Amanda whipped up a six-egg omelet running with fragrant melted cheese.

They talked a while longer. At length Caroline said, "I know it's early, but I'm beat. Jet lag. I've got to sleep."

"I wish you could come back and stay at my place," Amanda said with a wistful smile. "But there's no room except on the sofa."

"I'll be fine here. Tomorrow we'll take your navy brats shopping and buy them designer outfits at that overpriced children's boutique in Mystic. Then we'll eat ourselves silly at the Lighthouse Inn, and the next day I'll fly back to London."

"And we'll survive. . . . We'll go on," Amanda whispered.

"Maybe. Africa looks like a sure thing for Frank's next post," Caroline moaned. "Christmas in the Congo—how jolly."

Amanda felt emotionally drained as she drove back toward the base, away from the lovely gray clapboard summer homes of Groton's Eastern Point and back to her mundane military world of identical matchbox apartments. Drained but calmer and resolved to her loss. The sensation was similar to the way she felt after she'd finished a strenuous rehearsal with Nick, sapping every ounce of nervous energy, but somehow leaving her stronger in spirit.

She opened the door with her key. The house felt empty.

"Robert?" she called, crossing to the refrigerator where they left their notes. A discarded utility bill envelope, scribbled over with pencil, was stuck on the door beneath a plastic strawberry magnet.

Took kids out for supper.

"Probably to the club," she murmured, not caring for the atmosphere where her children would be dining. Undoubtedly, this once wouldn't hurt. In a way, she was glad to have the place to herself.

Amanda went to her bedroom closet and dug through several boxes of old clothes before finding her very first pair of toe slippers. Pressing them to her heart, she let the tears fall as she recalled Sara fitting them to her foot, showing her how to wrap her toes in lamb's wool. The tender knuckles of her toes had blistered and bled anyway, but she hadn't minded. To dance on her toes had been a dream come true.

She'd learned to cross-lace the satin ribbons over her instep, around her ankle, and tuck the knot invisibly behind the smooth pink strip of satin. She smelled the old sweat inside the shoes, ran her thumbs up the stiff leather shanks, and pressed the dusty satin to her cheek, weeping one final time for the woman who had gracefully ushered her through adolescence and into womanhood . . . and who would never leave her soul.

Doug temporarily closed the studio and told Amanda he'd call her after he hired two part-time instructors. A month slipped by, and she didn't hear from him. Amanda used the time to sew a slipcover for her tattered sofa, paint John's bedroom, and make a couple winter outfits for each child. After a while, she ran out of chores and grew restless. She tried to call the studio, but Doug didn't answer, and she began to worry about him.

Amanda popped John and Christy into the car one afternoon, drove to New London, and parked on State Street in front of the studio. Peering up at the dark windows of the second and third floors, she knocked on the street door. After ten minutes of pounding, she gave up.

"Come on, guys," she said, hauling the two kids out of the car. "We're going for a walk."

They hiked up the street in the late September sunshine to Kresge's. "Mr. Stevenson is no longer employed here," the manager told Amanda when she questioned him about Doug.

She frowned, confused. "When did he quit?"

"The week after his wife died. We were sorry to lose him. He was a hard worker."

"I know," she murmured, feeling incredibly dim-witted for failing to foresee the obvious. Doug was despondent, inconsolable after Sara's death. They'd been partners in dance, in love, and in life for so long.

Amanda quickly took John and Christy by the hands and marched them briskly back down the hill to the car. It occurred to her that she'd be wise not to take them into the studio with her, and she definitely couldn't leave them in a parked car in the middle of the city. She loaded both kids into the wagon, made a U turn, drove down State Street, and squealed around the corner, pulling up in front of her parents' duplex.

Olga sat in the parlor, sorting through old magazines: *Woman's Day, Reader's Digest,* and *The German News*— discarding most of the magazines and newspapers unread, clipping recipes she'd never cook.

"Can you watch the kids for an hour?" Amanda asked, ignoring John's pleading expression. He hated staying with his grandmother and made no secret of it.

"A person might like a little warning," her mother grumbled. "I have a busy day planned, you know." Amanda had never understood why her parents ever had a child; they'd never made adjustments in their lives to accommodate one. But she supposed she shouldn't have been surprised when they made no room for grandchildren. At least they were consistent.

"It's an emergency, Mother," she returned sharply. "Believe me, knowing how you feel, I wouldn't ask otherwise."

Olga cast her a petulant look and sighed. "Oh, very well. Where will you be?"

"At the studio—" She bolted through the door before her mother could unleash a second round of objections.

The studio door was still locked. Amanda banged loudly. It was hopeless. There was no bell, and if Doug was on the third floor, he'd never hear her. She thought for a moment and remembered the door leading from the roof down to the rear of the ballroom stage. Years ago, the latch had wobbled free of the decaying wood frame. Perhaps Doug had never replaced it. *Oh, God, please!*

Amanda had known the owner of the Puritan Diner since she was twelve years old. She pushed through the dusty glass door of the diner and rushed past the Lion's Club bubble gum dispenser and cigarette machine and down the length of the cracked Formica counter. A thick-necked, aproned man stood at the end, pouring coffee for his only customer.

"Raymond, have you seen Doug lately?"

"Hi, Amanda. Doug? No, not since three or four days ago. He was coming down for supper every night since . . . you know."

"May I use your upstairs door?"

"Sure. You can't get in the front way?"

"It's locked. I don't want to disturb Doug."

"Oh." He scowled at her from under greasy black brows. "Everything okay? He's not in trouble or anything?"

"I'm not sure. If there's a problem, I'll call down to you."

He suddenly looked worried. "Want me to come with you?"

"No. I'm sure he's fine," she lied. Her stomach was in knots as she climbed the musty steps from the back room of the diner, pushed open a trap door, and climbed up onto the tar-paper roof.

Blinking in the bright midday light, Amanda got her bearings, then hurried across the crackly surface between chimneys, steam vents, and smoke-blackened exhaust fans. She spotted the peeling green wooden door of the studio and grabbed for the knob. It came off in her hand, but the door swung easily open, and she dashed through, plunging breathlessly down the stairs behind the stage and into the ballroom.

Amanda stopped dead in her tracks. Nothing had been moved, nothing added or taken away since the moment Sara had collapsed during class. She swallowed over a fist-sized lump.

"Doug?" she rasped weakly. "Doug, you here?"

Her words echoed. No answer.

Slowly, she crossed the ballroom, gazing up at the sagging gilt-edged balcony where she and Caroline had hidden on Saturday nights when they were still too young to attend Sara's dance parties. They'd watched the sailors and cadets flirting and dancing with their young partners, and they'd painfully envied those girls who were only a few years older than they. In the last eight years the balcony had been used only to store scenery flats between recitals.

Memories, she thought briefly, *memories live all through this wonderful old place.*

Running beneath the balcony, she entered the dim hallway that branched off into four windowless practice rooms. Amanda opened doors, quickly checking behind each. The rooms were identical with worn wooden floors, marred by layers of masking tape to mark students' positions, full-length mirrors along one wall, a barre, a cheap manual phonograph, a simple wooden bench to sit on while changing shoes. They were all empty.

The stairs to the third-floor apartment curved upward in a dark stairwell. Amanda stood on the bottom step, more afraid with each passing second.

"Doug?" she called out again. "Doug, are you—"

"In here." His deep voice, coming unexpectedly from the second-floor office in the front of the building, startled her.

She swung around and flew into the room, her heart beating crazily. Sun streamed through the wide, bowed glass pane overlooking the street. Doug sat on the window seat in chinos and an old green sport shirt, his knees pulled up, his long arms wrapped around his legs, his back braced against one wall. He looked thinner than she ever recalled, and his eyes appeared more deeply set. But his face gave an impression of a soul at peace. No longer were his features ravished by pain. A cool river of relief flowed through Amanda's veins. At least her worst fears had turned out to be untrue.

"I tried to call," she said. "When you didn't answer the phone, I walked up to Kresge's. The manager told me you'd quit."

"I've been thinking," he said without offering any explanation.

Amanda held out her hand, and he absentmindedly took it between his. She sat down on the other end of the flowered cushion. How often had she and Caroline perched here, watching the Fourth of July parade pass below, spying on other girls as they necked with their boyfriends under a street lamp, or just passing time in companionable gossip while they waited for the Nesbits' limo to appear and whisk Caroline away after a lesson?

Had Doug seen her standing below, knocking?

"What have you been thinking?" she asked gently.

"That I should sell the studio."

Amanda's breath rushed from her lungs. "What?"

"Sell," he repeated deliberately. "I should sell this god-damn rattrap."

"But, what will you do? The studio is your livelihood."

"I don't see how it can be any longer. Sara did all the work. You and Sara, that is. She taught more than half the classes, kept the books, advertised, sold lesson packages. Even if you took over more of her classes, which would be difficult with John and Christy, I'd have to hire a bookkeep-er and at least two part-time instructors, then take on managing the studio myself. With the extra payrolls, I doubt I'd break even."

"Oh, Doug," she groaned.

"I know. It's going to be hard on you." He looked into her eyes with concern. "You've practically lived here since you were a kid. These last few weeks, I've been thinking a lot about that."

"Don't worry about me. I'll manage. What will you do?"

"I have a sister in Phoenix. She has four kids—three of them boys. Her husband cut out on her a couple years ago. She could use some help with her tribe."

"Phoenix?" It seemed the other side of the planet.

No studio. No Sara. And now no Doug Stevenson in her life. Her heart crumbled inside her chest. The people and habits that had held her world together for the past decade were a blink away from disappearing forever.

"Maybe whoever buys the building will keep it as a dance studio," he said hopefully. "If they do, they'll be looking for reliable teachers."

"Maybe they'll turn it into a warehouse," she murmured. "Or break it up into cheap apartments."

Doug gazed sadly at their linked hands. "Try to under-stand, Amanda. I can't stay here. Even if I were able to keep the business afloat, my heart wouldn't be in it. Everything reminds me of Sara. I have to make a new life away from here. It's the only way for me."

"I know," she whispered. "You do what you have to do."

That night Amanda stayed awake long after the children were asleep, long after Rob had nodded off, stretched out on top of the bedspread with his last drink in hand. Sitting on her sofa, she sipped a cup of blackberry tea while rubbing the bridge of her nose with thumb and forefinger and tried to sort out her life.

She had lost Sara. As painful as that was, it was a fact she'd have to learn to deal with. It also appeared she was going to lose Doug. And although she might try to convince him to stay, remaining in New London wouldn't be good for him. Doug was absolutely right. Everything in the studio was Sara. He would see her in the expanse of tarnished mirrors behind the long oak barres of the ballroom, hear her whenever he played music from the stacks of 45's and long-playing records she'd selected for her students. Every creak of the aging wooden floor would conjure up her sweet form, waltzing in his arms. He'd touch the scenery flats they'd spent long hours painting together and feel her hand in the raised swirls of pigment. Crossing the ballroom, he'd smell her delicate scent clinging to the walls, the curtains. And everywhere he touched would be a spot she'd touched.

No, it would be impossible to make a new start here. She couldn't ask that of him.

But what about *her?* Unlike Doug, she thirsted for the comforting memory of Sara. Sara, who'd been so many people to her over the years when there was no one else who cared about the things that were important to *her.* Even Caroline hadn't been as strong an influence on her life. To lose the studio was to lose Sara—forever.

Amanda wiped a tear from her cheek and drew a shaky breath. *Oh, Sara.* Without dancing, she didn't know if she could carry on with her life, such as it was.

She loved being a mother but only tolerated the role of wife to a navy man whose sole recreation was imbibing martinis. She felt abominably cheated. Rob had promised her a different sort of future—a partnership in which she would share in his business venture and he would appreciate the things she loved.

But reality hadn't worked out that way, and she was stuck in the present, with no changes on the horizon and a horrible feeling in the pit of her stomach that she was trapped forever by circumstances beyond her control. The truth was, Rob would never leave the navy, teaching for another studio would never be the same, and not teaching at all was unthinkable.

"If I only had money," she murmured to herself, dropping her head onto her folded arms. *Like Caroline. Caroline wouldn't be fazed in the least. She'd buy the damn place just like*—Her fingers snapped reflexively, and she gasped, "Like that! Oh my God!" Sniffling, she raised her head and stared blindly across her living room as the impact of what she'd just thought sank in. But how could she buy the studio?

Her mind raced ahead, grasping at possibilities that seconds ago had seemed as beyond her imagination as a rocket flight to Saturn.

Money. She'd need a great deal of money and a solid credit history. Well, she had only two hundred dollars stashed away in a pickle jar at the back of her kitchen cupboard for dire emergencies. Most of the time they lived on a rigid budget from one paycheck to the next with a little left over to put aside for Christmas. However, included in that budget was the three hundred dollars a month Rob had always pulled from his salary to save for his sporting goods business. Although she wrote out the checks to pay the household bills and kept track of everyday expenses, their savings account and filing of their joint income tax forms had remained his responsibilities. She expected that after all these years their nest egg must total close to thirty thousand dollars, which was certainly enough for a down payment on a small business. If that wasn't going to be a sporting goods store, why not a dance studio?

Amanda spent until three o'clock that morning making notes, trying to determine if her idea was financially feasible or just a tantalizing pipe dream. She'd never owned any real estate and had little experience with people of property other than the Nesbits. Somehow, they didn't seem to count. They were so far out of the ordinary they might have been Martians. Olga and Bruno had always rented. From the brief snatches of family history Robert had shared with her, she assumed that his parents had always lived in military housing.

As to credit, she didn't possess a charge card and suspected she hadn't much of a rating. Until this moment, paying cash for everything had seemed the most sensible way of managing money. Now that she dared to see herself in an entirely new light—as a prospective businesswoman —how would a banker view her?

No credit, no money of her own . . .

Wait! she told herself sternly. *I do have money.* Why did she automatically think of their savings as Robert's property? She contributed at least an equal effort to their marriage and family. In all fairness, half of that money was hers. She took a couple minutes to get used to that delicious concept while she made herself a pot of coffee. While it was brewing, she watched a red autumn sun poke a path up over the treetops outside her kitchen window.

Hunting up a pencil and paper, Amanda sat down again with a steaming mug in hand. She drew an arrow across the top sheet, at the end writing the figure fifteen thousand dollars, exactly half of their estimated savings. If Rob didn't think it wise to risk their entire nest egg, she'd have to go along with him. Suppose the building on State Street was worth fifty thousand dollars. No more than that, surely, as run down as it was. But it might be put on the market for that much since it was quite large and located in a prime area of town. If it were fixed up, the studio might resell for twice as much, which meant it was a good real estate investment.

Amanda caught a few hours' sleep on the sofa before John and Christy woke up.

The next day she spent in the public library, researching small businesses. She started by listing the special expenses the studio would require to reopen in proper shape, including a new heating system to replace the old forced steam radiators, which were inadequate for the high ceilings. Air-conditioning had never been installed, but she decided that wasn't a necessity. The breeze off the river, aided by a couple portable electric fans, was usually enough to enable students and staff to survive the hottest of Connecticut summer days. She continued listing major and minor expenses and was reassured that nothing overwhelming came to mind. Of course she'd have to ask Doug what to expect; there might be structural problems she was unaware of.

Amanda looked up briefly and observed John and Christy, cuddled up on a beanbag chair in the children's corner. He was reading to her, keeping her out of trouble, bless his heart. At nine years old he was a born peacemaker. His personality seemed naturally closer to Frank Donnelly's than his own father's, which seemed odd but pleased Amanda.

She went back to work. On the opposite side of her worksheet she listed the income she could expect to produce if the same number of students continued in classes that were registered at the time of Sara's death. Then, with the help of a kind reference librarian, she found a formula for computing the monthly principle, interest, insurance, and taxes on a mortgage with a payout of thirty years. She calculated tax advantages, chewed the eraser of her pencil, recalculated everything with the possibility of hiring one full-time and one part-time instructor, and finally figured her own total income after expenses, remembering belatedly to add her average annual earnings from competitions.

For five long minutes, she studied the resulting numbers. Amanda's pulse quickened. On paper she was solvent, not rich by any means, but she would actually be able to earn a slightly higher income than her current teaching salary. And, most importantly, she would *own* Sara's studio!

But she wanted still more proof to present to Rob, for she sensed that if he found any ground for doubt, he would react negatively, then nothing she could do or say would change his mind.

Over the next few days, she continued brainstorming, coming up with additional ways to increase the studio's income, and therefore her own, which would be her best chance of impressing Rob and selling him on her scheme.

She would begin hosting practice parties for her own ballroom students and their private guests. By limiting entry to serious dancers and not serving alcohol, she would eliminate the need to hire security. With only a moderate turnout of twenty couples at five bucks a head, she'd clear two hundred for the night.

Another option was to hire an experienced teacher with an established list of students from another studio, bringing more money to her own studio, because students happy with one teacher were apt to follow him or her to a new location. Nick! Might she be able to convince him to move to New London to teach for her? He and Susan had always liked the area.

Growing more and more excited, she could imagine aggressively managing the studio, ushering it back to its heyday, maybe even hiring a live band once a month and opening the doors to students from other area studios. If leisure activities were on the rise for the baby boomers, why not beat the curve and be ready for them in five or ten years when they began looking for gentler leisure activities in their mature years?

It all made perfect sense to Amanda. Suddenly, at thirty-one years of age, her life seemed to be coming together. *This* was what she was all about! Her drive for independence and creativity had found a practical channel: her own studio! Her own business!

After a full week of fact gathering to convince herself (and Robert, when the time came) that she could make all of this work, she called Doug. This time she let the phone ring eight times. True to his promise to answer his calls, he picked up.

"Have you listed the studio with a realtor?" she asked.

"A woman is coming by tomorrow to give me an estimate. I expect I'll let her show the place if her projected price seems fair."

"Just get numbers from her. Don't list," Amanda pleaded.

"Why?"

"I have to talk to you about something before you make any commitments. What time will she be coming?"

"About ten in the morning."

"I'll be there at eleven."

The next day, after getting John off to school, Amanda broke her own rule by leaving Christy in day care. However, she used a program run by a young mother in her home. It was expensive, but Amanda couldn't afford to be distracted by her lively daughter for the next few hours.

Doug met her in the studio office. "The realtor just left," he told her.

"Well?"

"She says sixty thousand as a fixer-upper. No more. The buyer will have to sink a good twenty thousand into plumbing, updated heating, and basic repairs and maintenance."

Amanda sucked in her breath. She'd suspected that her renovation estimates might be low, but not by this much. "What do you think, Doug? What will you accept if you can't get sixty?"

"I figure I'll be lucky to get fifty thousand. The place is in worse shape than that woman knows."

Amanda swallowed with difficulty. This was both good and bad news from her point of view: the possibility of a lower price but also of hidden expenses.

"Would you consider a private sale?"

He looked at her, taking a long time to absorb her meaning. "You?"

She nodded.

"Amanda, you don't have that kind of money, and . . ." Doug frowned, raking a hand through his hair in frustration. "You know I'd do anything for you, honey. But I can't *give* you this place. I need whatever cash I can salvage from the old dump to get out to Arizona and make a fresh start."

"I'm not asking you for a gift," she explained hastily. "This is strictly business. I have enough saved to put down ten percent on fifty thousand and begin making repairs. And I can make monthly mortgage payments once I reopen the studio and start taking in lesson fees. The difficulty is my credit. I suspect I have none."

"That is a real problem."

"With a bank, yes. But if *you* were to finance me . . ." She studied his expression, which was at first surprised, then skeptical.

"The only way I could do that would be to let you assume the present mortgage."

"I know that."

"You'd need to put up close to thirty thousand in escrow plus closing costs."

"That would be around thirty-five thousand dollars?" She blinked, stunned that the figure was so high.

"Do you have it?" Doug asked.

"Almost . . . maybe. It would clean out our savings, though."

Doug sighed. "I don't know how you could possibly swing this, Amanda. That's a lot of money, and believe me, starting out with no renovation money would put you right back where Sara and I were: scrambling to keep our heads above water. Besides, selling to you like this would put me at risk, too. You'd have to make your payments to me exactly on time so that I could pay my own expenses in Phoenix."

"I know it's not ideal for either of us," Amanda admitted, hoping beyond hope that she could somehow make this work. "But I promise I'll make good on the loan. Please, give me a week to work out the details, okay?"

Doug looked out the window, silent for several minutes, his gentle eyes full of unspoken doubts. "All right," he agreed at last, "one week."

Robert worked the next day. Amanda spent it organizing her notes. She intended to make a formal financial presentation to him, show him how the studio could be purchased, renovated over a period of two or three years, then start earning a strong profit by the fourth year.

She began to see the venture in concrete terms, as something already accomplished, as her future and a business that might provide a means to educate her children. Sara's legacy to her would be a gift of security and happiness she'd never dared to dream of possessing. All of her life she'd scratched and saved, only to make ends meet, with nothing left for herself except the love of her children, her friends, and her art. For the first time, she felt as if she were taking charge of her own and her family's future, and that made her feel wonderfully strong.

Amanda prepared Robert's favorite dinner that night: spaghetti with a meat and mushroom sauce that she simmered for three hours, garlic bread, and a spinach salad. She chilled wine and, when five o'clock rolled around, changed into a blue knit dress with a lace collar that, she hoped, gave her the look of a professional woman. She waited.

Rob came home on time. He immediately took in the fragrant kitchen, her attire, and the lighted candles on the table.

"Special night?" he asked, grinning.

"Very." She looped her arms around his neck and kissed him with unusual enthusiasm.

Drawing back and narrowing his eyes suspiciously, he studied her. "You're not pregnant again," he said.

"Good lord, no!" She laughed. "Come sit down. I fed the children early. We can eat a grown-up meal in peace." She'd let John take charge of entertaining his sister. They were watching cartoons for the moment. She rarely resorted to the TV as a baby-sitter, but this was a special occasion. She wanted nothing to interrupt her discussion with Rob. "Come sit down," she repeated softly when he seemed reluctant.

"What's the rush?" He turned away, heading for the bedroom. "I'd like to wash up and have a cocktail before dinner. Mix me a martini while I change?"

She let out a long breath as she watched his retreating back. "Okay." *One martini. Just one.*

Amanda was determined that her husband remain clear-headed so that she could present her case and receive a reasonable response from him. From her point of view, there seemed to be no logical reason why he should refuse her request. Never had she asked him to hit their savings. Even their holiday flights to visit Caroline and Frank had been scrimped for during the year, accumulating in the form of ones and fives stashed away weekly in a large brown envelope in the top drawer of her dresser.

When Rob stepped out of the bedroom looking fresh, having changed out of uniform into jeans and a sports shirt, she handed him a short glass of gin with a splash of Vermouth and one plump green olive bobbing at the bottom.

"We don't have to eat right away," she agreed. "But I do have something to show you. Come sit down with me." She took his free hand and led him to the kitchen, feeling prickles of excitement dance up her spine.

On the dinette table, she'd arranged her notes and careful

sketches she'd made of possible renovations of the studio. One showed a low wall dividing the expansive ballroom, which would allow for café tables and chairs as well as another bathroom at the end beneath the balcony. The changes would give the place more of a clublike atmosphere while only fractionally cutting down on floor space for dancing. She had figures for replacement windows and estimates from a plumber and electrician Doug had contacted a few years earlier.

"What's all this?" Robert asked, sipping his drink with an amused smile as he sat down. He picked up her top sketch. "Looks like the studio . . . sort of."

"I'm surprised you remember it. It's been years since you've been there."

He shrugged. "Part of our past, babe. I remember picking you up there when we were dating."

"Our courting days," she murmured, wishing she felt the delightful tingle she'd experienced back then. It seemed forever ago, another lifetime. Some days, she couldn't remember a time before her children entered her world. The thought of living in her parents' home was thankfully distant but still grim in her memory, for it reminded her poignantly of her failure in their eyes. She shoved that dissatisfaction out of her mind. The studio's new life and her own destiny were more important. She drew herself up and swung a chair around beside Rob's.

"This," she said, feeling a thrill at the words, "is our future . . . or it could be."

"Our what?" He looked puzzled.

"Doug is selling the studio and moving to Arizona to live near his sister."

"Good for him. He should be with family at a time like this," he commented blandly, sipping his drink.

"I agree. And this gives *us* a very exciting opportunity."

"What opportunity?" Rob set his glass down and leaned over the plastic tabletop, suddenly concentrating on her words.

"As I said, he's selling the studio." She swallowed, then plunged on. "I want to buy it."

"*Buy* it? Buy the dance studio?"

"Yes. You've always said that at some time you'd want to go into business for yourself, but for now you don't want to leave the navy. Well, we could use some of the money we've put aside for a down payment on the State Street property and take out a little larger mortgage to cover renovations." She slid her sketches in front of him. "I've consulted professionals in the area, studied the numbers, and everything looks promising. Within a few years, I believe we could be making a good profit."

"Wait a minute. . . . Wait a minute here." Rob's voice was already an octave above its normal range and cracking —both bad signs. "You keep saying, 'the money we've put aside.' You mean *my* money? The money I worked hard for—my savings—that's what you're talking about, isn't it? Let's get this clear." His tone had become antagonistic at the blink of an eye. He stood up abruptly, crossed to the bar, and sloshed more gin in the general vicinity of his glass, not bothering with vermouth.

Amanda cleared her throat, ready for battle, if necessary. "Rob, we agreed that that money was for our future. I've contributed to this family in a very real way by keeping a home for us, raising our children, and earning an income at the studio. I should have as much a part as you do in deciding how our savings should be used."

"Your job is a fuckin' hobby—always has been," he muttered after two long swallows of his drink. "What do you have to show for it? Do you have cash stashed in a savings account somewhere? No," he answered before she could respond. "You spend it as fast as it comes in."

"Yes, I do," she admitted angrily. "But only a very small percentage is used for comps or costumes. Most of it pays for clothes for the kids, something nice for the house now and then, for birthday and Christmas gifts, and our holiday trips and—"

"Extras!" he spat. "Stuff we could do without!"

"*No,* things we'd spend on anyway, except that, if I weren't working, the money would have come out of your paycheck, leaving you less to spend on booze and—and . . . whatever!" She brushed a hand in front of her eyes to clear away the haze of confusion he was creating. "Never mind. I just didn't think we were dividing things up this way. A family is a cooperative effort—or should be," she finished bitterly.

He rolled his eyes. "Jeez, Amanda, what has gotten into you? Do you think we'd be living in base housing if we could afford to buy property?"

"We've never really talked about it," she argued, aware that they were drifting away from her carefully planned discussion. A hollow feeling in her stomach warned her that his mood had turned too volatile for her to reason with him, but she couldn't give up. "Now is the perfect time," she continued firmly.

"This is crazy. Absolute insanity!" he railed. "Do you intend to keep on with this dancing thing like you're still a schoolkid? You've embarrassed me for years, disregarding my feelings on the matter!"

"I—"

"Shut up and listen to me for once," he growled, bringing his glass down hard on the table. "You're the mother of my kids, so I don't put up a stink about your adolescent whims. I turn my back and say, 'Go ahead, play your games.' But you're not touching a penny of *my* money. You understand that? Not a fucking penny!"

His face was inches from hers, flushed with anger and alcohol. She hated the smell of his breath, the slur of his words. If there had been two more inches between them, he'd no doubt have been jabbing an accusatory finger at her, and she'd have slapped his arrogant face.

Tears welled up into her eyes, but she refused to let them fall, not while he watched her for signs of weakness.

"Robert, this isn't fair," she pronounced between gritted teeth. "The money we've saved is, by all rights, equally mine. I work hard. I should be able to expect a future as secure as yours. I'm an adult, I can make decisions for myself. This is a sound investment—I *know* it can work."

"Fine. Make it work!" His tone turned from belligerent to theatrically nonchalant, and he allowed her a frosty smile. "But that bank account is in my name, lady. Mine alone, got it? You can't legally touch my money."

She spun away from him, furious, longing to scream and

strike out at him. Instead, she scooped up her papers and bolted from the room.

"Jeezuz!" he groaned loudly. "You sure know how to spoil a night!" He walked over to John who'd been surreptitiously observing his parents' argument from his seat on the floor. "Mommy sure is in a silly mood, isn't she?" Robert asked him, ruffling his dark hair. "Better stay on her good side, little guy. She's got a me-e-ean temper!"

Amanda swung around. "How dare you!" If there had been a weapon close at hand, she might have killed him without an ounce of remorse.

"Tell Mommy that I've gone to the club where I can eat in peace," Rob told John cheerfully. "See ya round, fella! You, too, Christy babe."

Until that moment she hadn't realized how coldly manipulative Rob could be. He'd twisted facts and emotions, rearranged their relationship to suit himself, cut her out of their savings, and now was attempting to turn her children against her.

Now, because Rob was being so protective of that money, she wondered if it existed at all. What if he'd let it dribble through his hands over the years, spending it as it came on his own amusement?

Amanda collapsed on the couch, hunched over, her aching head pressed into the heels of her hands.

Christy shook a finger at her from across the room. "Naughty, naughty," she chided, echoing her father's accusatory tone. She turned back to her TV program.

John stood up, walked over, and sat down silently beside her. She reached out one arm and hugged him, feeling desolate and angry with Rob but even angrier with herself, because she'd trusted him and naively allowed him to trap her in this impossible position.

Although Rob had his weaknesses, she'd always assumed that he would look out for her and their children financially. Now, even that hope was gone. She had, it seemed, nothing she could call her own.

That's it, she thought, *I'm leaving him.*

But, in the next second, Amanda knew she couldn't. Not yet. For as of this moment, she had no means of assuring that her children wouldn't starve as a result of her impulsiveness. She must be practical. If she were to leave Rob, she'd make sure John and Christy wouldn't suffer for her decision. Before taking any rash steps, she must first establish her independence. To do that, she had to create a reasonable income. She had no college degree, no clerical or professional training of any kind. She had nothing but her talent for dancing and the opportunity to buy a dance studio. But how?

She hadn't a clue. *There really is no one I can turn to for advice, is there?*

Unless . . . Caroline? Caroline knew about money. Wealth was her whole life!

Amanda wiped away her tears and told John, "Mommy's okay now. I love you, darling."

"I know," he said. "I love you, too, Mom." Then, with less confidence, "Dad loves you."

She smiled dimly. "How about some dessert? I made an apple pie."

They all three sat at the table with slices of warm pie topped with vanilla ice cream, accompanied by glasses of cold milk. After they'd eaten, Amanda put John and Christy to bed and returned to the kitchen. She cleared away the unused dinner utensils and plates, refrigerated the uneaten meal, then made herself a cup of hot tea.

While it was cooling, she retrieved her notes from the bedroom and curled up on the couch to look them over with a fresh eye. Despite Robert's criticism, she found her information sound. Then she retrieved Frank's last letter. He'd described how to reach them in Zaire in case of an emergency. It would probably take her most of the night.

She managed to reach an operator at the State Department in Washington, D.C., gave the woman Frank's location in what used to be Stanleyville in the Congo and was now Kinshasa in Zaire, then the radio call letters he'd told her to use. Reliable telephone communication was still rare in Africa. Few people had home telephones; radios were used to communicate within the country and with the outside world. But the department, Frank had assured her, could patch through a message from the States by way of European phone lines. She didn't understand exactly how the system worked after that point, but she assumed that the radio links could then be reversed to patch back through to her telephone.

Amanda told the operator that she needed to contact Caroline Donnelly on an urgent matter and left her number, then curled up with the phone nestled against her stomach. She dozed, waking only briefly when Rob came in and, without speaking to her, crossed the living room in a jagged weave to the bedroom.

At six o'clock, Amanda awoke to a brilliant sun. She splashed water on her face at the kitchen sink and made a pot of coffee. It was almost seven when the phone rang. She dove for it.

"Hello?"

"Amanda! What's wrong? Are you all right?" It sounded as if there was a pound of cotton wool between her and Caroline.

"I'm fine. So are the kids. Robert is driving me crazy."

Caroline laughed. "What is the old smoothy up to now?"

"Don't sound so amused!" Amanda snapped. "He's stepped way out of line this time." She explained how he'd hijacked her nest egg and that Doug was moving to Arizona and selling the studio, leaving her without a job. Whatever self-control she'd held on to during the first two minutes of their conversation, slipped away, and she started babbling. "I haven't a cent to my name! And I've decided I want to buy the studio, but Rob won't let me touch my money—if it even exists—and I'm sure he'd slit his wrists before he'd cosign a loan with me! My income isn't enough to secure a mortgage on my own. Besides, with the studio closed, I don't have an income anymore. Any bank would laugh me out the doors and onto the street. Oh, God, maybe this is impossible, but I have to try! What do I do?"

"First, you calm down," Caroline advised. "How much do you need?"

"At least fifty thousand. Sixty would give me some renovation money." Amanda thought for a moment. "Is there such a thing these days as a letter of credit? Could you or your father put in a good word for me with a banker friend? You know that I'd work myself to death before defaulting on a loan. I'd make the studio work."

"I know, honey. I know," Caroline soothed.

But there followed a space of dead silence from Caroline's end. A sinking feeling filled Amanda's stomach.

"Are you still there?" Amanda whispered urgently.

"Yes, just thinking." In a gritty government office on the second floor of the embassy in Kinshasa, Caroline shifted the radio receiver to her other ear. Frank had set up the communications link with the States for her, then left her alone in the room to talk with Amanda.

In a way she felt responsible for Amanda's plight. She suspected that the reason Robert was keeping their so-called nest egg to himself was exactly as Amanda had guessed: It was pure fiction. He flew all over creation to meet her three or more times a year. As a matter of male pride, he refused to let her pay for his plane fare, although she covered all of their hotel bills and meals while they were together. Nevertheless, his travel expenses added up for a navy man with a family. Somehow she'd never thought of the money as coming out of Amanda's pocket.

"I'll lend you whatever you need," Caroline said at last.

"What? No, you can't!"

"I can do anything I damn well please. And believe me, I won't even feel it. I'll just shift funds in a few of my portfolios. I don't give a damn whether I invest in Connecticut real estate or gold reserves." She tried to sound flip to throw Amanda off. Sixty thousand wasn't exactly pocket change, even for her.

"Really? You'd do that for me?"

"Sure. I'll write a check and post it in the diplomatic pouch today."

Caroline hung up with Amanda's cheerful thank-yous still ringing in her ear.

"It's the least I can do for you, honey," she murmured to herself, releasing the transmit button in the handset. "Guilt money . . ." She didn't care if Amanda never paid her back.

For the thousandth time, Caroline considered breaking off her long-term affair with Robert. She'd always told herself she could do it at any time. It wasn't as if she were

211

addicted to sex, even to Robert's delightful brand. She loved her life as a diplomat's wife. She didn't want to lose Amanda's friendship. Shouldn't she, by now, be able to choose?

Caroline ran her tongue over dry lips and gazed out of the window into the dusty streets of Kinshasa, and she wondered when she'd fallen in love with Robert Allen. God help her. Lust, she could satisfy, but love had no place in her life. She'd held a tight grip on her emotions in order to build for herself this special life. She'd shielded herself from caring too deeply about her husband and daughter, but Robert had slipped through her defenses.

And now, she really couldn't do without him.

12

Amanda received a check from Caroline the following week. She called Doug to make sure the price he'd mentioned was still acceptable. He surprised her by knocking off another five percent he would have spent on a realtor's fee.

"You'll need every cent you can lay your hands on," he told her. "An old building like this sucks up money like a black hole. The expenses are never ending."

But Amanda believed that her position as owner would be different from the Stevensons'. They'd been trying to squeak by, day after day, without putting anything back into their business. But, thanks to Caroline, she had the funds to make the studio beautiful again as well as efficient. And, if she introduced the new programs she envisioned, she'd make that investment pay.

"I won't be rich like Caroline," she admitted to Olga and Bruno when she revealed her plans to them, "but at least I'll be able to support myself and my children."

Bruno shook his head. "Dat's vot a husband is for," he informed her, as if she were a particularly thick-headed student.

"You haven't done anything to make Robert angry, have

213

you?" Olga asked, reverting to German as she did whenever she was upset.

Amanda saw no point in lying. "He doesn't approve of my buying the studio if that's what you mean."

"Den vy are you doing it?" Bruno roared. "Robert is a man of the world. He should know a bad investment. Vot are you thinking, Amanda?"

"I'm thinking I have to . . . to be able to stand on my own feet if I'm to be happy. After all, this is 1975!"

"Oh, dat's modern rubbish . . . women's liberationalist stuff. You have a husband, let him vorry about the money."

It was the first time her parents had defended Robert, and it didn't take Amanda long to figure out the true motive behind their concern. If she failed in her endeavor and her husband threw her out—destitute, with two children—she might have no choice but to return home to live with her parents. It must have been their worst nightmare. Olga undoubtedly envisioned her precious relics pawed by grimy hands, knocked asunder. Bruno feared the noise and emotion of children playing, distracting him from his somber papers and lectures.

She'd never felt so frightened yet, strangely, at the same time so free, so hopeful and childishly excited. Purchasing the studio was an enormous challenge, unexpected but welcome. Amanda had never imagined herself as a businesswoman, but when the opportunity had flung itself at her, she'd found it impossible to turn down. Nothing had ever before felt so right.

At home, Amanda found no more support than she'd received from her parents. Robert glumly surveyed bills marked with her name that arrived in the mail and tossed them wordlessly at her. He refused to listen to any of her plans or details of her hours spent resurrecting the studio. If she was exhausted at the end of a day and she let him see it, he observed her with an omniscient twinkle in his eye that she found infuriating.

"Bit off more than you can chew, huh?" he often taunted.

"Hard work doesn't mean I'm failing," she responded.

"You're going to feel damn foolish when this is over," he predicted. "Just don't come crying to me to bail you out when the bank comes banging at your door and you can't pay up." Amanda had asked Caroline not to mention their private loan when they got together at Christmas that year. Robert assumed she had gotten the money from a local mortgage company.

"I won't come to you," she assured him, finding it hard to endure his ridicule but counting on winning him over through her success. The proof is in the pudding, Olga used to say. Whatever else Robert was, he wasn't stupid. If the studio survived its first few years in her hands and started making money, he would be right there beside her to share in the profit. Whether she'd allow him to do so was something she'd have to think about.

She was puzzled by the energy that he put into attacking her dreams and wondered if his ego was so weak he built himself up by trying to lower her self-esteem.

She'd never lied to Rob before, never kept anything from him except her correspondence with Frank, which had always been entirely innocent. But now she felt the need to establish boundaries between Rob and herself.

He had started the process of separation long ago, she reasoned. He spent long evenings away from home with his drinking buddies, weeks on TDY she was no longer convinced were always official. He had branded their savings his personal property. When she asked to see bank statements and IRS records for the past years, he informed her that they were kept in a safety deposit box, under his name alone, for safekeeping.

She decided they'd probably end up filing separate federal tax forms from now on. He wouldn't want to associate his income with the studio's debts. That was fine by her, but the direction their relationship was taking saddened her. She had always wanted, still wanted, the kind of marriage Sara and Doug had had—shared triumphs and tragedies, assets and debts lumped together to be enjoyed or paid as necessary, a ready source of encouragement through the best and worst times. A true and loving partnership between a man and a woman.

Sometimes she wept, thinking how good marriage could have been with the right man. Then she remembered John and Christy and knew she'd never regret her decision to marry Rob. Besides, if she'd met somebody else, perhaps she wouldn't still be in Connecticut, starting this marvelous adventure, entering this challenging new phase of her life! She wasn't religious, but she held on to a kind of mystical faith that her life was somehow playing itself out as it should. She believed that everything had a reason for happening and that her patience and hard work would eventually pay off.

In the weeks that followed, Amanda tried not to dwell upon the lack of support from her parents and husband. There was, in fact, very little time to think about anything beyond the work that needed doing.

By the time she signed the papers at the closing for the studio and Doug left for Phoenix, Amanda had already contracted with a plumber and electrician. Next she met with a carpenter and discussed the structural changes she envisioned. They walked through the three floors of the old building, and Mr. Tempchick pointed out numerous sections of the wide oak floor boards and the cavetto molding that needed replacement. He suggested that the entire floor of the ballroom be refinished, including the stage and balcony. His estimate took her breath away, but she sensed that the figure probably wasn't unreasonable, given the size of the room. While he was there, she also asked for an estimate on stripping and replacing the crusty layers of gold leaf from the ornate art deco trim on the ceiling and balcony. This amount was staggering, and she immediately readjusted her sights.

"Maybe I can do some of the trim myself," she suggested. "A little bit at a time."

"It's hard work and you'll need scaffolding," he warned her. "Them's eighteen-foot ceilings."

She winced.

"Well," he said helpfully, "if you want to go that way, let me know. I can at least give you a list of stripping chemicals and paints to use so you don't muck up the job."

During the early months of winter, Amanda spent all day at the studio while John was in school. She and Christy kept the workmen company. Somedays she stripped wood until her fingers were raw from the caustic stripping solutions. Other days, she enlisted as amateur painters Sara's old pupils, who stopped by after school to ask how soon she'd be reopening. Many evenings she spent with a turpentine-soaked rag, sponging up the paint spills and spatters her eager helpers had left on the newly stripped floor. Weekends, John was with her. He was becoming an excellent painter, and together they got a lot done.

On mild days, she took John and Christy up onto the studio roof for their lunch and supper breaks. She pointed out what must have seemed like the entire world to them— the sand-colored obelisk on the far bank of the Thames River (a Revolutionary War monument); the shipyards, still managed by Caroline's father; a couple miles upriver, the navy base and across from it was moored the *Eagle*, an immense trimasted schooner that had once belonged to Adolph Hitler and was now a Coast Guard training ship. In the distance and across Long Island Sound were the misty silhouettes of Block Island and Orient Point, Long Island.

Amanda made friends with her neighbors. Raymond Gnatowski, owner of the Puritan Diner, was already well known to her. He introduced her to other merchants up and down State Street: Mr. and Mrs. Kaplan, who owned the jewelry store; Fred Barney, the clothier; Margot Simms, manager of Simms Shoes. The owners of the bridal shop, the news center, the two bars at the dock end of the street, and the managers of Kresge's and the Garde Theater.

As time passed, the workmen fell enough behind schedule to make a January reopening of the studio impossible. It looked as if February would be the earliest she could schedule classes.

She wrote to Caroline:

February 14, Valentine's Day, will be the big day! I'm sending out fliers to parents of all Sara's and my old students. And I'll post bulletins at the library and supermarkets. I even wrote ads for the *New London Day, Groton News,* and *Norwich Bulletin.*

Caroline responded:

> What about radio? It's cheap advertising. You can play different kinds of music in the background and advertise lessons for social dancing, not just ballet and ballroom. You know, appeal to the disco groupies as well as the folks who love a snappy foxtrot.

Christmas approached, and Robert seemed in a happier frame of mind. Frank and Caroline planned to spend the holidays in Connecticut, which meant that money Amanda had laid aside for airline tickets could be used for somewhat nicer gifts and to pay a few bills. In fact, Robert was in such high spirits that he took the kids off her hands while she worked at the studio during the week before Christmas and drove them every day to visit Jennifer Donnelly at Gray Cliffs.

On Christmas Day when they were all together, it was Frank who seemed unusually quiet and somber. His letters had come less frequently in recent months, and Amanda was concerned about him.

"He must be working too hard," Amanda remarked to Caroline after dinner. He'd excused himself to work in his father-in-law's study while the others adjourned to the massive parlor.

"He's become a workaholic—so dreary," Caroline complained. "Boring, cerebral, and aloof." She sighed, looking across the room at Robert, then away.

Amanda followed her gaze without surprise. Yes, her husband was still attractive, possibly even handsome in other women's eyes. But their arguments had sucked the life blood out of their love. And his drinking had taken its toll on his physique and health in ways perhaps only she noticed—the perpetually flushed complexion, softly glazed eyes, mornings spent in a semidaze. He often forgot things —where he'd left his keys, what time he was expected at the base commander's office, something she'd told him the day before about John or Christy.

They rarely made love, and when they did, it seemed

purely a function of habit. Amanda both feared and welcomed the possibility of Robert no longer reaching for her in bed. She didn't want him, but she was still a young woman and needed to be touched. If Robert wasn't going to be the one who satisfied her, who would? To be without sex as well as love . . . that seemed a horrible thought.

Now, sitting in the lovely parlor of the Nesbits' home, she looked at Frank and Caroline's wedding picture. Frank hadn't changed very much. He still had that wonderful compact body—no jowls, no beer belly like those sported by so many other men his age. He was still a striking, well-dressed man whose intelligence, charming sense of humor, and deep respect and love for people appealed to her immensely.

His letters had kept her sane on her worst days and exuberant on her best. He wrote about everything from routine briefings with colleagues to visits from celebrities and barely averted diplomatic disasters. She began to appreciate how one man might manipulate history with a word or conciliatory gesture. She thought he was brilliant and fascinating, and she regretted that they hadn't yet been able to chat in private this Christmas. Before she knew it, the day was winding to an end, and Caroline's mother pressed her toward the kitchen.

"Take leftovers for yourself and the children," she insisted. "Marta wrapped up some turkey and ham. The packages are in the refrigerator."

Amanda smiled and gave Mrs. Nesbit a hug, thinking how well Caroline's mother looked. She was an elegant silver-haired lady with erect posture, queenly bearing, and seemingly endless energy.

"Thank you. We'll enjoy them," Amanda assured her.

She walked through the kitchen door and surprised Frank reaching into the refrigerator, picking turkey meat from the carcass.

"Caught you," she teased.

He spun around and grinned, looking like a little boy caught with his hand in the cookie jar. He licked his fingers. "Guess you did."

"Can I make you a sandwich before we leave?" she offered.

"No. I just felt like snacking."

She handed him a plate and stood by while he piled it with strips of tender white meat. "I'm so glad you two came home for Christmas this year," she murmured.

"Tired of jetting all over the world every December?" he asked.

"Not at all. I love traveling, much more than I ever thought I would. But I think Caroline enjoys being home. And it's important for Jennifer, too. She likes being here."

"You're right. She does." He salted his turkey and nibbled on a piece of it. "I don't know if I've made clear in my letters how brave I think you are, launching this studio venture on your own."

"I couldn't have done it without Caroline's help," Amanda admitted.

"I'm sure you would have found some way. Don't underestimate yourself."

She blinked, pleased by his faith in her. "Are you enjoying your new post?"

"In Zaire? Very much."

"I gather from Caroline's letters that she doesn't feel quite the same."

He laughed. "You could say that. If I stay on for a second tour there, I wouldn't be surprised if she insisted on coming home for the duration."

"I don't understand. As much as she adores traveling, I would think she'd find living in Africa terribly exotic and exciting!"

"Not a polished enough social life for her, I'm afraid," he said dryly.

Amanda studied the look of disappointment on Frank's face. Beneath his expressive eyes were dark shadows. "Are you all right, Frank?"

"I'm fine. I just . . ." He lowered his voice. "I've known for a long time, you see, that what Caroline and I have is nothing more than a marriage of convenience."

"Don't say that," Amanda begged. "Things change."

"But not always for the better. I'm afraid I've lost her altogether."

Amanda gently touched his arm. It was the first time they'd spoken face-to-face of Caroline's infidelity. She felt moved anew by his confidences in her.

"You believe she's still seeing other men?"

"I'm certain of it. We no longer sleep together, and Caroline has always been a passionate woman."

Tears threatened to spill from Amanda's eyes. She felt ashamed that they weren't tears of sympathy for Frank and Caroline. They were for herself, for her own lost marriage.

"Hey, don't take it so hard," he said, offering his handkerchief, which she waved away. "Marriage is like that, I guess. You get sick of one another after a while. Then it's all for show."

"It doesn't have to be," she said, looking up at him. "You see older couples strolling the boardwalk at the beach, holding hands. Sara and Doug were like that . . . would always have been like that."

"Maybe. What about you and Robert? Are things any better?" One brow raised in question.

"We exist in the same house," she admitted with a shrug. "We're rarely there at the same time and then only to eat or sleep. I don't suppose that Robert suffers along without . . . without *affection* when he needs it."

"I'm sorry," Frank murmured, regarding her intently. She was such a warm, sweet woman and deserved to be loved. To have married such a selfish bastard was an inconceivable injustice.

"If things don't improve between us, I won't stay with Robert indefinitely. But the children are still young, and I have to think of them."

"If you need help—" Frank began, realizing even as he pronounced the words that she'd never ask. Regardless, he had to offer.

"Thank you, Frank. But I'll be fine. We'll all make it . . . really."

"So all four of us will just go along as we are—"

"Not perfectly happy," she agreed, "but fortunate in

many ways. I can't complain with so many good things happening in my life."

Frank looked at her, amazed. For some time, he'd listened to Caroline speak of her friend's marriage, which she considered destined for divorce. And he'd read Amanda's most intimate thoughts in her letters. All he'd been able to think was: *My God, this woman doesn't even know what a hellish life she leads! Her husband is an egotistical brute and a drunk who verbally abuses her. She lives on pennies, raises two kids with no help from him or anyone else, has no loving relations to flee to should she get fed up and leave the jerk. What the hell does she have to be so damn cheerful about?* But now he saw Amanda in an entirely different light. She *knew* her marriage was a catastrophe. She acknowledged that Robert was an alcoholic and womanizer. It wasn't that she didn't care. She must be hurt deeply. She simply chose to focus on other aspects of her life. She made her own happiness.

Knowing Amanda in this way gave him strength. She set an example of how he might endure his own life. He would rededicate himself to the two goals that had kept him going since Inchon; his wish to make a better world for people to live in and his love for his little daughter. If he accomplished nothing more in his lifetime than laying one or two stones in the foundation of peace among nations, he'd have done a great deal. And if his daughter grew up to be half as happy as Amanda Allen, he would die a fulfilled man.

Oh, he supposed if he'd met someone like Amanda ten years ago, before Caroline came along, he probably wouldn't have been able to appreciate her simple sweet strength and uncluttered intelligence. But now, he admitted with a fair amount of shock, he felt drawn to her. The tragedy was, she would never view him as anyone but her best friend's husband.

We could have had more, he mused as he studied her rich brown eyes. *We could have started as friends, like we are now, and gone on from there.*

But it was the wrong time in their lives for romance, the wrong time to fall in love again—he at forty-five, she at thirty-one, both with children—and he put any such possibility firmly out of his mind.

The first year after Amanda reopened the Stevenson School of Dance seemed, to her, to flash by like the swallows that bug-hunted over the rooftops of New London on a summer night. Her days were crammed full of telephone answering, bookkeeping, scheduling lessons, recitals, interviewing new teachers, teaching classes, studying for and taking her examinations for the Imperial Society of Ballroom Dance Teachers, cleaning, and working on the long list of repairs and renovations remaining after her fix-up money ran out. Her nights were a five-hour nap, then she was wide awake, on her feet, and dashing through the next day.

Amanda and Robert entered a stage in their marriage akin to laissez-faire politics. She spent most of her days at the studio. He was at sea, at the Officers' Club, or working on the naval base. For the most part, neither had anything to say about the other's life.

John and Christy both attended school now. Amanda sought special permission for them to transfer to a school in New London so that she could drop them off in the morning on her way to the studio, and they could take the bus to State Street in the afternoon.

Most nights, by the time Amanda arrived at home with the kids, it was after eight o'clock. Christy usually fell asleep in the car, and she'd carry her daughter to bed. John became accustomed to the late hours and often read for an hour before turning out his light.

Saturday nights were even later because of the dances. On these nights, Amanda tucked both kids into Sara's old bed upstairs.

Sundays the studio was closed. Amanda caught up on laundry, housework, took a long bath, and, sometimes, took Christy and John to a movie. It was a ruthless schedule, with painfully little time for herself, but Amanda wouldn't have given it up for anything.

When Rob was in town, he sedated himself with his martinis and wine, drinking himself into a drowsy torpor by nine o'clock. He was almost always asleep before his family returned home. On the rare nights he managed to wait up for Amanda, he was irrational and accusatory. They had terrible rows.

"When're you gonna spend some time with *me,*" he'd slur. "When're my kiddos gonna be home for their old man?"

"When we are here, you ignore us," she stated flatly. "You hardly look at John and Christy on your way to the liquor cabinet."

"My kids and I get along great! You're turning them against me!" he shouted. "Taking them away from me." Sometimes he was red-faced with anger. Other days, he approached her tearfully.

She supposed she *was* keeping her children from their father. If he offered to watch them for part of a day now, she was afraid to let him, because he was capable of terrible misjudgments. Once, he'd walked them down to the park, sat with them for a while, then wandered off to a nearby package store to replenish his booze, leaving them unsupervised and wondering where he'd gone. Or, he might leave them at home and sneak off to the club to watch a football game on the big-screen TV or insist he was capable of driving a car after downing three martinis.

"It's a miracle you haven't had an accident," she told him repeatedly. "Until you get professional help for your drinking, I'm not letting the children ride with you."

"Don't be ridiculous," he retorted. "You make me sound like some kind of lush." Indeed, from ten A.M. when his hangover wore off to three in the afternoon, he seemed perfectly normal. He rarely remembered things he'd said or done while drinking the day or week before. He was a different person—a fairly effective worker and quite a charming man when he put his mind to it.

"I'm serious, Rob. Get some help . . . go to AA . . . do *something.* We can't go on living like this forever!"

"What are you saying?" he demanded. "Are you going to take my children away from me?"

She met his troubled eyes, and the pain that engulfed her heart was overwhelming. "If I have to, I will. Yes."

"Look, if it'll make you feel better, I'll cut down a little. We'll compromise." He reached out and hugged her, while she held herself stiff, not trusting his promises but wanting to believe he could change. "It's not like I have to drink. I can stop anytime I want. It just helps me unwind. I'm under a lot of stress in this job."

For their holiday season in Africa, Caroline and Frank invited the Allens to Kinshasa. It was a trip Amanda hungered for.

Since the previous December, she'd thought often about her conversation with Frank in the Nesbits' kitchen. His sympathy and trust in her had meant a lot to her. They'd written throughout the year, but tricky telephone connections had made calls impractical. More than anything in the world, Amanda wanted to talk face-to-face with Frank, to hear how he was really doing, to tell him all about her year of adventure at the studio and watch his reaction in his strong, sharply lined face.

However, the first two days in Zaire were so busy that they didn't see much of one another. Amanda and Caroline spent most of the time shopping and visiting with women in the diplomatic community while the three children got reacquainted. French was the common language of foreigners and servants, and Lingala was the most frequently spoken tongue of the native population, so Amanda struggled along, understanding little of what was said around her. But it didn't seem to matter. Caroline interpreted, and they had a wonderful time.

Rob amused himself by prowling the streets of the exotic city.

Frank worked long hours at the chancery.

By the third day, though, Amanda and Frank assumed their familiar duties by taking the children on long excursions while Rob and Caroline, claiming exhaustion, stayed behind at the house to play cards or nap.

On this day, Amanda and Frank took their three lively charges to the nearby Ivory Market to bargain for exotic trinkets. The youngsters ran from stall to stall in the open square on the banks of the Congo River, from one colorful blanket spread on the dusty red street to the next, thrilled with every discovery, laughing with delight and commenting loudly on everything.

They spotted a medicine man, en route to visit a patient, dressed only in a wide leopard-skin belt with a vivid red loincloth. Around his neck was the traditional strand of leopard teeth. Jangling at his ankles were immense copper bangles. Christy was terrified of him and hid behind Amanda until he'd passed by. Then she was tearing after John and Jennifer, selecting bananas and avocadoes Cook had requested they bring back with them.

"They're wonderful," Frank said with a sigh. "Look at them, not a care in the world."

"I can still feel like that sometimes when I'm dancing."

"Can you really? I envy you, Amanda."

She smiled at him and took his arm as they walked at a more leisurely pace than their offspring. "Don't tell me you've forgotten how to play."

"Not forgotten. I do have enormous fun with Jennifer when we're together. We play tennis or go on long walks. But lately she's taken up her mother's sedentary existence and, more often than not, refuses to leave her room and books. I think she believes exercise is unladylike."

"That's a shame." They walked in companionable silence for a while before Amanda asked, "How much longer will you be in Zaire?"

"I want to stay on for at least one more tour. This is a beautiful country, and I love the people. They're so warm, and they've come a long way since 1964. A multinational force had to be sent in to rescue Belgian and U.S. citizens trapped in the country during the civil war."

"How . . . trapped?" she asked.

"It was a mess—tribal politics at its worst. Warriors slaughtered their enemies and foreigners indiscriminately."

"How horrid."

"Yes, it was." The fine lines around his eyes deepened at the memory. "I parachuted in with a Belgian contingent, not to fight but to debrief survivors. We used the information to locate foreign civilians hiding outside the cities and transport them out of the country. The whole affair was pretty grim."

"I can imagine." It had happened before she'd met him, before he'd married Caroline. Envisioning him parachuting into hostile territory to rescue the innocent added another layer to his persona, one she'd come to admire deeply over the years.

He drew a breath. "That sort of thing frightens Caroline. Every time rumors of unrest threaten Kinshasa or Brazzaville across the river, she panics. She thinks Jennifer should be back in the States, where she'll be safe."

"What do you think?" Amanda asked.

"Sometimes I agree. If our intelligence indicated more trouble, I'd put both of them on the first plane. But for the present, the country seems stable enough." He studied his hands. "I'd miss Jennifer terribly."

"Well, maybe the next few years will be peaceful ones."

They stopped long enough for Amanda to purchase a tub of jam, fresh butter, mustard—other items from Cook's list—and a shopping basket in which to carry her purchases. Then she couldn't pass up a pastry shop, where she purchased a sweet for each of them, and they munched as they continued walking. The pastries were surprisingly excellent.

"There is another reason Caroline wants to go back to the States," Frank said at last, licking his fingertips clean of buttery crumbs. "She's convinced her daughter should attend a private boarding school."

"But Jennifer is so young!"

"I know. Eleven years old. I suspect Caroline is trying to force my hand, hoping I'll turn down another tour here for some place more appealing to her. Another European post or a desk job in D.C."

Amanda felt for Frank and was torn. Her loyalty to Caroline tugged her in one direction, but she couldn't rationalize her friend's selfishness. This was a man who deserved to be loved and supported. He held wonderful ideals, dreams, values! Why did Caroline insist upon cluttering her life with other men as long as she had Frank?

Because, the answer came to her, *she's always been able to have everything she wanted.*

Amanda gazed at Frank and asked the question that had come to her mind hundreds of times but had never crossed her lips or appeared in her letters. "Why don't you leave her?"

He avoided her eyes. "Same reason, I suppose, you don't leave Robert."

"It's not the same—" she began, then stopped herself. The bottom line was, neither marriage was working. "The children?" she said consciously lifting her chin.

"Yes," he agreed. "I guess I'm afraid of that, too. If I left Caroline, I might lose Jenny as well." He turned to face Amanda in the busy street. "Your case, though, is different. I suspect John and Christy would be better off without their father."

She sighed, confused. "Sometimes I think that, then I watch them throw their arms around his neck on a Sunday morning with a 'Daddy, I love you!' It breaks my heart to think of separating them forever."

She thought for a moment. "He needs help, Frank. He won't get it for himself yet. I can't walk out on him until I'm sure he'll be all right."

"He looks perfectly fine to me," he commented dryly.

"I know. He's better when we're traveling. But he is addicted, if not chemically, then socially. He can't sit down to a meal without first having a couple drinks. He can't carry on a conversation without a full glass in his hand. I'm afraid it will get worse if someone doesn't nag some sense into him."

"And that's a wife's job?"

She smiled. "Right."

They'd walked from the market back to the house. She turned to follow the children inside, but Frank reached out and gently grasped her wrist, stopping her. For a moment they both focused on his wide fingers encircling her narrow wrist, then their eyes met.

"You don't have to do this, martyr yourself to save him," he told her in a hoarse whisper, although no one was close enough to overhear. "It's probably impossible anyway. He won't quit drinking unless he wants to. And he doesn't want to."

"I know, but a woman can't just abandon the man she loves."

"You love him?" He looked surprised.

"I did . . . once. Perhaps I could again if things changed."

He took in her words with a thoughtful darkening of his eyes. His hand remained around her wrist but loosened. "You realize the irony of our marriages," he murmured.

She didn't understand. "What?"

"In trying to marry sensibly, we've chosen the least suitable mate."

"Oh, I don't know—" she stammered to silence. "Yes, I suppose you're right."

"You and I have more in common than either Caroline and I or you and Robert."

Amanda laughed, shaking her head. "Oh, that would be stretching things a bit. You and I together?" He looked hurt, and she quickly explained. "You and I come from different worlds, Frank, and we exist today in those same different worlds. You've always had money, lived in exotic cities, you brush shoulders with people I only read about in the newspaper. Caroline knows how to hostess a luncheon for a queen. I'd be at a loss. I'm just a small-town dance teacher."

"You underestimate yourself." He sounded suddenly tense, his voice urgent. "You are a successful, self-made career woman with a business of her own. You love children, care passionately about all people. If you didn't, you wouldn't be so charitable with Robert or have put up with Caroline's snobbish idiosyncrasies all of these years." He bent closer to her. "You are strong and incredibly lovely and—"

"And we've become very dear friends over the years," she finished for him, afraid of hearing his next words. Amanda slipped her wrist out of his hand. She was shaking.

He looked away from her and hunched his shoulders in a gesture of resolve. "We'd better go along inside," he whispered.

Caroline and Robert were seated in the parlor, but the children had disappeared into another part of the house by the time Amanda and Frank entered the room. Robert observed his wife and the diplomat at her side over the lip of his brandy snifter.

Caroline stood up hastily and ran over to Frank, looping her arm through his, her eyes shining, fiery. Planting a kiss on his cheek, she beamed at him. "So tell me, darling, what were you two cooking up on such a long walk?"

"Just sharing family news," Frank said stiffly, looking distrustful at her sudden show of affection.

"Ah, family news—" Robert chortled, raising his glass. "Kissing cousins, dangerous diplomacy, boisterous boys and garrulous girls . . ."

Caroline laughed at him. "You're sloshed, Robert. I think that's all for you tonight."

"Shut up!" he snapped, his mood reversing itself in the beat of a second. "You're beginning to sound like *her!*" He jabbed a finger in Amanda's direction.

Frank shot him a disgusted look, but Amanda ignored her husband, expecting he'd stop acting the idiot when he got no reaction. He was like a little boy at times like these, seeking attention, wanting to stand out in the crowd.

But Caroline refused to let his comment drop. "Don't tell *me* to shut up! Maybe your wife takes that crap from you, *but I won't!*" She glared at him, fury sparking in her blue eyes.

"Geez!" Robert giggled, crossing the room to refill his glass from the bountifully supplied sidebar. He loved Christmases in Caroline's houses. Everything served was the best quality, an endless supply of luxury. But he wouldn't let her or any broad emasculate him. "Women," he grunted. "Turn 'em upside down and they're all alike, huh, Mr. Diplomat? Ever notice that? All bitches look alike! What a revelation!"

With lightning reflexes, Frank knocked the glass from his hand. It smashed against the leg of a table, the amber liquid leaking away into the thick pile of the cream carpet.

"You cheap drunken sailor! Don't you dare talk like that while you're under my roof!" Frank gripped the front of Robert's shirt, scrunching it in his fist under the navy

230

officer's narrow chin. "If you were a man, you wouldn't carry on like this in front of your family—here or in your own home."

Caroline instantly arrived at her husband's side and pulled at his elbow. "Please, Frank. Don't make a scene. Leave him alone."

He shook her off without so much as glancing her way. "I've never liked you, Allen," Frank continued tautly. "I don't care for the way you treat your wife or the way you look at mine. I don't like anything about you. You're a crude, sick man. The only reason I've tolerated you over the years at these family gatherings is because our wives are friends." He was grinding out each word between clenched teeth. Amanda had never seen Frank angry. The barely controlled violence of his emotions was thick in the air; her skin prickled with its intensity. "If you open your damn trap one more time, I'm jamming my fist down your throat and tossing you out for good!"

He released Robert, shoving him out of his reach, as if the man were an insect too repulsive to squash beneath his shoe. Robert fell to his knees.

Hunched over defensively, Robert glowered at Frank while tenderly rubbing his bruised throat. He coughed for several seconds before catching his breath. His eyes glowed with the irrational need to hurt back. "That's—that's not the only reason I'm tolerated in this hou—"

Caroline leaped at him. "Shut up! Shut up, you idiot! Just go upstairs and pass out, *go* before you say anything more!"

Silently, Amanda helped Robert to his feet, ashamed for him. "I'm sorry," she murmured to Caroline. Then to Frank, "I'm so sorry about this." Tears of humiliation spilled down her burning cheeks.

Robert pulled away from her and stomped up the stairs, falling against the polished wood banister twice.

John, Christy, and Jennifer stood at the top of the stairs watching as he staggered into his room and slammed the door. Their gazes swerved to take in the three adults at the bottom of the steps.

"Is Christmas over?" John asked. By now he was accustomed to abruptly curtailed social engagements.

"It's over," Amanda said weakly. "I think we'd better go home tomorrow if we can book a flight. Why don't you and Christy start packing?"

Frank turned with a disgusted look on his face and walked out through the front door.

Caroline rushed to her as soon as the children were out of sight. "Amanda, please, you don't have to—"

"Yes, I do. We can't stay after Rob behaved like that."

"Will you be all right?"

"Of course." But the words stuck in Amanda's throat, for she knew it was the last Christmas they'd spend together.

Later that night after the house was quiet, a knock sounded on her bedroom door. Amanda pushed up out of the chair where she'd been trying to sleep while Robert snorted in his alcoholic slumber, monopolizing the bed.

She cracked open the door. It was Frank.

"I shouldn't have blown up that way," he whispered through the opening. "As a diplomat, I'm supposed to be able to handle delicate situations."

She shook her head, absolving him of guilt. "Don't."

"Tact is somehow more difficult when people you really care about are involved," he said, looking into her eyes.

Something caught in her throat. She swallowed, swallowed again. It didn't go away.

In that moment, an acknowledgment passed between them that Amanda welcomed joyfully but also feared with all her heart. No matter where Frank traveled in the world, he was only a letter or phone call away. From a distance he had supported her through all of her dreams and difficulties. He cared about her as not even Caroline could, for the friend of her youth had never completely understood her. Perhaps Sara. Maybe she had understood her best. It had never occurred to her that a man might fill Sara Stevenson's shoes, might come to know her so intimately he would be able to see to the heart of her emotions.

Why now? she thought wildly. *Why him!*

She felt excited in a way that she hadn't felt in years. Excited by the nearness of this very special man who was leaning into the narrow opening of her bedroom door as if

232

by sheer will he could pass through it and into her life and she felt timid in the light of this new affection.

He belongs to someone else . . . to my best friend, a warning rang in her head. She let her eyes slip away from his and pressed softly against the door. "Good night, Frank," she whispered.

"Good night, Amanda," he said through the door.

Frank watched the British Airways jet rumble down the runway, then lift laboriously into the expanse of azure sky above Kinshasa. Caroline stepped closer and pulled his arm around her waist. She had chosen the worst time to display her attentive side.

All Frank wanted was to be left alone, to be allowed to think of Amanda in peace. To remember her as she'd been last night, pressed against the back side of her bedroom door, warily taking in his nearness, responding to his apology as if he'd shouted that he wanted her. Which he did—oh, Lord, did he ever. But he hadn't said so and never would. He had felt her trembling through the wood.

"What a fiasco!" Caroline moaned, squeezing his waist. "Well, so much for Christmases with the Allens."

Frank unwrapped himself from her long, bracelet-bedecked arm and started across the departure lounge toward the exit.

Caroline trotted to catch up with him. "Are you mad at me, Frank?"

"No."

"What's wrong?"

"I don't want to fight."

"No, really . . . tell me, darling."

He shook his head and kept moving.

She persisted as passengers and well-wishers rushed past in brightly swathed head scarves and tan tropical suits. "Please, tell me."

He stopped with a jerk. "It's everything that has gone unsaid for the past eight or more years, Caroline. Believe me, you don't want to hear it."

She looked convincingly bewildered. "I don't understand.

I thought you were just pissed off about Robert getting drunk."

"I think you understand only too well. It's just not politic to admit it. We've been living separate lives for a long time."

Suddenly, Caroline became fully aware of the nature of their discussion. Things were evidently more serious than she'd initially assumed. She took his arm and started walking again, wanting to move him into a less public area for the remainder of the conversation. "We wouldn't be like this if we moved back to D.C."

"No, Caroline. I mean, even when we're together, we're apart. The love, the gut-honest affection that should be here"—he drove a fist into his own stomach—"it got lost somewhere along the way. We stopped doing things together. We act only for ourselves."

She cast him a petulant look as they passed through glass doors into the bright December sunshine. "Are you accusing me of being self-indulgent?"

"I'm saying we both are, but you have taken it a step further." He held open the car door and she gracefully slipped into the passenger seat, feeling the knot in her stomach tighten as she realized what he was going to say as soon as he joined her in the car. He threw himself in and slammed the door. "You take lovers whenever you please, and we never make love anymore." She opened her mouth to object, but he cut her off. "Once in a while, we have sex. That's true. But I think you encourage a little passion now and then just to keep our marriage legitimate. It's impersonal and mechanical, and I'm convinced that neither of us truly enjoys it."

Tears filled her eyes. "Frank! How can you talk like this?"

"Tell me I'm wrong," he said stiffly, starting the car. He gripped the wheel and pulled away from the terminal with a burst of speed. "Tell me you've had no lover but me."

"Such a ridiculous accusation doesn't deserve a reply. You imagine a list of men, no doubt. They don't exist," she insisted, blotting her lashes with a lace handkerchief.

"They don't?"

"No." She went through the motions of searching for

another tissue in her purse, then her lipstick and compact, hiding her rising hysteria. Until this moment, she'd taken for granted she'd been clever enough to conceal her affair with Robert. After all, she'd gone to such great lengths, and Frank hadn't questioned her in years! How was she to know he was dangerously near the point of deciding to let her go? She would have to do something drastic to smooth his ruffled feathers.

They rode in silence to the house while she repaired her ravaged face. These days, the job seemed to take longer.

The car stopped in front of the low mud-brick building in the middle of Kinshasa's extensive international community.

"I have been thoughtless, darling," Caroline blurted out, stashing all of her cosmetics away. "Let's go upstairs and get reacquainted." She ran three fingers up his arm.

Frank bolted from the car but came around and opened her door. "I have work to do," he said rigidly.

She quelled her offense at being turned down and followed him into the house. "What are your working on?"

"Jeffrey Illing, the ambassador to Chad is looking for help with the situation there. My experience in this country might be useful to him there. Then there's Rami. He's trying to form an alternative government in Romania."

Caroline tensed. Frank's insistence upon working with dissidents and sometimes taking positions opposed to official State Department policy still frightened her. More than one of her friends had brought her rumors of Frank's growing unpopularity within the department and among powerful Washington liberals.

"Darling," she said quietly, "do you think it's wise to continue this friendship?"

"With Rami? Probably not. But I don't intend to desert him now."

Anger crept into her voice. "You're jeopardizing our future by taking up with that sort of person."

"What's your definition of our future?" He squinted at her. He had a feeling her vision of his future was far different from his own.

"Definition?"

"Am I threatening your status quo as a celebrated professional hostess with a nearly unlimited expense account?"

"You twist things. You make me sound like a petty bitch." She stormed across the parlor and tossed her purse down on a chair.

Frank followed her, no longer wanting to avoid a confrontation. He had to know where she stood once and for all. "If you care about me, about my career and goals, you'll understand that I can't sit back and let people suffer while others oppress them."

Tears filled her eyes again. "Darling, you can't cure the ills of the world! Let them fight it out among themselves. We have too much to lose." She flung herself into his arms. "Oh, Frank, it's been so long since you've said you loved me. Tell me now. I love you desperately. I don't know how we let ourselves fall apart like this. It doesn't have to be so hard. If we each give a little, it can be as good as it once was."

He looked down into her moist blue eyes, wanting to believe that, after all, he had chosen the right woman to share his life. The last couple of years must have been especially difficult for her. Morale among foreign service wives was generally low at African posts. Most women drank too much, tended to let themselves go, dressed dowdily, and became apathetic about entertaining. Caroline had somehow escaped that emotional snare and remained vibrant.

Caroline clung to him, afraid of his silence. What would she do if he asked her for a divorce this very minute? She must offer something he couldn't walk away from.

"I know I've talked about taking Jennifer back to the States," she said quickly, "but that's for her. What I really want more than anything is to stay in Africa with you. I'd just miss you too much." She drew a deep breath and observed the wary pleasure registering in his eyes. "It's true that Jennifer would be better off in a private school at home with a permanent set of friends. But she'll survive. And I love you so much. This dreadful suspicion is unhealthy." She ran her tongue over dry lips, hoping the token she'd offered would satisfy him.

Frank held her close, his arms rock hard, locked around her as if they'd never let go. She recognized the magnitude of his need for family, how he wanted to count on her devotion.

"There's nothing I'd like better than to have . . . my wife with me," he said, his voice hoarse with emotion. "But we have to consider this and future assignments on the basis of safety. Illing is considering evacuating nonessential personnel and civilians if the situation turns nasty in Chad. If that's where I'm sent next, I won't even try to take you and Jen. It would be too risky."

"Oh, Frank." Tears glimmered in her eyes, but she concealed the small smile that threatened to spoil the effect. She could almost hear the civilized tinkle of crystal at a Washington dinner party.

"We'll talk about it more later," he promised.

She nodded and curled into his body, wanting him. They walked upstairs, arm in arm, and made love. Only afterward, when Frank recalled their conversation did he remember that, although Caroline had made concessions, she'd never denied her affairs. He could only hope that she'd been thrown such a scare she would forego future liaisons.

He rolled over on the bed and twirled a lock of honey-blond hair around his forefinger as she dozed contentedly. The strand was the same color as Jennifer's but not natural. He suspected that Caroline had chosen it because she looked stunning alongside her daughter. She must have known how the sight of them together tugged at his emotions.

"We could have another child," he murmured.

She flinched, half awake, and turned her head. Her breasts rested full and soft against the sheets. "You still want another child?"

"Um-hmm." He smiled. "We could try for a boy."

She yawned. "We can talk about it. Maybe if you get a good post, near reasonable hospitals. It's so dangerous, being shuttled from country to country at eight months pregnant."

A lump caught in his throat. Would she really consider another baby? It was more than he had hoped for in years. But he'd have to be willing to take a tame post, maybe remain stateside for five or six years. Playing it safe would hurt his career, but he'd never been obsessed with climbing departmental ranks. Besides, straightening out his family would be worth almost any sacrifice.

Amanda's sweet smile drifted into his imagination, and his eyes stung with regret. One can't have everything, he thought.

13

John waited on the sidewalk in front of the brick school building for his sister. His mother trusted him to make sure Christy got on the bus with him. He was only thirteen now, but his sister was only eight and in third grade—still a baby really.

Today was his least favorite day of the week. Every Wednesday Mom had to stay late at the studio to practice with Nick after they'd finished teaching their own students. So, after they took the school bus to the studio, John walked Christy to the foot of State Street to catch a city bus that would take them across the river to the navy base.

John always tried to talk his mother out of sending them home early. He'd rather stay at the studio. He liked Nick. Nick was a trip. He had big muscles, and he picked up John even though John was almost as tall as his mother. Nick wrestled with him, called him Big Guy, was always cheerful, and told neat jokes. He'd taught John to whittle so he'd have something to do while he and Mom danced. Nick told him, 'Keep your hands busy, and you'll never be poor or get into trouble because you're bored.'"

John figured his family wasn't poor, but that wasn't good

enough. He wanted to be rich. He wanted to buy Mom pretty gowns so she wouldn't have to sew her costumes anymore. He also wanted to buy his family a big house like some of his friends at school had. Their dads were the same rank in the navy as his dad or worked at Pfizer's, the pharmaceutical plant, or in the shipyards, but they seemed to have nice houses in town with basements to mess around in during the winter and aboveground pools in the backyard in the summer. Apartments on base couldn't have pools.

He also didn't like Wednesdays because Dad came home to take care of them. That started when Dad no longer had sea duty. The navy gave him a desk job. He'd overheard Mom and Dad arguing about it. His father was upset because they wouldn't let him command a submarine anymore.

Mom said, "It's your own fault, Rob. You drink too much. They don't want you ramming your ship into an iceberg like you rammed your Corvette into that tree." The car had been totaled, and his father had replaced it with a used compact model because the insurance wouldn't buy anything better.

His father was very angry. "The accident wasn't my fault! There was a mechanical failure; the 'Vette went out of control. I'm seriously thinking of suing GM!"

Mom had looked like she didn't believe it wasn't his fault. John wasn't sure what to think.

One thing he was sure of: Dad didn't like baby-sitting on Wednesdays. He was grumpy all afternoon. But he did it because Mom said he owed his kids some time and ought to help her out one day a week. Even when Dad took him and Christy for a walk to the playground "to kill time," John would have preferred to stay home and mess around in his room with one of his friends, because Dad always took his little leather-covered bottle in his pocket, sneaked drinks, and stared at ladies a lot.

John thought he should stop him, but the one time he'd told his father that drinking alcohol was bad for him, his father had smacked him across the face and yelled, "Don't give me any lip!" The funny thing was, he'd never hit him before and probably wouldn't have even then if he hadn't been drunk. Just to be on the safe side, John never said anything about his drinking again.

John knew that Christy didn't like Wednesdays either. She said Dad never understood—like Mommy did—that half the fun of going to a playground was getting pushed on the swings or cheered when you reached the top rung of the giant slide. It wasn't just doing stuff by yourself. So John played with her, even though he felt like a baby and hoped none of the guys came around and saw him.

Other times, Christy didn't seem to care if Dad never paid any attention to her. She had loads of girlfriends at home, and they played dolls constantly.

But John ached inside for a guy to be with and talk to, someone older who knew what was going on. Nick was the best he had, although Uncle Frank was nice, too, except John had only seen him at Christmas. But since his fight with Dad in Zaire, it didn't look like he'd ever see him again.

Anyway, after the Donnellys moved back to America, Mom let him talk to Frank on the telephone sometimes. Uncle Frank told him how Jennifer was doing at her special school in New Hampshire where rich girls went. Chisolm School for Girls.

Jennifer came to visit once in a while. She was always quiet and nervous at first, but after a couple of days, she loosened up and he thought she was pretty cool for a girl. She was smart, too, but never bragged about it. She had a butterfly collection that she took everywhere with her, and she'd trusted John to touch the specimens without breaking their wings.

Sometimes he wished they all lived together—Frank and Caroline, Mom and Dad, Christy, Jen, and him. Dad had drunk a lot less when Aunt Caroline was around, except for that one last Christmas.

John looked up from his thoughts and saw Christy strolling along with three of her friends, taking her time. He waved for her to hurry up. If they missed the bus, Dad would have to drive to New London to pick them up. John worried about things like that because he didn't want to be in the new car if it had a mechanical failure and hit another tree. Wednesdays were so difficult.

Jennifer sat in her dorm waiting for one of her roommates to get off the phone so she could call home.

Because it was impossible get hold of her mother and father on weekends, she called every Wednesday, right after supper at six o'clock. That way they expected her, and Wednesdays being kind of boring in Washington anyway, Mother usually stayed home.

Caroline always answered the phone, and they'd talk for two or three minutes. Her mother always asked the same question: "Are you having fun with all of your little friends?" And she could never remember Jennifer's roommates' names. "Ginnie and Karen, Mom. I told you last time." And then she'd say, "Well, sweetie, I suppose you want to talk to your father now." It was as if she couldn't wait to get off the phone.

Her father picked up the minute Caroline summoned him because he'd be waiting at his desk for her call.

"Hello, Princess. How's the most beautiful girl in New Hampshire?"

"Oh, Daddy," she'd say, "I'm not beautiful." And she wasn't. She was fat, although she loved him for lying to her. Her weight was why she didn't have many friends, that and the fact she was klutzy. Grown-ups and a few polite girls at school told her she was intelligent and nice, but none of the girls invited her to parties or to go home with them on weekends or holidays.

Jennifer wished she looked like her mother. Caroline was awesome. When she put on her makeup, arranged her hair, and dressed up, she was the most gorgeous woman in the world, prettier than Miss America or even Farrah Fawcett.

They used to dress in mother–daughter outfits, but during the last couple years when Jennifer had put on a lot of weight, they stopped.

"She looks like a blimp in that dress. Take it off her!" she'd overheard her mother instruct the governess. "Everyone will laugh at me."

No, Mother, not at you, at me. Jennifer had often wondered if the reason she'd been sent away to a boarding school was because she was fat and an embarrassment to her mother.

"How's school?" her father asked.

"Okay."

"Do you want to come home this weekend? I'll arrange for a plane ticket."

"No, that's okay." She'd be in the way. They were very busy people with gobs of parties, receptions, and appointments to rush off to.

"Last time I talked to Aunt Amanda, she said she'd like you to stay with her again if you liked—for a weekend or longer."

Jennifer sat up on her bed and grinned, suddenly interested. "She did?"

"Sure. John would love to have you visit."

Her heart rumbled warmly. John was great. He never made fun of her, and even when they were little, he'd always shared stuff without being told to. "That would be neat!"

"You have her number?"

"Sure. I'll call her . . . next week maybe."

She could hear her father shifting the telephone receiver against his chin, his beard making a scraping sound. He coughed as if he were nervous. "Jen, remember I told you that sometime soon I might be going back to Africa?"

"Yeah."

"Well, I'm leaving for Chad in two weeks. I'll be deputy chief of mission in the executive section, second man to the ambassador."

"No kidding? That's super! Can I go, too?"

"Not yet . . . we'll see. The political situation isn't very stable over there at the moment. Anyway, it's important that you stay in a good school."

"Oh," she said, disappointed. But she didn't want to make him feel bad, so she didn't beg.

They talked for a while longer about things in the news. Jennifer brought up the headlines because her father knew everything that happened in the world and liked to talk to her about politics and coups and that kind of stuff. He'd met most of the men whose pictures she saw in the newspapers.

Some had posed with him for photographs, which hung in his study.

In her own bedroom back home, she had two photos of herself. In one she stood beside President Ford at a formal reception. In the other, she was shaking hands with Margaret Thatcher in front of a fireplace in Ten Downing Street. They were good pictures, taken before she'd gotten fat.

She said, "I gotta go now. Love you, Daddy."

"I love you, too, Princess. Don't forget to call Amanda."

"I won't," she promised.

As soon as Jennifer hung up, though, she knew she wouldn't call John's mother. She didn't want to be a bother or sound like a baby, looking for an excuse to get away from Chisolm. More importantly, she didn't want to attract attention to herself by writing her name on the weekend travel list on the bulletin board downstairs. She munched on a Scooter Pie and let out a long sigh. She might as well study; at least she was good at that.

The situation in Chad worsened considerably after Frank arrived in the capital city of N'Djamena in February of 1979. Ever since the country had received its independence from France in 1960, Christian southerners and Islamic northerners had clashed violently, and various groups vied for power. But now the Forces Armées Populaires and the Forces Armées du Nord united to drive the national army from N'Djamena with bloody results. The U.S. diplomatic corps remained in the city, on ready alert, monitoring radio transmissions from the embassy. At a base near the airport, eleven hundred French troops waited out the latest waves of combat. Their official role was to remain aloof from the country's internal affairs and to protect French civilians in the country. But unofficially they provided air transportation and helped maintain electric power and water supplies for the new, fragile government.

Communications from the embassy in N'Djamena to Washington were limited to radio transmissions at agreed-upon intervals or reports and memos sent in the diplomatic bag. At first, Frank welcomed the isolation. He didn't have to feel guilty about not telephoning Caroline. Conversations with his wife—either in person or over the phone—always seemed strained and artificial. So it was with mixed emotions that he found himself in Paris, attending a conference of African states, with a telephone in his hotel room.

He looked at the old-fashioned black plastic instrument and thought, *I should call my wife.* But he didn't want to. And then he thought of Amanda, her sweet voice, her excitement if he should decide to ring her up without warning.

The last few years since the fiasco in Zaire, the Donnellys had Christmased without the Allens, and it just hadn't seemed the same without the ring of children's laughter through the house, without Amanda's contagious smile. But he and Amanda still wrote to one another every month or so—long newsy notes that gave him as much pleasure to write as to read.

Letters and photographs, however, weren't the same as seeing Amanda's sweet lips curve upward in response to one of his stories or hearing her gentle voice. He missed even the small snatches of time they'd shared.

Nevertheless, the years flew by surprisingly quickly, for he worked hard through long days, leaving few spare moments to dwell upon Amanda or anything else not directly related to his job. Sitting in the hotel room now, though, he suddenly did have time on his hands to think about her. He hoped her days had been as full and satisfying as his had been. He hoped she wasn't aching for him, then, perversely, prayed she was. To have a woman like Amanda love him, even if it was a forbidden love . . .

He dialed the number for the studio by memory, then checked the time to be sure she'd be there.

A young voice answered. "Stevenson School of Dance."

He grinned. "John, is that you?"

"This is John," the boy answered politely. "Who is calling, please?"

"Hey, fella, this is Frank! How's it going?"

"Frank!" The transformation from rehearsed dialogue to familiar banter was instantaneous. "Hi! Where are you calling from? Africa?"

"Paris."

"Wow! Hey, thanks for the tribal mask. All the guys at school thought it was cool. I'm going to wear it for Halloween this year!"

Frank laughed. "You do that. Scare the evil spirits right back into their houses. Is your mother free, or is she teaching?"

"She's in class, but I'll get her. She'd kill me if I didn't tell her you were on the phone."

"Well, we can't have that, can we?"

"No, sir. Hold on."

Frank chuckled and hummed and ran his tongue over his teeth, waiting, anticipating the moment when Amanda's voice would sing in his ear. He imagined her hearing the news from John, assigning an older student to take charge of the class, imagined her breathless dash down the dim hallway to the office. He'd been there only a few times but recalled it implicitly whenever he thought of her in her world.

"Frank!" She sounded as if she might have been in the next room, and he had to remind himself that she was thousands of miles and half a world away. "How are you?" she gasped. "Oh, God, it's been so long since we've talked! Your last letter sounded grim."

"It's not a happy situation in Chad," he admitted.

"I thought there were no phones . . ."

"I'm in Paris for one week. The ambassador didn't want to leave N'Djamena while the situation was so volatile. He sent me to Paris to attend the Pan-African Congress in his stead."

"I've been following it in the newspaper," she said softly. "And the situation in Chad. Are you in danger?"

How different her tone of anxiety from Caroline's, whose main concern was that he might be chopped up into pieces before she enjoyed the benefit of another European post.

"We're all extremely cautious about where we travel in the country. During the last round of fighting, we took a few days off from work and stayed inside, playing cards mostly." He smiled, thinking of the pleasant hours he'd spent at a card table with Amanda. "Sort of a nice break," he murmured.

246

"Will you stay if the fighting continues or gets worse?" she asked.

"The ambassador and his immediate staff are the last to leave the embassy, under any circumstances."

"I see," she whispered. "Take care of yourself, Frank."

"That's my intention, lady," he said, trying to sound breezy for her benefit. Then he cleared his throat. "Well, on to cheerier news. Has Jennifer called you yet?"

"Why, no, she hasn't recently. Should I expect a call from her?"

"I would have said yes a few months ago. We had a conversation one day before I left the States. She said she was going to call and arrange to visit you."

"Oh, how marvelous! You know how much I love having her here with me! But why didn't she phone?"

"I don't know." A cloud passed over his mind. He rubbed his temple with thumb and forefinger. "She's a funny kid—so bright but maddeningly insecure. Having Caroline for a mother doesn't help, I'm afraid. Maybe she just chickened out."

"I'll call her tonight after classes are over. In fact, I was thinking of asking her to come for the summer or as much of it as she'd like if Caroline can spare her."

"I'm sure that won't be a problem. She and Caroline don't spend much time together." He hesitated. "But I don't see how you can have time for a third child—"

"Don't be silly. She's what? Twelve? Almost thirteen like John? I'm hiring four teenagers this summer in addition to John to work as assistants during our summer dance camp."

"You know she doesn't dance, at least not very well." He thought of how awkward his Jen was—chubby and uncoordinated. His heart went out to his daughter. To him she would always be beautiful, but he knew she sometimes felt self-conscious about her weight.

"Jennifer doesn't have to dance. She'll work in the office, answer the phone, schedule new students. As you said, she's a bright kid. She can handle it."

"That would certainly build her self-confidence." He was pleased with the unexpected plan.

"I can pay only minimum wage, and the hours will be

long. But she'll be with kids her own age all day long, get lots of exercise, and probably pick up a good deal of dancing if she cares to."

"Wonderful." He felt so grateful for her wisdom, at that moment, he could have kissed her. In fact, that thought seemed increasingly tantalizing the more he thought about it.

"I'll call Caroline and check it out before I speak with Jen," she promised.

"That's probably best, although I don't expect she has anything in particular planned for her this summer." He got up, crossed to the bar on the other side of the room, and poured tepid soda water into a glass. Holding the phone in one hand, he raised the glass and took two swallows. What he had to say next was going to be difficult.

"Amanda," he continued, then hesitated.

"Yes?"

"There's something I've wanted to say for a long time, I—" Damn it, he was a diplomat. He made his living with words, handling sticky situations, quelling high emotions. Why was this so different? "I appreciate having you for a friend," he blurted out.

"You're very . . . special . . . to me, too," she murmured, her tone sounding tight.

"It's more than special, our friendship. I think it's pretty near unique, at least in my experience. I would never have thought I could be friends with a woman without any of the usual sexual game playing involved."

"Perhaps it's because I'm not your type," she guessed simply.

He considered this possibility. Something in what Amanda had said rang true. She wasn't a socialite beauty like those women he'd always dated or the one he'd eventually married. But what if that wasn't "his type"? What if she, Amanda, with her sweet nature, her uncluttered natural prettiness, her joy with life and dedication to her art and her children, *was* his type. *What if—damn his soul—he hadn't realized it all of these years!*

On the other hand, perhaps she was just an excellent listener and a kind person, who naturally attracted good feelings. Knowing this about her, he felt thankful that Jennifer would be spending the summer with her and also a little . . . What was that prickly sensation crouching in the back of his heart? Jealousy? Of course not, he told himself. *Of course I'm not jealous of my own daughter.*

Nevertheless, the thought of spending an entire summer in Amanda's gentle, musical world tugged temptingly at him.

"I suppose you're right. You're not my type," he admitted at last with a touch of wistfulness. "And I'm not yours. As you said in Zaire, we're from different worlds. But I hope you don't feel uncomfortable about our continuing to visit long distance like this."

"Not at all. Although, I have to admit Robert would be upset if he were aware. I stopped sharing your letters with him years ago."

"I'd guessed that," he said. "If you'd rather I not write—"
Please don't say stop, please don't . . .

"Oh, no!" she gasped. "We're doing nothing wrong. If Robert can't trust me, that's his problem."

"How is he?"

"I've begged him to join AA dozens of times. He's destroying himself, and his relationship with his children is deteriorating. It won't be long before the kids start avoiding him. John already does in subtle ways."

"I'm sorry, Amanda. He's not abusive, is he? To you or the children?"

"He never gets physical," she stated carefully.

Frank closed his eyes and took a deep breath for courage. "Listen, tell me to shut up if I'm out of line, but . . . why don't you leave him? I'm serious. This has gone on a long time. You couldn't possibly still love the man."

He listened to the silence of the open line. Then he could hear her soft breath, in and out, in and out. *She's going to hang up on me. I've gone too far. Please, God, if you exist, don't let her hang up.* His knuckles ached on the receiver.

At last she spoke in very carefully arranged words. "I've asked myself that question a thousand times. But I keep coming back to one thought: Robert loves his son and daughter, and they love him because he's their father. I believe, deep down, he cares for me, too. If he wants us all to stay together, he'll change. Besides, there's no one else waiting for me. I see no need to rush into a divorce."

"No other men in your life?" he asked, holding his breath. *Why was he holding his breath?*

"None. Oh—" she laughed, sounding like a young girl—"I have opportunities. Students, fellow competitors in dance world, other officers, but I'm not interested. Don't get me wrong, I want to be loved passionately, by the right man. I'm just not sure that . . . that he exists . . ." she finished, almost too softly to be heard.

"If you left Robert temporarily, it might prompt a faster change from him," Frank suggested. *No, that's not what you really want. You want her to leave him, leave him now and forever. You want to be sure that even if she's not with you, at least she isn't sleeping with that bastard!*

"Robert needs his family, Frank," Amanda whispered into the receiver. "I can't take his children from him."

"Well, you know what is best for all of you," he forced the words between his lips. "Just don't make the mistake of believing you have to put up with his behavior indefinitely. There are plenty of men who'd give their kingdoms to be good to you, Amanda."

"Sounds like a fairy tale," she murmured, and he imagined her smiling.

He gazed out of the window at an intimate café across the street. Couples sat sipping wine in the late afternoon sunshine. "Perhaps it is. But you have to remember that at some point in his life booze will become all that Robert cares about. Then you and the kids will be better off on your own. If nothing else, remember that I'm always here for you if you need money, legal help, anything. Okay?"

"Okay," she agreed. "Good-bye, Frank."

"Good-bye."

Sunlight splashed through the high windows of the ballroom, scattering dust motes, warming the late June morning air. This was Amanda's favorite time of day—silent, promising activity but not yet ready to explode with the music, laughter, and learning. John, Jennifer, and Christy were upstairs having breakfast, and classes wouldn't start for another half hour. Amanda laid her hand on the long wooden barrel, stretched her calf muscles, arched her back, and let the sun warm her throat above the plum-colored leotard that covered her slim torso.

"Oh, Sara," she murmured, "life is good. Thank you, thank you for this wonderful place . . ."

It seemed strange that she should feel so content. For the past two months Robert had been on TDY in San Diego, and he wouldn't return until the first of September. She wished she could say that she missed her husband, but his absence was more of a relief than a hardship. She didn't have to clean up after him when he spilled a drink on the sofa cushions, didn't have to explain to him why she'd been late getting home from the studio, didn't need to make his dinner in the morning and leave it in the refrigerator, where he'd expect to find it when he returned that evening, didn't argue about how much she'd spent on groceries, while his choice of booze became increasingly expensive.

The navy was making strides in counseling its heavy drinkers, and they'd relieved Rob of all sea duties while firmly encouraging him to attend AA meetings. However, he stocked an extensive bar at home "for guests" and frequently cheated on his pledge of abstention.

"This cold-turkey crap is ridiculous. I can stop any time I like," he assured her. "Cutting back gradually makes much more sense."

His rationalizations no longer convinced Amanda, and she marveled that he continued to believe himself.

Hearing footsteps cross the ballroom floor, she turned around. John and Jennifer were walking toward her, and her world instantly brightened. They were so different, yet got along beautifully. He was dark, thin, and athletic. She was pale, blond, and a bit plump despite the exercise she was getting at the studio during the summer. Amanda made a mental note to try to supply her with more low-calorie snacks.

"Christy has her dumb cartoons on the TV," John complained. "It's my turn to choose, but she won't let me change the channel."

"Oh, dear," Amanda sighed ruffling his hair. She put an arm around each of them. "Major catastrophe?"

He grimaced. "Naw. I guess I don't have to make a stink about it."

"Good man." She was so proud of him. Despite his father's poor influence, he was turning out just fine. His grades in school were good; his friends all seemed to be great kids; he was running track for his second year and, according to his coach, showing a lot of promise.

Christy was the one she worried about these days. Her daughter was perennially lazy and invented excuses to get out of cleaning her room, for turning in homework late, or doing anything remotely taxing. She was a job to keep track of but a lovable little girl nonetheless.

"Do you need help setting up for the day?" Jennifer asked.

"I sure do. Driving back and forth between the base and studio eats up time. I wish we could get started earlier, but I can't bear to drag you three out of bed before seven o'clock on a Saturday."

John shrugged. "No big deal. I like it better here. The apartment is sort of . . . crowded."

"Anyplace would feel small compared to the studio," she said.

"You should rent out the upstairs apartment," Jennifer pointed out.

Doug and Sara's apartment remained much as it had been when they'd lived there. Doug chose to take only a few pieces of furniture on his move out West, and Amanda found the private third-floor rooms convenient. She and the children had stayed overnight a few times when Robert was away.

"Hey!" John exclaimed, "I know what we should do! We should move here, live here all the time!"

"Oh, yes-s-s-s!" Jennifer squealed, then clamped a hand over her mouth as if surprised at her own outburst. She lowered her voice. "That would be so fantastic. We could live here all summer."

"All winter, too!" John chimed in. "We could just move to the studio, permanentlike."

Amanda laughed at their fantasy. "You'd have to leave

your friends on the base," she said, expecting his balloon to burst.

"I don't care. I'd make new friends! Anyhow, everyone in my school lives in New London."

Amanda's smile wavered as she recognized a possible motive for John's enthusiasm. Could it be that he realized Rob would never agree to follow them here? Had the gulf between father and son become that wide?

"I don't think your plan is very practical," she said slowly.

"But Dad's in San Diego, and anyway we have everything we need here. Oh, Mom, why not? Just for the summer . . ."

"Just for the summer," Christy took up his chant without knowing why as she darted into the room, her curly brown hair falling in her eyes.

"Just for the summer . . . Just for the summer . . ." all three chorused.

Amanda shook her head, grinning at their silliness. She didn't tell them no, but she made no promises and sent them off to perform morning chores before students began to arrive.

All day long as she taught, though, Amanda thought about John's idea. And it stayed with her all through Sunday, her day off. At home in the apartment while she cleaned and loaded laundry into the washer, she mused, *I could do housework just as easily at the studio while I worked on my budget and planned lessons.* In fact, her time would be much more efficiently used since the studio ledgers, practice tapes, and records would be close at hand.

The following week Amanda telephoned SNETCO to ask if calls to the Groton apartment could be forwarded to a New London number. They could. She dialed Rob's number in San Diego to ask what he thought of the idea but hung up before he could answer, deciding she didn't really want or need his permission. He was a devoted misanthrope and never failed to crush her most exciting plans.

Amanda arranged for her phone to ring at the studio. She ordered the post office to forward her mail and informed a neighbor that she would be living at the studio until the end of August. She left the address and phone number in case of emergency.

It took the four of them no time at all to settle in. The first night at the studio, she felt as if she had truly come home. She only wished she didn't have to leave at the end of the summer.

The children blossomed in the atmosphere of activity and fun. When they weren't helping her teach, they ran errands: picking up a fast lunch of frankfurters, Greek salad, and homemade bread pudding from the Puritan Diner; hiking up to the supermarket at the top of the street for groceries or to buy a watermelon to take up onto the roof and cut into juicy slices at the end of a long, sweaty day. For a special treat they walked to the Garde Theater for a matinee.

Jennifer lost ten pounds of baby fat and seemed happier than Amanda had ever seen her. But during the last two weeks of August, she grew quiet again and seemed to withdraw into her old shell.

"I'm worried about Jen," John confided in Amanda.

"Why?" she asked, curious to hear his reasons.

"She's . . . I don't know . . . acting funny."

Amanda thought she knew what was troubling the shy teenager. "Are you worried about going back to school?" she asked when they were alone together.

Jennifer chewed her lip. "I like Chisolm. I get great grades."

"I know you do." Amanda hesitated, choosing her words carefully. "Do you have many friends there?"

"Sure—sure I do." Jennifer glanced at a nail poking up through the wood floor, at the kitchen table, out the window, anywhere but directly into Amanda's questioning gaze. "Can I go find Christy now? I promised to French-braid her hair."

"Of course."

Amanda watched sympathetically as Jennifer dashed out of the room. She too hated to see the summer end. They'd have to return to the base. In a couple of days, she'd drive Jen back to New Hampshire, and Rob would come home. She felt saddened by the loss of one dear little personality and reinstatement of a far less tolerable one and guilty for wanting more of what she should have appreciated as a gift:

one tranquil summer with her young people, free of the complications of caring for an adult who, she was finally beginning to understand, carried with him a lifelong social disease.

On the last night before their autumn relocation, Amanda couldn't sleep. She lay in bed, thinking about the trying months of readjustment ahead and worrying about Frank in Chad. His last letter wasn't encouraging. Although a general cease-fire had been proclaimed and some semblance of order restored to the larger cities of the struggling young county, armed factions still roamed the countryside. Revolutions were dangerously unpredictable, and Americans made easy targets. Although she wasn't religious, she prayed for him that night.

Giving up on sleep, she read for a couple hours. At last, she laid the open book on the sheets beside her and, without shutting off the light, let her eyes drift closed. Dozing restlessly, she was assaulted by visions of Africans slung with ammo belts and brandishing machetes. She sensed that she ought to be terrified, but, strangely enough, she longed to be in N'Djamena with Frank. Not that there was anything she could do to protect him. She just wanted to be there, to share whatever hard times he might be facing. A warm feeling swept over her, and at last, she slept.

It might have only been minutes or it might have been hours later when a nerve-tearing scream followed by a loud crash shattered her peace. In one motion, she whipped back the sheet and bolted from her bedroom.

When she reached the children's room, John was sitting up in his bed, blinking away sleep. Christy snored puffily in her cot.

"What was that?" John demanded.

"I don't know." Her palms felt clammy. Suddenly alert, all she could think was *A prowler . . . someone intent on mayhem . . . Oh, God, what do I do to protect the kids?* "Stay with Christy," she rasped. "I'll go see what it is."

Ignoring her directive, he leaped out of bed and ran silently on bare feet toward the stairs.

"John, wait!" Amanda hissed, aware of the utter silence of

the studio, which amplified their frantic noises. She glanced around the room as she tore after him. Jennifer's bed was empty.

"Oh, God, no!" The veins in her forehead felt as if they would burst. As she ran, she switched on lights, seized a broom with the vague thought of using it as a weapon, then heard John shriek, "Jen!"

He'd negotiated the stairs in threes, reaching the ballroom below well ahead of her.

Amanda's heart caught in her throat as she came to the stop beside her son. A chunk of wooden railing lay on the floor at his feet alongside the crumpled shape of the girl.

"Don't touch her!" she automatically choked out.

Kneeling, she placed two fingers gently on Jennifer's throat, felt the blessed pulse, saw the labored motion of her chest. "Thank you. Oh, God, thank you," she murmured. "John, call 911. She needs an ambulance!"

He stood rock still, gazing down with a stricken expression, his lip quivering. "It's m-m-my fault."

"Don't be foolish. The railing was rotted, she fell. Call for help. *Now,* John!" she shouted, knowing she sounded harsh but needing to shake him out of his stupor.

He turned shakily, then ran toward the office.

Jennifer's nostrils flared slightly, a first sign of consciousness. Amanda leaned over and brushed the trailing strands of hair from her pale cheek. "It's okay, darling. You'll be fine. We're getting a doctor for you."

Jennifer moved her head from side to side and began to sob. "I can't. I can't. Please, don't leave me . . ." she cried.

"I won't leave you." Amanda held her hand. "I'll be right with you the whole time. And as soon as we get to the hospital, I'll call your mom and dad."

After what seemed an eternity but was no more than fifteen minutes by the clock, an ambulance arrived. Amanda sat with Jennifer during the short ride to the hospital, through X rays ordered by the doctor on duty in the emergency room, then in the examination room while Dr. Crane, an orthopedist, checked her out.

"Tell me again how this happened?" he asked Amanda as he pressed, poked, and peered intently at Jennifer.

"I'm not exactly sure. She must have been leaning over the balcony at my dance studio and fell. A section of old wood broke away."

He nodded, looking at Jennifer who was calmer but in obvious pain. "Is that how this happened to you, young lady?"

Amanda realized with a flash of intuition that his concern was child abuse. She felt her cheeks flush hot with embarrassment but said nothing. He was just doing his job.

"Yes," Jennifer said, "my hair ribbon fell over the edge. I reached for it but I guess I missed."

"I guess you did," he said, his blue eyes twinkling now that he was sure he had nothing more than an accident to deal with. "Well, the good news is, it doesn't appear a head injury is involved. However, the X rays show two fractured ribs and a clean break of both wrist bones in the right arm to compliment a nice collection of bruises." He turned to Amanda. "Are you the mother?"

"No. A friend of the family. Jennifer stayed the summer with me."

"Can you reach her parents for permission to treat her?"

"I have power of attorney for her medical care." She reached into her purse, thankful she'd planned ahead, and pulled out the document.

"That simplifies matters immensely." Dr. Crane leaned on the heels of his palms over the examination table, his eyes solemn but reassuring, and spoke directly to Jennifer. "Now for the fun part, young lady. We're going to tape up those ribs so you can breathe a little more comfortably, then we'll set that arm." He grinned at her. "Afraid you'll be going back to school with a cast for all your friends to sign."

Instead of looking amused, Jennifer winced.

"Hey, a cast is a great conversation piece," the doctor told her. "You'd be surprised. Bet you'll be the most popular kid in the school first day back."

Jennifer gazed doubtfully at him.

While Jennifer's ribs were being tended to, Amanda

called John at the studio and told him that Jen was going to
be all right. Then she returned to the casting room to sit with
her, holding her uninjured hand while Dr. Crane and a burly
male nurse set her arm. The ordeal was as excruciating for
Amanda as for the patient. But Jennifer was remarkably
brave, letting out only one pitiful wail when the two men
tugged her misshapen arm back into line.

At last, Amanda took her temporarily adopted daughter,
pumped full of Darvon, back to the studio. After she'd
settled her into the roomy double bed in the master bedroom and checked on Christy and John, who had fallen back
to sleep, she made herself a quick cup of instant coffee and
went downstairs to the office.

It was by now almost five A.M. In Washington, the time
would be the same. In Chad it was three in the afternoon.
She decided she'd wake up Caroline and let her decide how
and when to tell Frank about their daughter's accident.

Amanda's hand shook as she dialed. She felt somehow
responsible for Jennifer's injury, although, logically, she
realized she shouldn't blame herself.

The telephone in the Potomac, Maryland, house rang . . .
and rang . . . and rang. She counted fifteen shrill jangles.
Finally, she hung up, pressed in the numbers again to be
sure she hadn't misdialed, waited for another dozen rings,
then hung up again, trying to think where Caroline could be.

She called Gray Cliffs on the off chance the Nesbits would
be able to locate her. Vincent Nesbit answered gruffly. But
his tone softened as soon as he recognized her voice.
"Amanda, what's wrong?"

She explained as calmly as possible about Jennifer's fall.

"But the child is all right?" Vincent asked, his voice stern
again.

She repeated Dr. Crane's reassurances. "I've called Caroline, but there's no answer at her house."

"I don't know where my daughter would be at this hour if
not at home. To my knowledge she had no travel plans."

A queasy feeling edged into Amanda's stomach. Of
course, Caroline wouldn't leave a forwarding address if
she'd arranged a cozy rendezvous with a lover. "I'll just
keep trying," she said hastily.

"I can be there in twenty minutes," Vincent offered.

"No," Amanda said quickly. "Jennifer is resting now. The doctor said she'd probably sleep all morning. He's medicated her pretty thoroughly."

"Well, at least let me settle up with the hospital."

"Thank you," she said, grateful to have at least some responsibility lifted from her shoulders. "I'm sure I'll reach Caroline soon. And I'll have Jennifer call you when she wakes up."

"Please do." Vincent paused. "You should probably put out a message through State Department channels for Frank. Or would you rather I do that?" he asked.

"No. I will."

Amanda pushed down the button and immediately punched in the extension at the State Department in Washington that Frank had given her.

The day following the accident was without students, being a Sunday. Amanda tried all morning to contact Caroline but never got an answer. She began to suspect she'd been right, that Caroline had taken off for a long weekend rendezvous. She felt furious for Frank's sake. He deserved so much more from a wife. She felt enraged for Jennifer's sake, for no child ought to be without her mother when she'd come so close to death.

All three children slept until eleven-thirty that morning. Jennifer woke only once, briefly, to ask for more medicine because her arm was hurting. Amanda gave her two pink-and-gray capsules with a glass of water to wash them down. She checked to be sure her cast was propped up high enough on a pile of pillows, as the doctor had instructed, to keep the arm from swelling inside the plaster shell.

While the children slept, Amanda tried to take her own mind off the uncertainty of Caroline's whereabouts by paying a few bills that had been awaiting her attention, then she planned the following week's lessons. She had trouble keeping her mind on her notes, though. It was one thing to know she shouldn't blame herself for Jen's fall, but another to believe herself.

If only I'd had that rail replaced instead of patching it when we remodeled! she thought miserably. *Why didn't I hear her get up? Why didn't I hear her walking around?* Since John had been born, she'd become accustomed to sleeping shallowly, alert to a muffled cry or subtle warning sounds of illness in the night. But she hadn't heard Jennifer at all, and that continued to nag at her conscience.

Jennifer telephoned her grandparents shortly after noon. They insisted upon seeing her and arrived at the studio a little after one o'clock. Amanda led them upstairs to her bedroom, and they spent a good ten minutes fussing over Jennifer, who only tolerated them.

Finally, Vincent pulled Amanda aside. "You've done everything you could, and we're grateful," he stated. "But since Caroline is temporarily out of touch and Frank is abroad, I think it best that my granddaughter come back to Gray Cliffs with us."

Amanda caught a flash of disappointment in Jennifer's eyes. Both of her lids had turned a rich shade of purple, and one cheekbone was swollen. She was quite a sight.

"Can't I please stay here," she begged timidly. "Amanda says that Daddy's coming for me. He'll expect me to be here."

"Frank is flying home?" Gloria Nesbit asked.

"The State Department got through to him and returned the message that he'd be flying back to the States immediately. Communications with Chad are even more primitive than they were with Zaire. I couldn't speak with him directly."

"I see," Nesbit said, exchanging a cloaked glance with his wife. "Well, once he arrives, I guess it will be his decision where Jennifer should stay."

Jennifer did nothing to prolong her grandparents' visit, and they left a few minutes later. Amanda had often suspected that Jennifer didn't get along well with them. During the entire summer she'd spent only two days with them in Groton, and then only after much convincing from Amanda.

She decided to bring up the subject later that afternoon.

"They don't really like me," Jennifer confided in Amanda. "They're embarrassed whenever their friends see

260

me. They think I'm fat and dull. I *am* fat, but they shouldn't care, should they? I'm their only granddaughter."

"No, they shouldn't, honey," Amanda agreed, wrapping an arm around her shoulders. "But you're wrong; you're lovely. You may be a little overweight, but not much. You wait, darling. In a few years you'll drop that last bit of baby fat and be a beautiful young woman."

"As beautiful as Mother?"

So that was it. "Yes, every bit as beautiful as your mother." Except, your heart will be purer. "You will be a lovely, intelligent, sweet person."

Jennifer hugged her too hard and broke away, laughing and gasping from the pain in her crushed ribs. "Guess I'd better not do that," she groaned. "When will my dad be here?"

"Soon, darling," she soothed, stroking her blond hair. "Soon."

It would have taken Frank at least forty-eight hours to reach Connecticut had he made commercial airline reservations. Instead, he caught a French military transport from the airport in N'Djamena to an air base on the outskirts of Paris, and from there hitched a ride on a NATO jet to Frankfurt, where he located a huge C-20 cargo plane due to leave for Andrews Air Force Base within the hour.

At last on the ground in the oppressive heat of a D.C. summer, he telephoned his in-laws, questioned them briefly about Jennifer's condition, and asked Vincent to have a car waiting for him at the commuter airport in Groton. He chartered a prop jet to fly him the final leg of his journey.

The Nesbits' limousine whisked him across the bridge toward New London. Thanks to his lucky series of connections and the time difference, it was only eight P.M. on Sunday.

He was inexorably tired, for he hadn't slept during the entire journey and he wore the same clothing in which he'd left N'Djamena. He'd eaten nothing the entire trip except for a couple of stale rolls he'd grabbed in Frankfurt.

His heart hadn't stopped hammering in his chest throughout the day of plane hopping, his mouth was dry with fear, and he was scared to death of what he would find when he reached the studio.

Jennifer, my Jennifer, please, let her be safe and well.

When he'd spoken with Vincent from Andrews, his father-in-law had described a confusing scenario of a fall and various injuries, interspersed with vague reassurances. But Frank had to see his daughter to convince himself that she was really all right.

Then there was his irritation with Caroline. Each time he'd landed, he'd found a phone and tried to call her. By now he'd contacted every girlfriend, resort, spa, and beauty parlor he'd ever known Caroline to visit. She was with none of them, but every person he spoke with offered to keep an eye out for her just in case she showed up.

The director of the illustrious Greenbriar in West Virginia told him, "She sometimes arrives on short or no notice, sir. Just a call on the way. Should she appear, we'll certainly have her contact you."

Should she appear? What is she, a fairy sprite who dazzles the world by magically popping in and out of reality? "Tell her to telephone Amanda in Connecticut. She has the number."

Then Frank was in the air again, wishing he had the nerve to pump the guy about his wife's stays at the posh resort. What did she do at the Greenbriar? Whom did she spend her days and evenings with? Caroline was not a loner. There would be doubles tennis matches, undoubtedly mixed. Who would be her partner? She loved riding horseback, and there were miles of secluded woodsy trails throughout the lovely West Virginia countryside. She adored dancing until the early morning hours.

As Frank rode through the dusky streets of New London in the backseat of the Nesbits' limo, he stared at the rows of discolored brick buildings along the river—windowless, crumbling, being razed to make way for new ones. And he realized something astonishing. His questions surrounding Caroline's fidelity weren't raised out of jealousy. They had become a function of pure curiosity. No tugs at the heartstrings. No pain at the vision of his beautiful wife in another man's arms. Incredibly, that was all in the past.

He blinked, surprised, yet relieved after all these years. As a test, he forced himself to imagine Caroline in a lacy negligee, her blond hair tumbling out of a sexy coiffure after a night at a Georgetown party, and he felt neither the bite of passion nor the pang of regret.

Frank dropped his head into his hands with a groan. But she still held an unarguable power over him through his career. Her influence in diplomatic circles was not to be taken lightly. She could do him great harm if she put her mind to his destruction.

Caroline's most potent weapon, though, was still their daughter.

Looking up, he took in the tidy small-town shops lining State Street. The studio was on the right, a green wooden door darkly wedged between a luncheonette and a shoe store. Gold letters stenciled on the second-floor window announced that this was the Stevenson School of Dance, although Amanda had taken it over years ago.

"I'll wait, sir," the driver said as he pulled up to the sloping granite curb.

"Don't bother getting out," Frank told him while opening the back door for himself. On second thought, he leaned back inside for his valise, which held little more than his one spare shirt. "I may be a while," he murmured.

The driver shut off the motor and leaned back in his seat.

The studio door was unlocked, and as tired as he was, Frank flew up the stairs. He'd been here a couple of times to pick up Jennifer. The renovations Amanda had made were a definite improvement but couldn't disguise the building's age. The musty odor of wood rot issued from somewhere deep in the bowels of the place. Dust gathered in thick pillows between cracks in the hallway floor, formed as the boards had slowly shrunken and separated. Music played from somewhere above him: a radio station . . . pop music. Singing voices seemed incongruous with his daughter's shattered bones and agony.

Amanda intercepted Frank before he reached the second flight of stairs leading to the private apartment. She was dressed in her working clothes: a sleeveless black leotard and pink tights that ended at the ankles, baring her tiny feet,

263

a loosely wrapped skirt of tie-dyed gauze that might have been a scarf.

"I saw the car pull up," she said in a quiet voice.

"Amanda—" He gripped her shoulders between his hands. "Is she really all right? Tell me!"

She smiled at him, warming his fear-chilled nerves. "Jen's making the most of being an invalid. John and Christy have been waiting on her hand and foot."

"You're sure there are no internal injuries, brain trauma, internal bleeding, nothing they've overlooked?"

"Dr. Crane gave her his seal of approval. Two cracked ribs, one broken arm, and a nice assortment of bumps and bruises. But everything has been set, taped, and bandaged. Oh, there is one other thing . . ." she added solemnly.

"Yes?" he asked, anticipating the worst.

"Busted fingernails." She grinned mischievously.

"Fingernails?"

Jennifer spent some of her hard-earned salary on fake nails from Kresge's. She glued them on herself and Christy. Three broke off in the fall."

He let out a howl of laughter. "Geez. Kids!"

His hands dropped away from Amanda's shoulders. He couldn't stop laughing. Since the cryptic message reporting his daughter's accident had reached him in N'Djamena, he'd been screwed on as tight as a lid on a jar of molasses. Despite his father-in-law's reassurances over the telephone, he somehow doubted he'd find his daughter in one living, breathing piece—until he'd seen Amanda's smile. At last, he caught his breath, quelled the inexorable giggles, and steadied himself against the banister.

"Has she been able to tell you how it happened?" he asked. "I mean, Vincent filled me in about the balcony rail giving way, but why was she up there in the middle of the night? Were the three kids playing rough or something?"

Amanda shook her head. "Jennifer was the only one out of bed. She said she was having trouble sleeping and was just walking around the studio. She looked over the balcony edge and her hair ribbon slipped off. She grabbed for it. Before she knew what was happening, she'd gone over the edge."

"Do you believe her?" he asked seriously.

Amanda frowned, puzzled. "Why shouldn't I?"

"You know how kids are. . . . They get horsing around, start playfighting. Things get out of hand."

"Christy was sound asleep when Jen's scream woke me. John was still in bed. I'm sure that's where he was when she fell." She hesitated. "They were all getting along famously, Frank. If you're thinking that one of them push—"

"I'm accusing no one of wrongdoing," he cut in hastily. "It just seems odd . . . the circumstances. But you said you believe her?"

"What other explanation is there? Besides, she won't talk about it. When I bring up her fall, she seems embarrassed and changes the subject. I think she figures this was the ultimate klutzy faux pas."

He nodded, still thinking. "I can imagine her mind working like that. She seems obsessed with what she views as her physical deficiencies." He stared past Amanda.

"As painful as the process is, they all outgrow these stages, Frank," she whispered gently. His eyes refocused on her and he smiled. "Do you want to see her now?" she asked.

"Of course." He followed her up the stairs, talking as they climbed the creaking boards. "I haven't been able to come home for months at a time. Kids change so fast. Since we can't talk on the telephone, I'm sometimes afraid she'll stop thinking of me as her father."

"You worry too much," she scolded.

They stopped side by side in the bedroom doorway. Jennifer was propped up on Amanda's bed with John and Christy sitting like bookends on either side of her. A bowl of dry cereal nestled in her lap, from which all three were snacking, their eyes riveted on a TV show. Slowly Jennifer's glance drifted from the screen to take in her visitors.

"Daddy!" she cried, spilling the cereal in a futile attempt to extricate herself from the tangle of sheets and pillows.

He crossed the room in two long strides and Christy ducked out of his way as Frank gingerly hugged his daughter. After a moment, he pulled back to examine battle scars.

"Well, you *are* in one piece just as Amanda promised. Not bad for bailing out at five thousand feet over a ballroom."

"Oh, Dad, it wasn't *that* big a fall!" she moaned.

"Still, you deserve a medal for bravery." He drew a small white envelope out of his coat pocket and pressed it into Jennifer's left hand.

"Ooh, what is it?" Christy gasped. She dove back onto the bed, her dark eyes sparkling with envy and curiosity.

"I bet it's a scarab," John teased. "That's an Egyptian bug."

"Is not!" Jennifer stated firmly. "My dad wouldn't play a mean trick like that." She fumbled, trying to break the seal with her good hand, refusing all offers of help. At last, she tore off one end between her teeth and shook out the contents.

A delicate gold locket spilled onto the blanket.

She held it out for Amanda to clasp around her neck, then admired it. "It's *s-o-o-o* pretty," she said wide-eyed.

"I bought it for your birthday but decided to give it to you a little early. There's a place inside for pictures," he told her. He'd imagined his and Caroline's.

"Can I put anyone I want in here?" she asked.

Frank looked at her, surprised. "Well . . . of course."

"Jenny's got a boyfriend! Jenny's got a boyfriend!" Christy chanted, giggling.

Jennifer threw a pillow at her, then mayhem broke out—pillows, stuffed animals, and cereal puffs flying. A few minutes later, Amanda restored order by talking the three combatants into a game of Monopoly. Frank stood back and marveled at the scene. The room looked as if it had been hit by a tornado, his daughter's face was black and blue, and he had no idea where in the world his wife was, but he felt happier than he had in years.

Amanda watched Frank's expression as he backed out of the room. Love glowed through deep layers of fatigue. She thanked God that Jennifer hadn't been more seriously hurt or worse. How could she have ever told this man that his only child had died while under her care?

"She's doing great, Frank. Relax," she encouraged after shutting the bedroom door behind them.

He nodded. "Thank you for taking such good care of her."

"She seems like one of my own," she admitted. "The three of them get along so well."

"I noticed." He shuffled his feet. "The car is waiting downstairs."

"Oh, I'd forgotten!" She shook off a pang of disappointment that he was leaving so soon. "Well, what are your plans?"

"Plans?" He seemed momentarily at a loss.

"Are you staying at Gray Cliffs for a while or taking Jen back to Potomac right away?"

He scratched his head, an effort that appeared the limit of his strength. "I hadn't thought. My brain stopped functioning somewhere over the Atlantic."

"Why don't you send the car back and stay here tonight. It's getting late and Jen's cot is free in the children's room. I promised her that she could sleep with me."

"That's motherly of you." He smiled.

She grinned back at him, her cheeks warming in response to the approving look in his eyes. "You're exhausted. Get a good night's sleep, puzzle things out in the morning. By then we should have tracked down Caroline."

"That sounds like an intelligent solution," Frank agreed.

He ran downstairs, spoke briefly with the driver, then rejoined Amanda in the upper-floor kitchen. She handed him a cup of hot coffee.

"I'm making myself a sandwich. I've been so busy today, I don't remember eating. Want one?"

"That would be wonderful," he answered gratefully. "Let me help, though."

They stood side by side at her kitchen counter. He sliced some ham from a leftover chunk of meat and found cheese in the refrigerator while she spread bread with mayonnaise, sliced tomatoes, and pulled leaves off a crisp head of lettuce.

Amanda was shocked that Frank seemed so at ease in a kitchen. As far as she knew, he'd grown up with servants in his parents' houses, and wherever his own home happened to be in the world, there was always a cook. Perhaps the Marines had taught him to be self-sufficient.

They chatted about his circuitous route home. She was

amazed that he'd made it to Connecticut in such a short time but was glad he was here now, for an enormous load of responsibility seemed to have been lifted from her.

"How did the summer go for the studio?" he asked.

"Great!" she responded brightly. "The dance camp program was full with a waiting list. The program brought us a lot of new students, many of whom will carry over into fall classes. And whenever we enroll a new youngster, that puts us in touch with adults in his or her family who might be interested in lessons for themselves."

"Ballroom?"

"Mostly, although we do have two adult ballet classes. But, yes, adults are mostly interested in ballroom dancing. A wedding comes up—their own or a family member's—and they want to be able to waltz with the bride or groom without stepping all over their feet. So they sign up for what we call survival lessons. Before long, they discover how much they enjoy dancing, even if there isn't the pressure of a public affair breathing down their necks. They continue taking lessons. Some go on to compete as amateurs, others just dance for the exercise and as a way of meeting nice people."

Frank listened, laying slices of ham over the bread she'd prepared. He was acutely aware of every movement Amanda made, only inches away from him. The turn of her cheek, the slim line of her arm as she reached in front of him for a plate, the way she stood on one foot with one hip slightly higher than the other. He was also aware of sounds emanating from the next room—his daughter and Amanda's children reacting to the roll of the dice, hooting when someone landed on Park Avenue—and *she* was so close.

He felt as if he could say anything to Amanda, anything except what he was thinking at this moment. Because then she'd despise him, for what he was thinking was wrong. He felt as if he were tumbling down through an interminably dark well with no other place to go but down . . . down . . . down. Maybe fatigue was conjuring up this hopeless image. Or maybe he felt close to her because they'd shared fear for the sake of his child. But as they talked into the night like old friends or new lovers, he felt more intimately connected with her than he'd been with any other woman in his life. And that included the one person he should feel close to—Caroline, his wife.

He argued with himself. *We've known each other for nearly fifteen years. It's reasonable that we should feel some amount of familiarity. She is thirty-five. I am forty-nine. Just right for old friends. All wrong for lovers. Be a friend to her.*

Frank reached out to close a sandwich at the same moment Amanda stretched her hand toward the top slice of bread, and their fingertips touched.

Amanda's hand froze midair. She didn't dare look at Frank. She felt suddenly short of breath, alive in every nerve, as if she'd been running on automatic for the last eight hours and only this second became aware of her surroundings. Every detail of the room sparkled with unusual clarity.

She expected Frank to withdraw his hand immediately, the way strangers or mild acquaintances do when they inadvertently brush against one another on a bus—an anonymous contact of flesh. But this was different. Oh, so different.

All of their letters, their shared joys, the birth and growth of their children, the confided embarrassments and worries —although they were more often than not separated by thousands of miles—conspired to fashion of them the dearest of friends. And now, as his forefinger slowly traced the delicate, tingling spaces between her fingers, she knew they were moving beyond the sort of closeness that she and Sara or she and Caroline had known. This was an intimacy only a man and woman could share.

Blood rushed into her head, her ears thrumming with its warm pulse, and her eyes dropped, mesmerized by the motion of his hand as it stroked hers with infinite tenderness.

She drew a shuddering breath. "What are we doing, Frank?"

"Making sandwiches." His voice sounded casual, innocent of emotion. She stared up into his face and saw that she had, after all, been right. His eyes were dark, intense, and troubled.

"Are you sure?"

There was a long silence while Amanda breathed in and out, in and out, consciously trying to slow her heart rate . . . not succeeding.

"Do you know how long I've loved you?" Frank whispered.

"Don't say that!" she choked out, panic swelling in her throat. *Move your hand, Amanda. Move your damn hand before it's too late!*

"It's true. I think I began to love you the moment I first read one of your letters." He looked into her eyes, and Amanda's heart melted. She couldn't force her hand to retreat even an inch while he continued stroking its soft hollows and mounds. "I have a confession. That letter wasn't even for my eyes. You wrote to Caroline soon after we arrived in Naples, but she left the letter out. So there I was, curious about my wife's best friend, maybe because I was attracted to you from the start or maybe because I thought you'd help me better understand Caroline, who was as much a puzzle to me then as she is today. And I learned who you were through the words you wrote in that round, flowing hand. I liked the person who'd written them. I wanted to know you better."

Amanda absorbed his words with mixed horror and gladness. But once said, there was no taking them back. It seemed to be her turn. "The first time we met, I was in awe of you," she admitted, no longer censoring her own thoughts.

His lips curled upward at the corners. "Why?"

"Because of who you were: a distinguished diplomat." She blushed, embarrassed. "And I thought you were all wrong for my wild, beautiful Caroline because of how you looked. Like a conservative New England banker. But of course I didn't dare tell Caroline she'd chosen the wrong man. You were her idol, her dream man in the flesh, the source of everything she wanted in life."

"And she was the woman I'd conjured up as my perfect mate."

270

Amanda swallowed, squeezing her eyes shut for a moment. "How can we be so wrong about choosing our life partners? Why do we make such terrible mistakes?"

"Because we're not perfect. None of us are."

Amanda started to move. She didn't know whether it would be away from or toward Frank. She couldn't breathe, couldn't think for the pounding in her head. *No, not toward!* She had to get out of the kitchen to escape both him and the question hammering at her mind, *What if I'd married Frank instead of Robert?*

He anticipated her bolting and stepped behind her, putting her between himself and the kitchen counter. His arms enclosed her, keeping her there.

With a sense of sweet resignation, Amanda rested her head forward on his chest. "Oh, Frank" was all she could manage.

A second passed, a minute, longer . . . They held one another in silence, absorbing the warmth of one another's bodies, drinking in an eternity of love although they'd found each other late in their lives. Gradually, Frank shifted a couple inches away from her to look into her moist eyes. Then he slowly lowered his head and kissed her on the lips.

Amanda sensed that he'd intended the kiss as both a hello and parting gesture. A sign to seal their confessions as well as to bury them. But her fingertips curled themselves around the back of his neck, and her mouth opened to drink him in, and the kiss deepened, carrying them away.

At last their lips separated by a fraction of an inch.

"I swore I wouldn't let this happen," Frank whispered. "I swore I would never do to Caroline what she's done to me."

"You mean, have an affair?"

"Yes. But then *this* . . . what you and I have . . . has become so much more serious than an affair."

"We can keep our friendship, just not do anything about the rest of our feelings," she said sadly.

He lifted her chin and looked into her eyes, his left arm still holding her close. "Can we, Amanda? Do you believe that's actually possible?"

"We must try. Ripping apart two families to satisfy lust is—"

271

His finger pinned her lips. "No, don't say that. Lust isn't what this is about."

Tiny tear droplets formed in the corners of her eyes. "Then why do I want you to make love to me? Why do I feel as if I'll dissolve into a billion molecules and sink through this damn floor if you don't love me this very minute?"

He shut his eyes, swallowed once with enormous effort, then looked straight at her. "I was praying you'd be the strong one," he rasped. "That you'd throw me out."

"I can't do that."

His mouth fell on hers, hot and urgent, and his hands smoothed upward over her ribs to rest on the soft sides of her breasts. Again they were lost in a long, deep kiss. Amanda's knees buckled, and her head spun with aching delight and agonizing sadness.

Too soon, Frank pulled away. "Then I have to do this for us. I'm going to Gray Cliffs for the night."

"Now?" she gasped.

"If I don't leave this minute, I won't be able to at all."

She nodded numbly, incapable of speaking.

"I'll come for Jennifer in the morning and take her home to Potomac. When will . . . when will Robert be home?"

"Next week. I'll go back to the apartment on the base," she said bleakly.

He nodded and stepped clear of her, breaking the warm connection between their bodies. "Take care of yourself, Amanda."

She turned away, grasping the edge of the counter, unable to watch him leave. Staring at the unfinished sandwiches, she heard him speak briefly to Jennifer in the other room, heard him say good night to John and Christy, then hurry down the steps. The street door clacked open and banged closed.

Amanda wondered how he'd get to Groton since he'd sent the car away, then realized how ludicrous her concern was. He'd come halfway around the world in one day without a ticket. He was capable of anything, she believed in that moment. He'd probably hike the half mile to the foot of State Street and pick up a cab from the line in front of the train station. And all the time she pondered these inconsequential details, she didn't shift one muscle, didn't breathe, but she was acutely aware of the rhythm of her own body, humming in high gear, needing this man who'd taken the only sensible action for both of them by walking away.

The following week, Amanda moved back into the apartment on the sub base. Robert returned from San Diego, restless and intent as usual on reestablishing his authority over everything and everyone around him. He was unhappy with the quality of their furniture, yet unwilling to use any of his savings to replace it. He was discontent with his continuing restriction from commanding a ship, yet unwilling to alter his lifestyle to accommodate the navy or anyone else.

Irrationally, the worse he behaved, the more guilty Amanda felt.

I've done nothing wrong! she told herself again and again. But she would have done something inexcusable if Frank hadn't left her after two kisses. She would have willingly, joyfully made love to her best friend's husband. And, she realized, she and Frank wouldn't have stopped after one passionate indiscretion. For she knew now that she loved him, had undoubtedly always loved him, and that once they'd consummated that love, she could never have gone back to a cold marriage that survived only out of habit.

She set out to erase Frank from her mind and heart. To that end, she threw herself into the fall schedule of classes at the studio, wrote fresh ads for the newspapers, suggested to Nick that they prepare for a more aggressive competitive year. But no matter what her body was doing, her heart kept Frank close. She wondered what he was doing at any given hour of the day or night, recalled how his wise hazel eyes had a habit of surprising her with illusive humor or a greedy passion for life.

She read the *New York Times* religiously, watching for articles on Chad. She scanned the lines of dense print for the chance mention of Frank's name, always glad when she didn't find it, for newspapers invariably focused upon victims. She didn't know if he'd gone straight back to Africa or had stayed in Potomac for awhile. She ached to call, to find out how Jennifer was doing, but was afraid Frank might answer, the sound of his voice pitching her back into the black void of needing him. Or, worse yet, Caroline might pick up and read her thoughts and hate her for wanting her husband. At one time they'd known each other so well they'd been able to decipher their most intimate emotions.

Amanda counted the hours, desperately trying by day to forget Frank, Caroline, and even Jennifer. But at night she pushed her pillow aside and pressed her cheek flat on her mattress to remind herself of how it had felt to rest against the firm muscles of Frank's chest. She imagined him holding her again, imagined his lips crushing moistly against hers, and her blood pressure shot upward in response. She prayed he'd be safe wherever he traveled and that Caroline would come to her senses and love him again, because he was such a good man and deserved happiness. Then she felt nauseous because she couldn't bear the thought of Frank making love to another woman, especially, most awfully, to her friend.

14

In the cab on the way from Dulles International to the house in Potomac, Jennifer fell asleep. For the first time in years, Frank carried her upstairs to her bedroom. He didn't undress her as he had done when she was little, knowing when she woke up she'd be embarrassed to find out that her father had seen her naked. She would always be his little girl, but she thought of herself as grown-up. He laid her on top of her bed, covered her with a light quilt, dropped a kiss on her forehead, and turned out the light.

He had a raging headache and took two aspirin, then made himself a cup of hot tea and took himself with his valise into his study. He'd brought work from Chad. Now that he was in the States, he would be pressed by the department to meet with scores of people. He had been appointed interim ambassador two months earlier when Ambassador Wilson had resigned. As the fatherhead figure of an American legation abroad, he felt compelled to return as quickly as possible to his post. The situation in Chad was too damn unstable to trust.

He would stay as short a time as possible in Washington. He'd brief the secretary of state on developments in Chad,

275

meet with the press, politic with several human rights groups that were concerned about atrocities rumored to have been committed by Rami's old enemy, Nicolae Ceauşescu. Life in Romania, according to recent underground reports, had become intolerable, although the old despot had somehow managed to remain lily white in the eyes of the foreign press.

But, above all, Frank needed to find Caroline and make sure that Jennifer would be properly cared for in his absence. When it came down to it, he didn't want to leave Jen at all, but he knew he had no choice. Chad, in these days of unrest, was no place for a young girl, and he must return to N'Djamena, for he had another family to protect.

He opened his valise on his desktop, took out a sheaf of papers, and stared at them while sipping his tea. He couldn't concentrate. Through the lines of type, he saw Amanda's lovely face turned up to gaze at him.

When he'd returned to the studio to pick up Jennifer the next morning, he and Amanda had barely spoken two words. She avoided his eyes, and he wished to God he could think of something to bring back the easy camaraderie they'd shared over the years in their letters and family visits. But he was at a loss. He'd weakened and kissed her and confessed to loving her. The price had been high.

She said only in parting, "Take care of yourself, Frank. Drop us a note when you can."

Us. The family. Safe words with a message: *Don't think of me as your lover. We're friends, no more than that.*

"I will," he promised. "You, too."

It was terrible. He'd felt physically sick.

He'd stayed with Jennifer at Gray Cliffs for most of that day, still trying to reach Caroline, still having no luck.

He had no idea what he'd do if she didn't show up soon. He didn't trust the latest intelligence reports that indicated northern and southern factions in Chad would likely reach some kind of accord in the next month. Pain sliced through his temple. He wondered if he should have taken something stronger.

Then he heard a car pull into the driveway.

Frank had two cups of tea on the kitchen table before Caroline breezed in.

"Darling! What a lovely surprise!" Looking genuinely delighted, she crossed the room to kiss his cheek.

"You don't seem particularly surprised to see me," he commented drolly.

"I saw the lights on. It had to be you or a rather stupid burglar. I was hoping it was you."

"How reassuring."

She frowned. "A little testy, are we? What's wrong? Is it something to do with Chad? Are the natives restless, darling?"

He could hold back his anger and frustration no longer. "I've tried for days to find you. No one had any idea where you were! Where the hell have you been, Caroline?"

She drew off her driving gloves, studying him calmly over the tips of the doeskin fingers. "I was at Mary Ellen's, in Denver. You don't know her, but we've become very close while working together on the National Art Guild fund-raisers."

"A ready enough answer."

"Call her and ask if you don't believe me."

"I'm sure she'll corroborate every word," he snapped coldly. Then he pulled in a deep breath, resisting the temptation to call her bluff. He must get to the point.

"Jennifer had an accident. You couldn't be reached, so Amanda sent a message to me by way of the department, and I flew in from Africa."

"She what? Oh—" she gasped belatedly. "Is Jenny all right?"

"Jen's going to be fine. She survived a nasty fall at the studio."

Caroline glanced petulantly toward the stairs leading to the second floor. "That child is so clumsy. I don't know what I'm going to do with her. What happened? Did she twist her ankle or something?"

"It was a little more drastic than that. She fell from the balcony."

"The balcony! How did she manage that?" Reading the expression of distaste in his eyes, she trapped a laugh halfway up her throat. "Well, I take it she wasn't seriously hurt."

"Two cracked ribs, one broken arm, and assorted bruises."

"Good grief, is she . . . is she here or in the hospital?" For the first time, Caroline looked truly concerned.

"Jen's in her room. She'll want to see you, then we have to talk."

He sat down at the heavy oak butcher block table, one of Caroline's prize auction buys, and waited, knowing she wouldn't stay long with her daughter. Jen was such a loving kid. He'd never understood why it was so difficult for Caroline to be a mother to her. Perhaps if their daughter had been born a mirror image of Caroline, his wife would have developed a genuine fondness for her.

He looked up when Caroline reentered the room. She had brushed her blond hair into shining waves over her shoulders, reapplied lipstick, and tidied up her travel-worn mascara.

Caroline turned on a brilliant smile. "Well, as you said, it looks as if she'll survive." She sat across the table from him. "How about something stronger than tea?" she asked. "This is one hell of a shock."

"Certainly." He went into the parlor, mixed her a Scotch and soda in a short crystal tumbler, and returned to the kitchen to hand it to her.

She sipped. "You said we had to talk. I assume that means there's another crisis of some sort."

She looked at him from beneath her long lashes, and he was struck anew by how beautiful she was. Too beautiful, perhaps, for her own good. She'd learned to use her looks, cunningly, calculatingly, and it repulsed him to observe her practicing her art on him.

"I'd call it a crisis," he pronounced grimly. "You were nowhere to be found when your daughter needed you."

She rolled her eyes. "Oh, for godsake, Frank, don't lay a guilt trip on me! How was I supposed to know the kid would break her arm?"

"You decided to remain in the States to be with her."

"Yes, and I have."

"But you were off with a . . . *a friend,* leaving no word of your whereabouts with Amanda, your parents, or anyone else in case of an emergency."

"Amanda's perfectly capable of handling anything that might come up. Anyway, she's better with kids than I am." She sighed, momentarily humbled, then winked saucily at him. "But then again, I have my talents, too."

He ignored her obvious attempt to distract him. "That's copping out."

"It's the truth. I admit I'm not an earth mother. That doesn't mean I don't care about my daughter."

"What about me? I needed you."

She looked surprised, then puzzled. "You did?"

"I shouldn't have left Chad at a time like this. Too many people are counting on me."

She shook her head. "If I know the kind of people you're talking about, they always scrape by somehow. I don't know why you let yourself get so emotionally wrapped up in these causes!"

"Anyone who had a heart couldn't help but sympathize with the people of Chad," he said pointedly. "But it's not just the Africans I'm concerned about, it's the embassy and the agencies under my jurisdiction. I'm responsible for those folks, Caroline."

"Oh, Frank." Casting him an irritated look, she put down her glass. "Do you think the world revolves around you? Just do your job and come home."

"They are human beings. They matter," he said simply.

"I suppose that's supposed to imply I'm a coldhearted bitch?" she retorted. "Listen, Frank, whether you're willing to admit it or not, you're treading a very thin line. It's dangerous, what you're doing. I was talking with Barry McKinley, last week." McKinley was assistant secretary of state. "A lot of department people are nervous about you. You've bucked policy all of your career. One wrong step now, and the word is they'll pull you out of the ambassador's seat and stick you with a home office desk job."

The muscles in the back of his neck hardened reflexively. "Let them try it."

"You'll destroy your career!"

A sense of cold truth settled over him. "Here we go again, Caroline. Is it my career you're worried about or your personal prestige?"

She straightened defensively in her chair. "If you want to know the truth, I've been humiliated more than once when someone mentioned your name at a party. You're developing a reputation as a troublemaker."

"Good, making a few waves often gets something accomplished."

She grabbed for her drink and gulped a long draught. "You are not the man I married," she muttered.

"And you have never been the woman I believed you were."

She glared at him furiously. Then, gradually, the light of logic returned to her frosty blue eyes. She'd recognized what she had, what she might lose, and took the necessary conciliatory step backward.

"So, we're even," she stated with forced mildness. "That doesn't mean we have to be enemies. You can do your thing, and I can do mine, as long as we're both discreet enough not to shake things up." Her eyes met his, conveying her meaning.

"If you want permission to sleep with whomever you choose, I won't give it," he said.

"I haven't said a word about infidelity. I just need my space. I'll still be your hostess. Just give me two weeks' notice, and I'll entertain a hundred, five hundred! I'm damn good at what I do, Frank."

She looked pleased now, as if she were striking a reasonable bargain for all concerned. As he watched, she rose from the chair, crossed to him, and knelt, laying a petal-soft hand on his knee.

"Come on, let's make up," she whispered.

"If this is your idea of a marriage," he said quietly, "I want out. I think we should get a divorce."

She looked at him with alarm. "There's another woman!"

"No, there isn't."

"I know you, Frank. If there were no woman, divorce wouldn't enter your mind. Well, forget it. I'm perfectly happy as things are." She stood up with a jerk. "And don't try to start anything with a lawyer or I'll have my father's attorney seek a restraining order. You'll never see Jennifer again."

Blood rushed from his face. He shot up out of his chair and glared into her angry eyes. "You have no grounds!"

She shrugged. "I'll sing a song of abuse to the courts and press."

"You wouldn't make up a lie like that!"

"Try me. Divorce would be a messy proposition, Frank. Take my word for it." She trailed a finger down the line of pearl buttons on his shirt front. "Think what it would do to your career, to your precious little Jennifer."

Suddenly he felt weak, defeated. He had no doubt she'd carry out her threat.

Returning to her own chair, Caroline picked up her glass. "Don't look so down, darling. I'm not asking for much. Status quo will do. Just watch the boat. Don't rock too hard."

Frank had a briefing the next day at ten A.M. with the secretary, a press conference at noon, and a meeting with an Afro-American group interested in encouraging Chadian refugees to immigrate to the United States. He ordered reservations for his return flight to Paris on TWA, from there on Air Afrique to N'Djamena. He knew Caroline would do nothing to physically harm Jennifer. Anyway, within a week she'd be back at her school in New Hampshire. There seemed nothing more he could do about their relationship, at least for the time being.

Wednesday morning at five, the telephone rang at his side of the bed. He reached for it, still half asleep.

"Yes?"

"Ambassador, this is Jay Sanderson, State Department. Sorry for waking you, sir."

He was instantly alert. "I remember you, Sanderson. What is it?"

"We've just received word that intense fighting has broken out in all sectors of N'Djamena. The international district is caught in rocket attacks and automatic weapons cross fire."

"Any news of casualties?" Frank demanded. He was on his feet, carrying the cordless phone with him out of the bedroom and toward his study.

"None reported yet. Mansfield Warner and Barney Smith are holed up in the embassy. Luckily, most of the staff were in their homes when the city was overrun. Warner is staying on the radio, warning all your people to stay inside and not try to reach the chancery, since it's located in one of the areas suffering the heaviest shellings."

"Good." Warner was his political section chief. Smith headed the U.S. Information Agency contingent in Chad. Both were good men. *But I should be there, dammit! I am the one who should be assessing the situation, planning an escape route if the shelling keeps up, negotiating with faction leaders for safe passage.* "What information does intelligence have for us?"

Intelligence meant the CIA. They weren't supposed to be there, but then, they were everywhere these days.

"The government radio station has been hit and silenced. A number of quadrants have fallen to the rebels. Casualties on both sides are high. No numbers yet . . . sorry."

Frank was pulling papers out of his desk as they spoke, stuffing them into his valise. "I'm heading downtown right now. As soon as I get there, I'll want to send a message to Warner, then I'll leave directly for Chad. Have you arranged for my flights?"

Sanderson cleared his throat. "I'm afraid we can't get through to Warner. We lost communications with the chancery at oh-four-hundred hours. And, uh, sir . . ."

"What about my flight?" He was losing patience with the young attaché.

"Well, sir, my directions were to inform you that a crisis briefing has been called for nine A.M. at the secretary's office. No reservations have been made."

A cold sweat broke out on Frank's forehead as he imagined his people struggling to survive a civil war that had nothing to do with them. A number of his men and women had families in country. Others had children in the States.

He didn't want to have to tell any of those kids their father or mother had been hit by a stray rocket.

Amanda woke up before John and Christy. The house was quiet and she could have dozed for another half hour, but she liked to watch the morning news on TV over a cup of coffee before the madness of the day began. She switched channels to the CBS morning show, curled up on the couch, wrapping her worn but comfy chenille robe around her bare legs and sipped her coffee. The mug was a heavy red-glazed creation decorated with lumpy white hearts. John had made it for her one Mother's Day. She studied the deformed proportions, smiling fondly.

Suddenly, her ears pricked up at a familiar place name, and her heart stopped. Kevin Matthews, one of the network's star political reporters, was reading a statement before the camera:

"Fighting has been ugly and endless in N'Djamena since the rocket attacks began sometime yesterday. Because all communications with the American legation have been cut off, we have little information. But a reliable source at the State Department tells us that at least thirty Americans are trapped inside the city."

Amanda's hands began to shake. She clunked the mug down on the coffee table and listened with her heart in her throat. But there were no reassuring details.

Amanda jumped up and ran into the kitchen. She grasped the phone, punched in Caroline's number, then let it ring ten times. When Caroline at last answered it was in a sleep-slurred voice.

"Is Frank all right?" she demanded.

"Amanda? Wha—why shouldn't he be?"

"Fighting has broken out in the capital of Chad. I heard on the news just now. Is Frank—"

"No. No, he hasn't even left yet." Caroline sounded a little more awake now. "Thank goodness he came home for Jennifer, otherwise he'd be in the middle of that. Talk about luck."

Amanda breathed again. "What will he do?"

"I don't know. Oh, wait a minute . . . I think I remember

him saying something about a meeting. . . . I was still asleep. He's probably gone in to the department." She sounded bored. "They'll draft an official statement, make policy decisions, the usual sort of thing."

"I see."

"Hey, sweetie, thanks for taking care of Jennifer. You saved my skin, let me tell you."

"No problem," Amanda murmured. A wave of guilt broke over her. How could she talk to Caroline as if nothing had changed? She'd almost slept with her husband! Which made her think about Frank and Caroline in bed. Had they made love last night?

"I have to go," Amanda blurted out. "Please call me if anything happens, if Frank goes over. I want to know."

"You think he might? But that would be crazy. He wouldn't walk into a war. Would he?"

"I think he would if it meant getting his staff out," Amanda said. She felt hollow inside, wretchedly guilty, and frantic to escape from the sound of Caroline's voice. "I've got to go, really," she gasped.

"I'll let you know how things turn out."

"Yes, thanks."

The secretary of state put his leathery fingers together and rested his chin on the perch. He looked worn, like an old rug. Life hadn't been easy on him. In the past six months Americans had been taken hostage in Tehran, the U.S. ambassador to Colombia had been kidnapped in Bogotá, and the Soviet Union had invaded Afghanistan. There were rumors that he was ill, and the death of his son in an automobile accident the previous summer still weighted heavily on him. Frank wondered how many ways a man could be stretched before he snapped.

Nevertheless, Frank refused to accept the secretary's advice of a minute earlier: "We all just sit tight and see what happens next."

"We can't do nothing!" Frank objected. "Every minute we delay could mean American lives!"

General Patrick Paulson knocked a chunk of ash off of his cigar. "The secretary is right," he said calmly. "This sort of thing happens all the time in African countries. In another couple of hours, one side or the other is bound to run out of ammunition and head for the hills."

"I'm not willing to take that gamble," Frank ground out.

"There's nothing you can do that the French army can't," Paulson pointed out. "They still control the airport. If the situation stays hot and your folks can make it across the city, the French have agreed to airlift them to Paris."

"But I should be there to lead them out. That's my job!" Frank insisted.

The secretary looked around the table at his advisors. No one risked bucking the old man these days. They sat quietly. His bleary eyes focused on Frank. "If I were in your shoes, I'd feel the same as you do, Ambassador. However, I don't think it prudent to throw one more of *my* people back into the fire."

Frank rubbed his jaw, he'd forgotten to shave this morning but hadn't realized it until now. He thought about Warner and Smith and the others. Anger boiled up in his veins.

"Damn it, Mr. Secretary, you have no way of knowing what's going on in N'Djamena at this minute. Habre's FAN troops might take it into their heads that Americans have been collaborating with the national army and butcher anyone they can lay their hands on. Malloum's faction might figure on the reverse but end up doing the same. Remember the Congo ten years ago? The rebels tortured foreigners and threw what was left of them off of the highest bridge they could find! The few they spared that fate, they slaughtered and *ate!* Is that what you want to see in Chad, Mr. Secretary?"

General Paulson glared at him. "You, sir, are out of line!"

"No, George, it's all right," the secretary said, holding up a hand. "Frank, I won't argue with you. But we're not going to throw you back into the fray. Nothing would be achieved."

Frank squeezed his eyes shut for a second. When they opened they were burning bright. "Then send in a squad to get my people out."

"You mean a rescue attempt?" the secretary asked.

"Exactly. It may be easier than you think. If my staff members have followed directives and stayed in their homes, it's a matter of a handful of U.S. Marines going door-to-door, picking them up in a Jeep, and whisking them off to the airport."

"But, if the rocket attacks have driven them from the international quarter, they might be scattered across the countryside by the time our men reach N'Djamena," the secretary observed. "Isn't that right, General?"

"Exactly, sir."

"I realize we'd be putting more American lives in danger," Frank said, desperately searching for the right words to convince. "But every minute counts. You can't depend upon a half-dozen determined armies in the heat of a centuries' old civil war to wrap things up in a couple of days. Even if they don't turn against Americans, stray bullets and shrapnel will take a toll on civilians."

The secretary looked at him, then around the rest of the table. "Frank, I'm sorry. I've made my decision. We wait this one out, at least for a while. Gentlemen, that's all for now. When further developments arise, we'll be in touch."

Frank left the building in a black haze. He saw nothing as he stalked stiffly down the steps and into a steel-gray Washington morning. He didn't bother to return to his office or speak with anyone of his home staff.

He drove back to Potomac and when Caroline cheerfully asked if his day had been good, he bit her head off.

"Thirty Americans, my friends and co-workers, with their wives and children, are caught in the middle of a ruthless shooting war, and you ask if I'm having a nice day?" he demanded. He knew he shouldn't take out his frustrations on her, but her solicitude was so plastic and she too had pushed him against a wall.

"I was just trying to be pleasant," Caroline responded. She chewed her lower lip thoughtfully. "Remember, the Spanish ambassador's reception is tonight. I'll lay out your tux on the bed. The car will come by for us at seven."

"I'm not going."

She bristled, her eyes sparking with blue electricity. "We have to go. We RSVP'd!"

286

"I don't care if we signed our names in blood!" he roared. "I'm not going to any dinner party while my people are trapped and in God knows what condition. Send our regrets . . . or, better yet, *you* can go and deliver my apologies in person. That way you won't miss a good party." He stormed out of the room.

No official calls came that day although the phone rang incessantly as Caroline's friends in diplomatic circles called, curious about the developments in Chad. Frank took advantage of infrequent lulls to telephone Stateside family members and try, as best he could and with almost no reliable information, to reassure them.

Later that day, Caroline made a call to Chisolm School for Girls, arranging for Jennifer's arrival there the following week.

Frank didn't hear Caroline leave for the reception but knew she must have when the Potomac house took on a different sort of quiet. He'd expected she would go. Spain was one of her favorite vacation countries, and she enjoyed the special treatment the wife of a dignitary always received in a foreign country.

He made himself a plate of crackers and cheese with a couple slices of apple to snack on, returned to his study with it, and sat at his desk writing the official orders for all U.S. citizens to evacuate Chad and for the closing of the embassy. *Paperwork*, he thought, *official statements that count for nothing*. He raged inside with restlessness.

The next day, Frank drove downtown again. He arranged for a press conference and drafted a policy statement for review by the secretary. He didn't rock the boat. *Caroline should be proud of me*, he thought grimly.

He hung out at the office all afternoon, waiting for word. But radio communications still hadn't been reestablished with N'Djamena. He feared the worst and was nearly mad with worry.

At the end of the longest day of his life, he drove home. Jennifer was walking across the living room, looking less in pain today. He hugged her and asked how she was doing.

"Okay. I guess you've been pretty busy. I heard about

Chad." She looked up at him. "Guess you wish now you hadn't come home," she said.

Frank shook his head. "It was just crazy timing," he told her.

"I'm sorry," Jennifer murmured.

"It's not your fault, Jen." *And it's not mine,* a voice reminded him. He couldn't allow himself to fall into that trap.

"I'll make you a sandwich if you want one," Jennifer offered.

He didn't feel hungry, although he had eaten almost nothing all day. But he let her build him a ham and cheese on rye so that she would feel useful. When she handed it to him on a white china plate, he couldn't help remembering his last sandwich, which he'd never eaten.

For the first time in almost forty-eight hours he thought of Amanda. Now, in his time of torment, he longed to talk with her, and the sense of her loss was overwhelming. Conversations with Caroline brought him no solace. The sound of his wife's voice disgusted him; he resented the hold she held over him.

Jennifer kept him company in the kitchen while he ate. He asked her about school. She avoided the subject of friends and hobbies and chattered on about dresses she planned to wear for dances she hoped to go to, asking his opinion of styles and colors. He got the impression she'd never been asked by a boy to a dance, and his heart went out to her. She asked his advice on a new diet, but again, he had no idea what to tell her.

"I just don't know, Jen," he said, confused and flustered by the utterly female nature of her questions. "Why don't you call Amanda," he suggested. "I'm sure she was good at helping you with stuff like this during the summer."

"Yeah. I will tomorrow. Well, I better go to bed. I'm really beat."

"Sure, sweetheart." He kissed her on the forehead. "Sleep well."

"You should go to bed, too," she told him in a motherly tone. "Sounds like you have a big job ahead of you."

288

Yes, he thought regretfully. *And part of that job may be recovering bodies.*

Frank sat alone in the kitchen, staring at white cabinets, white countertops, white table and chairs and ceiling and coordinated appliances. The mention of Amanda had made him itchy. Without thinking about what he was doing, he pushed up out of his chair, crossed to the phone on the wall, and pressed the numbers for the studio in Connecticut.

An answering machine picked up. Amanda's voice told him the days and hours the studio was open. The beginner classes still had openings. A new adult ballroom class would be starting in two weeks and would emphasize dances suitable for weddings and holiday parties. He listened to the whole recording, amazed that the calm tone of one woman's voice could slow his heart rate. Her constancy and caring bathed every word. His burning nerves cooled even as her voice invited the caller to leave a message.

After the beep, he cleared his throat and said unsteadily, "Hello, Amanda. It's Frank. I just wanted to . . . to let you know that I'm okay and—"

"Frank!" She'd been monitoring her machine. "Oh, I'm so glad you called. All day I've been listening to the news bulletins about Chad. Caroline told me you hadn't gone back when the fighting started!"

"In some ways I wish I had," he admitted.

"You couldn't have done anything," she said softly.

"I know . . . logically, I know that. But I feel so damn helpless. I broached the subject of sending in a special force."

"And?"

"No go. Official policy stands—we don't interfere with a host country's internal problems, unless they ask for help."

"But what if they can't—you know—work things out quickly and protect your people?"

"I don't know, Amanda." His head pounded, his heart ached, and he could no longer discern the pain of being away from his duty from the pain of being away from her. Somehow, illogically, they seemed tied together.

She was silent for several minutes. "Frank, you want to go back, don't you?"

"Yes."

"I guessed as much."

It was like her to understand. He sat in silence, twisting the receiver wire around his finger, at a loss for how to continue the conversation or end it.

"It's not easy," she whispered at last, "being apart from you. I swore I wouldn't say this but I can't help it. I—"

"Please don't, Amanda," he interrupted, unable to listen to her say that she loved him. The words would kill him. "It's just as hard on me. But Caroline and I—we've had a—"

"A reconciliation?" she guessed breathlessly when he hesitated for a heartbeat.

"No. Quite the opposite. I asked her for a divorce. She's made it clear that she's not willing to give me one. She wants everything to remain as it is."

"Maybe she still loves you," she murmured weakly.

"I doubt it. Not in any way I can comprehend."

She remembered her last conversation with Caroline. It had been brief, almost cool compared to those they'd once shared, baring their souls to one another. The reason for this was, of course, that neither of them was being honest. Caroline cheated on Frank and refused to admit it to Amanda. Amanda was in love with Caroline's husband. The impasse colored everything between them.

"As her oldest friend, I can talk to her about a divorce if you thought it might help," Amanda offered. "I'm sure, in the long run, she'd be happier, too. But it would seem self-serving, to say the least."

"Yes, I suppose so. Probably, it would do no good anyway. She's determined to keep me, keep Jennifer, keep her houses and social standing. We're all prizes to her. But, as long as my people are in jeopardy, I can't waste time agonizing over a dead marriage. I have to get them out of Chad before I can think of anything else."

Amanda drew a labored breath. "Frank, I'm scared. I don't want to lose you. I know that sounds strange because I don't really *have* you. You belong to someone else, and I do, too. But you've always been there for me. Always . . ." she ended in a plaintive whisper.

Frank flinched, surprised that she'd actually read his mind. And now he realized that it was *she* who had kept him going through the long day of waiting word. Her love was so strong, the miles dissolved between them.

"If I go," he promised, "I'll be careful."

"You do that."

He ought to hang up now, but he needed to drink in her voice for just another minute. "John and Christy are well?"

"They're getting ready to start school. John is enrolled in an honors class in political science. He talks about you all the time. I think he has ambitions to steal your job. Christy's auditioning for a special tutorial program for young dancers at Connecticut College."

He smiled. "Good for both of them."

There was nothing more to say. The future hung over them like a dark cloud.

At last Amanda spoke. "Frank, take care, please . . ."

"I will."

"I'll watch the papers and pray for your people over there."

"Thanks, they'll need it. I'll call or write when I can."

"I lo—"

He gently hung up the phone, unable to listen to the words. "I love you, too, Amanda," he whispered, safe because she couldn't hear him.

Caroline came home from the reception at two in the morning. She was evidently still angry with him for not accompanying her or for asking for the divorce or both. She took herself off to the bedroom without a word to him.

Frank spent the night in his study, drinking coffee and brainstorming possible ways of handling the situation in Chad. By seven the next morning, he'd made a decision, but it was too early to implement his ideas. Now that he'd determined his course of action, his appetite returned with a vengeance. He fixed himself a hearty breakfast of scrambled eggs, three slices of toast, sausage, sliced tomatoes, coffee, and orange juice. While he ate at his desk, he made notes.

At eight-thirty he called an old friend at Andrews Air Force Base, who made a few calls, then reported back to him that there was a cargo plane leaving for Frankfurt in a couple of hours. He made his own arrangements, not wanting to involve a junior officer and risk blame falling on his or her head for what *he* was about to do.

Amanda read the newspaper hungrily the next morning, but there was no word of the fighting letting up in Chad. All day long, she kept her radio tuned to an all-news station.

She tried to keep busy—shopping for school clothes and supplies, balancing the studio's bank statement, ordering ballet and ballroom shoes for her new students. Nick and Susan were expecting their first child. She brought John and Christy with her and dropped in on Susan at her apartment in New London to see how she was faring and to ask if there was anything she could do for her.

"I'm just fine," Susan said happily. She looked at Amanda with concern of her own. "Nick tells me you two plan to dance in eight comps this year. That's an awful lot, considering you have the studio and two kids to look after."

"I like to keep busy," Amanda said abruptly, offering no more explanation.

Susan shrugged. "Suit yourself."

They talked strategies for almost an hour while John and Christy played outside. Then Susan brought up an old topic.

"Have you decided whether you'll take up that offer to teach ballroom seminars at the University of Connecticut branches?"

"It's very tempting," Amanda admitted. "But I don't like the idea of leaving the kids with Robert for very long, even if he agrees to take them." His reliability hadn't improved.

Susan had offered her opinion of Robert only one time, and that was in succinct terms. "Dump him and find someone who'll treat you right. He's a jerk." But once that had been said, she never again mentioned him and now she approached Amanda's dilemma from another angle. "I could watch them," she offered.

"With a new baby on the way?" Amanda shook her head firmly. "No. I'll wait until the kids are older."

"Really," Susan insisted, "anytime you want to take off—for work or recreation—just say the word. I live so close to the school they could walk there and back. I'd love to have them for a while."

"We'll see," Amanda said. "Thanks."

Caroline didn't call, and Amanda didn't call her.

She tried to look forward to happier times when she and Frank might hope to be together. Possibly when Jennifer turned eighteen. She'd be old enough then to decide for herself where to live. Only then would Caroline lose her control over Frank.

But that wouldn't be for another five years and seemed an eternity away!

Then there was the matter of Robert and a number of very practical questions. The studio was holding its own but hadn't begun to turn much of a profit. If she left her husband, would she be able to stand on her own financially? She didn't want to have to turn to Frank for help, even though he'd offered many times over the years. She desperately wanted to be able to support herself and her children without anyone coming to her rescue. But if that wasn't possible right away, the only fair arrangement was for Robert to shoulder some of the burden of his children's support.

The following morning, while Rob slept, Amanda hustled John and Christy out of bed to get ready for their first day of school. She brought the newspaper inside and sat down with a cup of coffee at the kitchen table while the children dressed in clothes she'd helped them lay out the night before. When she unfolded the paper, a headline seized her eye.

AMBASSADOR DONNELLY RETURNS TO CHAD
TO LEAD AMERICAN EVACUATION EFFORT

Her hands shaking, Amanda reached for the phone. The line in Potomac, Maryland, was busy. She slammed down the receiver, her heart pounding. She dialed again. Still busy. She poured a second cup of coffee and rushed the kids to the table for breakfast, then popped them into the car. The drive to New London seemed to take forever. Sweat trickled down the crease of her back, although it was a cool September morning. She ran a stop sign without thinking about what she was doing. She pushed buttons on the radio as she drove, trying to find a news report.

After wishing John and Christy good luck on their first day back to school, she dropped them off in front of the red brick building. When she walked into the studio ten minutes later, the phone was ringing.

It was Caroline. "Have you heard?" she asked Amanda.

"Just now—I read in the paper." Amanda swallowed hard. "When did Frank leave?"

"Yesterday morning. I haven't heard from him since. Oh, Amanda, I'm so scared."

"I know. I—" She would have preferred for Caroline not to care. It was more like her old friend to say "The hell with Frank if he wants to get himself killed." It hurt to know that Caroline still cared for her husband, the man Amanda had let herself fall in love with. "What's happening?" she choked out at last.

"I haven't got a clue. The press doesn't have any facts yet either. And the department isn't telling dependents anything on the grounds of security. But the president is supposed to make a statement at noon."

Amanda nodded.

"Can you come down and stay with me, just till this is over?" Caroline pleaded.

Amanda was taken by surprise, but she couldn't say no to Caroline. She thought quickly about John and Christy. She'd call Susan and ask if she was serious about having the children visit. They'd much rather stay with her than with their grandparents. And she could get someone to cover her classes for her.

"I'll take Amtrak down. It's about a six-hour trip. I should be there tonight by six."

"I'll be waiting," Caroline said.

15

Frank arrived at the airport in N'Djamena. He was greeted by Garth Williams, attaché for agricultural affairs. Garth often dropped in at the chancery, but they normally had very little contact except during home-team meetings.

"I've put together a list of those not accounted for," Garth said. His face was drawn, and deep circles skirted his eyes. He had a nervous tick beneath one eye that Frank had never noticed before.

Frank read down the list of names. "According to this, at least half of my people are still in the city?"

"There or somewhere between the embassy and the airfield. There was no way to reach people other than shortwave radio. They may be receiving the broadcast directing them to meet here at the airport for evacuation but are unable to send. We have no way of knowing if they're on their way to the airfield or pinned down

Frank nodded. He had worked out a standard evac plan months ago on the chance they might need it. But because of the suddenness of this last outbreak, people had been caught in their homes sleeping.

"Are you senior officer?" Frank asked Garth.

"Until you arrived, sir."

"Right." Frank thought for a second. "We need to get everyone who's made it to the airfield together in one place. This hanger will be fine. We'll interview them, see if we can establish the last known locations of missing staff members and their families."

"Right." Wilson looked relieved to relinquish the reins of authority.

A half hour later, they were assembled in a hanger protected by the French army. Frank addressed his people —men, women, and children—feeling heartsick he'd deserted them at their time of need. If he'd been here, perhaps he'd have seen early warning signs and given the evacuation order before the shelling started. On the other hand, he'd had no way of knowing Jen would be okay. He'd had to see her for himself.

Frank spotted two young men who worked under Garth but were also CIA operatives. *Good,* he thought, *I'll be able to use you fellas.* There were also three Marine guards who, he was willing to bet, would prove invaluable.

While he and Garth questioned people about the missing staff members and their dependents, two of the secretaries took notes. At the end of an hour, they had a clearer picture of the quadrants of the city that should be searched first.

Again, he assembled the entire group in the middle of the French hanger and addressed them. "Thank you for your cooperation. I'm sure you want to know what will be happening next, how soon you can be transported to a safe location, and how we intend to find your co-workers and, in some cases, family members.

"Let me start by saying this: The French are staying out of this civil war. Their officers are under standing orders not to enter the city. That puts us in a vulnerable position. We can't depend upon them to rescue our folks. It's up to us." He looked around at frightened faces and spotted one little girl who appeared to be about nine years old. He gave her a reassuring wink.

"I need a total of eight volunteers to search the city in two teams—our three Marines plus five more, preferably people who have been in the military at one time or another and know how to fire a weapon. The French commander has already notified me that he'll unofficially lend us Jeeps and weapons, and we now have sound leads to follow up on. In the meantime, those staying behind will prepare to be flown to Paris and from there to the States.

The two CIA men volunteered immediately, as he knew they would—that made six, including himself. He turned down one of his staff because he knew the man had a bad heart and accepted a male attaché with the USIA.

Amanda stepped off the train at Penn Station in Washington, D.C. Commuters had long since departed, leaving the escalators that crawled up from the tracks thinly trafficked. Above on the dark street, she located the taxi line and asked the driver to take her to Potomac. The ride took nearly an hour, much longer than she had expected. She'd never been to Caroline's house before.

It was an elegant white-brick French Colonial, cradled in a circular drive and surrounded by lofty trees. Blue shutters, like butterfly wings, framed each tall window.

Amanda paid the cab and approached the double doors, solid mahogany from the looks. Shining brass carriage lights flanked them.

Then Caroline swung wide the doors and greeted her with a warm hug. "I'm so glad you could come. I'm insane with worry." Her hair hadn't been brushed, her makeup was smeared, probably a day old.

Amanda had never seen her in such a state. She swallowed over the guilty lump in her throat. *You do care,* she thought sadly. *Oh, God, why do we have to be in love with the same man?*

"Have . . . have you heard anything more?" Amanda asked.

"Nothing," Caroline stated as they crossed a soaring foyer with black and white marble squares underfoot and a circular staircase. On one side was a walnut-paneled library, floor to ceiling with leather-bound books. On the other, where they now adjourned, was a delicately decorated sitting room. "Apparently somebody leaked a few rumors to the press," Caroline continued, "but no one's sure what's going on."

297

"Oh." Amanda said. She wanted to leave, to run away from her anguish. But she'd promised Caroline . . . she'd promised her she'd come. "How is Jennifer taking this?" she asked.

"She's being impossible. I can't deal with her." Caroline threw up her hands in surrender. "You'd think *I* sent Frank over there. She says if I'd been *nicer* to her father, he wouldn't have gone back."

"She's looking for someone to blame for this madness," Amanda guessed, "trying to make sense of insanity."

"He didn't have to go, you know!" Caroline fumed. "His boss told him he was to sit tight. Frank ignored direct orders. Can you believe that? He'll either get himself killed or he'll be blacklisted in the department for insubordination! And on top of that, he leaves me with this nasty child who accuses me of sending him away!"

Amanda held her tongue. "Maybe I could speak with Jen?"

"I sent her back to school."

At first, Amanda didn't believe she'd heard Caroline correctly. But then, it was just like Caroline to ship off her problems, expecting someone else to sort them out later. Her heart swelled with pity for poor Jennifer, bearing the fear of losing her father on her own. She decided she would call her first thing in the morning to see how she was doing.

"Why don't you take your suitcase upstairs," Caroline suggested, "unless you need help." Amanda shook her head. She'd packed light, only necessities. "Good. Cook prepared us a late supper before she left for the day. I think I could eat something now that you're here."

When Amanda entered the kitchen, she found the table in the breakfast nook set with two shrimp salads arranged on tender arugula leaves, cantaloupe balls and cottage cheese, with crisp wheat crackers on the side. As the two women ate in silence, Amanda tried to force her emotions into some sort of order. She wanted Caroline to be happy. If her friend was happy with Frank, she should be happy for her— shouldn't she?

But regardless of Caroline and Frank's relationship, there

298

were some things that remained the same. And these were best discussed openly and immediately.

"I'm glad you called me to come down," Amanda began with difficulty. "I've wanted to speak with you about Rob for a long time. I guess I didn't know how. You and I seem to have gotten out of practice talking to each other."

"Rob?" Caroline picked daintily at her food, eyes downturned.

"I'm going to ask him for a divorce."

"Really?" Caroline didn't seem surprised, but a spark of interest shot through her blue eyes. "Why?"

Amanda glanced around the kitchen, a professionally decorated world of copper and stainless-steel gourmet pans hanging from long, clear brackets. The kitchen had a cathedral ceiling littered with glass skylights to let in the sunshine or starlight—as they did now—from above. Here everything was modern, bright, and ostentatiously expensive—just the way Caroline liked her kitchens. Her other rooms spilled over with antiques and old-world charm. It was as if she couldn't make up her mind who she was.

"I don't love him anymore," Amanda said at last.

"That's no reason for leaving a man. That's an excuse," Caroline stated.

Amanda drew a deep breath. "He's never grown up, Caroline. He doesn't love me or listen to anything I say, want, or dream. I'm part of his life but only to fill space, to keep his family intact. And he's so hard to deal with—"

"Aren't all men?" Caroline remarked dryly. She looked at Amanda's pained expression. "Oh, you mean the booze."

"Yes."

Caroline gnawed at her lower lip, her mind racing. She didn't want Rob roaming around unattached. He might take it into his head that he wanted *her* to dump Frank and marry him! He was fine as a lover. And, yes, she did love him, but he'd never make enough money to support her in style. She was a practical woman. The best she could do was to keep the situation stable.

If she could get Rob and Amanda back together, that would also extinguish any fires burning in Frank's heart.

And that was why she'd summoned Amanda to Potomac, to determine for herself the extent of their infatuation.

She had long suspected there was a lot more between them than an occasional letter swapping family news. She had found one of Frank's letters, half written, and months later discovered one from Amanda in her husband's briefcase. For years, their correspondence had seemed harmless. She kept tabs on Frank. She knew he hadn't been playing around. But she'd overheard his phone call to Amanda before he'd left for Chad. And now, looking into Amanda's eyes, she knew.

Amanda was in love with her husband. And there was nothing more appealing to a man than someone as sweet and pretty as Amanda gazing with open adoration at him. She could tolerate an occasional affair on his part—something heated and meaningless—but a serious relationship would poison her hold over him. She wouldn't relinquish him to anyone, least of all her old friend.

"Rob's a good guy, Amanda," she offered in his defense. "Why not give him another chance. You did love him once, didn't you?"

"Yes, I suppose," she admitted softly.

"Is there someone else?"

"Yes." Amanda had never been able to lie. "I can't talk about him though."

"No problem. Discretion is necessary sometimes."

"And you—" Amanda asked throatily. "Do you still love Frank?"

"Geez, is anyone in love with her husband?"

"I think it's possible," Amanda said carefully. "I think it's very possible to stay in love with the same person for a long time."

"Maybe that's what's wrong with your marriage, you expect too much." Caroline sucked the juice from a melon ball and swallowed it.

"How long do you suppose love lasts?" Amanda asked.

"Three months, six tops. If someone tells you different, they're lying. After that it's just sex or some other reason, like money."

"Is that why you stay with Frank? Money?"

"I stay with him for the same reason I married him. We're perfect for each other. We *need* each other, and that has nothing to do with love. At least I'm honest." She took in the agonizingly confused expression in Amanda's eyes with satisfaction. "He'd be lost without me," she stated conclusively.

Amanda stared at her as though unsure she was telling the truth. *Let her wonder,* Caroline thought with satisfaction. *He's mine and I'll keep him for as long as I want!* Suddenly, she wanted more than anything to inflict pain on her old friend, to pay her back for daring to imagine she might take Frank away from her.

"I take it that Robert and you are no longer . . . intimate?"

Amanda shut her eyes for an instant. When she opened them, she focused on her wedding band. "No. No, we're not—" She immediately changed the subject. "This is just a theoretical question, but if Frank ever left you—"

"I'd make him pay through his goddamn teeth," Caroline finished for her. Then she laughed lightly. "But he won't. We understand one another. Besides, who says a marriage has to be perfect to work? So the sex is sort of automatic sometimes; we can get off on other things."

From the flicker of shock in Amanda's eyes, she'd hit a bull's eye. "You mean, you are still . . . you make love?"

"Do you think the man could resist me?" Caroline laughed.

Amanda looked away, tears shimmering in her soft brown eyes.

"What's wrong, sweetie?" Caroline quickly came over to stand beside her. "Oh, I am an insensitive bitch. You're thinking about you and Robert. Sorry. Well, at least you have your other man. Right? The one you won't talk about—"

"I haven't had sex of any kind in over two years," Amanda blurted out helplessly. "And—and before that it was only once every couple of months or so."

"That stinks. And nothing from your friend on the side? I think you should find another guy who can take your mind off—"

301

Amanda jerked her head around and squinted up at Caroline. "Why would you say that? You know I've never slept around. Why aren't you encouraging me to seduce Rob?" She was angry and suspicious. "You want me to patch things up with my husband, give him another chance. Why not throw myself at him every night of the week?"

Caroline realized her error too late. The answer to Amanda's questions was simple: Caroline didn't want the man she was in love with sleeping with anyone but her.

"Changes are good," Caroline said quickly, struggling to save herself. "I could introduce you to some very talented young diplomats.

"No, thanks."

"You need a good fuck now and then!"

"I need a loving man, a man who honestly cares about me, my interests, my children—" With a look of horror on her face, Amanda dropped her head into the cup of her hands. She'd just described Frank. And they both knew it.

Time slid miserably, slowly by. At first, no one in the department even knew if Frank had arrived safely in N'Djamena, for he'd traveled outside of official circles. Then word arrived by way of the French ambassador to Washington that he'd made it as far as the French garrison near the N'Djamena airport. The news was small comfort to Amanda. It only meant that Frank was closer to the danger.

After staring at the phone for twenty-four hours and receiving no news at all about the condition of the Americans trapped in Chad, Amanda decided that she was incapable of sitting still any longer. Caroline agreed that they'd go mad if they didn't get out of the house.

They ducked a small contingent of the press corps that had staked out the house, drove into the city, and shopped at Woodward & Lothrop's. Two members of the Washington press corps caught up with them in the designer dress department. They enlisted the aid of a salesgirl to elude them. Slipping out a rear door behind the dressing rooms, they made it back to the car and drove to Carmichael's for a spectacular lunch that was supposed to take their minds off of Frank's jeopardy. Caroline nervously gobbled everything in sight, and Amanda nibbled, enjoying nothing.

Back at the house, Caroline called the department for an update and got nothing more than solicitous reassurances that everything possible was being done to remedy the situation. "They say that better lines of communications should open up before long. Maybe within a few hours."

Hoping for a call, they drank gallons of coffee to keep themselves awake. They played endless hands of double solitaire, poker, rummy, anything to preserve their sanity and pass the time. Night fell and grew thick and black. They made more coffee, switched to checkers.

When the cool, gray glow of dawn edged up over the willows along the Potomac River, the telephone rang and Caroline, who had fallen asleep on a couch, groaned and covered her head with a pillow.

Amanda pounced on the receiver.

"Mrs. Donnelly?" a woman's voice asked.

"If it's another reporter, tell the bastard to lay off," Caroline mumbled.

"Who is calling?" Amanda asked.

"This is Maureen Brown from the department. I have news of Frank Donnelly for his wife," the controlled voice said.

Amanda swallowed. *Tell me! Tell me this minute!* Her brain shrieked. Summoning up her strength, she held out the receiver for Caroline. "It's for you. The State Department."

Amanda sat tensely at Caroline's side, hearing only her end of the conversation.

"Yes. Yes . . . I understand . . . tomorrow. Then what? Thank you. Yes, I'll be there."

She hung up and only then cracked a smile. "The son of a bitch made it."

"Oh, thank God!" Amanda cried, hugging her as tears rolled uncontrolled down her cheeks. "Tell me . . . tell me what's been going on!"

"Frank found about half of his staff already at the airport. They weren't sure of the whereabouts of the rest. He led a contingent of volunteers in and got them out. The important thing is"—her eyes sparkled—"the vice president along with representatives from the department and Congress are meeting him at the airport tomorrow to give him a hero's welcome!"

"Oh, this is wonderful!"

Caroline looked suddenly sober. "This might just be a public show though. The fact is, Frank ignored direct orders. He'll probably be pulled from his ambassador's position."

"But he succeeded!"

"You don't understand politics, my dear. He made the department and military look like helpless fools. He ignored his superiors' commands. He broke rank."

Amanda shook her head. "That's not fair, he saved those people's lives."

"Fair isn't the name of the game. It was a stupid move." Her teeth were gritted, and then she brightened. "Well, the press will get word of this in a matter of minutes. Frank and the others are flying to Paris and will arrive at Andrews Air Force Base tomorrow at noon. Oh, God, I'll have to figure out what to wear. No white. The television cameras will make me look like a corpse."

Amanda stared at Caroline. She really was more concerned with her public image than the fact that her husband had survived.

"I'll help you pick out something appropriate," she offered dryly.

Caroline smiled at her, looking refreshed after only a two-hour nap, her spirits soaring at the prospect of being in the limelight. "You look terrible, darling. I can pick out my own outfit. Why don't you go on to bed and get some rest."

"I think I will," Amanda murmured.

At Andrews, Frank's diplomatic faux pas was treated as an unmitigated triumph. A band struck up the national anthem as the military jet eased down the runway toward a cheering throng of wives, children, parents, well-wishers, and members of the press. Military officers in dress uniform lined a hastily erected dias, the vice president and his wife standing among them.

Amanda hovered at the edge of the runway beside Caroline. She peeked at her friend's face as the plane rolled to a stop. Caroline was beaming, a stunning picture in her pastel pink silk suit with a flowered silk scarf knotted gracefully around her throat. Three airmen rolled stairs to meet the silver fuselage, and the door opened. Frank was the first to appear. He waved to the crowd, and a deafening cheer went up.

As the ABC camera swept the ranks of spectators, Caroline stepped from behind the Marine guards and ran toward the plane. Photographers swung around in time to catch her kissing her husband and weeping with apparent joy.

Amanda stood quietly within the crowd as she watched Caroline and Frank embrace. A jagged pain sliced through her breast, and she started shaking uncontrollably.

At last, Caroline released her husband and turned to toss the TV cameras a grateful kiss. Frank scanned the faces in the crowd as if looking for someone special.

He knows, Amanda thought. *He knows I'm here.*

She didn't move, didn't raise a hand to wave—it seemed too enormous an effort. But a moment later, their eyes met. Amanda could hardly bear the bittersweet pang of love that filled her every nerve. Frank was *alive!* And she'd never been more thankful for anything in her life. But he wasn't hers, and suddenly the choice of whether they could ever be together seemed to have been wrenched out of her hands.

An air force general approached Frank, and he turned away from her regretfully.

She watched as he shook hands with the line of officials offering congratulations for a job bravely done. Then the entire party retreated to the raised red-white-and-blue-bannered platform.

The base commander spoke briefly to the audience, describing a week of tense drama in Chad and the ambassador's part in saving American lives. Then Frank addressed the audience and press.

He summed up the rescue in as few and as simple words as possible. "This is not a time for gloating or slapping one another on the back, ladies and gentlemen. The evacuation from Chad was something that had to be accomplished.

Most of us made it out. For the loved ones of those who did not, I can only offer my sincerest sympathy and regret. We tried our best, I assure you." One of the Marine guards and a secretary, newly arrive in Chad only three weeks before hostilities broke out, had been killed in the shelling of the city.

Frank looked at Amanda. She gave him a tearful thumbs up. *I'm so very proud of you, Frank.*

Caroline stepped closer to Frank and took his hand as cameras whirred and flashes went off. Amanda stood, clapping her hands in heartfelt appreciation alongside men and women who didn't know Frank and Caroline and couldn't be expected to see that the woman at Frank's side sharing his glory would have stopped him from leaving the country if she could have.

But did that really matter? Watching Frank and Caroline now, Amanda was forced to admit that they *looked right* together, standing there on the dias. They were from the same world, bred for each other, complimented each other professionally and presented a public image that was perfect.

I am all wrong for him—too simple, nothing more than a high school education. I haven't a clue how to address a prime minister, book a caterer, or direct a staff of servants. All I can offer is my love. I belong in a little dance studio in Connecticut.

Too many differences existed between them, too many changes lay between now and some distant day when they could be together. Tears rolled down her cheeks as all the truths assaulted her at once, and she was too exhausted, too emotionally strung out to fight them off.

The base commander reclaimed the microphone to announce that a formal press conference would follow and then all evacuees and their families were invited to a reception at the White House. Then all hell broke out.

Before Frank could take two steps away from the speaker's platform, he was surrounded by wives wanting to thank him personally for saving their husbands' lives, by fathers who energetically shook his hand. Mothers embraced Caroline, believing they understood the personal sacrifice she'd borne.

A bitter taste coated Amanda's tongue. How little the public knew of the men who served them, of the people they admired.

Someone grabbed Amanda's arm as she wiped away tears with the back of her hand. "Mrs. Allen, I just heard from one of the embassy staff that you are a close personal friend of the Donnellys. You've been staying with Mrs. Donnelly throughout this ordeal." A young female reporter shoved a microphone into her face. "Can you tell our viewers how the ambassador's wife coped through these days of suspense?"

Amanda turned to the woman, considering the many answers she might give. *She loved every minute of it!* Instead, she blurted out, "No comment."

Breaking free, she ran through the crowd, toward Frank and Caroline, who were being escorted by a trio of Secret Service agents that looked like linebackers for the Washington Redskins.

Catching sight of her, Caroline tugged Frank by the arm and waved for her to join them. Forcing her way through the jostling crowd, Amanda tried to find the words she must somehow wring from her lips.

Frank turned to the agent on his right. "Mrs. Allen will ride with us back to the White House for the reception."

"No, no, I won't," Amanda said quickly. "You'll be busy, and I'm sure that when this is all over, Jennifer will need some of your time." She was flying home later that day to see her father.

"Please," Frank said in a low voice, his eyes filled with longing and a thousand messages that couldn't be spoken. "Stay. Stay with"—there was a catch in his voice—"with us."

Caroline cast her husband a displeased look but said nothing.

"I need to go home," Amanda explained. "I'll just collect my things at the house and take the next train." With effort, she dredged up a smile and stretched upward to kiss Frank lightly on the cheek in an appropriate friend-of-the-family gesture. "Welcome home, hero."

Before he could respond, she spun on her heels and started walking. Amanda couldn't see the tarmac beneath her feet through her tears as she rushed off. An official looking man in a charcoal suit caught up with her almost immediately and tapped her on the shoulder.

"I'm sorry to disturb you, miss, but the ambassador asked me to offer the use of a car to take you wherever you'd like to go."

"Thank you," she murmured.

In less than two hours she was on Amtrak's Patriot, headed north. Lowering the tray in front of her seat, she wrote the letter she would mail as soon as she stepped out of the station in New London. It was addressed to Frank at his office in D.C., where she'd written to him so many other times over the years.

Darling,

I'm so very proud of you. What you did was a wonderful, selfless gesture. Please remember that I love you dearly and always will—for all the simple acts of your life as well as the gloriously heroic ones.

And now comes the hard part. Seeing you today in your world with your family and friends around you brought a lot of my thoughts into focus. I can say now with assurance what I've always felt to be true. Our being together was never meant to be. I'll be happier going on with my life, knowing that you are able to continue your work and knowing that I can get on with my own life.

Do not call or write—for all of our sakes. I cannot stand the pain of continuing our friendship.

My sincerest wishes
for your happiness—good-bye,
Amanda

16

Amanda tried not to think about Frank. She kept busy. She taught an exhausting schedule of classes, practiced with Nick whenever they could, and competed in twice as many comps as during any other year.

There was one very important change that helped her pick up the tattered pieces of her life without Frank. Because Robert refused to be counseled himself or, in fact, to accept that he had a problem, Amanda started attending support sessions for codependents. Codependency was a new concept to her. It meant that she too had come to depend upon Robert's habit. As illogical as it at first sounded, she had learned to live in the shadow of his alcoholism and incorporate his behavior into her daily routine.

Marilyn Jacobs, the psychologist who led the group discussions, became an important person in her life. Amanda began to understand why she had stayed with Rob despite years of emotional abuse. Although her parents weren't alcoholics, their coldness and isolation had in some way prepared her for life with someone like Robert. Because he had his good days, his moments of warmth and caring, she had viewed him as offering an improved family life over her childhood. She had tolerated far too much for far too long.

It didn't matter that there was no other man waiting in the wings. To be able to determine the tone of her days, to be free of the emotional roller-coaster ride of living with a man whose personality seemed split into two people—the sober and the drunk Robert—would offer her peace of mind.

She banned all alcohol from the house, which infuriated Rob and precipitated terrible fights. But whenever he sensed that she was on the verge of pitching him out the door forever, he became sweetly conciliatory, apologized with tears in his eyes for all he'd put her through, promised to be a model husband and father, seek professional help, do whatever he must to keep the family together.

At first, she believed him. But six months passed, his promises fell by the wayside, and he drank more than ever, although on the sly. He took himself off to the club or a nearby bar after telling her he would be working or playing golf. She discovered a supply of booze locked in his car trunk.

Finally, with the emotional support of members of her group, Amanda made good on her threats. She took John and Christy and moved off of the base and into the studio apartment. At first they accepted the separation with open relief and a sense of adventure. The studio was an exciting and fun place to live. They were closer to their school and many of their friends. They loved living on what amounted to Main Street, USA, within walking distance of Kresge's, the Garde Theater with its one-dollar matinees, Franny's Candies (a yummy new shop carrying penny sweets and hand-dipped chocolates), the Puritan Diner, and the News Center, which stocked enough paperback books to keep even John happy.

However, as the months rolled past and Amanda's children saw their father only in the best light—during the daytime when he was sober and on his finest behavior—their attitudes changed.

"Daddy's so lonely without us," Christy complained. "I think we should go home."

"*This* is our home now," Amanda told her.

"It is not! Home is where Daddy is!"

"What makes you think that?" Amanda asked her mildly.

"He says so." A cruel spark lit the little girl's eyes. "He says you're being mean, taking us away from him. I think he's right."

Amanda's heart shriveled up like a slug sprinkled with salt. She took her daughter by the hand and sat her down in a sunny patch on the ballroom floor and looked into her eyes. "Your father is sick, Christy. We've talked about this before. He could get better with help, but he doesn't want help. I can't live with him anymore, and it's not good for you or John to live with him as long as he's the way he is."

"If he's sick, you should take care of him!" Christy complained tearfully.

"Alcoholism is a different kind of sickness. You have to want to change to get well."

Christy stuck out her jaw and glared at Amanda from beneath feathery bangs. "I don't believe you! I don't believe Daddy is sick. He doesn't look sick, and he takes me out to restaurants and the movies and buys me nicer things than you buy me." Tears filled her eyes. "I want to go home!"

"No," Amanda said firmly, well aware that Rob had been working on the two kids by treating them to special gifts while he pleaded his case to them.

He was obviously going to make divorce difficult for her and would question her custody of the children. But she wouldn't back down, wouldn't go back to him. Living as a single parent would be a struggle financially, but emotionally she already felt stronger, except for moments like this when she had to face her children's bitterness and confused anger.

"John and I aren't going back to the navy base, and I don't think it would be good for you to go alone," Amanda stated, reinforcing her decision. She tried to put a comforting arm around her daughter, but Christy pushed her away.

"You're so *mean!*" Christy screamed. "You're the meanest mother in the world!" Crying hysterically, she ran from the room.

Amanda sat in the middle of the wide wooden floor, crushed. What was she to do? How she wished she could talk

311

KATHRYN JENSEN

to Frank at a moment like this. He would reassure her that she was doing the right thing. But she'd dismissed him from her life, for his and for Caroline's sake. She'd had no business falling in love with him. None.

Amanda looked up slowly when John came into the room some minutes later. He wore his stern, adult expression. "Christy's being a jerk," he stated. "You all right, Mom?"

"I will be," she said, standing up with effort. She looked into his deep brown eyes, flickering with pent up feelings of his own. "What do you think of all this?"

He shook his head. "You don't want to hear it."

"I do. Please, tell me what you're thinking."

John shrugged one shoulder. "I don't think Dad's such a bad guy. He just likes to drink like a lot of guys, and that messes him up."

"Oh, John—" Amanda reached out for her son, but he stiffened, casting her a warning look. She took a deep regretful breath. He, too, resented her decision. "Darling, I know it's hard. I agree, your father isn't a bad person in many ways. But I can't love him the way a wife should. I can't live with him, and I have to think it would be pretty difficult for any woman to live under the conditions he sets."

John glared hotly at the floor. "Maybe Aunt Caroline could."

She frowned, certain she hadn't heard him right. "What?"

John's eyes were wide, dark, and liquid. He looked as if he'd been holding a hot coal in his palm and was eager to drop it. "Aunt Caroline likes Dad. She likes him *a lot,*" he stated with obvious meaning.

Amanda stared at him. "You think that Caroline feels more for your father than she should as a family friend?" Perhaps being a male, he was already old enough to pick up on Caroline's runaway sensuality.

"They were kissing," he stated blandly, observing her with interest. Evidently, he expected his mother to be moved to action by the threat of competition.

She choked out a hysterical laugh. "Kissing?"

"At Christmas, a couple times. He called her on the phone sometimes, too. Like when Christy and I were at home with him and you were practicing with Nick." His tone softened

312

as he witnessed the blood draining from her face. "They talked like . . ." He shrugged again, less sure of the emotional territory he was treading but determined to unburden himself. "They sounded like boyfriend and girlfriend, you know what I mean?"

Amanda's head reeled and her stomach dropped to her ankles as she thought back over the years, remembering the times that all of them had been together—two couples. Two couples with the wrong partners. For hours she and Frank had kept one another company while entertaining their children. In the meantime, Rob and Caroline, claiming boredom with playgrounds and juvenile games, lingered behind—alone.

She recalled with a bitter sting Rob's TDYs, unexpectedly extended cruises, the disputed savings account. Had the money ever existed? Or had he used it to pay his travel expenses for clandestine meetings with Caroline?

She'd assumed the existence of other women, especially once the intimacy had drained out of their marriage. But Caroline?

They were lovers before you met him, a voice reminded her. Intuitively, she now knew what in her heart she'd always sensed but refused to admit. *Yes, and they remained lovers.*

"Oh, God!" she gasped.

"Mom?" John whispered, looking suddenly concerned.

She couldn't respond to him. *Frank,* she thought wildly, *does Frank know?*

Yes, almost certainly he did. At sometime his general suspicion of Caroline's infidelity must have focused on Robert. He hadn't said anything to her. And he probably never would have, because he feared that by doing so he might hurt her more and would certainly destroy her friendship with Caroline.

In the light of all that had happened, Amanda was no longer sure how important that friendship was. Apparently, Caroline had put little stock in it.

"Mom?" John placed his hand on her shoulder.

Peering up at him out of her shocked daze, Amanda studied her son. He was taller than she now. *His features are*

313

*Rob's, but that intelligence and gentle light in his eyes are all
mine,* she thought proudly.

His face suddenly tightened with fear. "I shouldn't have
said that about Dad and Aunt Caroline. Forget it. It's okay. I
like Aunt Caroline, but I wouldn't go live with her. Even if
Christy wants a new mother, I'll stay with you."

Amanda dissolved into tears, and for a long time she
couldn't stop. At last she dried her eyes on her leotard
sleeve. John was still standing beside her, waiting helplessly.

"Let's go upstairs and have supper," he suggested. "I
know how to make spaghetti."

"I know you do, darling." She stroked his head.

They ate without any of their usual light-hearted conversation that night. Amanda had never been more thoroughly
miserable in her life, and she was sure her children were
equally unhappy. But she refused to back down. Returning
to Rob now was out of the question, and she would fight any
attempt on his part to take her children from her.

She spent two days writing him a letter. In it, she told him
she knew about Caroline, she wanted a divorce, she wanted
custody of the children, he could have limited visiting
rights.

A week later, Rob telephoned and sobbed to her that he
was sorry for everything. "Come home, Amanda! I miss my
family. I want my kids back. I promise I'll change. I
p-p-promise . . ."

But she could tell by his slurred speech that he'd been
drinking. By morning he'd forget everything that he'd said.
If he couldn't appeal to her sober, when he had everything to
lose, she held no hope that he'd ever change.

"I want a divorce," she repeated and hung up.

She contacted a lawyer and asked that he draw up the legal
separation papers, which were the first step toward filing for
the divorce. They were mailed to Robert; he did not sign or
acknowledge them. Duplicate documents were served on
him by an officer of the court. He still didn't sign them. The
lawyer advised her to proceed with the filing without the
benefit of preliminaries. She followed his advice.

Robert continued to call every couple of nights, always
after nine o'clock when he was thoroughly plastered, the

only time he was capable of humbling himself. She hung up on him. If he called back a second time, she left the phone off the hook. Eventually, he telephoned less often, and the children took out less of their resentment on her. Once in a while, a sense of blessed peacefulness visited her, promising happier times ahead.

But no matter how she worked to change her life for the better, one facet of it remained an unalterable constant. At some unexpected moment during every day, she thought of Frank. She desperately missed his friendship. She yearned for his quiet strength, his constancy, tenderness, and wisdom with an aching hole in her heart, and she knew that his absence was a loss she would never be capable of forgetting.

Another year came around. Two men in her codependency class showed a strong interest in her. They were both nice—one a dentist, one an insurance sales rep. Neither held any attraction for her. She fended off their invitations for a cup of tea after class or dinner before the next meeting. Somehow she went on, day to day. At night when she lay alone in the double bed above the studio, she pulled over the spare pillow and wrapped herself around it, imagining that the smooth linen was Frank's tightly muscled back.

Frank sipped a mug of coffee and listened to the sound of construction floating up from Virginia Avenue. He hadn't accomplished much today. But then there really wasn't a single paper on his desk that couldn't wait until tomorrow.

For several months after the crisis in Chad, he'd worn a hero's laurels. The American delegation had been withdrawn indefinitely from N'Djamena. Back in D.C., Frank was approached by Jerry Mandel, a mover in the local Republican Party. Jerry wanted to know his feelings about running for Congress in the state of Maryland. Frank had turned him down and squashed all the rumors about his plans for office. Newspaper photos of the brave ambassador became old news, and he, thankfully, faded from the public's eye.

But the State Department didn't forget Frank Donnelly. He had disobeyed direct orders of the secretary by returning to Chad. The outcome was irrelevant. As far as the department was concerned, he could no longer be trusted. Caroline had warned him not to rock the boat, and he'd pretty near capsized it. Now and for the foreseeable future, he was relegated to a desk job in D.C.

Frank sighed, sipping his coffee, which was, by now, stone cold. *I don't regret what I did,* he thought for the hundredth time. The bottom line was, he'd saved lives. He'd brought his people home safely. Given the chance to do it over, with the knowledge that his career would grind to a halt if he chose to ignore orders, he'd have made the same decision.

Lately, he'd given a great deal of thought to retiring from the department. Money certainly wasn't a problem. The difficulty was, what to do with himself when he wasn't working. He didn't like to spend much time at home—Caroline was there. Because his profession had always been a consuming passion, he'd never developed any hobbies.

However, he did have friends around the world with whom he'd been able to keep in touch over the years. He thought that he might like to travel, to see more of them as well as the countries where they lived. Perhaps he could land an instructor's position with an overseas branch of an American university and teach political science. Teaching had always appealed to him as a profession. He had a lot of experience to share, and no matter where he went, he would be near people he knew and admired. In fact, one very special man was due to have lunch with him—he checked his watch—in less than two hours.

Rami had arrived in the city several days earlier. He and his family were still working to free Romania from Nicolae Ceauşescu's tyrannic yoke. Over the years, he had lost a brother and two uncles in the struggle. Last month, his sister suddenly turned up missing. It was rumored that she'd been picked up by the secret police, and no word had yet come of her whereabouts or condition.

For the past six months, Rami, his wife, and their three children had been living in exile in Vienna. In Frank's present capacity, there wasn't a great deal he could do for his old friend except open a few doors and encourage a

316

sympathetic ear. He intended to do both with a great deal of energy.

Frank made reservations at Nathan's on M Street. He met Rami there promptly at one o'clock. They embraced like brothers, two men of one soul, and took seats. Frank ordered a grilled veal chop with wild mushroom sauce, and Rami chose the broiled Norwegian salmon.

As soon as the waiter left, Rami stated without preamble, "I'm going back to Timisoara." It was his family's home-town and not far from the Yugoslav border.

Frank was shocked. "You'll be arrested if the police discover you're in the country. They'll kill you!"

Rami shook his head, his dark eyes glittering like lumps of anthracite, his mouth drawn into a rigid line. "I can't work from the outside any longer. My people need me. You understand how it is, my friend. I cannot say no to them." He smiled a little. "Besides, we are beginning to see changes. The military is restless. They hate Ceauşescu. And Communism? It's only a matter of time before it dies. I want to be there when it happens."

"But if your timing is wrong, if you go back too soon—"

"Some things in life you simply must do when the spirit moves you."

How well Frank knew that to be true. In his case it had cost him an ambassadorship. In Rami's, it might cost more. "I would hate to lose you, my old friend. But I wish you well," he murmured.

Rami flashed him one of his old devilish grins. "We won't talk any more of death. Tell me, how is your family—Caroline, Jennifer?"

"Fine—no, that's a terrible lie." Even if he had a shot at deceiving the sharp Romanian, he didn't want to. "Caroline is the same."

"The ice princess. A woman like that is hard to love—she bleeds a man of his soul. But your charming daughter, she must be a joy! Almost a young woman by now."

"Jennifer is very special," Frank agreed, his heart warming with the mention of her name. "But I worry about her—"

"As all parents do."

"No, this is more than the usual worrying over skinned knees and braces. Jen has never really found herself. Caroline makes her feel inadequate, and I can't be close to her since she's away at school so much of the year. If I had to do it over, I'd insist she attend a school close to home and I would remain in country to better watch over her."

"We cannot foresee the future."

"I know, but I can't shake this terrible dread that I'm losing her."

"Somehow children survive their parents' mistakes."

"I hope so."

But Frank was not reassured. He decided he would put everything else aside and fly up to New Hampshire the very next weekend. As soon as he finished his meal and visit with Rami, he went straight to his office and dialed Jennifer's dorm.

She picked up the phone immediately, answering with a sullen "Hello."

"Hey, Jen! How are you?" he asked, forcing cheerfulness into his voice, although he felt none.

"Okay." Flat. No emotion.

His stomach clenched. "What's up? Tell me about your courses." It was the beginning of the new spring semester.

"Daddy, I—I don't have time. I gotta lot on me, loads of work to do."

He couldn't let her slip away that easily. Every other conversation in the past year had been the same. She brushed him off like a bothersome insect.

"Are you taking time out to have fun?" he persisted.

"Yeah, sure."

Say anything! Keep her talking! "I suppose this summer, you'll be going back to the studio again?"

"I don't see why I should," she said glumly.

"Why not?" He was surprised and disappointed. Jennifer had been virtually his only contact with Amanda for the past two years. When he'd dropped her off in New London or picked her up at the end of the summer, he'd at least caught a quick glimpse of Amanda. They'd spoken no more

318

than a couple of sentences apiece, but their eyes communicated worlds of tenderness and hopeless regret.

He had believed, after the initial jolt of her farewell letter, that he would get over her. Certainly, she would have an easier time banishing him from her heart. But seeing her for even those brief, breathless moments never got easier or less painful. He ached to hold her, to love her, to match his body's actions to his mind's wild ramblings.

But she had ended their relationship for sound reasons, and he felt bound to honor her wishes.

"Don't you want to see Amanda this summer?" he asked when Jennifer didn't answer the first time.

"Dad!" she groaned. "I'm getting too old for that kind of thing. Besides, Mother says I need to go to camp."

"What kind of camp?" It didn't really matter. Caroline was simply guaranteeing he wouldn't be able to spend much time with his daughter this summer. It had been so long since they'd had even a few days alone together—father and daughter. He no longer knew if her favorite color was still pink, if she still wanted a pony "more than anything in the whole world," if she dated boys, or—Lord!—if she was a virgin! "Is it a sport camp of some kind?" he asked hastily.

"Sort of . . . I can't explain now. Gotta run. Oh, John called. He wants to talk to you."

"John? Amanda's John?"

"Yuh." She sounded distracted. "He wants to know if there will be any student internships in D.C. this summer. Guess he's serious about majoring in political science and wants some experience for his college applications."

"Thanks, I'll give him a call." It was as much or as little of an excuse to call the studio as he needed. He hung up and immediately dialed by heart. Amanda answered on the second ring.

"Hello" was all he said. Not his name or "May I speak to John." Just hello.

There was a pause while she assessed his voice, as if making sure that it was indeed him. "Hold on," she murmured huskily. "I need to close the office door."

He ran his tongue over his teeth, waiting, his heart jumping about in his chest.

319

She came back on the line. "How have you been, Frank?"

"Well. And you?"

"Fine. Busy . . . you know."

"Yes." He cleared his throat, wondering if she meant the usual kind of busy or the almost insane busy a person makes himself to forget. "I've just finished speaking with Jennifer. Apparently she and John have been in touch."

"They call now and then," Amanda admitted. "Sometimes when I call her at school, she'll ask to speak with John or Christy."

He hadn't realized the connection still existed so strongly. It made him feel happy for Jennifer but deeply sorry for himself. However, Jen's refusal to spend the summer at the studio made even less sense to him now.

"Well," he continued, "John seems interested in a student internship with the State Department. I wanted to let him know that . . ." He had intended to say, I'll look into it for him and send the application forms. Instead, he continued in a breathless flood of words, ". . . a few positions are available. I'm heading up north this weekend. Why don't I drop the applications by the house on my way through."

There was a slight hesitation before Amanda's cautious response. "He'll be pleased. But come to the studio. We're here all of the time now."

All of the time?"

"The kids and I have moved off the sub base into the studio apartment. I've divorced Rob."

Frank's heart shot a mile into the sky. For over a full minute he was incapable of speech. When he finally regained control over his mouth, he tried to keep his voice level. "The three of you will be much better off."

"We already are."

"I'm glad. Well, I'm leaving D.C. early on Friday, taking a commuter flight to Hartford. I should arrive before six, if that's convenient for you."

"It will be fine. I'll tell John to expect you."

"Good. See you then."

He calmly put down the receiver, then sat for a moment tapping it with his left forefinger as a wide, boyish grin spread across his face, lifting and softening the age lines around his mouth. From some rarely tapped well of joy deep within his soul, a shout erupted, "Yes! Yes! Yes-s-s-s!"

His secretary Bess Murphy, convinced that he was suffering some kind of seizure and calling for her assistance, leaped up from her desk and threw open the heavy wooden door that separated their offices.

"Ambassador?" she gasped.

He observed her sheepishly from where he stood in the middle of the room, one fist raised triumphantly in the air. "I'm, uh, going out of town for a few days, Bess. Guess I need a break."

17

Amanda suspected that Frank's innocent-sounding plan to drop by New London was more than a side trip to help John secure summer employment. And it scared the hell out of her. She spent the next two days rearranging her Friday schedule so tightly that she wouldn't have ten minutes free all afternoon and evening. That way, she wouldn't be tempted to sneak away to talk with Frank alone, being with him even for a few minutes would be far too dangerous.

Frank's visit threatened to shake loose her resolve to carry on with an uncomplicated but pleasant life. Her divorce had become final. She hadn't yet confronted Caroline with the truth about her and Rob's longstanding affair, but she would, some day. There was no man in her life. Yet she was content just to raise her children and teach people, young and not so young, to dance.

Above all else, she had no desire to allow Frank to stir up old feelings inside of her.

When Friday finally did arrive, however, Amanda found herself reapplying lipstick and brushing her hair between every class. Each time she caught her own reflection in the tarnish-splotched mirrors, she tugged down the elastic at the tops of her leotard legs, smoothed the stretchy black fabric along her waist, and tucked a stray lock of brown hair behind her ear. Once, she imagined that she spotted a gray strand in the feathery bangs over her brow and impatiently plucked it out.

By five o'clock, she was far more tired than on any normal day. Her body felt like an engine throttled to the floor while the parking brake was engaged—racing at top speed but going nowhere. She couldn't seem to focus on any one task, couldn't catch her breath, but everytime she sat down to try to collect herself, she'd pop back up again.

Her five o'clock ballet class ended. Before leaving, all twenty of her students lined up in front of her to receive gold, silver, and sapphire stars (according to their effort) for their lesson cards. She chatted with the little girls as she licked and stuck, licked and stuck. Tossed encouraging comments to their parents. Laughed at one little girl's surprised shriek of joy when Amanda awarded her a gold star—her first.

Then Frank's face appeared over the young ballerina's head. He smiled, and Amanda's heart leaped in her breast, then slowly melted into a warm puddle.

"See you next week, girls," she murmured absently, her eyes locked with Frank's, knowing now that pretending was useless.

Nick stepped into the office and, taking one look at her face, demanded, "Are you sick or something?"

"No," she said.

He stepped in front of her, dismissing Frank as a waiting parent. "I can take care of the office. Go put up your feet for ten minutes. You've been tearing around all day."

"I said, I'm okay," she repeated. "Really." Why couldn't she stop gawking at Frank?

Nick ignored her and turned to the man who stood in the middle of a pink bevy of ballerinas.

"Can I help you? Interested in lessons for your daughter or—?" His expression transformed midsentence. "Wait . . . I know you."

"Yes," Frank said. He thrust out a hand and smiled. "It's been a long time. Hello, Nick."

323

"Well, I'll be—Ambassador Donnelly! This is a surprise." He glanced at Amanda. "For all of us, I suspect."

Amanda had never confided in Nick or Susan about her feelings for Frank. But the couple who'd known her for so long weren't blind.

Frank laid a manila envelope on the desk near Amanda's right hand. "These are the forms John will need to apply for the government internship. I've marked the positions that will give him the most exposure to the system."

"Thank you," she murmured, wrapping her arms in front of her, holding on to her elbows, as if she could, in that way, prevent herself from slipping any further into his eyes.

Frank nodded. "It's no big deal. He's a good kid."

"Sure is," Nick agreed heartily. "He deserves a break." His glance shifted from Frank to Amanda and back to Frank again. "Hey, listen, I have a class. Guess I'd better get moving."

"Good to see you again, Nick."

"Same here, Ambassador." He winked and started slowly back toward the door, watching them as the voices of little girls from the ballroom swelled to an excited crescendo.

Frank turned to Amanda. She held on to her elbows tighter. When he looked straight through her the way he was doing now with those piercing gray-green eyes, she wanted to throw her arms around his neck, hold him close, and never let go.

"How about dinner tonight?" he asked. "I have a car. It'll be too late to show up at Jen's dorm if I try to drive on through tonight." He was talking quickly, trying to explain himself before she could object. "I thought I'd stay at Gray Cliffs and drive up tomorrow."

Amanda shook her head three times before she could force a word over her dry lips. "No. No, I, uh, I have two more classes tonight. It would be much too late before I could get away."

"Hey, no problem!" Nick jumped back into the room and the conversation. "I'll pool your kids and mine. They'll love it. They can perform their recital routines . . . have an audience . . . great practice for them."

"Oh, Nick, I don't think—"

"Sounds like a grand idea," Frank interjected solemnly. But he winked at Nick.

"See?" Nick seized Amanda by the arm. "A super idea! The ambassador agrees." He pulled her into the hallway and toward the stairs. "Now you go on up, shower off all of that unladylike sweat, and put on a dress. I'll fill in here for the rest of the night."

"Thanks," she said dryly.

"Hey, what are friends for?"

They drove to Noank. Amanda couldn't think straight, couldn't stop herself from fidgeting in the passenger seat. She felt acutely sensitized to her surroundings—the car's interior, the shape of Frank's hands on the wheel, the curve of his chin and prickle of whiskers along his jaw where he had shaved too hastily.

She couldn't recall in her adult years riding alone in a car with any man except Rob or Nick. Rob had been, for a short time, her lover, for a longer time her husband. Nick was like a brother. Frank should fill one or another of those roles, shouldn't he? As close as they'd become? She no longer knew what he was to her. She was as confused as she'd ever been in her life. What kind of relationship did they have, if any?

Before she could allow herself to feel anything at all for Frank, she'd have to untangle her feelings for Caroline. And so it was Caroline she made herself think of as they drove, and the assault of emotions was overwhelming. How could her best friend have carried on a long-term affair with Rob? Not one isolated incident after too many drinks but repeatedly met him over the years, lying to and betraying the two people closest to her in life in order to keep on seeing him?

The answer wasn't easy to swallow, but it made perfect sense. *Because Caroline is Caroline, and she can rationalize anything.*

Caroline had always been able to make herself believe that whatever she chose to do was appropriate and necessary. She created her own morality.

Frank pulled the car to a stop, and Amanda looked around, surprised to find that they were in front of a crude, timbered shed beside an inlet.

During the summer months, the shabby structure served as a New England-style fast-food joint. It must have just opened for the season. Last year's hand-painted signs—Fried Clams, Lobster Rolls, Fries and Slaw—were lined up on the gravel beside the shed, providing impromptu advertisement while waiting for a touch-up of fresh paint.

"I wanted to talk more than eat," Frank confessed. "They serve up the best clams and cole slaw in Connecticut, though. Hope you don't mind the casual atmosphere."

She smiled. "I couldn't have survived a restaurant meal. Nothing's better than local seafood anyway."

They ordered two pints of clams and one each of slaw and fries, then went to sit on the rocks behind the shed and wait for their number to be called. The place wasn't crowded this early in the season. Schools were still in session, and families wouldn't set out on vacations for weeks. Two boys who appeared to be about ten years old were baiting strings and tossing them into the shallow brackish water.

"I used to crab when I was a kid," Frank mused. He clasped his knees with linked hands and pulled them toward him, looking boyish himself.

Amanda smiled, imagining him as a gangly legged boy with tousled sandy hair, barefooted and peering intently down the line as it zigzagged beneath the water.

"I never did," she said. "My parents were very strict. They wouldn't let me out of their sight. School and home. That was my world until I talked them into dancing lessons."

"Your ticket to freedom?"

"Yes. I suppose it still is."

Frank nodded. He ran the side of his thumb in a circle on his khaki-trousered knee and swallowed three or four times with visible difficulty. "I've missed you—" he finally choked out.

Then there seemed nothing he could do to stop the flow of pain-filled words that had been stored up inside of him all through the many long months.

"I suppose that makes no sense, Amanda. We never were together for more than a week or two at a time—family vacations, trips home between overseas tours."

"That's true," she whispered. Tears stung her eyes. She blinked them dry.

"I feel closer to you than anyone in the world today. Anyone in my entire life."

A loudspeaker rasped, "Number nine. Nine—pickup." Their order ticket, crushed in her left fist, was marked with a twelve.

"Frank, where is this leading?" she asked.

"I don't know. I—yes, I do. I want to marry you, Amanda. I don't want to share you with anyone. Not with Rob or with any man who replaces him. And as warm and beautiful as you are, there *will* be another man in your life as soon as you decide it's time. I'm going to be that man!" he pronounced between gritted teeth, then in one quick motion reached out and pulled her into his arms.

His lips pressed demandingly over hers. She opened herself to him, deepening the kiss that seemed to last for a sweet eternity, yet was over too soon. Amanda inched her head back and gazed wonderingly into Frank's feverish dark eyes. In all the years they'd been friends and that friendship had melted into admiration and love, it was the first mention either of them had made of marriage. For a slender moment, her heart did what any other woman's heart does when the man she loves tells her he loves her enough to pledge his life and future to her. She soared like the gray-winged gulls wheeling over their heads.

Then she envisioned Frank and Caroline standing side by side and holding hands on the dias at Andrews Air Force Base. "Frank, is leaving Caroline what you really want?" she asked, forcing herself back onto sensible ground. "She's a part of your life, whether you can admit it or not. She's good for your career. If we . . . if we were together . . . made love . . . and you . . ." She could hardly get the words out over the tears clogging her throat. The years of self-control crumbled. "If you made love to me once, then you changed your mind and went back to her, I don't think I could . . ."

"I'd never do that to you," he insisted urgently. "I'd never leave you, Amanda. But—"

"But what?" she demanded.

"Jennifer. I still need to protect her. She's so fragile. Caroline isn't above doing something vengeful."

"So, what do we do?"

He dropped one arm regretfully from around her shoulders and raked fingers through his hair. "I need you now. I can't go on not knowing how it feels to love you. It's too much to expect of any man." He looked at her. "I'll be able to work everything out in time. But for now . . . I have to see you once in a while to keep me going. Amanda, please come away with me tonight. We'll drive to a little cottage on Cape Cod that belongs to a friend of mine. It's quiet and private there. It will be for just a few days, but—What's wrong?"

She must have looked panicked. "You haven't answered me. What about your career?"

"My career be damned. I have plenty of time in service. If I wanted to, I could retire tomorrow. I've thought a great deal about doing just that." His glance slipped for an instant from her face, and he studied the waves lapping the rocks at their feet.

"Numbers ten and eleven," the loudspeaker crowed. "Orders ten and eleven are ready!"

Amanda took a deep breath. It was such a huge step, so many complications. "John and Christy," she murmured.

"I wouldn't do anything to jeopardize your custody of your children," he assured her.

"No." She smiled, tenderly touching his cheek with one hand. "I mean, how will I explain to them if I go away with you for the weekend?"

His face fell.

"Never mind," she said quickly. "I'll think of a way. Probably the truth is best." At last, her heart swelled with gratitude, and tears of happiness rolled uncontrolled down her cheeks. Then her eyes dropped away from his in a moment of regret.

"Don't think of Caroline now," he pleaded. "You're not betraying her."

"How can you say that?"

"Amanda, if she were the friend you've believed she was all these years—" He bit his tongue.

"She wouldn't have been screwing around with my husband behind my back?" she asked bitterly.

"That's what I wanted to say but didn't want to risk your coming to me only to pay Caroline and Rob back. How did you find out?"

"John. Children hear and see things we don't."

Frank shook his head. "I wonder if Jen knew, too. They thought they were protecting us, no doubt."

The breeze off the ocean grew snappy, penetrating her light sweater. Amanda cuddled within the warm, protective circle of his arms.

"If you love me, come," he whispered into her hair. "That's all. It's that easy."

"I do love you." She sucked in her breath. "But I'd feel better being up front with Caroline. I think I should call her, tell her that we want to marry. I don't feel right sneaking off like this."

"Do you think it makes me feel good?" he asked, pain filling each word. "Of course I'd rather just come right out and tell the world I love you. That's the way it should be done. But Caroline isn't a rational person. Jen will be the one to suffer."

Amanda tightened at the thought. Caroline was capable of doing great damage to the child.

"Yes," she whispered at last, "I'll come."

She was burning her bridges, pouring gasoline and tossing the matches, no longer considering the consequences or, at least, no longer taking them on her own shoulders. Robert would have to accept that their marriage was officially finished. John and Christy would have to adjust to a new man in their mother's life.

And she'd have to scrape together enough money to pay off Caroline's loan on the studio fast. For Amanda was most certainly going to lose her benefactress. Once Caroline became aware that her husband was leaving her for her old friend, she'd lose no time calling in her chips.

Amanda hoped to God that Frank was serious about marrying her, for she'd have precious little left of her old life once she'd made her intentions clear.

God help them both if it didn't work out.

The broad-leaf maples and oaks along the Connecticut shore whispered past the car windows. Glimpses of water—the harbor at Mystic where whaling ships once made port, the bays at Newport, Rhode Island, and Burlington, Massachusetts. Interstate 95 buzzed with weekend traffic—folks getting away for a long weekend after the damp, dreary winter, hoping for sun and clear skies. Then the maples turned to squat salt marsh evergreens struggling to survive in the thin, sandy soil, and the cities came fewer and farther between.

Amanda had said almost nothing as Frank drove.

He was the one to, at last, break their silence.

"The house is very little. A two-bedroom cottage in Hyannis beside a cranberry bog."

She turned her head and smiled at him. "That doesn't matter. We'll be together."

Love and longing shone in his dark eyes. Although gray-tipped hairs framed his ears and forehead, Frank's wrinkles were more like smile lines. His age and the turmoils in his life didn't show.

Incongruously, Amanda found herself trying to imagine what he must look like naked.

"What are you thinking?" he asked, eyes still fixed on the road.

She felt blood rush into her cheeks. Clasping her hands, she berated herself for reacting like a teenager. After all, she was a woman who'd been married most of her adult life and now had a nearly grown son. How could the mere thought of a man's body affect her like this?

"I was thinking . . ." she said slowly, preparing a fib. She looked at him, and he pulled his eyes away from the road for an instant to meet hers. Then she was incapable of lying. "I was thinking that you probably look wonderful with your clothes off."

Frank flashed her a wicked smile. "Glad to hear that. I hope I live up to your expectations." He chewed his lower lip. "I confess that I've dwelled on similar thoughts myself . . . many times."

He turned away for a moment as they crossed a bridge to Sandwich and became entangled in the first of Cape Cod's infamous traffic rotaries. Cars seemed to come at them from every direction, and it took him a minute to find the right exit onto Route 6, heading east again.

"Amanda, I don't know what you're feeling just now. Maybe confusion and fear. You've been very quiet, and that isn't like you." He slid a peek at her. "But I hope, above all, that you love me." He reached over and clasped her left hand, drawing it off of her thigh and into his palm. Gently, he raised her fingertips to his lips and kissed them, turning her insides liquid. "I need you to know that I want to spend the rest of my life with you and that I realize it will mean some adjustments for both of us. But I won't ask you to give up anything more than you wish to."

He meant her dancing. "The studio?"

"You should keep it, of course. You should always dance."

"It will be difficult to do . . . and spend any time with you."

"I'll commute from D.C. on weekends," he said.

"What about overseas jobs? You've always loved working abroad. I wouldn't want you to turn those down and resent me because of it."

"I told you, I've been thinking seriously of retiring. There are a few loose ends, though. I need to finish the work I started long ago."

She nodded, understanding. Over the years, he'd written of the friends he'd made, the plans he'd laid to help in little corners of the world. These personal pledges meant everything to him, and she'd never dream of asking him to break them.

"Sometimes," she confessed, "I ache to be at your side. I actually hurt inside. I don't know how we'll work it out— our lives."

"We will," he assured her, squeezing her hand. "We'll

manage to overcome the distances and difficulties. Time is on our side. It's been with us all along, Amanda."

She smiled gratefully at him. Like a child who blindly trusts adult wisdom, she trusted Frank. A better man, she knew, simply did not exist. With the rest of their lives stretching out ahead of them, she rested her head on his shoulder and thanked God they'd finally found one another.

That evening, they walked along the narrow, twisting streets surrounding Hyannis Harbor. Sportfishing and excursion boats were returning to the docks. A whale-watching cruise, filled with senior citizens and schoolchildren, disembarked. Amanda spotted a pretty little restaurant called the Captain's Chair, which overlooked the water, and they went inside.

Remarkably, the lobster was less expensive than many of the other dishes, so they indulged in boiled lobster dinners with drawn butter, crusty rolls, and tossed salads with homemade blue cheese dressing.

They slowly walked back to the cottage, arm in arm, watching stars appear in the black sky overhead. Amanda thought, *I've come home. This man is my home. Wherever he goes, wherever he chooses to live, I must be with him.*

Somehow, she no longer worried about logistics. This weekend trip with Frank was so different from her trip to Maine so long ago with Rob. The sexual excitement that had driven that earlier relationship hadn't been a good enough foundation on which to build a solid partnership.

There was every bit as much anticipation building inside of her now, and she could sense Frank's passion, but he seemed to be intentionally pacing their union, letting her adjust to the idea that they were inevitably, tonight, going to make love and that they'd be repeating that act of supreme devotion over and over as the years ebbed and flowed.

They'd unpacked the car, changed out of driving clothes and into dinner clothes, eaten, held hands while watching the sun set, and now walked in the thick, moist darkness of spring on the Cape.

At last, they returned to the cottage. Frank locked the

doors and made sure the windows were secure, for the night promised to be chilly. Amanda put a kettle on for tea, and when the whistle sang, her soul sang along with it for sheer happiness.

They sat snugly together on the couch, watching the middle of an old Bill Holden movie, a tearjerker set during World War II in the Pacific. Neither of them could remember the title or the name of the pretty blond actress with him, and pretty soon Frank took the empty teacup from her hands and said in a sweetly husky voice, "Amanda, it's time."

"I know," she said.

He took her hand and led her into the bedroom.

When she turned to him with her hand on the top button of her blouse, he whispered hoarsely, "No." Reaching out, he moved her hand away. "I'd like to undress you, if you don't mind."

"I don't mind," she murmured with a pleased smile.

He gently unfastened each tiny button, the button at the back of her skirt, those at the cuffs of her blouse that she never bothered undoing. He slipped the silky blouse from her shoulders, carressing her skin as the fabric slid fluidly away, planting a kiss at the tops of her shoulders, at the base of her throat, and at the soft cleft between her breasts.

Amanda let her head drop back, closing her eyes, concentrating on the delicious sensation of his hands as they removed all of her garments. It seemed as if the years of distance and loneliness slipped away, too. All that mattered was now—this slender moment in time—while they had one another and their dreams of the future.

Amanda stood naked in front of Frank, her chin high, eyes meeting his. She wasn't at all embarrassed as she'd feared she might be. Years of passion held in check bubbled up inside of her, and she began to undress him with as much care and reverence as he'd taken with her.

When they at last embraced, standing before the old iron-railed bed with its homey patchwork quilt, her breasts fitting neatly into the hollow beneath his softly furred chest, she lapped her arms around his neck. He kissed her with an ardor that spanned lifetimes, and they made love like a promise, never to part, never to let the events or people of their lives come between them again.

Jennifer sat in her dorm, staring out the window at the cold spring rain that fell across the quadrangle. In another week, Easter break would arrive with all the bustle and excitement of a holiday. The girls would shout and squeal at one another across the hallways. They would telephone their parents for permission to bring their roommates home with them. They'd flash photographs of boyfriends they were dying to see, of brothers just right for a friend, of loving parents waiting anxiously for their return.

It's all so depressing, Jen thought. *The absolute worst.*

Another horrible struggle with Mother. Caroline would reassess her as she always did and find her miserably inadequate as a daughter. Rush trips to a dietician, to a dressmaker to order garments to conceal the additional six pounds she'd put on since Christmas, to a doctor for another argument with him over prescribing the pills she insisted Jennifer take to control her appetite.

The doctor had refused on the last trip. He didn't think it wise to send a teenager whose medical history included bouts of severe depression off to boarding school with a potentially dangerous, lethal drug. Caroline had been furious with him.

"She's as big as a house!" she shouted. "Something has to be done! I can't take her anywhere like . . . like *this!*" She waved a hand at Jennifer's fleshy pink stomach overflowing the silk bikini panties Caroline had given her for her birthday. Typically, they were Caroline's lacey style and two sizes too small.

Jennifer didn't think she could face one more holiday.

It wasn't just her clothes that she didn't fit. She was out of place everywhere—at school, at home with her parents. It had always been that way. She was fat and ugly, an embarrassment to everyone. Even her father's blind adoration couldn't disguise the truth. Even summers at Amanda's failed to heal the pain.

Slowly Jennifer eased herself up off the bed, tears rolling down her cheeks. She walked over to the student desk, one of three in the little room, and slid open the top right drawer. Behind stationery, envelopes, and stamps were two full bottles of aspirin. She popped the child-safe cap with two thumbs, removed the white cotton puff, and dumped the contents into her palm. Fifty tablets, the label read. Better take both bottles.

From the tiny fridge, she pulled a can of regular Coke. It was her roommate Laura's. Laura weighed ninety pounds, wore a size three, and ate anything she liked without gaining an ounce. Laura always looked at Jennifer with a forced smile to cover her pity and disgust. Jennifer hated her and all the girls like her who breezed through life without knowing what it was like to hate yourself.

Jennifer had hated herself for a long time. She had tried to change, to diet, to exercise. She'd even tried to kill herself once before, a couple years ago. She had been staying with Amanda for the summer and at the end had been so miserable about having to leave the studio and return to school, she'd thrown herself off of the balcony. But she'd failed at that, too. All she'd managed to do was break a few bones and make a fool of herself. Luckily, this time she wouldn't leave so much to chance. She knew exactly how many aspirin she'd have to swallow and how long it would take.

She tried swallowing half a bottle all at once, gagged and coughed them back up into her hand. Methodically, she swallowed the soggy tablets two at a time. Then she opened the second bottle, repeated the process, and stretched out on her bed. Laura and Marcie wouldn't return for at least four hours. They had signed up to go on a nature hike with the boys from Andover, the neighboring prep school.

Jennifer sipped her soda, swiping at tears as they trickled down her cheeks, and waited. She considered writing a note to someone to explain why she was ending her life. But she figured if they couldn't figure it out on their own, nothing she said now would make them understand. She reviewed her short sixteen years. The few joyful instances couldn't outweigh the daily pain, torment, and self-disgust.

As the drug began to work, she stopped crying and set the

Coke can on the floor beside her bed, so it wouldn't spill and make a mess when her muscles went limp. For the first time she could remember during her short life, she felt at peace.

Now I lay me down to sleep, God bless Daddy. God bless Amanda and John and Christy. God bless me . . .

And she fell asleep.

18

For the two days Amanda and Frank spent on Cape Cod, Amanda felt as though she could, at last, breathe all the way to the bottom on her lungs. She was like a deep-sea diver who'd finally come up for air. She gulped in their happiness, unable to get enough of it.

Amanda woke each morning with a smile and curled into the warm male body beside her in bed. They made love in the early morning light, still drowsy from sleep, sweet, lazy love, and again during the day, with tender passion, and again at night, in any way that pleased them. Amanda's energy level soared, and she felt a full ten years younger.

She and Frank held hands everywhere they went—while strolling the tiny beach at the foot of the street, while eating, sharing a cup of coffee at a quaint breakfast nook, or sprawled on the couch as they read the Sunday newspaper— only releasing their warm grasp to negotiate a doorway or turn a page. To not touch one another left an uncomfortable void. She tried not to think of leaving and returning home, but even that prospect failed to dampen her spirits, for they had begun a new life together.

Amanda started searching for ways to extend the weekend. "Let's go see Jen together. I'll take tomorrow off. Nick can handle the studio—Mondays are always slow days."

Frank's face brightened at the suggestion. "An excellent idea. We'll stay here tonight and drive to Chisolm in the morning and surprise her."

"We should call the school, though," Amanda suggested. "I'm sure they have regulations about visitors."

"Good idea," Frank agreed. "But that can wait until morning." A demon sparkle in his eyes tipped his hand. "The more I have of you, the more I want you."

"Say that to me always," she whispered.

"Always," he promised.

The telephone rang at five A.M. *It's a wrong number,* Amanda thought groggily. Then, *No, it's not.* Nick had the phone number in case of an emergency.

"Promise I won't use it unless the kids burn the studio to the ground," he'd teased.

Amanda sat up in bed and stared at the old-fashioned heavy black instrument with its worn rotary dial, a chill descending her spine.

Frank stirred in bed, waking slowly from a deep slumber.

She sat up, tenderly removing his arm from around her naked waist, then reached over and picked up the receiver on the fourth ring. "Hello?"

A voice on the other end coughed before turning into words. "Sorry for disturbing you, Amanda—Nick here. First off, John and Christy are fine, so you can start breathing again."

"Thank God," she murmured.

"Yeah, well, something's come up—serious I'd guess. Jennifer Donnelly's school called a few minutes ago. They've been trying to reach her parents." He paused. "Guess you're on the emergency card."

She recalled giving Jen permission to include her name and number as a backup for her parents.

"Is she sick?" she asked.

"I . . . listen, you'd better have Frank telephone the school. The headmistress is doing the calling, and she won't talk to anyone except the immediate family. I didn't know the grandparents' number or I'd have given her theirs. She sounded upset for one of those hardened school administrator types."

Amanda wrote down the woman's name and telephone number as he read them to her. "All right. Thanks, Nick."

Frank raised himself up on one elbow, took in the worried tightening around her mouth, then looked at the piece of paper in her hand. "Jen?"

"The headmistress wouldn't tell Nick what the problem was. You'd better call," she said tensely.

Amanda pulled on a robe and sat on the edge of the mattress beside Frank while he dialed. He reached the woman directly—she was answering her own calls—and that seemed a bad omen to Amanda.

She could hear only Frank's end of the conversation, but she witnessed a man thrown into a storm of agony on the wind of a few words. His face grayed and seemed to shrivel up like a time-elapsed shot of a withering blossom. The life faded from his eyes.

"Jennifer? She w-wouldn't . . ." he stammered. "No, of course, I believe you . . . Not your fault, I'm sure, but I had no idea. I'll come right away. Have you contacted her mother? If you do, tell her . . . tell her . . ." He dropped his head into the palm of one hand. "Never mind, I'll be there as soon as possible."

He sat with the receiver limply cradled in his free hand. Amanda lifted it out of his fingers, listened for a dial tone, then hung up. She swallowed hard, a roaring filling her ears, the sound of impending doom.

"Frank, please tell me. What's happened?" *It can't be any worse than what I'm imagining now,* she told herself.

Frank's voice came to her as if from a dead man—dry, emotionless. "Jennifer swallowed two bottles of aspirin. They found her early this morning. My little girl is dead!"

Amanda gripped Frank's arm for support as they walked out of the headmistress's office, through the vaulted vestibule of the administrative building at the Chisolm School for Girls. Outside, the spring sunshine seemed a cruel reminder that however tragic life might be, nature carried on.

"You can't blame yourself," Amanda murmured dully.

"Blame myself? Of course, I should blame myself!" Frank roared, shaking Amanda's hand off his arm. He hadn't said a word to her all the way to New Hampshire, as if by his silence he could keep reality in check or negotiate the facts into a less horrible truth. "I should have seen this coming!" He glared at her in disbelief, his emotions running wild with helpless fury. "Dear God, my daughter!"

"Frank—" Amanda sobbed. "There is nothing any of us could have done."

"I could have insisted on keeping her near me. I could have stopped Caroline from sending her away. I could have done a hundred things!" he ground out.

"I loved her, too," Amanda cried. "If blame is to be passed out, I'm just as much at fault. I was closer to her geographically, and . . . she was like a second daughter to me."

"You weren't her mother, though," he stated sharply.

"So my loving Jen didn't count? My grief doesn't matter? Is that what you're saying?"

"It's just not the same."

The click of high heels on the brick path crisscrossing the quadrangle between buildings drew Amanda's attention. She looked up to see Caroline striding up the walk. Even in this moment of supreme loss, she looked elegant in her suede pumps with matching handbag, designer pastel suit, and meticulously applied makeup.

"Oh, darling, tell me it's not true!" she wailed, flinging herself at Frank with open arms. "My baby—"

Frank cut off his wife's embrace with stiffly extended arms. "Don't ever speak to me again," he pronounced in a deadly tone. Turning to Amanda, he said, "Take the car home with you. I'll have someone from the rental agency come for it."

For a long moment, Amanda stood helplessly frozen to the spot on the mossy-encrusted bricks where she stood, watching Frank walk away. The shoulders of his blue argyle sweater were bowed, his head down. And she knew that going after him would do no good.

Caroline said, "He's . . . he's upset. He'll calm down."

"I don't think so," Amanda murmured.

"He always . . . always comes back . . ." She looked at Amanda. "I love him. He can't possibly blame me for this . . . *I wasn't even here.*"

"I think that's part of the problem," Amanda said, tears clogging her throat. "He blames you for treating Jen so coldly, me for taking him away when he should have been with her, and himself for not having the insight of God." She started to move down the path.

"Amanda, don't leave me now!" Caroline pleaded. "I was wrong. I admit it. What should I do? Tell me."

"Go away. Marry Robert. He obviously loves you as much as he can love anyone other than himself . . ."

Caroline ran to catch up with her. "Robert? What are you talking about? Why would I want to—"

Amanda shook her head. "I know about the two of you, and so does Frank."

"Oh," Caroline breathed. It took her only a moment to recover her composure. "But—but he's a drunk and he has absolutely no—no . . ."

"Money?"

Caroline smiled grimly. "The most important ingredient in the martini of life."

"That's tough," Amanda said dully. "Guess you'll have to go it alone for a while."

Caroline reached out and stopped her. "No. You can't leave me, too. Not after all we've been through together."

Amanda stared at her. "Our friendship should have meant a lot. But it's one of those things that doesn't work one way. Good-bye, Caroline."

Amanda, John, and Christy attended the funeral on Long Island. It was a cold, somber affair matched in mood by the weather. No comforting hugs between parents and grandparents. The air was rent by the suspicion and anger of one family blaming the other. Tranquilizers and bitter silence stifled a sense of barely restrained hysteria.

Amanda nursed her own grief and comforted Christy, who didn't stop crying through the church service or the graveside prayers and benediction. John clamped his teeth over his lower lip and stared with intense emptiness at the coffin while the minister spoke words her son probably never heard.

Across Jennifer's coffin, Amanda glanced at Frank as he stood with his parents. Caroline's side of the family was stationed well away from him, toward the head of the slim white box. Amanda waited in vain for some signal from Frank that he wanted her at his side—a quick glance, a soft word—but none came. She had just enough inner strength left to realize that he was punishing himself, not her, for Jen's death. But that didn't make her feel any better.

The summer announced itself with a week of torrid, thunderstorm-shattered days—unusual for Connecticut. Frank neither called nor wrote.

Amanda sent him a card on his birthday on June 8. On the back of it, she wrote

I mourn Jen, too. But please, let life go on. I miss you.

Love,
Amanda

She received no answer.

On June 20, she packed up the car and drove John to Washington while Christy stayed at home to attend a program for young dancers at Connecticut College under Nick and Susan's watchful eyes. John had received his student internship and would be staying with a host family —Steve and Jane Murphy—who lived in the district.

Amanda kissed him good-bye outside the Dupont Circle condominium, despite John's objections at being fussed over by his mother in public. She drove north on I-95 feeling as if all of her men had now left her. More than anything, she wanted to drop by Frank's office, only a matter of blocks away, but she couldn't do it. If their love had been destroyed with his daughter's suicide, there was nothing she could do to restore it, for Jennifer was never coming back.

Frank stared out the eighth-floor window of the State Department and into the sizzling July sunlight. Every other time he let his eyes drift toward the window, he never really focused on anything beyond the glare of glass and light and sooty smudges. But today he saw something that caught his attention: a slender young man in a neatly pressed navy blazer and gray slacks standing on the curb beside a government limo. At first he looked only vaguely familiar.

After a couple minutes, though, Frank recognized him. John—Amanda's son.

For some reason, he'd forgotten all about the boy's coming to work in D.C. for the summer. For Frank, life had stopped on the day his daughter took her own life, and it seemed inconceivable that anyone else should continue with the mundane routine of life.

A young man's first summer job. Frank remembered how scared he'd been on his first paying job, and he had worked for his old man at Chase Manhattan in New York, a city he was already intimately familiar with. Eventually, he had learned something about the world of finance, enough to know he didn't want to spend the rest of his life ensnared in it. The following year he'd enlisted in the Marines and fought in Korea.

But it seemed impossible that the little boy who'd played on the parlor floor with Jen in Vienna was now a young man, starting his career. For the first time since her funeral, he wept. This time, not for himself, this time for Jen and for the woman she might have become.

When he lifted his head from his desktop, Frank felt somehow different, not necessarily better, just different. On an impulse, he put on his suit coat, walked past the Chippendale benches lining the corridor, past the bust of Benjamin Franklin, America's first foreign diplomat, to the elevator, which he took down to the lobby.

When he reached the sidewalk, John was still leaning against the side of the long black car. He must have already been in town for several weeks, but he looked abysmally nervous, and Frank had to cover a sympathetic smile.

"Hello there," he called out, and to his own ears his voice sounded almost happy. He had to control the urge to ruffle the boy's hair and pat him on the shoulder and say, It'll be all right. You'll do fine.

"Ambassador!" John cried, his face lighting up.

"How's the job going?"

"Okay. I sort of thought I'd be working in an office. But since I'm seventeen and have a driver's license with a clean record, they've been using me as sort of an errand boy." He shuffled his feet worriedly and squinted up at Frank. "Today they're short on drivers, though, and I'm supposed to chauffer a couple of dignitaries around town."

"You'll do fine," Frank assured him. "And it's all very important work. Keep your eyes and ears open; you'll learn a lot."

John grinned. "I already have. I know my way around D.C. pretty well. I memorized the locations of all the federal agencies." He gestured at a road map and handwritten notes lying on the front seat.

"Good deal," Frank said, laughing. "When do you take your lunch break, that is, if you have one?"

John glanced at his watch. "In forty-five minutes."

"Meet me at Dino's on M Street. My treat."

"Okay! Great!" John stuck out his hand to shake, looking almost grown-up.

Frank took himself for a walk. Down C Street to the Lincoln Memorial and past the Washington Monument before doubling back to the restaurant.

John beat him to Dino's and was standing outside when Frank approached along the sidewalk. They had to wait their turn along with the rest of the lunchtime crowd to be seated, but they passed the time chatting.

Until Jennifer's death, Frank had often come to Dino's with colleagues or alone.

John sat rigidly in his chair, looking around, his eyes wide, conscious of how he moved at the linen-draped table. He rearranged the heavy silverware in front of him, took a drink of water, clasped his hands in his lap, and gazed around the noisy but posh dining room with interest, his eyes stopping for an instant to recognize a prominent senator from California, the speaker of the house, and, finally, two lobbyists for the Teamsters Union.

"Nice," he appraised. He was already learning. This was a place where power hung out.

"Yes, it is," Frank agreed.

John was so like Amanda—his inquisitiveness, intelligence, and dark, strong good looks were all her. Suddenly she was there with them whether or not he could handle that emotional jolt or not; she was there with them.

"How's the family, John?" he asked tightly.

"Christy's studying dance with the José Limon Company at Conn College." He looked up when Frank didn't comment. "Oh, you mean Mom."

Smart kid. Frank smiled. "Yes. How is she?"

"Okay, I guess. Not very happy."

"No?"

"I guess she thought of Jen as one of us kids. Her own."

A lump rose in Frank's throat. This wasn't fair, those words coming back at him. "I remember her saying that once." He also recalled how he'd shut her out with his grief. He doubted she could ever forgive his selfish coldness.

John swallowed hard, blinked, and took a long drink of ice water. "We all . . . *I* miss her too. Why'd she go and do that?" Now he sounded angry, bitter, hurt. "It was stupid! She didn't need to. She could have talked to me!"

It felt strange, now months later, to be put in the position of explaining Jen's suicide to somebody else when he himself still hadn't succeeded in getting a handle on it.

"I suppose she thought she had no other option. She was that unhappy, John. I—I didn't know . . ."

"Me either." The boy blinked rapidly, denying tears a chance to form.

"We have to . . . to release her and go on."

John nodded thoughtfully, then looked straight across the table at him. "When are you going to call her?"

Frank nearly choked. Amanda had evidently taught him not to pull any punches. "Your mom?"

John nodded.

"I'd like to. I've thought about it, but she's probably very angry with me. I didn't treat her very fairly when Jen died."

"I don't think she's mad, more like sad." John took a deep breath. "I think she sort of . . . likes you."

Frank smiled, warmer inside than he'd felt in months. "I think I sort of like her, too."

During lunch, Frank made several decisions. He would first of all do what he'd toyed with many times: turn in his resignation and officially retire from the foreign service. Then he'd call a few friends on the faculties of select universities—Yale, George Washington, Columbia. They should be able to give him some idea of the possibilities of securing teaching positions in their political science departments. Yale would make an easy commute from New London. He liked the idea of Yale.

That night, he dialed Amanda's number. When she answered, he found it impossible to speak over the lump in his throat.

"Hello?" she said a second time, sounding unsure that anyone was on the line.

"I'm coming home," he choked out without introduction.

"Frank!"

"If you don't want me—"

"Thank God!" she whispered. He could hear her crying.

"Don't . . . please. I love you, Amanda. I need to be with you. All of the rest . . . we'll work that out. I'll be there Saturday morning. What time do you start teaching?"

"Nine o'clock."

"I'll make it by six A.M. We'll have a long breakfast. I'll bring pastries."

"I'll make the coffee," she said, sniffling. "I love you."

He shook his head in wonder. "You must."

Amanda didn't dare let herself feel too happy all at once. This was a mechanism she'd developed over the years to protect herself from disappointment. If you expected little, you were less likely to be hurt. Old habits were hard to break.

She tried to work through each day, taking them one hour at a time, not daring to anticipate Frank's return to her on Saturday. Nevertheless, Susan noticed the difference.

"You've lost weight . . . or gained it in just the last couple of days. Whichever it is, you look great!"

Amanda smiled to herself. "Must be the weather."

Which wasn't entirely implausible. The rare burst of early summer heat had moderated itself into sunny days in the high seventies washed over by pleasant breezes from the ocean. The half-barrel oak planters that lined State Street were blossoming with red geraniums reminiscent of those Sara had once grown on her rooftop. Shoppers appeared in record numbers, cheering anxious merchants.

As Saturday approached, the magnificent atmosphere won Amanda over. She let herself believe in a future with a loving, admirable man. A good friend who had become her lover but would always remain a friend at heart. It was the best of all worlds. She went to bed on Friday night, her heart singing so clearly in her ears she was unable to sleep at first. Gradually, she drifted off and must have been so deeply asleep by the time the telephone rang at her bedside that it took a dozen warbles to wake her.

Drowsily, she reached for the phone and only opened her eyes when she recognized John's voice at the other end. She stared at the glowing digits of the clock: 6:08.

"What's wrong, John?"

"The ambassador," he said tightly, "he's gone."

She smiled, relieved. "Yes, he's on his way here."

"No . . . I mean, I know he was supposed to be driving up to see you. He told me. But—" His voice became urgent, deeper than a boy's ought to be, older. Amanda closed her mouth, fearing the worst. "Mom, I just drove him to the airport. He said to call you after he'd left, that he couldn't. He's on his way to Romania."

Amanda's stomach sank. She gripped the bedsheets, telling herself she was still half asleep and hadn't heard right.

"Did you say, Romania?" she demanded urgently.

"Yvetta Grazi called early this morning. Her husband, Rami, has been taken into custody by the secret police in Timisoara." The Grazis had visited Frank twice while the Allens had been staying with them. Once in Vienna, once in London. Amanda would never forget the couple's poignant dedication to their cause.

"Oh, God, no," she breathed.

347

John spoke softly. "She asked the ambassador for help."

And Frank had answered an old friend's call. She felt cold inside, helpless and desolate. To come so close—

"Thank you for calling, John," she whispered.

"Mom, are you all right?"

"I . . . I will be." Not if she remained in New London, though. With a devastating shock, she realized that her years of biding time were over. Action was her only recourse, either that or she sensed that she might lose Frank forever.

"John, are you working today?"

"Yeah. Why?"

"I'm flying down."

"Mom," he objected, "you can't do anything to help him."

"The hell I can't. I think there's a commuter flight on Allegheny Airlines. I'm going to try to get on it. If you can meet me at Dulles Airport, please do."

"Mom—"

She hung up.

Romanian borders had been closed at Ceauşescu's orders for months. Rami's wife and children were staying with friends in Belgrade, Yugoslavia.

"Rami went in under cover of darkness three weeks ago," Yvetta explained. "I couldn't stop him. His sister, she was still missing, and there were reports that she'd been seen in a prison camp near Timisoara."

"He went to the prison?" Frank couldn't believe his friend's bravery—or stupidity. Right into the lion's den. But then, he would have done the same for his family—for Jen—or for his new family—Amanda, John, and Christy.

"Can you do something?" she asked, looking at him hopefully.

"Nothing official can happen quickly, even if I call in favors within the State Department. But I can follow Rami into Romania, travel as a tourist, and fish for information. If I'm able to determine that the secret police have detained him without cause, I can plead to the U.S. government to file a formal complaint of violation of civil rights."

"That will do no good. Nicolae doesn't care what Americans think."

"Public opinion worldwide is a powerful force, though. You'd be surprised. Only last year, crafty old Nicolae received the Iron Cross from Queen Elizabeth for humanitarian efforts outside of his country. If she and other world leaders suspect him of gross human rights violations, we might force his hand—" He reached for her hands, sending her a message of strength through his firm hold. "Pray, Yvetta. I'll do what I can."

Frank crossed the border that night but only after six hours of stalling tactics by the Romanian border guards. These days, it seemed that no one was passed through without ridiculous scrutiny and endless questions. He drove to the outskirts of Timisoara and checked into a small hostel rather than stay with the contacts recommended by Yvetta.

If one of them had betrayed Rami, he didn't want to fall into the same trap. But he also wanted to avoid jeopardizing lives by asking people to shelter him. If everything worked out as he hoped, in a week or so he'd be flying home to Amanda.

For three days, he worked his way through the city, gathering information from people short on food and clothing and crammed into inadequate housing with poor plumbing and unreliable power. He discreetly arranged contacts from a list of names Yvetta had supplied—sympathizers within the Socialist government who might know of Rami's whereabouts. Most denied knowing him at all. Several stated that he was definitely *not* being held. Two suggested that, although the secret police couldn't possibly have him, perhaps the immigration board had detained him for standard questioning.

"For two weeks?" Frank asked.

"Anything is possible" was the response.

Then he met Boris Orlevski. Boris was a *Pravda* correspondent who surprised him by pulling him aside in a café.

"We met the other day," Boris reminded him, "although you probably don't recall. I was in the chancellor's office, waiting for an interview."

"I do remember," Frank replied warily. Russians he'd met before had generally been good people but lied facilely and without apparent regret.

"Your friend is in grave danger," Boris stated. "The police have him whether or not they admit it. They have been interrogating him."

"Then he's still alive?"

"I believe so. My sources are fairly certain," Boris added mildly. "They also tell me that you are at risk. You should leave right away—tonight."

"I can't leave without Rami."

"Then you will not leave," Boris said sadly.

Frank looked at the man. He could be a Ceaușescu plant.

"Rami goes with me," Frank stated firmly.

Boris shrugged. "That is your decision. If it were me—being a Soviet citizen and learning to deal with governments such as this—I would never have come. Friend or no."

"That is the difference between us," Frank said.

He returned to the hostel. Tomorrow he would change accommodations, switch to a smaller boarding house on the other side of the city. He'd call his contacts in D.C. and apply pressure on the people who could most subtly apply pressure on their leader. The U.S. ambassador to Great Britain was one way, he thought. He'd call him, too. Rami probably wouldn't be released immediately, but death by slow torture might be avoided for fear of international scandal.

Sometime during that night, Frank woke out of an exhausted sleep, aware of someone in his room. He didn't move but cracked open his eyes just enough to see two shadows passing in front of the windows. Even as he reached under his pillow for the short-bladed knife, the men fell on him.

Clutching her purse to her breast, Amanda stepped out of the glass-and-marble foyer of the State Department building onto the heat of Washington's C Street. She took five unsteady steps into the bright white sunshine and stopped to lean against the first of a row of towering flagpoles that displayed the Stars and Stripes.

She gazed blankly at passersby, her heart hammering in her chest, her eyes burning. As traffic poured past in a liquid blur, she clenched her teeth to keep from bursting into tears.

"Oh, God!" she gasped, feeling at that moment as if her soul had been wrenched out of her body. "It can't be!"

John had been right. Since Frank had formally retired and was acting as a private citizen, the State Department had no control over his actions or official knowledge of his whereabouts. After the news broke that former Ambassador Frank Donnelly had been kidnapped in Romania, it had taken Amanda two days of pounding on bureaucrats' doors and pleading with zealously protective secretaries to make herself heard by the people who should have had the power to help Frank. All she got for her efforts were some pretty fancy handwashing tactics and a flurry of denials that anyone knew anything about his whereabouts.

From the building behind her, John walked toward her. He stopped at her side and put an arm around her quivering shoulders.

"He had to go, Mom," he murmured comfortingly in her ear. "Rami was in trouble. Ceaușescu's thugs don't fool around."

"Why him? Oh, John, why *him?*" was all she could choke out, trembling within her son's embrace.

On hearing the news minutes earlier from a newspaper reporter, her heart had shattered into tiny shards, as if it were a priceless porcelain vase cast onto the floor at her feet. The man who'd been a dear and exciting friend for almost two decades, who'd stood by her through life's pain and joy, who'd made her heart sing at the sight or sound of him. The only man she'd ever truly loved was missing. And now all she could get out of the damn State Department was a bland statement that reliable information hadn't yet been obtained.

However, unofficial sources reported that he'd last been seen in Timisoara, being dragged from his room at the hostel by police loyal to the country's ruthless dictator. The same dictator who, in the past few days, had been accused of the brutal torture and murder of thousands of his own people who had defied him. Frank's string pulling might not have oiled the workings of the State Department, but he'd certainly caught the interest of the American press, which was always on the lookout for a good mass-murder story.

"All we can do now is pray," John said.

No! a voice inside her shouted. *Praying isn't enough!* Until the news that Frank had been captured, she'd been willing to work through the system. Now she could wait no longer.

"Is the car nearby?" she asked.

"Sure. Why?"

"Take me for a ride. Please, John."

He knew she was terribly upset and therefore didn't question her. Maybe a slow drive around the city, visiting familiar sites, perhaps stopping to shop in the Watergate boutiques, would soothe her. He might even be able to coax her into a quiet lunch at the Occidental Grill, a favorite with many of the men and women on Capitol Hill. But he was unprepared for her next request, which came as soon as they were settled inside the sleek, black diplomatic limousine.

"Head for Dulles Airport," she ordered, her voice sounding somewhat stronger.

"Mother, you can't—"

"And on the way, phone TWA for the time of their next flight to Athens or Belgrade, or whatever the hell airport is nearest Timisoara! I'm going to find him. Somehow."

Sitting rigidly on the front seat of the limo beside her son, Amanda shut out his objections, which were many and completely logical and had absolutely no effect on her. Finally he capitulated, took the car phone in hand and punched in the airline's number from memory as he drove.

19

Amanda took a taxi to an apartment house in a working-class section of Belgrade. Although there were signs of five or six people living in the two tiny rooms, they had evidently left the apartment to Yvetta so that she could meet with Amanda in private.

"I'm sorry I couldn't pick you up at the airport," Rami's wife apologized as she waved Amanda toward an aging sofa with tattered upholstery. "I have to be careful. I'm being watched."

Ceauşescu's agents apparently ranged beyond Romanian borders. She poured each of them a glass of tepid tea, sat across from her on a bare wooden chair, and looked at Amanda solemnly over the lip of her glass as she sipped.

"I'm sorry that you've been pulled into this horrid situation. And, Frank—I feel responsible for what has happened to him."

"None of this is your doing," Amanda assured her.

Yvetta shook her head. "In a way, it is our doing, mine and Rami's. We knew the risks. But we are fighting to save our country. Romania isn't Frank's country. He shouldn't have to d—" She broke off and bit her lip, her eyes filled with pain. "If Rami is still alive, he will never forgive himself if Frank . . . suffers."

Amanda swallowed and squeezed her lids shut for a second, willing away useless tears. "I'm going into Romania to try to find Frank. To do that I'll need your help."

"No! I won't allow you," Yvetta whispered urgently. "You know nothing of the country! You don't speak the language. You have no protection!"

"I've thought this all out," Amanda stated, trying to keep her tone calm. "I used to contribute short articles to a dance publication, sort of a regional newsletter." She fished through the roomy carry-on bag she'd brought with her on the plane and produced two issues. "You can put me in touch with someone in or near Timisoara who dances, someone willing to be interviewed. That will be my excuse for traveling to Timisoara."

"No!" Yvetta snapped, her eyes bright with fear.

"It's the only way," Amanda insisted softly. "With or without your help, I'm going. I can't abandon hope for Frank without even trying to reach him."

How often had she watched a network newscast, amazed by the courage of the wives of American hostages who journeyed halfway around the world to plead for their husbands' release.

And now, she was one of them—on an errand of mercy.

"I'm determined," Amanda stated through gritted teeth. "I will find Frank and find Rami, too, if I can."

Yvetta sighed. "I wish I could go with you, but a long time ago Rami and I agreed that should one of us be taken, the other would remain with the children." They had three young ones to raise.

Amanda nodded. "I understand." She swallowed more tea. It was strong and bitter, but she found it fortifying. "Besides"—she looked up with a dim smile—"I think I'll be better off on my own. You have a reputation in your own country."

Yvetta grinned. "As a rabble-rouser and insurrectionist?"

"Some day you and Rami may be hailed as heroes of your people."

"Only history will tell," Yvetta uttered softly.

Two days later, a young blue-jean-clad woman with waist-length straw-colored hair, whom Yvetta introduced only as Gretza, drove Amanda out of Belgrade. Gretza's car was a squat blue Fiat amply ventilated by rust holes—convenient for use in the stifling summer heat but, Amanda suspected, less comfortable during the Balkan Peninsula's frigid winters. From the capital city they drove east to Pancevo, then turned northeast across the vast fertile Serbian plain through Alibumar and along a rough, semipaved road amidst corn and wheat fields, past thatched-roofed peasants' cottages to Vrsac on the Yugoslav–Romanian border. Timisoara, where Frank and Rami were thought to be held, was only another hour or two.

First they had to satisfy the border police.

Amanda presented her passport and visa to a guard and explained that Gretza would be driving her to the Institute of Iron and Steel at the Academy of the Socialist Republic of Romania in Timisoara. There, she would be meeting a man and his wife who taught there but who had also been involved for many years in amateur ballroom dance competition. Since Ceausescu seemed especially eager these days to polish his country's image and present himself as a civilized man of the arts, it seemed logical that Amanda would be allowed in.

The guards discussed her papers, scowled at her sample newsletters, and kept her waiting for hours in the sweltering summer heat while they made numerous telephone calls to consult with various officials.

Night fell. Although Gretza had long ago been cleared, Amanda still wasn't allowed to pass. They ate a cold supper of bread and spongy cucumbers, washed down with *smederevka,* a local greenish wine, then spent the night sleeping on a hard bench in a steamy, overcrowded waiting room.

It wasn't until afternoon of the following day that Amanda was allowed to enter Romania.

As they drove, Amanda observed Gretza. She looked to be about twenty years old. She had gray eyes, which seemed mismatched with her straw-colored hair. A dense black birthmark the size of a dime marked the right corner of her mouth. She told Amanda that her family lived in Romania, but she had been a student in Belgrade for two years and so regularly commuted back and forth between the two countries.

"What part of Romania are you from?" Amanda asked.

"Constanta. It is a huge port on the Black Sea. A very industrialized city. But not far along the coast is Mamaia, one of the most popular resorts in all of Europe." Gretza's eyes shone. "Mamaia has beautiful hotels, beaches, and wonderful restaurants."

However, the area they were driving through now was neither beautiful nor thriving. Hilly farmland, unlike the tidy Yugoslav cooperatives, had been left fallow or inadequately tended. Vegetables grew among weeds, and broken-down farm equipment oxidized in unkempt fields.

Gretza took in Amanda's puzzled expression. "The state does this to us. Everyone works for the state, you see. But no matter how hard we work, there is never anything to show for it, for the state claims it all. Your house never gets any bigger. There is never enough food to lay on the family table or better clothing to put on our backs. People stop caring about the quality of what they produce. We have a saying here, The turnips are as soft as the tractors."

The heat grew intense. Amanda's clothes clung damply to her. They stopped beside the road and sat in the shade of an ancient tree with massive limbs, drinking more *smederevka,* eating cold *jesetra,* a small piece of poached sturgeon that Gretza had brought with her from Belgrade.

It was midafternoon before they arrived in Timisoara, and Gretza stopped the Fiat in front of the institute.

"While you are making your story look good by interviewing the dancers, I will find us a place to stay. In two hours, I will meet you here."

"When can we look for Rami and Frank?"

"Soon." Gretza looked away, her face expressionless. "I should have more information when I return."

John gazed up at the layer cake of sandstone and glass: the U.S. State Department building in Washington, D.C. He was scheduled to drive the Bolivian legation back to their hotel after an Organization of American States meeting. But he had other plans.

He consulted his watch and frowned.

For two days, John had talked with other drivers, gathering information, waiting for his chance to use what he'd learned during his few weeks of internship in Washington. Somehow, he had to help his mother and Uncle Frank. As time passed, he was growing more desperate.

Miraculously, ten minutes later, a familiar Lincoln Continental pulled up behind John's limo. He had seen the chairman of the House Foreign Relations Committee riding in it several times in the past week.

Perfect! he thought.

Congressman Mark Holliman climbed out and disappeared into the lobby of the office building, and John knew that this was the opportunity he'd hoped for. He left the limo and casually sauntered over to Holliman's car.

"How's it going?" he asked the driver, an older man with a bulbous nose and bored eyes.

The man laid the sports section of the *Washington Post* on the seat beside him. "All right, considering it's Monday. You?"

"I've been covering the OAS meetings. Got an easy ride for the rest of the day." John lounged lazily against the car, his head tilted back to warm his face in the sunshine as if he were on vacation. "I deliver the Bolivian delegation to the Hilton, come back for two more short runs, then I'm done for the day."

"Lucky," the other driver mumbled. "I've been all over the city with Holliman today. The Capital . . . White House . . . Executive Offices . . . I'll probably be driving in circles for another five hours. The guy never stops."

John shrugged. "I wouldn't mind that. Gives me a chance to memorize more streets. That's my hobby," he explained.

The driver slanted him a speculative look. "You're kidding."

"No, really. I'd switch assignments with you, but we'd probably get into trouble."

The man sat up straight, looking interested. "Not necessarily. If I have car trouble, I call the congressional motor pool to get a substitute. Holliman doesn't care what he rides in just as long as he isn't kept waiting."

John pretended uncertainty. "Gee, I, uh, I don't know . . ."

"Come on, kid! You said you'd have fun."

Trying not to look too pleased with himself, John nodded. "Okay. Why not?"

When Holliman and his secretary rushed out through the wide glass doors, John was standing on the sidewalk near the limo and he flagged them down.

The congressman strode over quickly, scowling. "Where's my car?"

"Engine trouble. I'm filling in, sir."

"Well, let's get a move on. We're heading back to the Capitol next, son."

"Yes, sir!" John ran around to the driver's seat since the secretary, a hulking guy who doubled as the congressman's body guard, held the rear door open for his boss.

John pulled cautiously into traffic, then glanced up into the rearview mirror. In the backseat, the secretary was busy annotating a fistful of photocopies. Holliman studied a stack of papers spread on top of his open briefcase.

John had intentionally left the clear privacy panel open between the driver's seat and the passenger area. He chewed his lip, then took a deep breath for courage and began.

"I've met you before, sir."

Holliman didn't look up. "You have, have you?"

"Yes, sir. My family was at the Nesbit home in Connecticut—Gray Cliffs—a couple of years ago. You were there, too."

Holliman glanced up, puzzled. "A Republican fund-raiser . . . yes. Why were you there? You would have been too young then to drive."

"I'm a friend of Ambassador Frank Donnelly," John told him proudly.

The secretary looked up, too. Frank's name and picture had been in every newspaper and on every television screen across the country since the press had caught wind of his disappearance. Journalists emotionally reminded their readers of his heroic rescue in Chad, and, before that, of how he'd fought for his country in Korea. Public furor was rapidly gathering momentum.

And nothing was more attractive than a rolling snowball in Washington, D.C. If you were smart, you got out of its way while it grew and picked up speed, then you claimed credit for starting it.

"Ambassador Donnelly," Holliman repeated thoughtfully. "His kidnapping is an outrage. A good man like that being dragged off the street by thugs and no one able to do anything about it."

"I think *you* can do something, sir," John stated.

The congressman let out a low chuckle, sounding flattered. "Well, of course, I would if I could. But I don't quite see how at this point. The State Department's trying to locate Donnelly, of course, but so far no official in Bucharest will admit that the government is holding him."

"But that's just *us*, Congressman. *You* know a lot of other heads of state, sir," John pointed out quickly. "Before Frank Donnelly left, he said something about the Queen of England putting pressure on Ceauşescu to release his friend, Rami. I didn't think then that he was serious. But now I believe that he was." John took a deep breath and plunged on. "Couldn't everyone sort of gang up on this guy and demand that he let these people go or . . . or we'll do something to punish him?"

He could tell that the congressman's mind was racing a mile a minute from the way his eyes darted around without really focusing on anything. Being labeled a peacemaker these days was almost as great for attracting press coverage as being the released hostage.

John didn't let up. "If important people make a big enough stink, threaten to take away their trade, advise tourists to steer clear, stuff like that . . ."

Holliman chuckled low in his throat. "It would have to be a really big *stink,* as you put it, son. President Reagan, the queen, maybe President Mitterrand of France, Willy Brandt, and the pope, all screaming their heads off."

"So?" John prompted.

"So . . ." Holliman said slowly. "I think it's worth a try."

To have come so close to happiness at this time in her life—thirty-nine years old. That, Amanda thought, was the tragedy. Not her husband's wasted life and infidelity, not her best friend's deceit, not even the loss of little Jennifer, had sent Amanda into hopeless despair; she'd survived each of these trials. But to now lose Frank—the only man who'd ever really loved her, the only man she'd ever truly cared about . . .

How could she go on?

Amanda ached through every nerve, every muscle in her body from weariness as she interviewed the two young professors in a dreary faculty lounge in the basement of one of the buildings of the Academy of the Socialist Republic of Romania.

Yes, they said, they had indeed competed in ballroom competitions throughout Romania and had traveled to three championships in the Soviet Union, where international-style ballroom dancing was extremely popular and taught in the schools. But as they spoke to her excitedly of their many experiences, and she made a show of taking notes for her "article," Amanda's mind and heart wandered.

At last, she walked back outside to the quadrangle where Gretza had left her. The young woman was waiting for her in the car.

"Have you found anything out?" Amanda asked tautly as soon as she'd climbed in.

"Unfortunately, the word is not good," Gretza replied. She started driving. "Ambassador Donnelly was seen being taken by the secret police from a student hostel in the northern part of the city. He had been beaten and was nearly unconscious.

A lump formed in the back of Amanda's throat, making it impossible for her to speak for several seconds. At last she rasped out, "Who can I speak to, who has the power to release Frank?"

Gretza shook her head. "The police are thugs. They act on direct orders from Bucharest. And Bucharest, these days, is Ceauşescu. He is unreachable."

Amanda thought for a moment. "Do you have any idea where Frank is being held?"

"Most certainly in a cell within the ministry buildings . . . if he's still in Timisoara at all. By now, he may have been moved, though. I suspect that Rami and his sister are no longer . . . no longer here," she finished sadly.

Amanda clutched her hands to try to stop them from trembling. "What do you mean, *no longer here?*"

Gretza took a deep breath. "I will show you, and then you will go home to America. You can do more from there than you can do here."

"I'm not leaving without Frank," Amanda insisted.

Gretza blinked, then drew a deep breath. "We'll see."

They drove through the city and another eight miles east into heavily wooded countryside. Between two peasant villages, Gretza turned off of the highway onto a narrow dirt road skirted by tall grass and tangled undergrowth.

"I have never been here myself," Gretza explained. "My uncle and aunt, who live in the village we just passed, told me about it."

The fir trees were tall and regal, the air fresh with the pungent scent of growing things, the pollution of the city gone. Amanda looked around, her skin prickling with anticipation as she wondered what Gretza wanted her to see in this lovely parklike setting.

Gretza continued in a reverent voice. "We will leave the car here and walk the rest of the way."

Gretza led the way down a dirt path through the woods. It suddenly occurred to Amanda as she walked that she might have been smart to insist that Gretza first take her to a hotel in Timisoara. At least she could have left a note or dropped a word to someone about where she was going and with whom. It was entirely possible that her young guide was in league with the secret police. If Amanda Allen disappeared in the middle of this forest, no one would ever know what had happened to her.

She pushed aside a bramble that had grown across the

path and, when Gretza wasn't looking, stooped to pick up a heavy stick. Keeping a wary eye on the girl's back, she followed deeper into the woods.

At last, Gretza came to a stop. She said nothing, only lifted her hand and gestured eloquently toward an opening between the trees. "There," she choked out, tears clinging to her lashes. "I had hoped they were wrong."

Amanda studied the clearing, at first thinking it strange that a farmer would choose this isolated patch to cultivate, for it was the only piece of broken ground for at least a mile in any direction. Then she noticed that the soil wasn't level. No attempt had been made to plow the area to break up the rich, moist chunks of earth.

On one side of the field, the soil was scraped into a low mound, and weeds had begun to poke up through it. On the other, the earth had been roughly hollowed out, then partially filled back in with dirt. When a hot breeze blew across the clearing, a sweetly sickening smell wafted over Amanda, obscuring the pungent woodsy scent.

Amanda dropped the stick and covered her mouth and nose with one hand. "Oh, God!" she gasped. "These are . . . mass graves."

Gretza nodded. "This is where my people are brought after the interrogations."

A wave of nausea overcame Amanda. Sour bile rose in her throat, and she swallowed it. For what seemed a very long time, she was incapable of speech. She stared at the ditch, at the mound.

Frank! Oh, Lord, please, don't let his life have ended like this!

"We should leave," Gretza said gently. "It would very bad for us to be found here. It's almost dark. That is when they will return with more."

Frank stared at his hands. If he held them six inches in front of his face, he could just see their dark outline against the slightly thinner darkness of the room where he'd been kept for the past five days. In fact his hands were really about all that he could see, for there were no windows to let light into the room and the thick metal door was always closed.

He sat in a corner with his back pressed against the dank cement wall, and he thought about Amanda. By now someone would have gotten word out of Romania that he was missing. She must be going crazy back in Connecticut.

Tears stung his eyes. To give his life for a friend—that was something a man sometimes had to do. His only regret was that he and Amanda had never found the chance to be together for more than one sweet weekend.

His attention was drawn back to his hands. They throbbed horridly where they'd been cut in the struggle at the hostel. Thinking his attackers meant to kill him right then and there, he'd grabbed the blade of one of their knives. But the secret police had other plans. They wanted information and had kept him alive. At least for the time being.

Frank's mouth felt as dry as an autumn leaf. His captors allowed him eight ounces of water, one serving of cold, skinless spiced sausages called *metitei,* and a fist-sized hunk of moldy bread each day. Just enough to keep him coherent.

His ribs ached furiously and the insides of his stomach felt as if they'd been rearranged. The police hadn't beaten his face, which left him hope that they were being cautious about leaving scars in case they should later release him. Unfortunately, they'd punched and kicked him everywhere else.

He doubted anyone knew where he was. He understood that if he told them what they wanted to hear about Rami—probably so that they could publicly execute his friend and declare him a traitor to his country—they still wouldn't release him. No matter how many times they promised Frank his freedom, he told them nothing.

The door opened, blinding him momentarily from the bare lightbulb dangling in the corridor. He turned away, listening with a sinking feeling in his gut to the sound of steps crossing the cement floor toward him.

He cringed involuntarily. It couldn't have been more than an hour since they'd last questioned him. He'd thought they would stick to their usual pattern and leave him in peace for the night.

Apparently not.

Two men grabbed his arms, hauling him to his feet.

363

"I demand to be allowed to speak with a counsel of the United States Embassy," he ground out for the hundredth time.

The men didn't respond. They dragged him down the hallway. As the trio neared the interrogation room door, Frank tensed.

But they continued on past the dreaded door.

"Where are you taking me?" he asked tightly.

No answer.

They passed into an underground garage and handcuffed him to a seat in a dark-windowed van.

Frank wished he knew where Rami was and if he was still alive. Maybe he'd been protecting a dead man all along. Maybe they were just trying to fill in gaps of information, and he was prolonging his own agony for no reason. He could make up something to satisfy them, then let them kill him.

The van bucked and swerved through the empty streets of Timisoara. It must have been quite late at night, for so few people to be about. Then the scenery changed to open fields, followed by forested land—primeval and foreboding. He wondered if this was the way to Bucharest.

Again, he thought of Amanda and felt a pang of regret that he'd never see her again, never touch her, never taste her sweet kisses, or ever, ever again be able to watch her float across a dance floor.

Amanda stared straight ahead through the Fiat's windshield, fighting the impulse to scream out her despair. For the first time since she'd arrived in the Balkans, she feared that she'd already lost Frank.

She sensed Gretza tighten beside her in the car.

"What's wrong?" Amanda asked.

Gretza studied the rearview mirror. "We're being followed." She pressed the accelerator to the floor. The little Fiat leaped ahead with a wild clatter of loose parts, but the car behind them—obviously a larger, more powerful vehicle—continued to gain on them.

"They're going to catch us," Amanda gasped. "What do we do?"

"I don't think there's anything we can do, except try to keep moving. If we can make it back to Timisoara . . ."

Amanda gripped the armrest beside her and held on as Gretza attempted to block the pursuing car from passing them. For several minutes, she was successful. But, as the narrow road curved sharply to the right, the larger car squeezed alongside the Fiat.

The man on the passenger side of the sedan signaled for the two women to pull over.

Gretza gritted her teeth, glared intently at the snaking road ahead, and kept her right foot pressed to the floor.

The chase car swerved sharply into the side of the Fiat, knocking it into the soft shoulder of the road. The Fiat's tires spun in the loose gravel, and they skidded out of control into a ditch. The car rumbled to an abrupt halt.

Amanda's head struck the dash at the same moment she heard Gretza shriek. When Amanda slowly lifted her head, a swarthy man in shirtsleeves was hauling the young woman out of the car.

"No!" Amanda cried. "Don't hurt her!"

A second man flung open the passenger door and dragged Amanda from the Fiat. She flailed at him with her arms and kicked him viciously in the shins.

He grunted, momentarily losing his grip on her.

With a sudden burst of adrenaline, Amanda broke away from her captor. But before she'd run a dozen desperate strides, he'd tackled her from behind, knocking her to the ground. Her face slammed into the rough gravel road. The blow to her nose stunned her, leaving her dizzy and disoriented.

In another second the man had pinned her arms behind her back and was straddling her. Breathing raggedly, she turned her head to one side and spotted Gretza.

The college student's eyes were wide with fear as the hulking driver of the other car pulled her toward the middle of the road, away from the car. He shouted something at the girl, then, to Amanda's surprise, released her.

Gretza staggered away a few steps, then turned to look questioningly back at Amanda. Her shirt was torn, and her face was smeared with tears and filth. She hesitated, staring hopelessly at Amanda.

"Go! Run!" shouted Amanda.

Casting the American woman one last regretful look, Gretza ran into the darkness.

Amanda's heart sank. She was glad that the girl had been allowed to leave, but now she was alone.

The two men conferred gruffly in Romanian. Amanda couldn't understand a word, but they seemed to be discussing what to do with the Fiat. At last, they just left it in the ditch, probably figuring it would do Gretza no good until she found a truck to tow it up onto the road.

One of the men climbed into the driver's seat of the sedan. The other shoved Amanda into the back, then slid in beside her. She swung around and struck him in the chest with her fists. He retaliated by smashing her across the face with one huge paw. Falling against the door, she slumped on the seat, dazed, realizing that she was wasting her energy. Obviously, she'd never be able to outfight these two goons.

They drove through the night, deeper into thick groves of trees.

I'm going to meet Frank, she comforted herself. *It may not be the way I'd imagined it would be, but if there is another life after this one, we will at last be together.*

The sedan pulled off of the highway and onto a two-lane road. A dense strand of trees lined both sides of the road, like silent sentinels, Amanda thought. Even if she somehow escaped from the car, she had no idea which way to run, how far she'd have to go to find help, or who she could trust in this country torn by hate and suspicion.

The inside of the car smelled of stale cigarette smoke and body odor. She wrapped her arms around her ribs and held on, terrified but also confused. If the two men weren't taking her back to Timisoara, which seemed to be the case since they'd driven around the city instead straight back into it, where were they taking her? If they were part of some elite hit squad, they would have already killed her. Perhaps she was being taken to a private house somewhere in the country where their commanding officer would question her.

Then a chilling image returned to haunt her: the little clearing in the woods Gretza had shown her. Perhaps there were other places just like that, scattered across the Romanian countryside.

To end up like that—raped, tortured, and thrown on a heap of other hapless bodies in a foreign land—oh, God! Her stomach churned sickeningly at the thought.

The sedan pulled off of the road and dimmed its headlights. The amber courtesy light flashed on over her head. For endless minutes they sat, neither men speaking to the other or to her. She thought she'd go mad, waiting. Still, she didn't dare move, didn't dare breathe too loudly, as if she might make herself invisible.

At last, she felt compelled to break the agonizing silence.

"What are you going to do with me?" she gasped.

No answer.

She tried German. *"Warum sind wir da?"*

A flicker of irritation lit the eyes of the man beside her on the backseat, as if he understood her but chose not to reply.

He mumbled something in Romanian to the driver, who nodded solemnly.

Then, gradually, the road behind the sedan brightened.

Amanda turned. Two lights, moving closer, illuminated the gnarled tree trunks outside. Amanda turned and gazed into the white pinpoints as they grew larger. Beyond their glare, she was unable to make out the driver of the approaching vehicle.

Transfixed, like a wild animal by the lights, she shuddered at the thought of yet more goons arriving. Why was *she* such an attraction? What did these people want from her?

A van pulled alongside the sedan. As soon as it stopped, the side door ground open and a burly twin to her own abductors pulled a smaller-built man in handcuffs into the road.

Her heart racing in her breast, Amanda flung herself against the window. "Frank!" But her scream was muffled by the thick glass.

The man beside her shouted something at Amanda, grasped a handful of her blouse, and dragged her across the seat, then out of the door on the far side. She struggled, trying in vain to break free, wanting only to run to Frank. If it was indeed him.

In the short, dimly lit glance she'd caught of him, he'd looked different—gaunt, devoid of spirit or hope. Perhaps she'd wanted so badly to see him in these last few moments of her life that she'd imagined some other unfortunate victim of the death squad was him.

She couldn't run to him, for her guard wrapped an immense paw around her upper arm and restrained her, moving at a deliberately slow pace around the end of the car until she could, at last, see the other prisoner up close.

It was Frank.

He squinted at her, as if noticing her for the first time. Then a spark lit his eyes, and with a burst of strength from some deep reserve, he shoved the man beside him out of his way.

"Amanda!" he moaned. "What are you doing in—"

His guard recovered his footing and, in one swift motion, drove a melon-sized fist into Frank's stomach. With a groan, Frank doubled over, clutching himself, his face twisted in agony.

"No!" Amanda shrieked. Still held back, she was unable to go to him. Helplessly, she watched as Frank slowly recovered his breath and straightened. In spite of whatever secret hell he'd been through in the last five days, he now stood with dignity and gazed at her lovingly.

"I prayed I might see you one more time," he whispered. "I didn't want it to be like this."

"I know," she choked out, hot tears flowing unchecked down her cheeks.

"Are you all right?"

"Yes. You're hurt?"

"It's nothing," he said quickly. "Do you know where we are?"

"No. But it looks a lot like a place I saw earlier today . . ." Her voice drifted off as yet another set of headlights approached from the opposite direction. "More of them?"

"Our escorts are probably just local boys. This must be the varsity team, from Bucharest."

She frowned, blinking. *No. We drove to the north and then*

west of Timisoara. This car was coming from the direction of the Yugoslav border.

As soon as the vehicle stopped, a man stepped out of the passenger's side door, took two steps toward them, then halted in the middle of the road. Amanda couldn't make out his face in the glare of three pairs of facing headlights, but unlike the men who'd brought her and Frank here, he wore a European-tailored business suit.

Without a word, Frank's guard unlocked the handcuffs and unceremoniously shoved him forward. At the same moment, the man holding Amanda pushed her roughly toward the stranger.

She had visions of tragic movie scenes—fleeing prisoners shot in the back while trying to escape. Was this a trap, some kind of sick game?

"What are they doing?" she whispered.

"Don't ask, just walk," Frank said tightly.

Staring straight ahead, he reached for her hand and started moving forward. Amanda put one foot slowly in front of the other. Together they cautiously crossed the stretch of pitted pavement. Amanda's spine tingled in anticipation of the inevitable whizzing bullet or hissing knife blade.

Slowly, slowly, another step crunching on dry gravel. Another. Until they were less than ten feet away from the stranger in the dark suit. From this close, she could see that he had thin, brown hair, a tidily groomed mustache, and clear, perceptive eyes.

"Ambassador Donnelly?" he asked with a strong British accent. "Mrs. Allen?"

"Yes," they answered in unison.

"I'm Mark Whitman, assistant to the British consul in Belgrade." His mustache lifted in a slender smile. "May I offer you folks a lift?"

20

Amanda clipped the emerald necklace around her throat and turned toward the full-length mirror to admire the deep green stone, cut in a large oval and surrounded by two-point diamonds. This time it wasn't costume jewelry. The gems were real and exquisitely beautiful, just like the rest of her life.

The gown she wore was a pure, milky white with a delicate froth of marabou at its hem. Tiny iridescent beads sparkled across her fitted bodice. Wings of opalescent fabric swirled from her wrist to the soft ruffle perched on the delicate crest of each of her shoulders.

"Are you nervous?" a deep voice asked.

Smiling, she turned to Frank. "Not as long as you're here."

In fact, after they'd walked across the Romanian–Yugoslav border nearly a year ago, nothing frightened Amanda. She had lived through an impossible trial and won a love so deep that the rest of her life and whatever it might hold seemed quite manageable.

Only a few hours later that same night she and Frank had been led to safety by the British consul, Rami and his sister had also crossed to safety. The next morning the Socialist government in Bucharest had officially announced that four dangerous anarchists had been expelled from the country. Frank predicted that Ceauşescu's days were numbered. He'd destroyed his country through greed and oppression. It was only a matter of time before his people revolted.

Amanda had been stunned that night by what seemed a miraculous reversal of fate. But in the next few days, she learned that their release had not been due to chance. A number of powerful people in Washington had acted swiftly to make key European political figures aware of the cruel atrocities being carried out at Ceauşescu's command. The old dictator had been confronted by representatives of no less than eight countries within a twenty-four-hour period. Rather than lose trade and be ostracized from the political community, he'd capitulated and released four troublemakers. Amanda had been doubly surprised to find that John had even played a part in the drama. She'd never been prouder of him.

Impulsively, Amanda touched the liquid green stone nestled in the hollow of her throat.

"Do you like it?" Frank asked.

"I love it," she murmured. "My birthstone will bring me good luck. It's a wonderful present, darling. Thank you."

He reached out and pulled her into his arms, and she was overwhelmed with the pungent male scent of musk and a surge of love far too grand to be contained in one heart. Oh, how she loved this man!

And what a fascinating man he continued to be.

Frank was now teaching at the U.S. NATO base in Rota, Spain. They'd flown from Rota to Blackpool, England, for the International Ballroom Championships. Nick had met them there and would return to New London afterward. He manged the studio while Amanda was away.

After the end of the semester, in three weeks, they'd return to the States for six months or so before leaving for another teaching assignment. This one would be in Weisbaden, Germany.

Meanwhile John had enrolled as a freshman at Yale. He was majoring in political science and doing extremely well. Christy had traveled with them to Rota, thrilled to be sprung from traditional school routine. Instead, she studied each morning with a private tutor, then, in the afternoon, took equestrian instruction and ballet lessons from a marvelous teacher who'd once danced with the Ballet Parisienne. She'd also exuberantly flung herself into the international lifestyle after learning enough Spanish to know when a boy was trying to pick her up.

Amanda melted deeper into Frank's arms and felt his palm come up to rest softly on the back of her bare neck.

"I have to go now," she whispered. "We're on next."

"I'll be cheering for you," he promised, dropping a kiss on her lips as she reluctantly stepped away.

"I know . . . you always have."

And that night she danced as she'd never danced before.

Printed in the United States
By Bookmasters